Kate Clayborn is the *USA Today* bestselling author of *The Other Side of Disappearing* and *Georgie, All Along*. She is a lifelong reader of texts of all kinds and a passionate advocate for the romance genre. A Midwesterner by birth, she now lives in Virginia.

VISIT KATE CLAYBORN ONLINE

KateClayborn.com
KateClayborn.Author

The Paris Match

KATE CLAYBORN

PIATKUS

PIATKUS

First published in the US in 2026 by Berkley,
An imprint of Penguin Random House LLC
First published in Great Britain in 2026 by Piatkus

1 3 5 7 9 10 8 6 4 2

Copyright © 2026 by Kate Clayborn

The moral right of the author has been asserted.

*All characters and events in this publication, other than those
clearly in the public domain, are fictitious and any resemblance
to real persons, living or dead, is purely coincidental.*

All rights reserved.
Penguin Random House values and supports copyright. Copyright fuels creativity, encourages diverse voices, promotes free speech, and creates a vibrant culture. Thank you for buying an authorized edition of this book and for complying with copyright laws by not reproducing, scanning, or distributing any part of it in any form without permission. You are supporting writers and allowing Penguin Random House to continue to publish books for every reader. Please note that no part of this book may be used or reproduced in any manner for the purpose of training artificial intelligence technologies or systems.

A CIP catalogue record for this book
is available from the British Library.

ISBN 978-0-349-44272-3

Printed and bound in Great Britain by Clays Ltd, Elcograf S.p.A.

Papers used by Piatkus are from well-managed forests
and other responsible sources.

Piatkus
An imprint of
Little, Brown Book Group
Carmelite House
50 Victoria Embankment
London EC4Y 0DZ

The authorised representative
in the EEA is
Hachette Ireland
8 Castlecourt Centre, Dublin
15, D15 XTP3, Ireland
(email: info@hbgi.ie)

An Hachette UK Company
www.hachette.co.uk

For Jackie
Ma meilleure amie, pour toujours
May we have many more Parisian adventures

YOU ARE CORDIALLY INVITED TO
A PARISIAN ADVENTURE FOR OUR MOST HONORED GUESTS
CELEBRATING THE WEDDING OF

Michael Plackett & *Emily MacKenzie*

Monday

Suggested Arrival
Hotel Rooms at Group Rate Available

Tuesday

Cocktail Hour Boat Cruise Along the Seine
Paris Dinner

Wednesday

Day Trip to Versailles

Thursday

Musée Rodin
Musée de l'Armée, Hôtel National des Invalides
Picnic Lunch, Champ de Mars

Friday

Ladies' Spa Morning / Gentlemen's Surprise
Full Guest List Open House, Cocktails and Music

Saturday

Rehearsal Breakfast
Wedding Ceremony
Reception Dinner

THE PARIS MATCH

Chapter One

I am calm ⇌ *Je suis calme*
I am unbothered ⇌ *Je suis indifférent*
I am thriving ⇌ *Je m'épanouis*

Of all the many psychological tricks Layla Bailey had played on herself in preparation for this—only her second trip ever to her favorite . . . well, was it better to say, former favorite? onetime favorite? nostalgic, painful, heartbreaking favorite? . . . city in the world—typing positive affirmations into her translation app was possibly the most personally embarrassing.

Worse than the hours she'd spent not just packing, but *planning* her packing, complete with careful searching online for aggressively neutral outfit ideas, the kind that she thought would make her seem quietly sophisticated, quietly committed to not pulling any awkward focus.

Worse than the Google Doc she'd labored over on late nights after long shifts, a color-coded itinerary that did little to soothe her, especially when her eyes encountered the blocks of time she'd turned bright yellow, unignorable reminders of the unavoidable.

Worse even than the breezy, dishonest text reply she'd sent off to Cara before the cabin doors closed.

I genuinely feel fine, I promise! she'd written to her closest friend, whose asks about this trip had grown increasingly concerned over the last two weeks, and whose most recent message had read, You can use me as an excuse if you want to cancel.

But this translation app trick?

This translation app trick had her feeling as though all her preparations had been in vain.

Breezy lies she'd been telling herself for weeks.

She pressed the button on the side of her phone to darken the screen, then leaned her head back.

Je m'épanouis, she could still see behind her now-closed eyes, a mocking afterglow.

A translation app probably couldn't even be trusted with an expression like that.

But then again, Layla thought, *she* probably couldn't be trusted with those translation app sentiments at the moment, either. After all, maybe it was impossible to feel like you were thriving when you were six hours into a transatlantic flight, in a middle seat way in the back because you waited too long to book your ticket, the people on either side of you absolutely dominating your armrests, your eyes dry and your neck cricked, your wireless headphones long since lost their charge.

Maybe this was simply a mind-over-matter moment.

And Layla liked to think she excelled at mind over matter.

She took a breath through her nose, imagined wiping those silly affirmations from the whiteboard in her brain. She didn't really need affirmations, anyway. She had neutral outfits. She had that itinerary, which would actually be perfect if she swapped out the yellow for something less loud. A pale green, maybe. A beige, if such a thing was available in Google Docs.

And Cara could simply take her texts at face value.

She wouldn't—*couldn't*—understand all this, anyway. Cara had never been married, and the thing was, marriages were their own universes. Hers and Jamie's especially, she'd always thought.

They had been a family.

This trip was about *family*.

The family she'd vowed was forever.

And the family she'd been doing her best to avoid for the better part of two years.

Another shaky breath, another clearing wipe across the busy whiteboard of her mind. Better not to think too much yet about family and what you owed them, about Jamie, about universes and how they ended. Those things, you needed fresh air for. Available armrests, at the very least. The flight was nearly over, and for the next ninety minutes or so, all Layla needed to do was keep her mind as clear as she could. Keep her hands off that app.

Except then the announcement came.

It was muffled at first, a crackle in the plane's speaker. French to start, like all the announcements had been throughout the flight, and Layla's fingers twitched on her phone, though she knew the flight attendant's lightly accented English would follow. It was probably about customs procedures for landing, or another pass through the cabin to collect trash, or—

Médecin, Layla heard.

She didn't need the app for that.

By the time the flight attendant switched to English, Layla had unbuckled and leaned forward, clearing her throat delicately at the armrest hog in the aisle seat, who turned to look at her with an expression of surprise. Layla gave him a polite smile, the sort that sat as naturally on her face as a pair of scrubs on her body. She'd call it her professional smile, but what boundaries she had between the personal and the professional weren't all that clear to her these days.

It just felt like her smile. And maybe it wasn't the kind of smile that said she was thriving, but she was pretty sure it said calm and unbothered in any language.

So when the man stood from his seat to let Layla pass, she didn't need any psychological tricks at all. In the aisle, she Face ID'd back into her phone, swiped out of the translation app without even thinking about it, and pulled up the copy of her medical license she kept in her photo library. In this moment, there was no Paris, no Jamie. No family she'd failed, and no universes ending.

There was only this plane and this patient, and that sounded near enough to how she'd been living her life lately that she felt right at home.

By the time she made her way to the closest flight attendant, Layla wondered if perhaps she might not be needed—this was a big plane, a full flight, and she imagined that there was at least one other qualified physician on board. But judging by the plain relief on the uniformed man's face, Layla was going to be doing this solo, and while a little pulse of adrenaline thrummed through her—this had never happened to her before, and she'd taken a *lot* of flights over the last couple of years—she still felt perfectly in control.

She was good at her job. Good at keeping a cool head in a crisis.

In as hushed a tone as the white noise whir of the cabin would allow, the flight attendant—Marc, his name tag read—told her there was a young woman in business class who fainted on her way back from the plane's lavatory. She was awake now, but quiet, a little confused. She was traveling alone.

"She is American," Marc said, in that beautifully French way. *Ah-merry-ken.* "So we will not need to translate."

Layla nodded, but heat rose to her cheeks as he turned to lead the way up the aisle. She hoped he hadn't somehow seen her doing the affirmations.

In business class—despite the pleasant accommodations, especially compared to the sardine can where she'd been seated—Layla felt something familiar in the air, a tense temperature she knew from walking into hundreds of hospital rooms. A silent, *someone is sick* restlessness that was an infection all on its own. A couple of passengers craned their necks to look at her and Marc, brows furrowed in anxious concern. They'd probably seen the young woman faint.

Don't worry, Layla thought, silently telegraphing comfort to all of them. *I'm calm.*

And when Marc gestured toward one of the curved half pods in the middle row, another flight attendant rising from the crouched position she'd been in beside the seat, Layla proved it.

She blocked everything out but the girl in front of her, and did her job.

It was quiet work, the kind Layla excelled at: observing, listening, prompting. There was a small black kit left by Marc at her feet, but Layla didn't open it yet. Instead, she talked to fifteen-year-old Willa: not only about how she felt ("Better now. Sort of woozy still"), but also about where she was headed (to visit her aunt and uncle and cousins, her first time doing this trip alone), and about the book she was clutching in her lap ("There's this fae prince," she told Layla, voice pitching into liveliness, "and he's in love with this mortal girl").

Layla watched Willa's face carefully as she talked, looking for—but thankfully not seeing—abnormalities that would suggest something amiss with her cranial nerves. She noted the grayish tint to Willa's skin; she listened to the arid clicking sound the girl's mouth made during a particularly long sentence.

And when Willa was ready—when she was detailing how the fae prince's mother gave the mortal girl a dose of deadly poison—Layla made use of the subpar tools in the kit. She listened to Willa's chest, checked her blood pressure, measured her respiration and heart rate. Layla asked mild questions about Willa's trip and her book and the five friendship bracelets she had stacked on her right wrist, but in between she asked other things: could Willa squeeze two of Layla's fingers, did she take any medication, how much had she had to eat and drink today.

It wasn't complicated, as cases go, and one thing about Layla's line of work was, she was well acquainted with complicated. What Willa needed was some snacks and a drink and probably a longer adjustment period with the new meds she'd started last week for her ADHD before taking a transatlantic flight. Since the ship on the latter had long since sailed, Layla focused on getting Willa hydrated and fed.

"The food on this plane is *not* good," the girl said at the suggestion, so dramatically that Layla had to press her lips together to stop a laugh.

"Let's try a little something anyway," she said smoothly, switching from her crouched position to sit fully in the aisle. She kept her face placid through a disturbing thought about an airplane floor's cleanliness, then smiled up at Willa when she was newly settled.

By now it felt different than simple doctoring: Were this a hospital room, Layla would have already made her exit, leaving someone else to take over the logistics of treatment. But here, Layla's responsibilities were more complicated—now that she'd treated Willa, she wouldn't leave her until she could place her in the care of the aunt and uncle. Even without those obligations, though, she wouldn't have minded staying, wouldn't have minded the opportunity to distract Willa with conversation, to watch color come back into the girl's cheeks as her blood sugar stabilized and her nervousness eased.

It was the most calm and unbothered Layla had felt in days.

By the time Willa asked her what she was traveling to Paris for, she didn't even need to take a meditative breath before answering.

"A wedding," she said—*breezily*—and thought: *I genuinely feel fine.*

She thought of Emily, her beloved and now former sister-in-law, thought of the handwritten note Emily had written to accompany the elegant save-the-date that came in the mail to Layla's barely lived-in apartment in Boston, the earnest phone call they had not long after, both of them trying not to cry. Emily had only been a few years younger than Willa when Layla first met her all those years ago, back when things were brand-new with Jamie, and now Em was getting *married*, married in *Paris*, and that would be wonderful for her, and Layla could be for her what she was being right now for Willa.

Not a doctor, okay, but still. A pleasant, supportive guest. Unflappable and selfless.

She owed Emily that. She owed the entire family that, especially after staying away so long.

Willa practically beamed at her, and Layla felt it like reassurance, a warranty seal on the fact that this trip would be okay. She would walk into this entire destination wedding week like she'd walked into this part of the cabin only a few minutes ago. The best possible version of herself.

"I love wedd—" Willa began, and then everything pretty much went to hell.

* * *

It started with a voice—too loud, too angry, and, if Layla had to guess, alcohol soaked.

"If she's sick," some man boomed, "she should be moved to the back of the plane!"

Like that, Layla's focus widened again. If she'd managed to lower the temperature of the cabin at all with her care for Willa, it ticked up again in response to this passenger's belligerence. She could sense bodies shifting in their little luxury pods, the tops of heads rising above curved plastic to peer at the source of the noise. From Layla's vantage point, she basically only had a clear view of Willa, who'd blanched gray-white again.

"I didn't pay for a seat up here to get whatever she has!" the man bellowed.

Layla rose to her knees. She put the placid smile back on her face and set a hand on Willa's forearm.

"You're okay," she told the girl, patting softly and nodding at the cup of ginger ale in Willa's hand. "Have a little more."

"Don't go," said Willa, a note of desperation in her voice.

"I won't." Still, she got her feet beneath her, lifted herself enough from her knees to see better.

The voice was so loud because it was only a row behind them—a window seat, opposite side of the plane, and Layla could see Marc leaning down, speaking softly. When he moved slightly, Layla got a look at the owner of the belligerent voice—a florid-faced, mussed-looking older man in a wrinkled, sweat-ringed blue dress shirt. He pointed at Marc accusingly.

"This better not get in the way of deplaning on time," he shouted.

Someone else—maybe someone at Layla's back—said the word

Ah-merry-ken again amid a torrent of irritated French, but this time it certainly didn't sound all that beautiful, and Layla thought that was fair enough.

Beneath her hand, Willa tensed, and Layla patted again.

But it was one of *those* situations—the kind Layla hated most, a mind-under-matter collapse of a little mob of people at odds. Another passenger turned in her seat to snap at the drunken man, then another flight attendant came over. There was increasing use of the word *sir*, a mention of getting the pilot involved. There was pointing and more shouting. Marc and his colleague seemed to lose the battle against this man's flailing, unfocused rage—now, he was ranting about the growing unavailability of peanuts in public spaces—and Layla felt like she was having that warranty seal from Willa ripped right off. She knew, rationally, that there was no connection to this asshole's mess and the week she had ahead of her, but it still pressed on everything she wanted to avoid, the exact opposite of all her affirmations.

She felt responsible somehow—the doctor called to settle a situation, and now it had escaped her control. If she could let someone know that Willa was fine, that there was no indication she was contagious, that the whole matter was resolving easily and that there would be no cause for any delays . . .

"Willa," she said quietly, leaning down. "I'm going to speak briefly to the flight attendant."

But before she could, another man stood from his seat.

Also one row back from Willa's, also along the window, but closer to Layla—directly opposite the shouting. To Layla, he was in profile, facing the disturbance, but . . . but god, it was a striking profile. Thick black hair pushed back from a face that looked carved from stone—strong brow, sharp nose, full lips set, and a stubbled jaw cutting horizontally across the line of his neck. The hair on his head, on his cheeks, matched the clothes on his lean body—black long-sleeved T-shirt, loose-fitting black pants, a black ball cap fisted in the hand Layla could see.

Her breath caught, her heart thumped. She saw his mouth move, no sound that she could hear, but still, it made her skin prickle with warmth.

Well, it was the circumstances, obviously—this reaction in her, this heat in her. It was the tense scene across the aisle that had started because of poor Willa, and Layla was responsible for Willa, and now this man was part of it, too . . .

His mouth moved again.

She heard him this time.

"Quiet," he said. "Be. *Quiet*."

It was a white-hot blade, that voice. She couldn't even say if it was particularly loud, if anyone across the way could actually hear it. But it was *cutting*. All edge. A voice like his face, like the way he held his body. Angles everywhere.

It worked for a few seconds—slicing right through the man with the red face and the boozy voice, silencing Marc and his stressed-looking colleague, who both stared in shock across the middle seats. If the drunk man's anger was a thick, cloaking cloud, this man in black's anger was a lightning bolt.

Bright and electrifying.

"Sir," Marc finally managed. "You'll need to return to—"

"If you want off this plane quickly," the man in black said to the drunkard, as though Marc hadn't even made an attempt, "you will be quiet. Because if this disturbance carries on, it will be me who needs medical attention, and you'll be stuck on that runway for however long it takes for me to get it."

Layla blinked up at him—up, because she now realized she'd somehow sunk back down to her knees—in surprise.

It will be me who needs medical attention.

She *shouldn't* be surprised, of course she shouldn't—she knew sick didn't always look a certain way. She was just rattled, not thinking straight.

She was shocked through by the big-bang, lightning-bolt effect of him.

She looked quickly at Willa, whose nerves had apparently eased off long enough to get interested in the show—she was practically leaning out of her pod to get a look at the man. Layla waited, kneeling there, thinking, *This can't possibly be the end of it*, because he was just some handsome man with sharp words of censure and an unnaturally still posture after he said them.

That *couldn't* be enough to silence or sober up the man across the way.

But after several seconds, it was still so *quiet*, only the regular hum of the cabin again, and the man in black kept his eyes straight ahead until he saw something that satisfied him enough to turn away, his whole face toward Layla now—the full effect of it striking in a different way.

He was scarred, she could see, and severely, if not recently, so: a whorl of pink raised texture at his temple, along his cheekbone, pulling the left side of his brow lower and disrupting his hairline. Along his jaw, a patch of similarly terrained skin, completely bare of stubble.

He met her eyes and she thought again of what he'd said—*me who needs medical attention*—and she reached for the placid smile, the cool control, the secure knowledge she'd had only a few moments ago that she was calm enough to do her job. She would ask if he needed help, be the best version of herself again, get that warranty seal reaffixed before this flight ended and she had to face the week ahead.

But in his gaze she was a stunned and smoking tree trunk, rooted to the ground, her mouth open as if poised to speak, except with nothing available to come out. She thought of her phone, her translation app, thought of a language she would call *Lightning-Struck*, and how to make it English again.

She watched as he raised the hand not holding his cap, saw that it was scarred, too. In a swift motion he smoothed back his hair and lifted the hat onto his head, pulling it low over his eyes so she could no longer tell if he was looking at her.

It helped, a little. She could finally get a word out.

"Sir," she said, like Marc had, and she hoped it didn't sound scolding. "Do you need—"

"I said *if*," he snapped, and she blinked in confusion before she could translate herself back into his earlier words.

If this disturbance carries on, he'd said.

Since it hadn't, he didn't have need of her.

She pressed her lips together and swallowed, strangely unrelieved.

When he began to lower himself back into his seat, Layla thought he'd released her from whatever spell he seemed to cast.

Fae prince and mortal girl, she thought briefly.

Wildly.

But before she could turn her attention back to Willa, the man stopped himself, halfway to sitting, and lifted his head again to look at her.

"Get up from there," he said, scalpel-sharp. "The floor is probably disgusting."

Then the brim of his hat lowered again, his lanky form folded back into his seat, his face turning toward the window.

Like nothing had ever happened at all.

For Layla, though . . . for Layla, *something* had happened, something she couldn't mind-over-matter herself out of, something that she wasn't sure she could ever explain. She thought—she *hoped*—she spent the rest of the flight hiding it from Willa, from Marc, from any other passenger who might've noticed her.

But she couldn't be sure, because she couldn't seem to affirm herself into any more lies.

They had been shocked right out of her body.

She was not at all calm about attending Emily's wedding.

Certainly not unbothered about seeing her ex-husband again.

And somehow, for some reason she couldn't begin to explain, everything about that interaction with the man in black made her feel as though Paris was the last place in the world where she would thrive.

Chapter Two

"Layla? Layla, oh my god, you're *here*!"

Layla had barely taken two steps into the hotel lobby before she heard Emily's voice: that clear, bright-as-a-bell voice, as excited as Layla had heard it probably a hundred times before, at a hundred different family gatherings.

It's happening, she thought, surprisingly relieved. *No turning back now.*

She could admit that her brief, pretty much one-sided interaction with the man in black on the plane had been difficult to shake off, even after the whirlwind that followed: landing and deplaning and passport control, all with Willa, followed by maybe the most chaotic meeting Layla had ever had with a patient's family. Willa's aunt and uncle—an effusive, quick-to-tears American woman and an elegant, fast-talking French man—showered her with a truly overwhelming amount of praise and gratitude, insisting that Layla simply *must* take some tangible form of thanks for helping and staying with Willa. At one point, the aunt had so forcefully tried to shove a stack of euros into her hands—"I insist, I *insist*!"—that Layla had cringed in embarrassment, and the uncle took over with a more sensible offer: a hired car to take Layla wherever she needed to be, to make up for whatever extra time she'd taken to wait with Willa.

In the end, agreeing to take a chauffeured car was better than taking a stack of cash, and once it pulled up—glossy midnight blue, with tinted windows and a brand-new smell—Layla decided that it couldn't hurt to have a few private moments in that sort of pristine comfort.

The opposite of *The floor is probably disgusting.*

The opposite of that man in black's expression, like it was Layla herself who inspired such revulsion.

But in the butter-soft back seat of the car, Layla still couldn't forget it. Even as central Paris came into view, she couldn't forget it. She wanted to see the panorama of the city with a mature, settled fondness, wanted to re-familiarize herself with its domes and spires and its great soaring tower, its rooftops and windows and balconies trailing flowers, its awnings and café tables and glass cases of delicious beauty.

Instead, it was the universe crashing into her.

These were streets she'd walked and sights she'd seen as a newlywed, with Jamie at her side, Jamie as the more experienced, well-traveled guide.

Disgusting, Layla kept thinking, and every time she did, she felt a rush of renewed frustration and shame.

No man should be able to ruin *Paris*.

At the very least, not some random man on an airplane who she'd never really met.

Out of the car and inside the hotel lobby, though, with Emily's voice ringing in her ears—*You're here!*—Layla was reminded of the immediate task ahead.

So she smiled as Emily bounded into view, wearing a flowing knee-length dress so pale pink it looked almost white, perfectly bridal. It wasn't the sort of boho style Emily used to favor, but Layla knew on sight that Manon—Emily and Jamie's mom, and Layla's former mother-in-law—had probably picked it out. Layla could remember standing before a dressing room mirror in a similarly blush-colored sundress a week before her own wedding shower, Manon nodding in approval from behind her.

"Em," Layla said, and opened her arms.

Emotion clutched in her throat immediately as Em hugged her—tightly, fiercely—and for Layla, it felt like having the wound from the plane wrapped.

This was *right*. It was right to be here for Emily.

As they both pulled back, Layla smiled, determined not to show Em the strange mix of relief and guilt and happiness and sadness that welled up in her. But Emily's eyes brimmed with wetness, and when two big drops spilled over, Em didn't bother wiping them away.

"You can't know how much it means to me that you came," she said, voice soggy, and that mix of emotion in Layla's body reconstituted itself, dominated now by guilt. "You really can't know," Emily repeated.

But Layla *could* know. She'd met Emily almost fourteen years ago now, when Layla was twenty and Emily was turning eleven, both of them on very different thresholds of growing up, and their bond had been quick, concrete. Layla was the big sister Emily never had, and Emily a sibling who—unlike Layla's one, much older half brother, Vaughn—actually seemed to care meaningfully about Layla's existence. When Layla and Jamie had finally told the family about their split—together, of course they'd done it together—Emily had been devastated. No one cried harder; no one asked more questions.

But why?

What did he do?
How will we stay close?
Will you promise to still be my sister?
Will you promise nothing will change?

By then, Em had been twenty-three, probably too old to be asking such grasping, desperate questions. But it was always there, that big- and little-sister dynamic between them. Layla remembered every one of her calm, dry-as-a-bone big-sister answers.

It's not any one thing.
This isn't his fault.
Of course I'm always your sister.
The important things won't change.

She hadn't intended for all of those answers to be a lie.

"Of course I came," Layla said, though the *Of course* felt like another lie, given the last year and a half of pretty much avoiding everyone, so she added, "I'm really happy to be here."

As she said it, she let her eyes wander to take in the lobby for the first time, and felt a rush of gratitude for its sleek, luxurious blandness: overwhelmingly marble-white with touches of black and brushed gold, oversize columns segmenting the space that looked more like sculpture than architecture, the furniture low-slung and uninviting.

It didn't feel even a little like the Paris she once fell in love with.

"I wish you could've come to my shower, too," Emily said, interrupting her thoughts, and Layla met her eyes again, looking for accusation there, a sort of *A sister would've been at the shower* judgment.

But Em hadn't ever been the judgmental sort, and all Layla saw in her face was genuine regret.

"My job," Layla said automatically, defaulting to the excuse she had used so often with the MacKenzies since the divorce, until they all eventually stopped asking for things that required an excuse. "It's hard to get time away during my placements."

"Right," Em said cheerfully. "How is it? Still going well?"

"It's great."

It was the answer she gave to everyone who asked, and she was sure she meant it, despite what had prompted her to take her current position as a locum tenens physician. When the recruiter had first reached out, the job—basically, being a doctor who took temporary four-to-six-week placements at hospitals where there were staffing shortages or doctors on leave—had appealed as an escape hatch, a way to avoid the crushing, hard-to-keep promises she'd made in the wake of the divorce.

A year and a half in, she could admit that there were other real benefits to the work. The money, of course. Seeing different parts of the country. Time off whenever she wanted it.

That she hadn't really taken advantage of any of those perks yet—that she spent little, got out even less, worked more than she could ever remember—well.

Well, that wasn't for Emily to know.

Em nodded and clutched Layla's hands, and then Layla was being pulled over to one of those low-slung sofas, its fabric lush and its cushions more comfortable than they looked. Still, once she was seated, she looked longingly over at the small luggage cart with her suitcase and carry-on that the hotel's porter had left by the reservations desk.

If she could only have a little time to check in, to freshen up...

"I'm texting Michael," Emily was saying, her face tipped down to her phone, her thumbs flying over the screen. "I can't wait for you to meet him."

Layla stared, her brain sluggish to catch up. She maybe shouldn't have sat down, because it was hitting her now, an overnight flight without sleep, and the adrenaline-rush ending of it.

"On the . . . on the cruise tomorrow, right?" she said, calling one of those yellow itinerary slots up in her mind. Today and most of tomorrow were meant to be no-yellow-at-all adjustment days for Layla. If it'd been up to her, she wouldn't have run into anyone— even Emily—before things officially got underway tomorrow evening.

"Well, yeah, but he's on his way back here!" Em's phone pinged and she looked down. "He'll be here in like ten! That's so *great!*"

"Oh, um—maybe I could change first, or—"

"Oh my gosh, *no*, you look great. This tonal dressing is very you. Quiet luxury!"

Layla looked down at the beige lounge set she'd worn for the flight. *Aggressively neutral.* But also, Em was being generous. It did not look quietly luxurious right now; it looked crinkled and saggy. And she hadn't really taken a close look to see whether she'd picked up anything from that *disgusting* airplane floor.

"Please wait?" Emily said. "I really want you to meet him."

You would have met him already, she imagined another version of Emily saying. *You would have met him, if you'd kept all your promises to me.*

I meant to, she imagined another version of herself saying back. *I meant to have the most amicable divorce in history; I meant to stay so close to all of you. I meant to keep showing up for friendly monthly coffee dates with Jamie, I meant to come to every single family gathering, I meant to be the kind of sister I was to you before.*

I meant to be better at all of it.

"Sure," she said instead. "I'm so excited to meet him."

Emily smiled brightly, but almost immediately, her smile

dimmed, and she grabbed Layla's hand again, her eyes suddenly pleading.

"Let's just do it," she blurted. "Let's talk about it before Michael gets here. You know that when I invited you, I didn't know, I didn't ever think Jamie—"

"Em," Layla interrupted, knowing exactly where this was going, and not wanting to dwell there for too long. "It's really okay."

Jamie had called Layla last month to tell her he was bringing someone, of course he had. A call she'd let go to voice mail at first, even though she hadn't been busy when she'd seen his name—just "Jamie" now, changed from the smug "Husband" nickname she'd added to her contacts the morning after their wedding—come up on her screen. His voice had been cautious when she finally listened to the message. *Lay, can you call me, please? It's really important. I don't want to text.*

She had a sense about what he'd say. Embarrassingly, she'd already clocked that he'd stopped posting on his social media recently, and she'd been speculating.

He's seeing someone. He doesn't want to flaunt it, not yet. He's trying to be respectful. Kind.

Amicable.

She'd been right. She knew Jamie, knew him in her bones.

So of course she'd been right.

By then, she'd already accepted Emily's invitation, and couldn't bear the thought of how it would look to back out after his call. Couldn't bear to take him up on his offer to not bring his new girlfriend at all, *if it would make things too hard for you.*

"I'm really happy for him," she added now, hoping she wasn't laying it on too thick. "We're all here for *you.*"

Emily nodded and her eyes welled up again, but she rolled them upward in embarrassment, pulling her hand from Layla's so she could press the sides of both of her index fingers gently against her lower lids.

"I'm so emotional!" she said, with frustrated laughter, and Layla laughed, too. It felt good to release some of the anxious air trapped inside her. She thought of those moments with Willa on the plane, and remembered who she wanted to be for Emily this week.

Pleasant, unflappable.

Supportive.

"I'm sure that'll happen a lot this week," Layla said knowingly, slipping into something approaching that big-sister role. Easy enough to maintain it for the next few minutes, for meeting Michael.

Emily dropped her hands and shook them dramatically in front of her, like she was drying them out.

"Okay, but! It's not going to happen *tonight*, because we are going *out*!"

Layla blinked, the Google Doc's blank spaces a photograph in her mind.

"My parents and Jamie and, you know, everyone"—a deft sidestep, that *everyone*, Layla thought—"don't get here until *way* late tonight, and Rosie and I have a dinner planned. I would love for you to join, really! Rosie *adores* you!"

Rosie was Emily's former college roommate and best friend. Layla had always liked her the few times they'd met, but not enough to abandon the blank space of her Google Doc. Right now she was thinking about getting a baguette from the nearest bakery and eating it like a turkey leg while fully under the covers in her hotel bed.

It would be disgusting.

"I think I better take it easy tonight," she said.

"Oh, but you can't! Rosie will absolutely die if you don't come; she'll be so mad. And I'm already in the doghouse because I'm pretty sure she hates the bridesmaid's dress I picked for her, but you know how Rosie is, so particular about her style!"

As far as Layla could remember, Rosie's style could be best characterized as "Add a piercing to it," so probably there were a lot of ways for Emily to go wrong with her choice of bridesmaid's dress. But either way, Layla was not in any condition to find out for herself this evening. She needed alone time, not dinner with two twenty-five-year-olds.

The baguette, the bed. That was the itinerary.

But as she was gearing up to make her excuses—she even thought about bringing up Willa and the bit of work she'd done on the plane to earn herself some more fatigue points—Emily practically vaulted from the couch.

"Michael!"

Layla stood, uselessly smoothing the front of her saggy lounge set, expecting to raise her eyes and see the blond, blue-eyed, and warmly smiling man she'd become superficially familiar with from Emily's various social media posts.

Instead, her eyes clashed with someone else's.

Oh no, she thought. *No, it can't be.*

But it was.

It was the man in black.

He was, unfortunately, as striking as he'd been at first sight.

He was also looking at her with that same unimpressed—no, not unimpressed . . . *scornful*, maybe?—expression that he'd leveled down at her from beside his business-class seat.

There was a buzzing, electric-shock feeling all along her spine.

Was she hallucinating him?

Had the disgusting bed-and-baguette plan brought it on?

But no: He was really there. She knew because he blinked—flinched, maybe—when Emily bounded to a stop beside him, throwing her arms around the other man Layla now noticed for the first time. He was a little older than Layla expected, older than he had looked in those probably filtered photos—a slightly receding hairline, deepish crinkles around his eyes. But when he smiled and bent his tall form to embrace Emily, he looked younger. He looked like the sort of person who recognized how great his fiancée's hugs always were.

She probably would've been able to appreciate that more about him, but she was too busy snapping her eyes back to the other man, who now stood with his hands in his pockets. A sentient column of smoke.

This was not a coincidence.

Not two separate hotel guests entering simultaneously.

He was *with* Michael.

He had come here with Michael.

How?

"Layla, hi," a deep, gentle voice said, and then Michael was in front of her, arms out tentatively for a hug, the sort of introductory embrace you give someone you have a built-in bond with, a *we've-been-waiting-to-meet* connection.

Even through her shock, Layla could tell that he was like Emily: friendly and confident and kind.

She leaned in, her return embrace feeling awkward and stilted. She knew the other man—the man in black—was still watching. Taking in, perhaps, that she had never been a natural at hugging someone new.

"I can't say enough how much it matters to Em that you came," Michael was saying as they parted again, his voice soft, as though making his best effort at discretion. "It was a huge ask, I know."

Closer up, Layla could see that those eye crinkles framed a world-weariness, and she wondered whether he was nearer to her own age than Emily's, maybe even a little older. Were she able to think about anything else but the stranger still watching her—she was certain he was still watching her—she would've been curious about this, maybe concerned about it. Would have been eager to learn more about what had brought Michael and Emily together, what their relationship dynamic was like.

"Let me introduce you to my best man," Michael said, and Layla's stomach flipped. "This is Griffin Testa."

She moved her eyes to him again, because it would have been rude not to. But he didn't smile. Didn't take his hands out of his pockets. Didn't acknowledge that he had been introduced to anyone at all.

"Hi, Griff," Em said, in the pause left there, and for the first time, the man broke slightly, shifting his gaze to Emily and offering the smallest tip of his lips. The very barest imitation of a smile.

"Em," he said, nodding. His voice was less like a lightning bolt for such a small syllable, but that didn't seem to matter to Layla, who felt the clutching silence from the plane grip her again.

Emily, it was clear, could not abide it.

"This is my . . ." She trailed off for a second, made a wincing recalibration. "This is my friend Layla," she finished gamely.

The man—Griffin—said nothing.

And suddenly, that electricity that had been humming through Layla took on a new cast.

It animated her, spreading from her spine out, sparking into her fingers and toes and behind her teeth. She'd spent the last couple of hours doing her absolute best to *be* her absolute best, and this man was so needlessly rude for *no reason*, right here in front of the person he was supposed to be the actual best man for?

It made her... it made her *angry*.

"We've met," she found herself saying, wishing she could manage something like the cutting sharpness he'd used back on the plane. But still, she could hear a faint coolness in her tone, and that was a victory of a sort.

"What?" Emily said, eyes darting between them now. "Where?"

Layla waited a beat to see if he would answer.

He didn't.

"We were on the same flight," Layla supplied.

Emily looked delighted, and then disappointed. "Really? I wish I would've realized! Michael could've met you at the airport, too. You could've all ridden—"

"It's fine," Layla said quickly, waving a dismissive hand. She wanted to feel judgmental of Griffin getting a personalized pickup in a city where public transit options were easy and abundant, but then again, her own public transit plans had folded pretty quickly in the face of that luxury car windfall Willa's uncle provided.

"Were you sitting near each other?" Michael asked. Layla detected a note of concern in his voice.

"No," Griffin said. Flat and final.

Layla thought a *nice* person, a normal person, would follow up with more information, but Griffin Testa was obviously not a nice or normal person.

He was a human black hole.

She cleared her throat delicately. "There was a medical issue near where he was seated. I did some light intervention."

Emily gasped dramatically. "Oh! Was everyone okay?"

"Everyone was fine," Layla said smoothly.

Because I handled it, because I was calm and unbothered, mind over matter, like I am now, no matter how this man standing here now made me feel in the moment.

"Just a bit tense," she added. "You know how flying is these days. Short tempers."

Michael's expression changed from interest to suspicion. His gaze snapped to his friend.

"Griff," he said, making no effort to conceal the note of frustration—of disappointment—in his voice.

But Layla was too busy noticing something else: the slight, nearly undetectable grimace that passed over Griffin's face.

She hadn't meant to suggest that he'd *started* it.

In fact, if she was honest, he'd ended it for pretty much everyone else on that plane.

Except for her.

She waited for him to say something to defend himself in the face of his friend's censure, but he didn't. And she shouldn't care about that, not after how he'd treated her.

How he looked at her.

But as though her mouth had a mind entirely of its own, she found herself speaking again.

"He helped defuse the situation, actually. It was sort of . . ." She trailed off, searching her mind for a word that was not *electric*.

"Heroic," she finished, and then wished she could sink straight into the marble floor.

Griffin looked at her as though she had betrayed him.

She swallowed, at war with herself. Should she stay in this . . . in this staring contest with him? Should she drop her eyes, a form of apology for what anyone else would take as a compliment?

Michael's hand clapped heavily onto Griffin's shoulder, and this time, he more than barely grimaced. He winced, his face contorting unevenly.

"Really, bud?" Michael said, seemingly oblivious to his friend's discomfort.

"It was nothing." A dull knife, now, that voice, but it still scraped all along Layla's skin.

"It was something!" said Michael, and then he turned to Layla. "Griff is afraid of flying. Terrified, really."

Layla swallowed, her mind flashing to Griffin's words from before: *It will be me who needs medical attention.*

She wondered if he had anxiety, if he had been on the verge of a panic attack, if he maybe had—

But when their eyes connected again, it was like she could feel him beaming his other words directly into her brain, his curt, dismissive *I said* if.

He didn't want her help or her concern. He didn't want her to know anything about him.

And that was fine by Layla. She had enough on her plate, dealing with the guests she already knew this week. She didn't need to spend any of her time learning some other man's minefields.

She didn't need someone looking at her like she had something to be ashamed of.

She would have to get used to ignoring him.

But when Michael and Emily both laughed, Layla realized she'd lost herself again in Griffin's piercing, disdainful gaze, and she knew ignoring him wouldn't be easy.

And when Em asked her again if she'd come along to dinner, if she'd *please please please* come, she thought of that bed-and-baguette plan again and could only hear the word *disgusting* in Griffin's sharp voice.

She couldn't have him wrecking her bed or a lovely baguette. She couldn't have him taking another part of Paris from her.

Not tonight.

So she smiled and looked at her former sister-in-law, and calmly said, "What time?"

Chapter Three

In the mirror, Layla looked precisely the way she wanted to.

She looked *polished*.

It had been stressful, choosing an outfit for this unplanned outing—she would need to figure out what to swap in for one of the other wedding events—but for now, she was happy with the navy, a satin midi skirt and matching fitted cotton boatneck top. It was the sort of outfit she'd admired when she'd been in Paris all those years ago, watching elegant women sit at cafés—granted, very unconcerned about the deleterious effects of cigarette smoke on every major organ of the body, but Layla could overlook that in her honeymoon haze—or strut down uneven streets in heels that spoke of their coordination, their command over themselves.

Layla would need to be careful in her own heels, but at the moment, she was determined.

She'd been determined pretty much since that moment with Griffin Testa in the lobby.

She grabbed her phone from where it rested on the room's bed—a full size, because while the hotel itself was big, this was still Paris, and the rooms ran small—and opened her camera app. She was not a particularly skilled selfie-taker, but she saw an opportunity here. A few awkward, unsuccessful attempts later, when she finally managed a shot in the mirror that did not make her question whether she'd ever managed to stand attractively still in her life, she sent it off to Cara with an accompanying text.

> Dinner tonight with the bride! Paris is great so far.

That was a white lie. If Paris was great, she wouldn't really know yet, because she hadn't left the hotel, not even for the baguette. Instead she'd taken a long, hot shower and a not-recommended-for-staving-off-jet-lag nap, then did a very self-indulgent skin care routine. She'd carefully filled out an elegant little card left on her bed about preferences for her stay, selecting mature and sensible things like having an English-language newspaper delivered outside her door every morning.

But that was not the kind of information that would suggest to Cara that she was *thriving*, so she left it out, adding a red heart emoji and a French flag before pressing send. On reflection, that probably would seem suspicious to Cara. Layla was not prone to emoji use.

It was still early back in Boston, still well in the realm of Cara's workday, so Layla was surprised when the little dots bounced on her screen immediately.

STUNNING!!!!!! was the first reply, and Layla smiled. Cara loved an exclamation point. Or several.

More bouncing dots, then, Gotta go deal with a GSW. Text me later!

If Layla was the emoji type, she would've sent that face with the crooked grimace and flushed cheeks. It was very awkward to have texted someone who was going in to treat a gunshot wound with a mirror selfie. Especially when said mirror selfie was probably more about proving something to Cara than it was about sharing something genuine.

But before she could think of anything to write back, there were the dots again.

    Take care of yourself, ok?

No exclamation.

Layla's smile slipped. She could read a world of concern in that text. She didn't want to text *Stop worrying* again, so she slid her phone into her clutch and decided she was ready to go.

In the hall, she waited in front of the elevator doors, surprised by the pulse of optimism that gathered in her middle. The nap had done her good; the night out would do her good. In fact, going out was the far better plan for avoiding jet lag, so she could be at her freshest tomorrow, and spending some time with Emily without the rest of the MacKenzies would be its own way of easing into the week.

C'est bon, she thought to herself. She knew enough French on her own for that.

Then the elevator doors opened.

And there was Griffin Testa.

Layla wished she could remember how the French said *Fuck*.

She stood at the threshold, hesitating. It would be weird not to get on; she knew this.

But you didn't ride the elevator with a lightning bolt.

Except then—then he stepped slightly to the side, as though to make room for her, and she caught her reflection again in the mirrored interior of the elevator, looking polished and maybe a *little*

Parisian, and he seemed to still be wearing the same clothes from the plane, so actually, who was the lightning bolt here?

She stepped over the threshold.

"Hello," she said coolly.

He didn't say anything back, which by now was unsurprising.

Layla *tried* not to look at him; she really did. But it was impossible with all these mirrors, and once she did look, it was hard to stop, because...

Because there was something wrong with him, she was pretty sure.

For one thing, his breathing was labored, a quick rise and fall she could see in his chest. She couldn't hear a wheeze, which was good, but when she turned her head to look at him directly, she saw a splotchy redness covering his neck. A bead of sweat trailing down his temple. His jaw held so tight, as though he was bracing himself.

She opened her mouth to speak.

"Don't tell Michael you saw me," he said.

She blinked at him. "Oh . . . kay?"

His shoulder jerked slightly. An involuntary spasm. When he reached forward to press impatiently at the button for the lobby, she thought he might've done it to cover the movement.

He pressed it again. Forcefully.

"I don't think that's going to make it go faster," Layla said.

He lowered his hand again, blew out a breath. Shoved it back in his pocket.

The elevator started to move—an annoying validation of his frantic button-pressing—and maybe the corner of his mouth ticked up. Maybe.

Foolishly, it felt to her like an opening.

"Listen, are you all ri—"

"Are you the ex?"

Layla stared, stunned.

"The brother's ex-wife, I mean," Griffin clarified.

"I'm—" She paused, cleared her throat. God, had *she* wheezed? "I'm Emily's friend."

"Right. But you're her brother's ex-wife."

His voice was different than it had been on the plane, even than it had been in the lobby. Quieter and raspier, but not any less effective. Less of a slice, but definitely a death-by-a-thousand-cuts situation.

Her silence must have served as an answer.

"It must be uncomfortable," he said, and it felt like an indictment. Like he was saying, *Don't pretend you're calm, don't pretend you're not like me on the inside, panting and splotchy and sweating and twitching to be out of here.*

She could not look at him directly anymore. Only in the mirror, where they stood side by side, her in navy, him in black.

We look like a bruise, she thought.

But she said, "It's not. It was amicable."

In the mirror, she saw his mouth move enough to make room for the noise of derision—of denial—that he made. He was watching her, too.

He could strip the polish right off her with his gaze.

"*What* is your problem?"

It was strange saying it this way, to the mirror and not to him. She could see too much of herself in it.

He didn't answer. He just waited as the elevator slowed to a stop, as it offered up a pleasant, mechanical ding that felt far too light for the moment.

For the two of them.

When the doors slid open, Griffin Testa kept his gaze straight ahead and said, "I'm not afraid of flying."

Then he stepped out, striding quickly across the lobby. Out of the glass doors.

Into the falling dark of the Paris night, alone.

"What. An. *Asshole!*"

Rosie made the proclamation so loudly that Layla had to stifle a groan of embarrassment. They were in a small restaurant in the Marais, not far from the hotel, crowded and rich with animated conversation. Still, Rosie—who had maintained her fashion for piercings, including a fresh one on the shell of her ear that was simply too red and puffy for Layla's professional comfort—had the sort of giddy shriek to her voice that called attention.

Layla did not think this was the sort of restaurant where people yelled the word "asshole." Plus, since Rosie was speaking in her brash American English, Layla was pretty sure she shouldn't be yelling anything.

Just to avoid playing so much to type.

But it was hard to hold it against her. The truth was, Rosie was *fun*. Distracting. Her elfin face full of shiny jewelry and her brain full of shiny thoughts, changing topics so frequently that Layla's own mind couldn't land on anything for too long, which was a relief after the elevator.

Beside her, Em laughed but also shushed Rosie mildly. "He's *not*, not really!"

Emily's defense of her future father-in-law was sweet, even if the description she'd provided of him over the last few minutes was really making Rosie's case for her.

"He's just like . . . *very* military?" Em added.

Layla soaked this up, another detail she was glad to have about all things Michael and Emily. So far, even amid Rosie's chaos, she'd managed to steer the conversation that way, and she was grateful.

It was good to know more about the man Em would marry: that he and Emily first met in a coffee shop in Beacon Hill, when Michael had been in town for work, a story that involved a spilled latte and a small dog in a purse (the dog was fine), which Rosie had proclaimed in advance "a meet-cute for the ages!"; that he worked for the government, though Layla got the sense that Emily wasn't allowed to say too much about precisely what he did; that he was warm and sensitive and doting in spite of having a father who seemed the opposite; and that his hands shook with nerves on the night he proposed. He was, in fact, quite a bit older than Emily—about a decade—but Emily mentioned it only as the most passing, insignificant detail about their relationship.

"Michael used to be in the military," said Rosie. "And *he's* not an asshole."

Emily shrugged, sipping her wine, her lips stained slightly red. Layla took a drink from her own glass, marveling at the reality of sharing wine with someone she still thought of, in some ways, as a kid. She remembered one early weekend at the MacKenzie home, introducing Em to *Mean Girls* over a bowl of popcorn and too many cans of Coke.

It was bittersweet to clock how much Emily had changed—obviously, in the many years since Layla first knew her, but also in this comparatively short span of time that Layla had stayed away.

The essence of Emily was still there—her optimism, her cheerfulness—but she had matured, too: She spoke confidently about her work as a freelance technical writer, had taken the shifting tides of Michael's job in stride. A couple of months after the wedding, they'd be relocating to Germany for two years, and Emily's research on and preparation for the move seemed impeccable.

More than that, she was more in command than Layla had ever seen her. When they met in the lobby, Layla still buzzing from that strange interaction on the elevator with Griffin, she worried that she'd fail at the sort of pleasantries required of a dinner out where she didn't know one of her companions very well. But Emily had smoothed the way for her and Rosie effortlessly—engaging them about their respective jobs, finding overlapping interests. And when they sat down at the restaurant, it was Em who took the lead, reading the menu where Layla and Rosie couldn't, speaking in slow but competent French to their server, holding the line with her efforts even when the man spoke back to her in English.

"I've been practicing my French and German a lot since Michael and I made the decision on the relo," she said, by way of explanation. "I want to feel comfortable getting around on my own."

Frankly, Layla was in awe of her transformation.

And more than a little rueful that she'd missed watching it as it had happened.

The server came to clear their entrée plates—Layla had eaten a truly astounding piece of fish, reminded on her first bite that it was Paris that taught her to genuinely love butter—and Emily raised her eyebrows at her and Rosie in question about dessert, and suddenly, Layla felt so *glad*.

Yes, she wanted dessert, because it was dessert *here*, in a city that was basically hallowed ground for desserts, and also because she was having fun, and shockingly didn't feel like she had to rush back to the hotel to recover from all this, and—

"Oh my god, okay," said Rosie, slapping her hands down on the table as soon as the server retreated back into the crowd. "As much as I've loved listening to you catch Layla up, Em, we need to move on now."

A little finger of foreboding tapped on Layla's shoulder.

"To this *best man* Michael brought along." She waggled her eyebrows. One, predictably, was pierced.

Layla swallowed, the taste of wine in her mouth turning sour.

The brother's ex-wife, he'd said. Somehow it felt more like a censure than any single thing Cara had said to her leading up to this trip, all her different versions of *You don't have to do this*.

When Griffin Testa said *the brother's ex-wife*, he said it like she was the stupidest person alive.

On the one hand, Layla did not want the topic to turn to Griffin. But on the other, she did not like thinking about him already knowing something about her, and her knowing nothing about him.

Maybe she needed some kind of ammunition to be in the same room with him again.

And when Emily responded to Rosie with an uncharacteristic eye roll, a dismissive hand wave, Layla felt her curiosity pique.

"Emmmmmmmyyyyyyy," Rosie said pleadingly, jutting her bottom lip out.

Em shrugged again, for the first time tonight looking unsettled. "The truth is, I don't know much about him. He and Michael grew up together, and he's very . . ."

She trailed off, took another drink.

"Very what!" Rosie practically shouted.

Layla loved Rosie, to be honest.

"Very private," Emily said. "I don't think he leaves home much. He's like, a billionaire."

Rosie slammed her hands on the table again. "WHAT."

Layla was stuck in staring mode.

"A billionaire?" she finally echoed, her disdain obvious. Being an even moderately aware adult in the twenty-first century had taught Layla that pretty much every billionaire belonged in prison, or at the very least kept in some kind of island confinement with other billionaires, where they could circle-jerk each other all day with their evil, society-destroying ideas.

"Okay, he's not actually a billionaire," Em clarified. She paused again while the server returned with more wine, as though she couldn't say any more until they were alone once more.

Layla flashed back to Griffin's words on the elevator.

Don't tell Michael you saw me.

"But he's wealthy," Em continued. "Like, big-money wealth."

The clarification, Layla knew, was speaking. As a MacKenzie, Em had grown up with money—well-to-do grandparents on both sides, the MacKenzie side especially. Jamie's dad, Robert, ran a successful financial management firm; Manon was a professor at BC. When Layla first met them, they were buying a second home in the Berkshires, having recently come into an inheritance from Robert's late mother. They regularly talked about having a pied-à-terre here in Paris—Manon's dream—when they retired.

So if Em was saying *big money* about Griffin Testa, she meant business.

"What's he do?" Rosie asked, and in the growing fog of her wine-brain, Layla considered options that made sense given her experiences so far of Griffin.

Extremely mean vampire who has amassed money over the course of centuries. Crime boss who sells organs on the dark web. Inventor of nuclear-grade weapons.

Instead Emily said, "He doesn't work, I don't think."

Rosie's mouth was hanging open. "He doesn't *work*?"

At this point, Layla felt more hungry for information than she did for the dessert she'd ordered. It was chocolate mousse, so that was really saying something.

"I think he has passive income, maybe? A . . . patent or something?"

Layla put a little mental check mark next to her nuclear weapons idea, but then Em waved her hand again.

"I'm honestly not sure. I know he doesn't leave his house that much. Like I said, he is *really* private. Michael protects that."

Layla wondered if she was imagining the slightly irritated note in Emily's voice.

"Passive income," Rosie said, her voice awed. "Let me get my vibrator."

Emily snorted a laugh, but then her face grew serious again as she shifted her gaze to Layla.

"I am sorry," she said, "that he was so rude to you in the lobby earlier."

"He wasn't," Layla said smoothly. It didn't really feel like a lie, because he'd been ruder in the elevator, though Layla was not going to mention that.

"I'd let him be rude to me," Rosie said, gesturing vaguely to her face. "He's got a real beast-in-the-castle vibe."

Layla grimaced. It was cruel to bring up someone's scars.

"That's unkind," she said, trying to gentle her voice so it didn't sound too much like a scolding.

But Rosie seemed unfazed. "I don't really mean because of his—" This time, she simply pointed at her face before continuing. "Just, you know, the being filthy rich and nontraditionally hot and also not leaving the house part."

Strangely, the only part of that Layla seemed to be able to focus on was *nontraditionally hot*. She guessed Rosie meant the scars, but honestly, if the man didn't have some kind of apparent fetish for cutting Layla down to size, she probably would have been willing to argue that he was completely, entirely, *traditionally* hot. All that thick, dark hair, those cheekbones. In that soft-looking black shirt he'd been wearing, Layla could admit she'd noticed his build: lean and muscled, like a distance runner, or maybe a swimmer.

"You're such a little dirtbag, Ro," Emily said affectionately, and they laughed and then oohed as the server set down their various desserts.

For a second, Layla left her spoon sitting on the table, her brain curiously unable to let go of everything she'd learned over the course of the day. A man in black with some kind of medical condition. Griffin Testa. *Not* afraid of flying. Rich and private and homebound.

Traditionally hot.

"You okay?" Em said, snapping Layla out of her reverie, and she hoped the pink in her cheeks read like a wine flush.

She smiled and shoved Griffin Testa out of her mind and suggested that they get champagne with dessert.

And Layla thought it turned out to be her best idea, that champagne, because for the rest of the night—two more hours at the table, lingering like real Parisians—she and Rosie and Emily laughed and talked and drank until there was no chance of wandering into any more awkward topics, all of them giddy and silly, Layla just drunk enough not to worry about whether they all seemed too American to everyone around them.

When they spilled out onto the narrow sidewalk, Layla continued to absolutely nail it in her heels, a moral victory. Around her, this corner of Paris at night practically sang with life: lights on, doors open, tables crowded. Even the plumes of cigarette smoke didn't annoy her. She steadied her two companions and confidently led them back to the hotel, barely needing an assist from her maps app.

Fuck Griffin Testa, she thought when she got into the elevator to go back to her room, and she thought it again when she crawled, a little drunkenly, into her hotel bed.

She was not just the brother's ex-wife. She was full of good food and good drink and she and Emily were okay, she and Jamie and the whole family would be okay, and this city was beautiful.

This wedding was going to be beautiful.

"C'est bon," she whispered aloud to herself, having no idea that, the very next morning, she would wake up to find that she had apparently ruined everything.

Chapter Four

Outside her door, he hesitated.

Hand raised to knock. Mind racing, heart pounding. He had not thought of what he would say if she answered, which was—when it came to having to do anything in front of another person, at least—unlike him. Even on the plane, he had practiced his intervention in his mind before he stood up. He'd begun practicing basically as soon as he heard the man across the way barking out his displeasure over the sick girl.

Be quiet
If you want off this plane quickly
If this disturbance carries on

But in the roughly twenty-five hours since he had first seen the woman he now knew as Layla Bailey, he had not managed to practice anything when speaking directly to her. He said things like, *Get up from there* or *Are you the ex* or *I'm not afraid of flying*. He did not like the way she looked at him, keen and curious. He did not like the way she blanked her eyes and smiled when she looked at everyone else.

He did not want to knock on this door.

But then he remembered Michael this morning: four a.m., tears in his eyes, elbows on his knees, every part of him sagging.

"I don't know how this could have happened," he'd said, and Griffin's entire body flared with white-hot pain.

How could this have happened? Michael had cried to him once, and Griffin hadn't been able to say anything.

Hadn't been able to *do* anything.

He could not do that again. He would never do that again.

So, he knocked.

Even though he had no plan.

Only after, as he waited, did he consider how this might look to her: a strange man at her hotel room door, a man who had been rude to her by all normal standards of human behavior, a man who only knew her room number because they'd checked in at the same time, both at the mercy of desk clerks who didn't speak quietly enough for his comfort.

How could this have happened?

He did not *care* how it would look to her. He cared about Michael.

He stared accusingly at the pale gray paneled door. Why weren't there peepholes on the doors of these rooms? Did the French think they were too good for peepholes?

Well, if Layla Bailey was smart, she wouldn't answer.

He heard a soft thud and a few rustling movements.

She opened the door.

And for a few seconds, he forgot what he came for.

She was wearing the same robe that hung, unused, inside his hotel room's closet, a fluffy white thing that he bet felt the right sort of soft to her. Her dark brown hair still had traces of the waves she'd worn last night on the elevator, flatter and more uneven. Makeup smudged beneath her eyes, a pillow crease on her cheek. Her full pink lips parted in surprise.

"I thought you were the paper," she said.

"They don't knock for the paper," he said. "You shouldn't answer this door."

He thought they might've blinked at each other in perfect sync.

"Why are you here?" she finally said, which was the more appropriate first thing to say. An opportunity to reset the entire exchange.

Unfortunately, as she said it, she raised her hand to the front of her robe, clutching it closed tighter, not that it was gaping. Now, though, there was her hand, right there, and that distracted him, because it was her hands he'd noticed first. The girl had fainted, and the flight attendant had called for a doctor, and then she'd come, walking by his seat, and it was such an old habit, to look first at a doctor's hands, at any medical professional's hands. He didn't think it made sense, but a lot of things about the habits he'd developed over the last decade didn't make sense.

She had nice hands, he'd thought then. Long fingers, short nails. When she knelt to talk to the girl, she pressed her palms together, occasionally twisting one against the other, re-clasping her fingers. She was warming them up, he realized, before she started her exam. Temperature was very important, in his experience. She was probably very good at her job.

Now, she cleared her throat. Loudly.

Pointedly.

He snapped his eyes back up to hers. Her eyebrows—she had thick eyebrows, a shade darker than her hair—were lowered accusingly. He should somehow indicate that he hadn't been looking at her breasts, which he could not even see in the robe, but it wouldn't be less strange to say he had been staring at her hand, probably.

"Get dressed," he said instead.

"I beg your pardon?"

She was using that same indignant tone from the elevator. What *is your problem?*

Well, part of his problem was that he had no idea how to start a conversation with her. His brain still felt full of the four a.m. pitch-darkness. His body was still disoriented from the chaotic hours the trip here had required.

Michael, he thought desperately, and grabbed hold of the memory of this morning. The knock on his own door. His best friend's pale, shocked face. The stunned, disbelieving note to his voice as he'd told Griffin everything.

He reset himself this time.

"I need to talk to you about Michael and Emily. And what happened last night."

Impossibly, her eyebrows lowered a little further. "What do you mean, what happened last night?"

"When you were out with Emily."

"Nothing happened when I was out with Emily. We had dinner and came back here, all together." Something panicked crossed her face. "Is she okay? I walked her and Rosie to their rooms."

"She's fine," Griff said.

He almost asked, *Who walked you to yours?* but that was a stupid question to ask of a woman who opened her hotel room door when there was no peephole. In fact, it was a stupid question to ask of a woman who had absolutely no sense—judging by the fact that she was attending this wedding in the first place—of self-preservation.

"If she was fine you wouldn't be here. What is going on?"

He didn't want to talk about this while she was in a bathrobe. Her door was open enough that he could see part of the unmade bed over her shoulder. Her room was very small. He would not be comfortable in there, not that it mattered. He would never have occasion to be in her room.

"Hel-*lo*?" she said, clearly frustrated.

Well, he was *more* frustrated. With her, specifically.

"Emily told Michael she's having doubts," he said, pitching his voice low. In addition to not having peepholes, these doors were not very soundproof. Last night, when he finally came back to his room, he thought he could hear every step that went by in the hallways. He hadn't been able to fall asleep, of course. When Michael knocked, Griff had only been dozing, his mind hazy with fatigue but his body—still shot through with pain—not quitting even for a second. He maybe should have stayed out walking for longer, but he'd been so tired.

Layla stared at him. "When?"

"When what?"

"*When* did she tell him that?"

He ground his molars together. Had he not made that clear already?

"Last night. After your dinner."

He could admit she looked genuinely confused. A blankness to her face that did not, for once, look like a practiced effort.

"I don't—we had a nice dinner," she said.

He could see her mind running in the background, sifting through memories. His own mind couldn't help a crude, invented mimicry: He wondered if the restaurant was candlelit. If the folds of her skirt touched the floor when she sat. If she left lipstick behind on her glass. If she *actually* smiled, at any point.

What was he *thinking*?

This time difference was killing him; not sleeping was killing him. Being away from home, away from his things, out of his routine was—

No.

No, this morning with Michael was killing him.

"You said something to her." He could hear the frustration in his voice, mostly at himself, but he didn't care if she thought it was all directed at her. "She told Michael it was something you said."

He watched it all pass over her face: more confusion first, then a swell of disbelief. Finally, a pulse of fear.

"Something I . . . ?" she said quietly, not finishing.

The way she looked at him—this searching, desperate look, these seconds where she forgot the plane and the lobby and the elevator and his fucking *face*. Her robe, her mussed hair, her hand still held at her heart.

She looked like she just needed some *help.*

But he was not here to help her. He was here to help the man who was basically his brother. His best friend, his best friend who had come to his room before dawn, worried that he was about to lose the woman he loved.

That could not happen.

Griff had not come all this way—an entire *ocean* away from everything he needed to be comfortable, everything he needed to *survive*—to see this fail because of some loose-lipped woman with an axe to grind against the family Michael was marrying into. He needed this wedding to happen.

When this wedding happened, Michael would be happy.

He set his jaw against that look on Layla Bailey's face. He would not let her get away with ruining this. He would make her fix it.

Somehow, he would make her fix it.

"There's a courtyard off the lobby," he said. "They serve breakfast. I'll meet you there in fifteen minutes."

He didn't wait for her reply.

He walked away, and didn't look back.

Chapter Five

Something you said. Something you said. Something you said.

The phrase pounded in Layla's head as she made her way to the hotel courtyard, the same way it had every second since Griffin Testa walked away from her again, this time leaving her slack-jawed and frozen in the doorway of her room. She only managed to snap out of it when another door on the hall opened; so startled by the noise, she slammed her own and turned to face the mess she'd left behind last night. Her shoes tipped to the side on the floor by the room's narrow, shallow armoire, her skirt draped messily over the lone chair, her white pillow bearing a smudge of last night's not-fully-washed-off mascara, her phone on the nightstand face up, not plugged in to charge.

That was so unlike her.

Something you said.

She'd washed her face, brushed her teeth, dressed herself in some combination of clothing she was sure wasn't on her spreadsheet. Last night's champagne was a curse, a fizzy cast over every conversation she'd had the night before. She could remember speaking more about Michael's family, and a long detour into the sordid, steamy history of Rosie's on-and-off relationship with a colleague. She could remember that she was careful to keep any conversation about herself focused on work.

But not according to Griffin.

According to Griffin, it was something she said. Something that made Emily have *doubts*.

She didn't want to believe it. She *shouldn't* believe it, not from a man who knocked on her door at eight in the morning, scowling and staring and demanding.

But still, she kept thinking: *What if it was something I said?* A little champagne-bubble-like utterance, rising to Layla's always-still surface. Something so small she'd already forgotten it, but not so small that it hadn't somehow popped in Emily's face with the force of a cork coming off.

And now, *doubts*.

Layla paused at the threshold of the courtyard. Maybe she shouldn't have come down here. Maybe she should have waited until her memory was sharper, her mind clearer...

Her phone pinged from the back pocket of her pants, and her heart thumped. She wanted desperately for it to be Emily, responding to the trying-to-be-casual text Layla sent before leaving her room. Did that champagne hit you as hard as it hit me? she'd typed, hoping the reply message bubble would show up immediately. That Emily would respond with something equally casual like *lol yessssss*. Proof that Griffin Testa was mistaken, that Emily was completely fine, not having any doubts at all.

But there hadn't been any reply, and now, Layla let her hand hover for a moment over her pocket, living in suspended hope that relief was only a swipe away. She imagined a world where she would get a text from Emily and know everything was okay. She would breathe easier. She would turn right back around and go up to her room, fix her face and her outfit, and follow her original plan for the day.

Without having to face Griffin.

But when she finally took out her phone and tapped her screen, the notification wasn't from Emily. It was from Cara, a curt question disguised with an exclamation.

Have you seen him yet!

Jamie, she meant.

Layla's stomach flipped, the anvil in her brain taking on a new pounding rhythm: her ex-husband's name. The thought of Jamie arriving here to find out that his little sister was having doubts about her wedding, doubts that Layla had somehow prompted?

It was an awful thought.

She shoved her phone back into her pocket and stepped into the courtyard.

Her eyes went to him immediately: the man in black, *again*, a piece of carved touchstone in the airy, uncrowded space. He sat at the opposite end of the courtyard at an ironwork table for two, nothing but a bottle of water and two glasses on its surface. His head was tipped down, his thumb swiping lazily up the surface of his phone. No hat today, but pants and a shirt that looked remarkably like what she saw him in yesterday.

Burglar chic, bank robber chic, she thought. *Billionaire chic.*

Bring-you-terrible-news chic.

He had practically been *seething* when she opened the door to him.

Layla put her shoulders back, gathering her strength. She crossed the courtyard's slate-gray pavers, passing more sharp-edged tables like the one Griffin sat at and potted green shrubs shaped into rectangular pillars.

She watched as he raised his eyes, noticing her approach. He stood, tall and lean, the napkin from his lap now in his hand.

Her brain supplied another worthless observation: *Jamie never stood up when I came to a table.*

"I said fifteen minutes," were his first words to her when she reached him, which pretty much canceled out any of the points he got for his standing-up manners.

He was an appalling person. Rude and arrogant and needlessly demanding.

"I had to get dressed," she replied.

A part of her was ashamed of the half lie: Of course, she *did* have to get dressed, but Layla had been a board-certified hospitalist for nearly five years now, trained in a residency program at one of the busiest hospitals in the country. When she wanted to, she could get showered *and* dressed in seven minutes flat. She was proud of this available efficiency. Usually, she didn't mind showing it off a little.

But quickness was beyond her this morning. Everything had taken longer in the face of Griffin's accusation.

"By all means," he said to her now, a mocking edge in his voice, "take your time."

Pop, pop, pop, little bubbles in her brain went, and for a few seconds, all she could do was take her time, her gaze locked with his across the table. He still hadn't shaved, the patch of bare, scarred skin along his jaw more noticeable as a result. Beneath his dark eyes, there were grayish-purple crescent moons.

She let him win this staring contest she'd never agreed to, dropping her eyes and gripping the back of the chair at her side. As she moved to sit—taking her phone from her pocket and setting it on the table—she couldn't help but notice the way he waited, not returning to his own seat until she lifted her own folded napkin, placing it across her lap.

Take your time, she wanted to snark back, if only to help her ignore the strange trilling feeling she got in her stomach from having him stand there like that. Above her, same as on the plane.

When he finally sat, though, he wasted no time.

"I need to know what it is you said."

I need to know what it is I said, she thought. At the very least, she assumed *he* knew; she assumed if Emily told Michael, Michael told Griffin.

Then again, despite being Michael's best man, Griffin didn't seem the type of person it would be easy to open up to. Maybe Michael kept the details vague.

Which was terrible news for Layla and her champagned brain.

"To Emily," he clarified unnecessarily, that blade of impatience back in his voice. It cut her so completely down to size. Answering his question—*I don't know*—would make her feel so *small*. Messy and out of control.

"Bonjour, madame," a voice interrupted, the most welcome two words of French Layla had ever heard in her life.

She looked up to find a server by their table, two thin rectangular menus in hand, which she set in front of both Layla and Griffin, who tensed in his seat. Layla could not follow the rapid French from the server that followed, and at whatever look she saw on Layla's face, the woman smoothly shifted to English—a word about the day's quiche, the croissants that would be out soon, a request for Layla's drink order.

"Coffee," she said, suddenly so desperate for it that she couldn't bother attempting even a word as simple as *café*. Dark, heavy. The anti-champagne, really. Coffee would help.

The server nodded and turned to Griffin, who . . . who, *for the love of God*, spoke back to her in French.

Not like, French-person French. But still. *French*.

"Je prends un déca, s'il vous plaît," he said carefully, the blade dulled with his effort.

"Bien sûr," the server replied, not looking at Layla as she turned and left them alone again.

"You speak French," Layla blurted.

"Not really," he said. Then he added, sharp again: "I practiced before I came."

Each word an indictment: as though practicing the language of the country she would be visiting was the very *least* she could do. She thought of her still-unused itinerary, her already-fallen-apart outfit plan. She thought of clutching her phone in her hand on that plane, typing in her silly affirmations.

She could not even remember how to say *I am thriving*.

Why *hadn't* she practiced French before she came? She could've used one of those apps, like she'd done before her first trip here, little badges she would show off to Jamie. She could've taken time after work, or in between cases, or—

A clear memory from last night finally bubbled to the surface, and in her frazzled, defensive state, it didn't matter to Layla that it wasn't the one she needed most at this moment.

"Some of us have to work," she snapped back.

Passive-income Griffin, all-day-long-to-practice-his-French Griffin. Gross.

Oh, he didn't like that, she could tell. His jaw ticked, his teeth clenching behind the tight, flat set of his lips.

But he would not be distracted. "You don't know, do you?"

She swallowed, twisted the clasp of her hands back and forth in her lap.

"You don't know what you said," he added.

"I didn't say anything," she finally answered, overloud, which immediately betrayed her lack of confidence in this answer.

She pressed her lips together long enough to take a breath through her nose, then tried again, keeping her voice down this time.

"Emily was fine when I left her last night."

This, at least, was the truth. Emily had walked through the hotel's hallways with her arm looped through Layla's, her cheeks pink and her smile huge and natural. She'd joked that Rosie and Layla were Chaos and Order, two poles that would keep her centered this week.

"She was laughing and excited. We didn't talk about anything unusual. We . . . caught up."

"Did you talk about your divorce?" Griffin said, a sneak attack. Plunging that blade right into the heart of her.

"Absolutely not," she bit out.

"Right, why would you," he said, his eyes doing a slow circuit of her face, checking for cracks. "It was *amicable*."

In that moment, Layla hated him.

Hated him.

It was such a shocking, uncomfortable feeling for her—hot and unbounded and all-consuming—that she shifted in her chair. The truth was, she was not sure if she'd ever really hated someone: hatred, she had always thought, was another one of those mind-under-matter collapses in the human experience, a failure of reason at best and a failure of empathy at worst. In the hospital—in *whatever* hospital Layla was in, no matter whether she'd been working there for a day or for weeks—people could tell this about her instinctively. They sent her into rooms with the most belligerent patients, or worse, the most angry loved ones of patients, and she'd come out largely unbothered, offering some soft justification for their behavior.

They're scared; they're hurting; they're hungry; they're sad.

But she couldn't, at this moment, think of any justification for Griffin Testa staring at her like this. *Speaking* to her like this. Saying *amicable* to her as if it was something to sneer at.

"Listen," she said, barely recognizing her own voice, "I don't remember saying anything that caused any particular reaction in Emily. Certainly nothing about her wedding, or her relationship. I told you she seemed fine last night, and I was telling you the truth. Maybe you misunderstood something Michael said. Or maybe he was confused."

"He was not *confused*." He said the word with the same sneer in his voice as he did with *amicable*. As if it were completely impossible for Michael to ever be confused about anything.

She lifted her hands, palms up, in a sort of *Well?* gesture. "Then maybe *you* misunderstood."

In the face of his disdain, this version of events started to take hold in her, to make more sense than any of Layla's fizzy panic. This hatred was clarifying, better than whatever coffee the server would bring out. Layla had been buzzed last night, but not drunk. More than that, she knew she'd never really stopped being attentive to her own performance in front of Emily and Rosie. She knew she played her role, supportive-still-sort-of-sister-in-law.

And she would've known if something was wrong with Emily.

But Griffin? Griffin was the kind of man who stood in the aisle of a transatlantic flight and shut everyone up with a wild look in his eyes. He sweated in elevators, pressed buttons like they offended him, strode out into the Paris night as if he had a hound from hell biting at his heels.

Another clarifying thought, one that Layla didn't enjoy even a little: Maybe the hound wasn't metaphorical. Maybe Griffin had been going out onto the streets of Paris to find something chemical, something illegal—

A clink of dishes interrupted the grim thought, the server back with coffee. Layla blinked down at her tiny cup, the liquid inside darker and heavier than the watered-down drip she was used to in the States. On her honeymoon, French coffee—espresso, really— had been a revelation to her, its compact package a delicate contrast to the punch it packed. At sidewalk café tables with Jamie, she had studied other patrons and their small, pursed-lip sips, the way they made that tiny cup last for as long as they wanted to linger. She had imitated them so carefully, feeling grown-up and sophisticated and *married*.

Now, she had an embarrassingly American pang for a to-go cup.

She could feel Griffin watching her, waiting until the server left again.

"I did not misunderstand," he said, when she was gone.

As though he'd never experienced a fizzy brain-bubble in his life.

"Michael woke me up at four o'clock this morning," he continued dispassionately, methodically, as if he was proving to her a sobriety she hadn't dared question out loud. "Emily came to his hotel room at midnight, a half hour after you, apparently, got back from dinner. She explained to him that having you here was . . ."

He paused, obviously considering his words before going on.

"Very important to her," he finished, and Layla decided that he hadn't really been considering his words. He'd been gearing himself up to say something that he so clearly found unbelievable, like it was impossible for him to imagine Layla—*aren't you the ex?*—being important to anyone.

She faked a pursed-lip sip, letting the espresso touch her lips but not taking any in. She just wanted an excuse to lower her eyes.

"She told him that you and she talked a lot at dinner, and that it got Emily to thinking about this week. She told him this"—he lifted an arm, cut his hand through the courtyard air quickly before lowering it again—"*planning* had taken up so much of her energy that she'd barely thought about their marriage."

"I said *nothing* about marriage. *Nothing*."

There was a frantic note in her voice, and she wished desperately that she could call it back, because she worried it made her sound unsure, when this was the part of the conversation she should be most sure about. Once the papers were signed, she avoided the topic—marriage in general, and hers in specific—with surgical precision, and had tried to train everyone she spoke to regularly in her life to do the same. Sure, Cara still might ask *How are you, really?* with a furrowed brow, or text things like *Have you seen him yet!* but for everyone else, Layla had made it vague, indistinct. A universe scattered across multiple dimensions. Too big to contemplate.

"Nevertheless," was all Griffin said in reply.

Nevertheless, it was you.

His eyes, so relentlessly *on* her, were the same rich brown-black as her espresso. She replayed everything he'd said so far—that having Layla here was important to Emily, that they'd talked a lot at dinner, that it got Emily to *thinking*—and had a horrible, heartrending thought.

What if it hadn't been something she said at all?

What if it was merely the fact that she'd come here in the first place?

What if, despite Emily's very best hopes and intentions in inviting her here, all Layla could ever be was a reminder of the way marriages—even the ones where two people really loved each other—could fail?

She pushed the tiny cup and saucer toward the middle of the table. She had no appetite for its jolting lucidity anymore.

"Brides get nervous," Layla said numbly, the kind of blank platitude that was entirely meaningless in the moment. A stalling tactic, a dodging tactic.

"Did you?"

Not even a little, she thought automatically.

She had been so calm from the moment Jamie had knelt in front of her, a ring in his hand, a shy smile on his lips. On the day of their wedding, she had waited patiently in the beautiful guest room at the house Jamie and Emily grew up in, her vows tucked into a cleverly hidden pocket at the side of her creamy, delicately pleated vintage skirt. She wouldn't even need to look at them. When she walked down the aisle set up in the MacKenzies' backyard, her eyes never left Jamie's.

She was so *sure*. She was walking to her future, a future where she would be a part of something, of someone. A settled and forever part of a unit.

She didn't answer Griffin's question—it was a taunt, more than a question, she thought—and after a few tense seconds, he spoke again.

"Emily wants to cancel tonight."

Layla swallowed, suddenly feeling hot and hangover-sick. The plan for tonight—an evening appetizer cruise along the Seine, followed by a group dinner at a restaurant in the 16th—was meant to be a welcome for the small group of guests who were here for the whole week.

It was also meant to be the first event where Layla would prove to everyone that she was fine.

That she was thriving.

And she'd ruined it with something she couldn't even *remember*?

"She can't," Layla said quietly, not even really speaking to Griffin now, and yes—yes, too much of it was selfish, too much of it was about Layla's pride and fear and guilt and determination to do this week in Paris exactly the way she'd planned.

But underneath all of that—at the core of Layla's heart—there was something else, something concerned and loving. Layla thought of the light in Emily's eyes last night as she'd talked about Michael, her genuine excitement and happiness about being here, about beginning a life with him.

Layla had to believe—she *wanted* to believe—that this desire to cancel tonight was an anomaly. Emily's version of a temporary, fizzy-brained panic.

"I agree," Griffin said.

She met his eyes again, jerked out of her thoughts. They stared at each other across the table, Griffin's jaw ticking again, and his stare ruthlessly hard.

She felt a creeping sense of unease at agreeing with him on *any* aspect of this situation.

She cleared her throat, a limp defense of Emily's right to do whatever she wanted gathering there.

"I mean, she *can*—" she began, but Griffin spoke over her.

"You need to fix this," he said, so flatly that it sent a chill through her.

She thought of Emily saying that he didn't leave his house very often, and she pictured it now: a dark, echoing mansion, a storybook sort of place with beams in the ceilings and furniture covered with white sheets, drafty and inhospitable, populated by stoic, quiet servants who heard directives like this from him all the time. He probably only practiced French for this precise reason.

To order people around.

She didn't want to be one of them, but she also didn't want this thing getting called off.

Apparently, he took her brief silence as resistance: He leaned slightly forward in his chair, resting a forearm on the table's surface. Even beneath the black sleeve she could see it was flexed from the tension of the way he held his fist, his knuckles rippling. He was pulsing his fingers against the fat of his palm, like he was getting his veins ready for a blood draw.

"Michael is very important to *me*," he said, borrowing his friend's words about Layla. "And this wedding—Emily, marrying Emily—she is the most important thing to him. He—" He broke off, those knuckles fairly bulging now. "This has to happen for him. The wedding has to happen."

For a few seconds, Layla's own rising sense of desperation at the possibility of being responsible for ruining Emily's wedding receded, sucked under by the sheer force of Griffin Testa's intensity. She wanted to stay under this heavy, churning water for a minute and drown out her own anxiety about how she would fix this—because she would, of course, fix this; she *had* to fix it, for Emily and Jamie and her former mother- and father-in-law and for *herself*—and only think about Griffin's words and the way he said them.

Not a matter of marriage, but a matter of life and death.

This has to happen for him.

The wedding has to happen.

What in the world would make a man like Griffin Testa have a stake like this in someone else's wedding?

When he leaned back, that fist retreating again, she realized that she had been staring—that she'd given up even bothering to look like she was coming up with an answer for him. He blinked and swallowed, as though he'd surprised himself, and Layla thought, dimly through the dark water, that this was an opening: his sword dropped, his guard down.

She wanted to say, *What happened to you?*

But he was faster than her: He stood suddenly from his seat, their cups and glasses vibrating slightly against the table's surface. He reached down, steadying it or himself; she couldn't be sure. But she was sure his hand shook as he did.

"I'll fix it," she said, inexplicably. "Tonight will happen."

He looked down at her—always, he was looking down at her—and nodded once.

"Your breakfast is on my room tab," he said.

And then, for the second time in a single morning, he turned and left her alone.

Chapter Six

He'd forgotten his fucking sunglasses.

Outside, the Paris morning had turned bright. Clear-blue-sky bright, no sign of the gray clouds that had hovered over the courtyard he'd sat in to wait for Layla Bailey. He paused outside the hotel's doors, fighting with himself about whether to go back up to his room to get them.

But if he did that, he might run into her again.

So, no fucking sunglasses.

He took his phone out of his pocket, squinted down at the screen, where he'd mapped directions to the spot Michael had texted him to meet. Ignored the way his fingers still felt shaky. Memorized the route: a half mile from here, a few turns down streets where he'd have to look for the dark blue signs stuck to the sides of gray-white buildings, not always easy to find. Those signs had been a real pain in the ass while he walked last night, if he was honest. Form over function, that was the situation with those signs.

He put his head down and started walking, not even really having to try at tuning out the unfamiliar surroundings.

What the fuck was he going to say to Michael?

He didn't know if he could admit to the full truth of what happened during his fleeting meeting with Layla. Bad enough that the woman had no idea what she'd said to rattle Emily MacKenzie enough to have doubts; worse that Griffin himself was rattled enough just by sitting across from her that he'd fled the scene after barely ten minutes, not getting the specifics of her promise to fix it, not even getting her fucking phone number so he could find out when she had.

The thing was, she'd put her hair up. The russet-brown mass of it, streaked through with lighter strands, gathered at the back of her head. A loose swoop at the front that kept falling over one of her muddy green-brown eyes. She wore tiny pearl-drop earrings in her lobes. If they were a gift from the ex-husband and she was wearing them here, to this week of events, that would be the most psychotic thing Griff had ever seen.

He supposed he had no room to judge.

But he *did*, he thought, as he crossed another street. He did judge her. He judged whatever she didn't remember about last night, that she said things like *Brides get nervous* even though he could tell she didn't mean a fucking word of it, that she never once looked away from his face.

He made one more turn, and now it was a straightaway to his destination—a relief to walk faster, to be a blur to everyone else on these sidewalks. He stepped off a curb, passing someone who trailed the smell of cigarettes. He didn't care for that, but he'd already learned last night it was part of the perfume here. Cigarette smoke, urine, car exhaust. Occasional butter and sugar.

He wondered if that server at the hotel ever brought out the promised croissants.

If Layla Bailey was still sitting at that table alone.

He stepped into a dark, cool corridor of stone arches, and paused. Behind him, sun-drenched Paris streets he'd walked through and not really seen. Ahead of him, his destination: some kind of park, but not any kind of park he'd ever seen. A cream-and-green tile of effortful perfection, boundaried by black wrought iron and trees trimmed into unnatural, elegant little cuboids. Surrounding it all, a great square of old redbrick buildings topped with steep blue-gray roofs and bolstered at the bottom with arches like the one he stood beneath.

He didn't like the look of it. Too fussy, too pretty.

Under here, beneath the arch, where the stone was stained dark and marred by the occasional stripe of graffiti, Griffin could pretend he was in a little dungeon of his own making. He should text Michael and tell him to meet him here. A more fitting location to recount that conversation with Layla, and anyway, no need for sunglasses.

Tonight will happen, she said, but he wasn't sure he believed her. Mostly, she still had that dazed, anxious look in her eyes.

A burst of rapid, laughing French startled him—a small pack of teenagers passing quickly by, jostling him slightly. He could not text Michael to come under here. Too dark, too depressing. Too on the nose.

He stepped into the sun, squinting as he crossed toward the park's entrance. A sign on the fence: STOP AUX RATS. It gave him a little satisfaction to see it. Rats, in a perfect-seeming place like this.

Good.

Griff found Michael easily in the still-uncrowded space: He sat on a patch of grass, his jacket beneath him, his shoulders slouched. It was a sorry-looking state of affairs, a grown man sitting on the grass like that. The sun shone on the exposed skin of Michael's receding hairline, and Griffin hated the way it made him seem even more vulnerable.

He strode over, watched as Michael plucked listlessly at the pristine grass, oblivious to everything around him. Griffin had to announce his arrival.

"Michael," he said.

Michael lifted a hand to his brow and looked up. No sunglasses, which meant Griffin could immediately see hope in his friend's still-reddened eyes.

"How'd it go?" he said.

Instead of answering, Griffin tipped his head toward one of the park's outer edges. "We gotta go sit on one of the benches. I can't manage the ground today."

Michael's face fell at the evasion, but he got to his feet immediately, bringing his jacket with him. He didn't need to ask about the not-sitting-on-the-ground thing, and that gave Griffin a guilty pang.

His only friend, his friend who knew him best, his friend he never had to make explanations to.

And what good am I to him? Griff thought. *I didn't even get her number.*

They fell into silent step with each other, crossing toward a bench. When they got close, it looked like a couple was on their way to the same one, so Griffin stared, a stare that felt perfectly natural to him, and they diverted themselves.

That was a satisfying thing, at least. About forgetting his sunglasses. About his fucked-up face.

When they sat, Michael went, as always, to Griff's right.

"What did she say?" Michael asked, before Griffin could even fully arrange himself. He hated this stupid French bench. The back on it cut him in exactly the wrong spot.

"She said she doesn't remember."

Michael sagged, and Griffin tightened his middle.

"Not anything?" Michael said.

"Not anything unusual."

Recounting this conversation to Michael was somehow worse than actually *having* the conversation. It only reminded Griffin of how badly he'd done it from the beginning: storming down to Layla Bailey's room without a plan, sitting across from her and bullying her into making a promise that he didn't even know the plan for.

"She did say she never mentioned her divorce," he added, as though that was a profound piece of intelligence.

Michael shook his head. "Well, she wouldn't, probably. I'm pretty sure that situation was—"

Griffin faked a cough, drowning out whatever word Michael said next. If it was "amicable," he probably would have destroyed this park with the blast radius of his annoyance. He'd watched Layla Bailey's face in that elevator mirror when she first said the word, and he didn't buy it for a second.

"Anyway, she said she'll fix it," Griffin said. "The thing tonight, it'll happen."

He could feel Michael's eyes on him. An anticipatory gaze. *Why hadn't he gone back for his sunglasses?*

"How?" Michael finally asked.

Griff swallowed. He could not bring himself to say the truth: *I don't know. I didn't ask. I ran.*

This time, when Michael shook his head, he swiped a hand down his face.

"I'm supposed to—what, wait for Emily to call me? I'm trying to give her the day; she said she wanted the day to think, but we're meant to be on a boat with her family in like ten hours, man. And then what about everything else? My parents get here tomorrow. What am I—"

"It's going to be all right," Griff interrupted. Before he could stop himself, he added, "Brides get nervous."

Jesus Christ. Borrowing *that* from Layla Bailey, of all things.

"You didn't see her last night. She's *never* asked me for space. She really means it with this . . ." He trailed off, shuffling one of his shoes against the fine-grained, chalky surface beneath their feet. Even the dirt here was sophisticated.

"Questioning," Michael finished glumly.

"She's young," Griffin said, which was better than saying something empty and dishonest like *Brides get nervous*, but not by much. If anything, it was too full, too honest: an insight into Griffin's own doubts about Michael and Emily, which he'd kept to himself ever since Michael had called him with the news he'd met someone, was serious with someone. The years between them probably would've felt pretty substantial to Griffin no matter who it was, but in the case of Michael specifically . . . well.

Well, Griffin didn't know a lot about Emily MacKenzie's life, he supposed. But he knew about his best friend's, and Michael hadn't had an easy thirty-four years. Griffin himself felt like an old thirty-four, and certainly when it came to some things—loss, heartbreak, grief—Michael had cause to feel even older.

"Don't do that," said Michael. "Don't dismiss her like that. She's a grown woman. Smart and mature. She's not *young*. Not the way you mean."

Griffin didn't bother protesting. He set his jaw and looked out over the park, waiting out the response that hovered right on the tip of his tongue.

It's not mature, he wanted to say, *to do this at the eleventh hour. It's not smart to do it when we are in a different fucking country for this, when there's a boat rented and a restaurant booked and a half dozen other spaces and events bought and paid for for the next seven days. It's bratty and thoughtless and if she leaves you over some forgotten conversation with a woman she's not even related to anymore, then maybe you're dodging a bullet.*

"I'm sorry," he said instead.

Michael gave a curt nod, and the silence stretched between them, taut and frustrated.

Then, after barely thirty seconds, Michael sighed, and spoke again.

"It's nice here."

Griffin looked over at his friend, who was gazing across the park, taking in the squared-off trees, the fountain nearest them, the people passing through. Anyone else would think the change of subject was strange, but not Griff, because Griff knew Michael, and Michael hated to fight. Hated a harsh word, a tense moment. Even now, when his fiancée was basically threatening to call this whole thing off, when Griffin had said something to make it worse and not better, Michael wanted to keep the peace.

It's nice here was basically his way of saying, *I'm letting what you said about her go. I'm going to talk about something else while the tension wears off.*

"Mm," said Griffin.

"Don't you think?"

Griffin narrowed his eyes at the ankle-height arches that surrounded each patch of grass, tiny fences like those hard-to-see signs on the sides of buildings. Form, form, form.

"It's fine," he said.

Michael scoffed, kicked Griff's foot lightly. "You should be appreciating this. Paris. Traveling. This is a big deal for you. Don't let—"

"I didn't come here to sightsee."

Griffin had always been terrible at peacekeeping. But also, he was sensitive to this—Michael's concern over how infrequently he left home. For a few years now, Griff had been cultivating the lie about a newfound fear of flying, which had worked pretty well for forcing Michael to come to him for occasional visits. For this wedding, though—Michael's wedding—of course there was no question about whether Griff would come.

Another, shorter stretch of silence, and then Michael took out his phone, swiped across the screen, and tapped something in.

"Used to be called the Place Royale," he said, reading off whatever page he'd opened. "This park, I mean."

Griff said nothing, an electric pain shooting from his left hip to his left shoulder. This was suddenly so familiar: this pain, sure, but also this conversation. He thought of Michael, sitting in a teal-colored vinyl chair in an antiseptic-smelling room, reading aloud. His own life split in two, and he would still sit there, sometimes for hours on end, trying to sew up Griff's.

"It's an actual square. That's interesting, right? 140 by 140."

"Yeah," said Griffin, a catch in his throat now. He breathed through the pain in his side.

He should have asked for her number. Her plan.

"Victor Hugo lived in one of these places," Michael said, looking up from his phone and squinting at one of the facades, as though he knew which one. "Know who that is?"

Griff shook his head, but he squinted at the building, too.

"He wrote *Les Misérables*," Michael added.

Mizz-err-ah-blays, he pronounced it, which Griff was pretty sure wasn't right. He'd listened to a lot of French people talking into his earbuds, ever since he'd heard about this wedding.

But Michael always tried. Tried so hard at everything.

No matter what, he kept trying.

"Don't know it," Griffin choked out, but he was thinking about the last twenty-some hours. Being on that plane, checking into that hotel, walking a city with street signs that made no sense, Michael knocking on his door at four a.m.

He was disoriented, overtired, aching. His mind scattered and susceptible, forgetful of the things he'd worked on before he came here. He'd been focusing on the wrong things.

He hadn't been focused enough on being Michael's best man. On being the best for Michael.

He hadn't been trying hard enough. Knocking on that door without a plan, not getting her number. How was that being there for Michael?

"*Hunchback of Notre-Dame*, too. You know that one, dude. We saw the Disney movie," Michael said. "At my cousin's that year for Easter, remember? When we were like nine."

Griffin did remember. Michael's parents had included him in a lot of stuff, once upon a time, including some holidays with their extended family. At first, it was awkward, the introductions around unfamiliar rooms, usually made by Michael's mom, Paula. *This is Griffin*, she would say so cheerfully, everything a pleasant exclamation. *He's a friend of Michael's from school! His mom is working today, so he's hanging with us!*

People always made a little noise at that, an intonation to their welcomes that suggested their pity. But Griffin never felt like he needed anyone's pity, because he had Michael for his best friend, and that was more than a lot of people had.

I shouldn't care about the way she looks at me, he told himself. *I shouldn't care about her hair up, her earrings, her nerves on the day of her wedding. I shouldn't care about that anxious look she's trying to hide.*

"The bell tower, yeah," Griff said, picturing the movie now, the redheaded, crooked-faced cartoon sitting on top of a gargoyle, looking out at a pink-and-purple-washed city Griffin could barely acknowledge he was actually in. "I remember."

Michael nodded, and it was as easy as that: a settled truce between them. Griffin's criticism of Emily, his sharp reply about sightseeing—all of it, forgotten. Sometimes, Griffin thought, this kind of conflict resolution was all that he and Michael were capable of now. Any other option had been scorched away on a single, horrifying night fifteen years ago.

Michael's phone had gone dark in his hand, the distraction of playing tour guide for Griffin faded. His gaze gone to the middle distance.

Layla Bailey, Griffin thought, like an idea he had to get used to.

"I can't imagine losing her," Michael said.

Griffin watched as his friend's throat bobbed in a thick swallow.

And he knew, he *knew* what would come next: could almost see Michael's next words before he said them, little flutters of black ash blowing across this blue sky.

Griffin braced himself.

"Or maybe the problem is that I can," Michael finally said, his voice quiet.

And right then, Griffin was glad to have forgotten his sunglasses. Glad to stare out again, unsquinting, into this too-pristine park and the huge, gallant buildings that surrounded it, all of it bathed in a ruthless brightness that made his eyes water. He would burn this place, this moment, into his mind. He would have an impression of it every time he closed his eyes, so that he wouldn't be able to forget it next time, no matter whether Layla Bailey was near him or not.

No more nighttime walks or knee-jerk reactions, no more

stomping down windowless corridors to knock on some woman's door without a plan. No more longing for a dark dungeon to hide in.

Not for the next week.

What Michael needed now was a different Griffin: a daytime Griffin, a Griffin who'd *trained* for this, a Griffin who slowed down enough to think straight, a Griffin who showed his full face in the light, no matter who stared at it.

And if that was a Griffin he couldn't quite remember, then he would remember the other things: the teal chair next to his hospital bed, *The Hunchback of Notre-Dame*, the reason Michael could imagine losing Emily.

He would find Layla Bailey again, and if she couldn't fix it alone, he'd find a way to fix it with her.

He could do it for one week.

Chapter Seven

"Thank god you're here."

Rosie said it with one slight, precise emphasis, exactly where Layla needed it.

Thank god you're *here.*

That emphasis—it put Layla back into a version of herself she better recognized.

Not a version where she sat alone in a courtyard café, staring at a man's coffee cup, heart racing, wondering what in the world she had agreed to.

Instead, a version who didn't waste time wondering. A version who got the job done.

She had Rosie to thank, because Rosie was the one who texted her: a vibration that finally got Layla's eyes off the coffee cup, the dark, untouched drink like the lightest part of Griffin Testa's eyes.

Come up to Emily's room, the text said.

Then, another. It's Rosie, btw

And one more, when Layla was standing from her seat: 😬

Obviously, Rosie's texts did not have much in common with the sort of texts that most often got Layla moving with the kind of no-nonsense purpose that had propelled her across the courtyard and into the hotel's lobby, pressing the elevator button with a specific tap of her knuckle that was so familiar it felt like teleportation to another time, another place.

But still, they had the same effect: like she was getting a room number in a less luxurious accommodation, a nurse or doctor's name, a code more specific than a cringe face.

Now, standing at the threshold of Emily's room, staring into Rosie's real-life wide-eyed *Yikes* face, Layla felt like she was doing a handoff. An official transfer of care.

"What happened?" Layla said, half expecting Rosie to reply with a heart rate.

"What *didn't*!" Rosie said, her voice pitched strangely between a whisper and a shout. She reminded Layla of a sweaty first-year resident.

"Start at the beginning."

Rosie swallowed and looked over her shoulder, then leaned in, committing to the whisper.

"She's in the bathroom. *Again*. Her stomach is upset. Because she is doing something *crazy*, absolutely *crazy*, and this is *me* saying that, so you know—"

"Rosie," Layla interrupted.

"Well everything was *fine* when I went to sleep!" She paused, then added guiltily, "I didn't fall asleep, okay? I passed out! Because of the champagne; I should never drink champagne, *god!* I know better. New Year's 2023!"

Layla blinked, and Rosie mumbled, "Never forget," like an outloud hashtag.

This was absolute chaos, but it was also revealing: Rosie had said nothing about Layla's role in this, no *I need to know what it is you said* from her, not that a sentence like that—bossy, precise, tinged with cruelty—was Rosie's style.

But Rosie's style would have been to say something immediately, if she thought Layla was responsible.

So, Emily hadn't told Rosie what prompted all this, at least not yet.

"And when you woke up?"

"When I woke up, it was three-something in the morning and Emily was getting *sick* in the bathroom! Which I thought was the champagne, because what did I say? New Year's 2023, know what I mean? But it was *not* the champagne. It's that she says she doesn't want to *get married*!"

Layla swallowed. That was more forceful than having doubts. More final than canceling tonight.

Before she could stop herself, she thought of the faces of her former mother- and father-in-law: the way Manon pursed and then crooked her lips when she was trying not to cry, the way Robert got a tipped-to-the-right trench between his eyebrows when he was worried. She thought of Jamie when he looked disappointed: a sort of hangdog passivity that overtook his handsome face, eventually pulling his whole body downward.

She'd gotten so familiar with those expressions during that final, wrenchingly sad part of her marriage.

Thinking of them now wouldn't do Emily any good.

She took a breath, trying to clear her head again, but instead, her brain conjured the sight of Griffin Testa's clenched fist on the table. The sound of him saying, *The wedding has to happen*.

"I think I should come in," Layla blurted.

"Yes!" Rosie sagged with relief, releasing the white-knuckled grip she'd been keeping on the door handle. She stepped back and waved Layla inside.

Thankfully, the room itself went a long way to distracting Layla from rogue thoughts of brokenhearted former relatives and coldhearted current acquaintances. It was big—twice the size of Layla's—but the current state of it muted any grand impression it might've made. Five suitcases out that Layla could see, all open and partially unpacked. Two queen-size beds, both unmade, and one covered in more wadded-up tissues than Layla had ever seen outside of a wastebasket. The thick drapes were pulled shut, darkening everything, and the air was close—a dorm room after a secret night of drinking.

Part of Layla was appalled. This sort of square footage in a central Paris hotel, two beds, and what was—if she had her sense of direction right—almost certainly a great view, treated like *this*?

But another part was strangely, tenderly jealous. This was a room where two best friends had gotten ready for a night out, a room where one of them had cried enough to turn a bed into a wastebasket while the other probably sat beside her and spoke soothingly, a room where the shameless messiness spoke of the sort of intimacy Layla had been missing in her life—had *avoided* in her life—since the divorce.

The muffled flush of a toilet jerked her back to the moment, and she turned to Rosie, who had slumped onto the tissue-less bed as though her strings had been cut. Layla remembered that the champagne had been her idea, and almost apologized.

Instead, she heard the faucet turn on in the bathroom and thought about the apology she was maybe going to have to make for saying something she couldn't remember.

There were the MacKenzie faces again, shocked and sad. *Layla?* she imagined them saying, a cocktail of disbelief and pity and dismay. *Layla told Emily not to get married?*

Frankly, she would rather think of Griffin Testa's fist. His pure, undiluted anger, all of it directed at her.

"Rosie," she said, keeping her voice low. "How about you go pick up a couple of croissants? Some hot tea?"

Rosie stood again, wobbly but with a little light in her eyes.

"Yes! Pastries! That is such a good idea! I will be in charge of pastries. And tea!"

She was already shoving her feet into a pair of thick-soled sneakers, not bothering with socks. She had on a pair of flared yoga pants and a neon-green T-shirt cut off into a crop top that absolutely looked slept in. Her hair was . . . not brushed.

Layla thought, *You can't go out into* Paris *like that!* but then the faucet shut off, and Rosie's eyes widened with panic as she looked up at Layla again.

"She knows you were on your way up," she said. "Just tell her I'll be right back. I need fresh air before I see her again, so I don't say the thing about her being crazy! I'm *literally* on the verge!"

Clearly, she meant it: Right as the bathroom door opened, the door to the room closed softly behind Rosie's retreating form.

Leaving Layla alone to face whatever she had done.

At first, mostly it was more crying.

Emily came out of the bathroom and crumpled against Layla's shoulder, fresh tears soaking through her shirt within seconds. When Emily finally lifted her face long enough to swipe a hand across her reddened, puffy nose, Layla gently guided her toward the non-tissue-splattered bed, patting her back and encouraging her to take deep breaths.

Patience, Layla knew, was a virtue—an important part of getting to good information, *true* information from someone in a crisis. Were they really staying away from cigarettes, had they truly been consistent with their medication, was there some symptom they were too embarrassed to mention?

But as the minutes ticked by, patience started to feel like a liability. Like Emily would never manage to dam up her tears, like tonight would get canceled purely because she'd drowned in them.

Layla decided to be proactive.

"Em," she began, ignoring the nerves that crested inside her at the thought of confronting this directly. "Whatever I said last night—"

It was all she managed to get out before Emily swung her wet, devastated gaze straight at Layla's face.

"You talked to Michael?" she said, her voice high and anxious. "What did he say? Did he . . . How is he?"

Talk about a symptom Layla was too embarrassed to mention.

But she wouldn't lie, not now.

"I didn't talk to Michael," she admitted. "I talked to Griffin."

Something shifted in Emily's expression. Less devastation, more . . . frustration.

"Oh, I'm sure *he's* thrilled," she said, an ironic little laugh escaping her, and Layla felt her brow lower.

Griffin Testa was definitely *not* thrilled.

Not about this, and also probably not about . . . anything, actually. Layla could picture him being presented with a birthday cake or a box of puppies or a straightforward solution to climate change, and simply staring at all of it in bored, judgmental disgust.

"Why would you say that?"

Emily shrugged. "I don't think he likes me. He's never been all that nice to me."

You should see him with a box of puppies, Layla thought.

"Some people aren't nice," she said instead, annoyance leaking into her tone.

This has to happen for him, she could hear him saying.

"He mentioned that it was something I said," she prompted again.

Emily's eyes dropped to her lap, her shoulders curving. A guilty posture, if Layla had ever seen one, a *Yes, Doctor, I've smoked a few cigarettes* posture. If Layla had any hope of Michael or Griffin misunderstanding this mess, it evaporated at the sight of Emily now: It *had* been something she said.

Layla watched another fat tear drop onto Emily's clasped hands.

"It's just—the thing with you and Jamie," she finally said, and Layla's stomach turned over.

I didn't say anything about Jamie, she wanted to scream, so certain she would swear on it.

"I know you didn't say anything specific about it," Emily continued, as though she could read Layla's mind. "I know you wouldn't. You never do."

There was something in Emily's voice for that last bit. Nothing quite like the ironic scorn of her *I'm sure he's thrilled*, but nothing particularly complimentary, either.

Layla opened her mouth to reply, stalled between the familiar, bland withholding—*It wasn't any one specific thing*—and an automatic, generic apology, but Emily spoke first.

"But remember when Rosie was asking you about your job?"

It took a second to register the question, since Layla was still stung by that *You never do*, but once she did, fresh confusion rose within her.

She *did* remember Rosie asking about her job, because when Rosie asked about her job, Layla felt like someone had lifted a weighted, itchy shawl from her shoulders. It was so *easy* to talk about her locum tenens work, so natural to sell it in the same way the recruiter had sold it to her. She remembered rattling off the names of all her placements so far, and playing up her enthusiasm for the next one—six weeks in Chico, California, a part of the country where she'd never spent any time.

"Yes," Layla said, and it came out inflected. A question.

"She asked why you became a hospitalist."

"Right," Layla replied slowly, even more baffled now. Another thing that had been easy to talk about. She loved inpatient work, loved coordinating with other physicians and PAs and nurses and techs. She was proud of her specialty, for all it was lesser-known by the world outside of the medical profession.

"You said you *were* going to be a surgeon," Emily said. "A general surgeon, you said."

Layla rifled through her memories of this part of the conversation: only a couple of sips of champagne in, a curl of rich chocolate mousse on her spoon. She'd made a casual gesture with it as she answered Rosie's question. *The original plan was general surgery for residency, but I wanted to stay in Boston for med school, and I knew it would be easier to get an internal medicine residency there.*

That was . . . a very normal answer. Also, a true one. What was the problem?

Bewilderment must've shown on her face, because Emily clucked her tongue, exasperated.

"You changed your residency plan for *Jamie*," she practically yelled. "So you could stay in Boston with Jamie!"

For what felt like a long moment, Layla couldn't say a word. She simply stared. For the last couple of hours, ever since Griffin had come to her door, she had lived in anxious anticipation, readying herself for some huge, catastrophic—forgotten—revelation to come crashing down on her.

But this?

This was *nothing*.

She was so relieved she almost laughed.

See? she wanted to shout to Griffin. *I told you; I* didn't *say anything!*

Instead, she softened her voice again and said, "Em, no. It wasn't like that at all; it was much more complicated than—"

But she didn't bother finishing, because Emily stood from the bed suddenly, throwing herself into pacing back and forth in front of the two beds, wringing her hands, her eyes swollen and her cheeks splotchy, her neck flushed.

Any relief Layla felt about her own culpability for this dissipated in the face of Emily's obvious distress. She had never seen this version of Emily: wild-eyed and restless and unpredictable. Like a downed wire on a rainy, windblown street, spraying off sparks intermittently.

"Emily," she tried, still soft, but her former sister-in-law barely seemed to hear her.

"I'm moving to *Germany* for him," Emily said, the word *Germany* like it was a big, shocking arc of those electric sparks, and this time, when she paced back Layla's way, Layla stopped her— reaching out a hand and touching Emily's forearm.

"Emily," she said again, firmly now, a real *We're going to talk about those cigarettes* tone. "What's really going on here?"

For a beat, Emily simply looked down at Layla's hand on her arm, her chin quivering, her shoulders slumping again.

"I don't know," she finally admitted weakly. "I—I promise you, Layla, I haven't ever felt unsure before now, before last night. It was like, you said the thing about doing your residency in Boston, and I thought, *every decision I make from now on has to do with Michael*."

A pretty late-breaking revelation! Layla thought, in the kind of exclamatory tone that reminded her of Cara—of Rosie, too—but she tried to keep her face serene, leaving Emily the space to say more.

"And then once I thought of *that*, I snowballed, I guess? Like, all this stuff I've been doing for the move, and the wedding, is that avoidance? Am I avoiding the reality of what I'm doing? Marrying Michael, and moving abroad? Moving abroad as a newlywed?"

"Well, I—" Layla began uncertainly during the pause that followed, still processing all this, but as soon as she started to speak, Emily burst forth with more.

"But like, what am I going to do about it *now*? We are *here*, right?" She flung a hand toward the still-closed drapes. "Paris is *out there*, and you know how my parents are about Paris, and there's all these activities we planned and people coming, so what am I going to do? Once I started thinking of that"—she pressed her palms to her eyes—"I panicked more. You can't get married just because you made a plan to, you know? It's not an *event*; it's a *marriage*. Marriage is forever!"

In the aftermath, there was an awkward silence—Emily dropped her hands from her eyes, looking guiltily at Layla as her eyes welled again.

"I'm sorry!" she said quickly. "I can't believe I—"

"It's okay," Layla responded, even though it did smart, hearing it. Hearing her own years-ago naivete mirrored back to her.

Her mind wincing away from the sting, Layla landed on a more practical thought. A more bureaucratic one.

"Wait," she said. "Haven't you and Michael already done the paperwork back in the States? Aren't you, you know . . . already married, technically?"

Emily shook her head, deflating onto the wastebasket-slash-bed across from Layla. "We were going to do the courthouse ceremony when we got back home, so the official date would be exactly a year from when we first met. I thought that would be really special, you know? Kind of a bonus anniversary. Now I can't decide if it's a blessing or a curse that nothing's legal yet."

Layla was quiet, caught for a moment in her own indecision about all she'd heard. On the one hand, everything Emily had said so far could be the sort of bland *Brides get nervous* bullshit Layla had offered to Griffin Testa back in that courtyard, when she was still flailing from shock and fear over what she'd potentially screwed up.

On the other, though—well, on the other, Emily's anxieties *were* real, prompted by real things. Moving abroad was big. The MacKenzie lore about and love for Paris was big.

And marriage was big.

Not really because it was forever, but more because sometimes it wasn't, and that was the biggest thing to reckon with of all.

For the first time since she arrived in Paris—maybe for the first time since *before* she'd arrived in Paris—Layla was able to truly block out everything except Emily. She didn't, for once, think about her divorce and how she'd failed at it; she didn't think about the MacKenzies' disappointment in her, or Griffin Testa's angry desperation.

She didn't think about this hotel room like it was a hospital, about Emily like she was another version of an anxious Willa on the plane, or an embarrassed patient who'd been sneaking cigarettes after a surgery.

She thought only about the Emily who had once been her sister.

The Emily she'd known for years, earnest and kind and genuine; the Emily she'd seen yesterday morning, full of excitement;

the Emily from last night, so authentically in love that Layla was grateful to witness it.

She did not want that Emily to make the sort of decision she couldn't take back.

So she leaned forward and took her hands, ducking her head to meet Emily's eyes.

"Honey," she said, using a word she'd only ever used with Em, back when they were so much closer.

Emily sniffed and smiled weakly, as though she recognized the gesture.

"You have to know," Layla said, "how much pressure you are under right now."

Emily nodded miserably.

"And I know you feel overwhelmed, and tonight and the week ahead feel like a lot."

"So much," Emily whimpered.

"But is it . . . is it possible that making another huge decision right now—calling off this whole week, this wedding—when you're this upset, might be a mistake?"

Emily sniffed again, soggy and uneven. "It's possible."

It felt like a huge victory, like stopping something from catching fire. Part of her wanted to stand up and open the curtains, let some natural light in, but then she thought of the view again, and decided it was too soon: that crushing pressure of Paris perfection all spread out before a bride who'd planned her whole wedding around it.

So she stayed where she was.

"I think you need to take some of that weight off yourself, as best you can. Yes, there's a week of events planned, and people are coming . . ."

Emily's fingers twitched in hers—sparks weakly trying to make their way back into the fight.

"That's happening," Layla said calmly. "There's nothing you can do about that. But you can focus on *today*, okay? Today, there's the boat, and the dinner, but that's it, right? That's all you need to think about. There's no rest of the week right now. No other Paris plans, no rehearsal, no ceremony, no paperwork back home. There's not even Germany! There's *just today*."

"Just today," Emily repeated.

"Right, and today, you will see Michael, and you need to remember, that's what this is about—you and Michael. You can keep your focus on you and Michael, and what's right for the two of you."

Emily's face softened at the mention of her fiancé.

"I do love him. So much. He is—everything. The very best man. I don't want you to think I don't love him."

At that, Griffin nudged his way back into Layla's consciousness. She thought of the fierceness in his eyes, his voice, when he spoke of his friend.

She thought of his tight fist, his white knuckles.

Michael is very important to me.

This has to happen for him.

She wondered again what Michael—this man Emily loved—could've done to earn the unchecked loyalty of someone like Griffin Testa, who seemed like the sort of person who would only have loyalty to himself.

"I don't think that," she said, squeezing Emily's clammy hands, bringing herself back into this moment. Away from the ones she'd had with Griffin.

Just Emily and Layla, she thought, her own version of the *Just today* refrain. Honestly, it was better than any affirmation she'd come up with on the flight over here. She should put it in the translation app.

Emily squeezed back, and then she said, in a near-whisper of vulnerability that might as well have been reading Layla's mind: "I really missed you, Lay. I really missed having you in my life."

At that, Layla's throat thickened with emotion, the weight of her absence from Emily's life, the weight of her broken promises since the divorce so heavy now.

Again, she was struck by the urge to apologize—to say that she hadn't meant to become someone to be missed—but she didn't know if she could get it out.

So instead, she kept it simple. "I missed you, too."

They gave each other shaky smiles.

"I'm still not sure," Emily said finally, pulling her hands from Layla's, fanning her face for a few seconds before gesturing widely at the room—the suitcases full of wedding-week clothes, the still-covered windows. "About all of this. But today, I can do. I want to do. Or, I don't know—I want to try doing? For Michael and me."

Layla thought, again—against her will—of Griffin, and of the promise she'd made to him.

I'll fix it. Tonight will happen.

And the fact that she'd kept it.

She tried to imagine his reaction when he found out. Would he give her that are-you-the-ex face, the-floor-is-probably-disgusting face?

Or would there be that split-second look of vulnerability that passed over his features in the courtyard, before he stood to leave her? Would he look at her like that again, would he soften his voice long enough to say thank you, would he—

"I mean, I'll need your help, of course."

Emily's now-more-normal voice cut through Layla's extremely fantastical train of thought.

"My . . . help?"

"I feel like"—Emily began, rising to pace again—"you're kind of . . . the *person*, you know? The only person who really understands where I'm at with this. With how I'm feeling, and with the whole 'just today' thing. If that's what I'm going to do—if I'm really going to give me and Michael a chance to work through this over the course of the week, I can't have everyone knowing about it. Adding their opinion in. I need this to be between you and me and Michael."

"And Griffin," Layla said, automatically, and wanted to kick herself for it. She cleared her throat. "I mean, he knows, too."

Emily waved a hand. "Well, fine. The four of us, then."

Layla did not like where this was headed.

"What about Rosie?" she said hopefully.

Emily shook her head. "I'm going to tell her it was a blip. That the champagne got to me, which she'll believe, because she's had beef with champagne for years. If she knows I'm still thinking about all this, she'll watch Michael and me like a hawk all week. It'll be so obvious. And there's no way she won't crack and blab about it to my parents or Jamie. You know how she is."

Layla wanted to object to this claim about *knowing how Rosie is*, but then again, one night in a restaurant with Rosie was pretty revealing. She probably would blab. Loudly.

"Your parents would understand if you talked to them," she said instead, though *understand* might not be the right word, when it came to the MacKenzies. *I don't understand*, Manon had said, about a million times, when Layla and Jamie had broken the news of their split. Robert had stared worriedly, deepening that confused, tipped-over trench between his eyes.

Emily pivoted, paced a longer path this time, and shook her head.

"This wedding—they've invested so much into it. It means a lot to them, especially after you and Jamie . . ." She trailed off, winced.

Layla swallowed, ignored the gut-kick feeling of what Emily left unsaid. "Okay. I won't tell anyone."

It would be easy enough, she supposed. She could redo her itinerary to make it so she attended fewer of the wedding-related outings. Tonight's welcome event, Friday's open house, the wedding itself on Saturday night—all that was required, but most everything else had been pitched as "optional, but encouraged!" Layla had put about half those optional-but-encouraged things on her itinerary, wanting to show she was making a genuine effort.

Now, maybe Emily would want her to scale back even more. To prevent any accidental disclosures.

It could be a blessing in disguise. A reason to be even more scarce than she'd planned. God knew the MacKenzies were used to her being scarce by now. Maybe there'd be more of the *I don't understand* stuff when Layla didn't show up for things, but this time, all of it would be secretly in service of Emily's needs. A favor to the family, really. Nothing for Layla to feel guilty about at all.

"And you being here for everything," Emily said, "will help keep me grounded."

Here for everything, Layla repeated back to herself nervously.

"Em, your family will be here. Rosie." *Your brother's new girlfriend*, she thought, but swallowed it back. "It's okay if you want to keep this between us, but those people can still be a support system for—"

"It's not the same," Emily said. "It's not the same as you."

Emily sat across from Layla again. This time, she was the one to lean forward, to take Layla's hands and grip them tight.

"When I was doing the save-the-dates—god, the way I went

back and forth on whether it was unfair to ask you to come to Paris. Especially with the memories you must have here. And the way you'd pulled back from the family after everything with you and Jamie. Like you—like you couldn't be around us anymore."

Layla could not meet Emily's eyes now, because her own were weighted with tears. She stared down at their tangled-together fingers, as if she herself had been called out on sneaking more than a few cigarettes.

"I debated for weeks," Emily continued. "You can ask Michael. But the morning they went out, I . . . I had this *feeling*, Layla. I had the envelope for you in my hand, and I felt deep down it was the right thing to ask you to come. I knew you *needed* to be here. And maybe this was why. Maybe I knew I couldn't do this week without you. Maybe I knew I'd really need you."

In that moment, Layla wanted nothing more than to be the version of herself that had first walked into this room: the no-wasting-time version, the get-the-job-done version. A monument to mind over matter.

She thought Griffin had been asking a lot of her, but . . . but this?

Being Emily's bridal shadow, being a built-in buffer for her former in-laws, her ex-husband?

It felt beyond her.

It *was* beyond her, as the last year and a half of her bolting out of their lives, going from job to job—doing anything, basically, to avoid the promised continued closeness—had proved.

"Emily," was all she said.

"Please," Emily said back, a single, desperate-sounding syllable that was almost as effective as seeing Griffin Testa's white-knuckled fist curled on a café table.

Only almost, though, and it was as if Emily knew it. As if she could see that Layla was about to bolt again.

So she added something else.

Something that she must've known would get Layla to agree.

Something that Layla imagined would feel exactly like having a white-knuckled fist driven right into her stomach.

She said, "You promised you'd always be my sister."

Chapter Eight

Griffin had not thought it possible to stand in front of another one of these hotel room doors and feel more uncomfortable than he had a few hours ago, when he was standing in front of Layla Bailey's.

But it was.

It was definitely possible.

"You good if I leave you here?" he said to Michael, who'd raised his hand to knock.

Michael dropped his hand and looked over at Griff.

No, Griff gathered. Michael was not good. He had not been good since this morning, and especially not since Emily's latest text had come through ten minutes ago, during his and Griff's slow walk back from the park.

Can you come? it said, when Michael showed Griffin his phone. And then, another: I love you.

He and Michael had both stood still on a narrow sidewalk next to the display window of a closed chocolate shop, staring down at the screen like two dumb American tourists who couldn't get anywhere without a map and without also interfering with the flow of pedestrian traffic.

"What does that mean?" Michael had said, his brow furrowed.

The meaning, Griffin thought, was pretty straightforward in the abstract, but also, he knew what Michael meant. Was *Can you come, I love you* good news or bad news? Was Emily asking him to come so she could call it off, or so she could put it all back on?

Had Layla kept her promise, or not?

"Let's go," Griffin had replied, getting moving again, but he hadn't counted on Michael taking that *Let's* so literally. He hadn't counted on Michael asking him to come up to Emily's room with him.

"Just, you know," Michael said nervously as they'd gotten closer to their destination. "For a few minutes."

A vulnerable ask, Griff knew. A brave one.

Michael had never given Griffin the chance to ask a question like that. He'd always been there before Griff even had to contemplate the prospect of such naked vulnerability.

So, now, with Michael's wounded eyes on him, he kicked himself for being so selfish again. Hadn't he *just* sworn to himself that he'd be a different Griffin this week?

He said, "Never mind," and lifted his own hand to knock on Emily's hotel room door.

Then he squeezed Michael's shoulder and stood slightly back, waiting. The way a best man should.

Layla Bailey opened the door.

Goddammit, Griff thought.

Hair still up, the rogue swoop by her eye, those little pearl-drop earrings.

She was not yet an idea he'd gotten used to.

Especially not when her eyes went straight to his, instead of

Michael's. As though part of her expected to see him. Dreaded to see him, probably.

Had she been *crying*?

Inexplicably, he took a step forward, but as he did, she snapped her eyes to the right. To Michael.

"Emily's washing her face," Layla said, and then she made a sort of stutter-stop move: a step back to widen the door, as if to invite them in, followed immediately by a narrowing of the space again. The little customer-service-type smile she'd given to Michael dropped from her lips, and he could see her nibble at the inside of her cheek.

"It's, you know—a little . . ." She trailed off, and Griff looked past her shoulder, the way he had this morning. He couldn't see much of this room, either, but what he could see finished Layla's sentence for him.

Were those tissues on the bed? A whole fucking lot of tissues?

He looked up at Layla again, narrowed his eyes.

"Is she okay?" Michael said, his voice weighted with concern. Griffin figured he'd spotted the tissues, too.

Right, it was probably Emily who was crying.

That made . . . a lot more sense.

"She's doing okay," Layla said, her voice gentle now, like it had been while she'd talked to the girl on the plane. "She was really glad you were coming."

Her eyes flicked to Griffin's, her lips flattening. *I don't mean you*, she seemed to be adding.

There was an awkward silence where both Michael and Layla seemed to register the oddity of their respective positions: her keeping the room closed off, but now unsure about doing so; him eager to see Emily, but unwilling to show any impatience.

"You could—" she said, gesturing at the room behind her, at the same time Michael said, "I can wait out—"

To tell the truth, Griffin did not know why his being here was particularly helpful. It wasn't like he had a talent for making situations like this less uncomfortable.

He did, apparently, have a talent for noticing that Layla's cheeks had turned the faintest shade of pink.

"Oh," interrupted a new voice, and Griffin had the sense of his and Michael's and Layla's synchronized head-turn toward the source of it.

There, a few steps down the hallway, stood a woman who was probably Emily's age, wearing a color of shirt so unnatural that it made Griff want to close his eyes. She had two gold hoops in one nostril, enough earrings to cover the entire curve of one ear, and also what looked like a small diamond chip in her cheek, right where a dimple would be.

"Rosie," Michael said, and Griff connected the dots, the piercings, whatever. This was Emily's maid of honor. *Kind of an alternative type*, is how Michael had described her on the drive in from the airport yesterday, which was a very Michael thing to say.

"What's happening now!" Rosie half shrieked, and Griffin winced. Everyone would hear that. Layla needed to stop being so sensitive about the goddamned tissues and invite them into the room.

"Everything's okay," Layla said, in her airplane voice.

Rosie's gaze bounced between Layla and Michael, clearly unsure. She lifted a white paper bag in one hand and a cardboard tray of small to-go cups and said, "I got hot chocolate, too. To go with the croissants."

Craw-sawnts. Griffin wondered if he was the only guest at this wedding who'd actually practiced the language before coming here.

"That's great," said Layla. "I'm sure Em will want some while she and Michael talk."

Griff felt Michael tense beside him at that ominous word—*talk*—but Rosie's expression lightened, as if she knew this boded well.

"They were pretty pricey!" she said, which seemed like the wrong tone for the moment, but what did he know.

Then she shifted her gaze to him. He'd give her credit for not being shy about it, but she was a starer. Not the kind who let disgust betray on her face while she looked, but still. A starer.

He stared back.

"All this cost thirty-two euros," she said. Pointedly.

Okay? he thought, bewildered, and then he heard it—a little noise from where Layla stood. A huff of air, but with a touch more noise behind it.

Was it . . . a laugh?

He turned his face toward her, but already, her face was expressionless. Still pink, but blank again.

He found it unaccountably frustrating.

"I'll Venmo you," she said to Rosie.

Rosie snorted and stepped past Griff and Michael, toward the door. "Well, fine. You're a doctor, I guess."

As she nudged her way past Layla into the room, she added, inexplicably, "But not a *billionaire*."

Layla's cheek tucked in again, a little bite she was taking from the inside. Trying not to laugh was better than crying, but he didn't see what was funny about getting price-gouged by a person with a diamond chip stuck in their face.

A door clicked open behind Layla, and seconds later, Emily was there beside her, her puffy eyes locked on to Michael's.

"Hi," she whispered shakily, and Griffin watched as his best friend's chin quivered a tiny amount, right as his arms opened.

Emily stepped straight into them, tucking her face against Michael's chest as his head lowered toward hers, his lips pressing against her mussed hair.

Griffin did *not* look at Layla.

"It was the CHAMPAGNE!" Rosie shouted randomly from inside the room, but Emily and Michael didn't seem to hear. Emily murmured something against Michael's shirt, and he nodded, then separated from her only long enough to start guiding her away.

"Uh," Griff said, which was not one of his finer moments, in a lifetime of not-fine moments.

"They need some time," said Layla, because neither Michael nor Emily was bothering to look back.

He turned toward Layla again. He didn't like the way she said that. It had none of the unbothered optimism of Rosie shoving her way into the room, yelling about champagne.

"Did you fix it?" he said.

Her jaw ticked. Better than the blank stare. "I'm going back to my—"

"Layla," Rosie interrupted, coming up behind her and holding out the white bag, "take the rest of these croissants. I already ate a donut thingy on the way back. One of those long ones. With cream inside."

An éclair, Griffin thought, at the same time Layla said, "An éclair."

Fine. Her pronunciation was not terrible. Based on his little Rosetta Stone lessons.

"I felt like I was in a porno eating it," Rosie said, and Layla practically snatched the bag out of her hands, muttering something Griffin didn't catch.

Rosie snickered, then added, "Want one of these hot chocolates? I think it's basically a war crime here to take them to go, so you might as well enjoy the spoils of my ruining a French barista's morning."

"Sure," Layla said. Griffin thought it sounded like she was speaking through clenched teeth.

Rosie handed over the cup, and Layla managed a quick "See you later" before stepping fully into the hallway, using the hand still holding the bag to close the door behind her.

When she looked up, Griffin raised an eyebrow. He was not, generally, the lesser of two evils in any given interpersonal environment. At least Rosie made her laugh, which he would most certainly never manage to do.

It was subtle, but he saw it—the way her shoulders drooped the smallest amount. A clear confirmation of his not-the-lesser-evil status. Standing with that gray door behind her, no natural light in the narrow passage of the hall, she looked washed-out, tired. The pink in her cheeks from before drained away now.

He cleared his throat, about to offer to pay for the croissants. Just so he'd have something to say.

But she spoke first, her voice as quiet as Emily's had been. "I don't know."

He stared at her, confused. "What?"

"I don't know if I fixed it."

Oh. Right.

"Tonight is on," she added. "But I don't know about everything else."

He waited for a familiar feeling to come over him—frustration, impatience, irritation. If they were there—in his body, his mind—he couldn't access them.

But if she was waiting for *him* to say something consoling, something kind—something like, *It's okay*—he couldn't access that, either.

He thought of sitting in that strange, squared-off park with Michael, everything pretty and pristine, the clear sky a rare robin's-egg blue.

He thought of Layla Bailey's cheeks turning pink in the sunlight.

No. He thought of the promise he'd made to himself while sitting beside Michael: If she couldn't fix this alone, he'd find a way to fix it with her.

And that's what he'd need to do now.

"Let's get out of this fucking hallway," he said abruptly. "This hotel."

She blinked up at him with her big, muddy-brown eyes, and he watched as her lips rolled inward, her throat moving in a heavy swallow. He did not think getting out of the hotel was such a terrible idea, but he supposed she had reason to be nervous about going to a second location with him. Fine, they could go back to that courtyard with the terrible chairs, or—

"Okay," she said.

He hoped she wouldn't notice him letting out—very, very slowly—the breath he'd been holding. But just in case, to cover his bases, he thought it would be wise to distract her.

"Sun came out," he said curtly, turning to make his way down the hall. "You'll probably need sunglasses."

He waited for her in front of the hotel, trying not to pace for fear of further disturbing the doorman, who was a starer of the "showing disgust" variety. Normally, Griff took that sort of thing as an opportunity to be defiant, even scary, but he figured the doorman could be a good first test of the daytime Griffin he was trying to be.

So instead, he simply stood what he thought was a few polite steps down from the hotel's wide, sleek glass doors, staring across the street at a building that looked much more like it belonged here, based on what he'd seen of this city so far. That cream-gray stone, shutters flanking old, tall paned windows, each with ironwork railings, and beneath them all, two huge arched and paneled entry doors painted a rich dark blue, a brass knob right in the middle of both.

He was thinking about how that was the sort of door that actually deserved a doorman when she stepped up beside him.

"Hello," she said. Businesslike, which he guessed was better, for him personally, than doctor-like.

He turned to look at her, felt a stupid degree of satisfaction that she'd taken his advice about the sunglasses, though he thought they were a little big for her face. He couldn't even see all of her eyebrows.

Not that he needed to see much of her face.

The sunglasses were a blessing, to be honest.

She had a purse over her shoulder but nothing else—not the hot chocolate or the little bag of croissants.

"Did you eat?" he said, for no good reason. Except that twice this morning, he and this woman had been in the presence of French pastries, which no one ever stopped going on about, and he hadn't seen her have one. He hadn't, either, but his body still felt too jet-lagged and outside-of-time for food. It wasn't the same for him.

"I'm not hungry," she said.

He nodded in the direction that he'd walked this morning on

his way to meet Michael. There's no way she wasn't hungry. "There's a bunch of cafés down that way."

He was just being *polite*.

"I don't want to go sit in a café like this."

He looked her over, bottom to top, grateful that he'd stopped first in his room and had his own eyes covered now. She was wearing the same thing she'd had on earlier. Sneakers and wide-legged black pants and a white button-up that looked a little wrinkled, but otherwise normal.

"Like what?"

"I'm not . . . dressed."

He stared. Not in disgust, obviously. More in bewilderment. In fact she was maximally dressed. This morning he'd seen her in a robe, for Christ's sake. And last night he'd been able to see a glimpse of her collarbones. Her slim, muscular calves in that skirt, flexed in the heels she wore.

Maximally dressed was also a blessing.

"Let's go this way," she said, and then marched right past him, in the opposite direction he'd suggested.

He had to hustle to catch up, his leg smarting ominously with the quick movement.

She crossed the street at a diagonal, one hand clutched around the strap of her bag, her strides long and purposeful, avoiding random puddles, occasional dog waste. On account of the sunglasses, he couldn't tell if she was taking much in around her, but there was no way she'd seen those big doors. He thought she would've at least paused if she had. There was no arguing that they were interesting, especially compared to the hotel ones.

When she finally slowed, it was at the curb of a busy street, a crosswalk right in front of them; on the other side of it waited the gray stone walls that flanked the river he'd seen, somewhat piecemeal, last night. She kept her head up, and when the traffic slowed, she stepped off the curb immediately. He almost grabbed her elbow, not trusting these speedy little cars and scooters that honked and swerved seemingly at random, but once again, she eluded him—straight out into the street, confident. A stride like she had a specific destination in mind.

Something got his back up, then. A twinge of suspicion like that pain in his leg.

"You seem to know what you're doing," he said when they made it across, the worst of the traffic noise fading behind them.

Layla cut to the right, and he followed, watching as her jaw ticked. He thought maybe she wouldn't answer, and the twinge transformed into something more forceful.

But when she turned again, a left into a gap in the wall, and started to make her way down a steep ramp that would lead them to the river, she finally spoke again.

"I've been here before."

That wasn't strange, he supposed. People—other people, at least—traveled. And he didn't know Layla Bailey's life; maybe she was a frequent traveler. Maybe the city of Paris was some kind of second home to her. What did he know?

Except there was something in the way she said it. Something in how she slanted herself into the ramp's descent, a stomping desperation that he recognized.

When they got to the bottom, the greenish-blue stripe of the river waited, momentarily distracting him. He could admit, he liked this better than the fussy park from this morning. Here, everything pretty was also slightly pockmarked: the soft gray pavers that formed a walkway along the water dotted with three worse-for-wear trash cans, set strangely close together; the canopies of bright green leaves of the thin-trunked trees on the opposite bank crudely interrupted by big gaps of uneven growth; the white and cream of the elegant buildings that rose up behind them capped with sooty, sometimes crooked chimney caps.

He felt, for once, like looking around for a minute.

But Layla Bailey stepped straight in front of him, turning her back on it all, and that suspicion reared up again.

He thought, *Just ask her about Michael and Emily. Ignore the suspicion, and figure out what needs to be done next about Michael and Emily.*

He said, "When?"

"What?"

"When have you been here before?"

She pursed her lips, and suspicion became a full-on presumption.

She'd been here before with the ex-husband. He'd bet on it.

He curled the fingers of his right hand into his palm, pressing hard.

Awfully fucking *im*polite of Emily to invite her to this.

Awfully fucking cruel.

"So, Emily," Layla said, and then, without giving him a chance to say anything stupid and snarling and irrelevant, like *Emily, who shouldn't have asked you to come to this wedding?*, she launched into the sort of report that made her sound more like a doctor than anything she'd said since he met her.

And he tried to listen; he did. He heard her say that she had not, in fact, said anything disparaging about marriage to Emily, that Emily was feeling skittish about the move abroad, and about the shape the rest of her life would take. He heard her say that Emily loved Michael, but that she was "nervous"—this word, Layla said pointedly, an *I-told-you-so* holdover from their aborted breakfast—and that she knew calling the wedding off was too extreme for today, but that she still felt tentative about whether she could get there by the end of the week. He heard her say that Emily wanted to try focusing on time with Michael as much as she could.

But like a lot of times in his life where Griffin had listened to doctors talking to him, his mind was more than half on something else entirely. Usually, it was his pain—the sort of pain that made words seem meaningless to his ears, the sort that had him thinking he could feel individual particles of dust settling on his skin, the sort that somehow made him wish he'd never have to listen to anyone, anywhere, ever again.

Right now, though, he was thinking of how strangely she was holding herself as she talked: her shoulders set so deliberately parallel to the river, her neck stiff like she couldn't turn it. When that loose swoop of hair blew slightly across her cheek, strands catching across the lenses of her enormous sunglasses, she didn't even lift a hand to brush it away. Twice, people passed right behind her, too close for comfort, and if she clocked them, he couldn't tell.

Before, when he'd been with her, what he hadn't liked was the way it seemed as though she was seeing everything.

Now, she seemed as though she couldn't see anything at all.

And he didn't like that, either.

When exactly? he wanted to ask. *When exactly did you come here with him?*

But that question didn't have anything to do with Michael, so he tried to think of a Daytime Griffin question. A polite question.

"So, what? We all . . . wait around until she decides?"

For the first time since she started speaking, she moved: crossing her arms over her chest, cocking a hip one way while her head tilted to the other. A posture of such evident annoyance that he knew he hadn't managed anything approaching politeness.

"We *support* them until she decides."

I'm not supporting anyone but Michael, he thought.

"We're the only two people who are going to know," she added. "That things are still . . . tentative."

He stared at her through his own sunglasses, watched as she shifted again. Tightening the arms she'd crossed, repositioning her feet. In his own body, he felt familiar, echoey pains, which he tried to ignore.

"She's not telling her family?" he said.

Her throat bobbed in what looked like an uncomfortable swallow at that last word.

"No," she finally said, and then—as if to divert him, she added quickly, "You can't tell anyone in Michael's family, either."

Before he could stop it, his face contorted—the unsightly twist he knew it made on the rare occasions he almost laughed. One minute of meeting Michael's parents with Griffin in the room and Layla would find out that there was no risk of them hearing anything at all from him. They could barely look in his direction, let alone talk to him.

The little bit of the eyebrows he could see on her face disappeared as she lowered them, and when her lips parted as if to speak, he preempted her.

"I won't say anything."

He hoped it came out with the finality he intended. He did not want to talk about Fitz and Paula. They wouldn't be here until tomorrow, and for Griffin, that was a temporary source of relief.

"Good," she said, with a quick nod, a little *doctor-getting-ready-to-leave-the-room* nod that he knew very well, and for the first time in all the times of seeing that stupid nod, he didn't feel as though he was about to get a reprieve.

He may not want to talk about Michael's parents, but also, he did not want her to leave yet.

Because of the promise you made, he told himself firmly. *Because you still haven't worked out how to fix this for Michael.*

"Support them how?" he blurted.

She uncrossed her arms then, lifting a hand to reposition the strap of her bag. He thought, for a second, that she might finally look around—turn her head one way or the other, remind herself that they weren't in a hospital room, the cabin of an airplane, an elevator, a hotel hallway.

Instead, he watched her shoulders lift slightly, a tiny intake of air he thought she didn't want him to see.

"Just—you know. Show up to the wedding stuff. Be there for them. Act normal."

It wasn't much of a plan, and he knew—he *knew*—that's what he should be focused on. There should be some strategy, some timeline for it all—a way to give Michael and Emily more time alone, a firm answer by a particular day, *something*.

But Griffin was long out of practice at making plans like that, and anyway, he still couldn't stop thinking about how still and shut-off she was being: a woman he'd first seen in motion, a woman he'd watched take in every single detail about a scared girl on a plane.

"Is this how you act when you're being normal?" he said.

"Is it for you?" she snapped back, and for a few seconds, neither of them said anything.

But he was thinking: a hundred answers, all at once, flooding his brain. *Normally, I don't travel. Normally, I don't go out much during the daytime, not where there's a lot of people around. Normally, I only eat food I've cooked for myself. Normally, I only see Michael when it's just me and him. Normally, I lie in my bed on a set schedule, even if I don't sleep. Normally, I don't see anything that looks as soft as that swoop of your hair—*

"No," she said, barely audible, and for a second he wondered if he'd imagined it—conjured a little light scolding for himself for thinking such a stupid thought about her hair.

But no—she had said it, and after a brief pause, she added, almost as if he weren't there, "This is not how I act."

Then, she finally did it: She turned her head. Looked to the left, westward, toward the river's long unrolling through this city, toward all the things people came here to see. Her chest lifted again, a bigger breath this time, enough to smell the mossy dampness that came off the stone lining the water, the smoke that trailed at least every tenth pedestrian.

She didn't turn her face back to him.

She said, with a finality more dismissive than any doctor's nod, "I'll see you tonight."

And after she walked away, it was long minutes before he finally realized: He still hadn't gotten her number.

Chapter Nine

"So that is a *huge* fucking boat, right?"

For at least the tenth time in the last tense seven and a half minutes, Rosie's boisterous voice pierced the heavy silence that kept falling thickly over the leather interior of the SUV.

Layla counted to six: one second for each of the passengers in this car, an unlikely crew. Rosie in the front passenger seat, wearing a burgundy-pleather corset top and matching pleated miniskirt, chunky black boots laced to her shin. The young, clean-cut, dark blue suit–clad driver, who had stared in seeming awe at Rosie's appearance outside the hotel, and then haltingly introduced himself in English as Matthieu, his one and only effort at speaking on this short ride.

Michael and Emily behind them in two captain-style leather seats, him in a crisp white shirt and tan suit, a complement to Emily in bridal cream, a color Layla thought made her—pale-faced as she still was—look wispy and indistinct. Michael's arm awkwardly extended across the narrow space to keep hold of Emily's hand, even though she kept her gaze out the window.

And finally, her and Griffin, in the back bench seat. Both of them pressed as far as they could get to their respective sides, him in all black again, dress pants and a long-sleeved knit crew neck shirt that seemed too casual for the occasion, her in a loose-fitting, latte-colored midi dress that had seemed perfect for her strange position at this wedding when she'd ordered it, and now—given the mood of everyone in this car except for Rosie—seemed overly dour.

Six seconds, and no one responded.

So Layla said, "It *is* big," which sounded absolutely inane. She wasn't even sure whether Rosie could hear her from back here. In her periphery, she saw Griffin shift, a body annoyed or impatient or—the worst possible option—embarrassed for her, and she clenched her hands around her (dour) clutch.

When have you been here before? he'd asked as they'd walked toward the river, and that's when she first heard it . . . the embarrassment. It was worse than the scolding disgust of his *Get up from there* on the plane, or the angry accusation of his *something you said* early this morning.

He'd asked her when she'd been here before as though he already knew.

As though he knew, and he felt *sorry* for her.

It wasn't as though he asked her nicely, or softly, or even with a gentle head-cock that might indicate sympathy. He said it the same way he said everything else, which meant he said it tersely, shrewdly; he said it like he had time for nothing but to rip out and hold in his hand the bloody, still-beating heart of any matter.

As she stood there across from him, Paris pressing tauntingly against her back, she realized what she would have to do before this already-awkward evening, and that was to face the city full-on, by herself.

So when she left him, she walked and walked—all along the

Seine, from the Pont de Sully to the Trocadéro and back, her head up as she treated landmarks like Band-Aids to be ripped off, one by one, so nothing could strike her fresh on this boat cruise. By the time she stood as close as she could to the Eiffel Tower, she felt numb to it. Tired and hungry and thirsty, enough not to care about sweatily ducking into a small Carrefour City to buy an apple and a bag of chips and a big bottle of water, as though she was in a nameless town that had nothing else worth eating on offer.

She had not, of course, abandoned Emily so soon after her new promise—Layla texted her before getting too far into the walk, making sure Em and Michael were still safely ensconced in their requested alone time, asking whether Em would want to meet up after. This time, Emily replied immediately, a cryptic We're talking.

"It's like, *too* big, am I right? Shipwreck big. Aren't there only like . . . a dozen of us going on this?" Rosie continued.

Michael finally cleared his throat.

"We don't have the whole boat," he said as the car slowed to a stop beside a great behemoth of a building that was built close to the river, ultracontemporary, with a gigantic and jutting structure that wrapped around the front, a girded glass walkway that was shockingly lime green.

"What the fuck is this," Griffin said, sort of under his breath. She chanced a glance and saw him staring skeptically out at the green structure. Frankly, she also felt a little *What the fuck* about it, but would not say that out loud.

"We kind of have the whole boat," Emily chimed in, and Layla was glad to finally hear her speak, too. Since they'd all met in the lobby, Emily had been quiet, not a good start to keeping this whole situation hidden. So far, Rosie still seemed to be attributing Emily's subdued mood to the champagne ("I swear to god I put like a cannonball of bronzer on her," Rosie had whispered to Layla, as though they were longtime coconspirators, "but she still looks like that Moët sucked out her soul"), but Rosie was not Robert or Manon MacKenzie, and Layla had to assume *they* would notice Emily was way off.

At least they won't really notice you, then, a nasty little voice inside her said, and she felt herself wince.

This is not about you, her better angels scolded back. *You are here for Emily, to be a sister to Emily. You will be the most normal you have ever been in your life, and you will buffer the hell out of this situation for the person who needs you.*

"The top level is ours," Emily added, and Layla looked again in the direction of the boat that awaited them on the banks. She could not, from here, see anyone milling around up there, but maybe that was because, on closer inspection, it *was* sort of shipwreck big.

Layla squinted at it, surprised. It was extravagant, and she'd never known the MacKenzies to be that. But she remembered what Em had said about their *investment* in all this, and felt a renewed pang of stress for her. This was so much pressure: this boat, this event, this week, this city.

This marriage, after the breakdown of Layla's own had apparently upset the family so much.

"Well, how great!" she said, desperate to be cheerful. "So much space to spread out and see the views."

She could sense Griffin turning his head to look at her, but she ignored him. Instead she focused on Emily, who looked over her shoulder and gave Layla a grateful smile.

Up front, Rosie was opening her door, shocking poor Matthieu, who said, "Attendez, s'il—" and then trailed off helplessly. Michael followed suit, opening his own door and turning gallantly to help Emily out.

Which left Griffin and Layla stuck awkwardly, waiting for Matthieu to come around and release the seat so that they, too, could make their way out. Griffin was looking at his phone, and she stopped herself from rolling her eyes. But she thought, *Guess this is you "acting normal."*

"It's a school," he said, puncturing her snide train of thought.

"What?"

"This building. There's a fashion school in there. Art exhibits. Some restaurants." Matthieu came to stand at the open door, reaching down beneath the seat Michael had been in. "In case you were wondering," Griffin added.

Was he . . . maybe trying to *actually* be normal? Conversational?

The seat in front of Griffin's knees folded forward, Matthieu pushing it into the floor with a satisfying little *thunk*, and Griffin stood in a crouch, murmuring a hasty *Merci* to the driver as he stepped down from the car.

And then he turned back toward it, extending his hand.

To Layla.

She stared, stunned.

It couldn't be called a mimicry of what Michael had done for Emily, since Michael looked at Emily with softness and concern and adoration, whereas Griffin was only managing a look of obligation. Of barely mustered tolerance.

But it was better than pity. It was *something*.

Something that spoke to their shared purpose tonight, the secret they were both keeping for the sake of Emily and Michael.

So, she took it.

Her fingers sliding against his palm, then his fingers closing around hers, warm and dry and enveloping, and for a second, as she leaned forward and stepped toward the open door, she was relieved. She was thinking, *He's not a lightning bolt; he's a man, a regular man, and I've—*

But then, as she stepped down, the rough pad of his thumb moved across her knuckles—an accident, she was *sure*, a small stroke of momentum and not intention—and she felt it, the electricity of him moving through her again, like it had when he'd first looked at her on the plane. Her spine practically jolted from it, every joint in her body humming and vibrating from its force.

When her foot hit the pavement beneath her, she wobbled.

He tightened his hold on her hand. Their eyes met: hers, probably wide with the renewed shock of this; his, pitch-dark and steady and *seeing*.

Pitying, she thought. *He pities you.*

"I'm fine," she said sharply, sounding like him, yanking her hand from his and immediately smoothing it down the front of her boring brown dress—no, her *blending into the background* dress—and turning her attention to the boat, to the wooden ramp Michael was helping Emily across, to the metal stairs Rosie was already halfway up, to the top deck where, she could now see, Robert and Manon MacKenzie stood waiting.

"You're sure?" Griffin said, not at all pitying now—just doubtful, judgmental, suspicious. His *You need to fix this* attitude back in full force.

It was such a relief that she almost turned to thank him, except that she didn't trust herself to take him in again—his set, handsome face, scars and all, and his lean, steady body.

Instead, she raised her arm to wave at two people who had once been her family, and smiled widely, hoping that from here it looked completely authentic. She remembered every Band-Aid she'd ripped off today. Remembered Emily was her priority.

She shot a glance toward Griffin and said, in the same tone of challenge he had already so frequently leveled at her, "Watch me."

D oing it like a dare was—to start, at least—shockingly easy.

Layla kept her own words in mind as she did the thing she'd been dreading and dreading and building up in her head for months: greeting her in-laws after a too-long stretch of avoiding them.

Watch me hug Manon tightly, watch me as I let her kiss both of my cheeks and then cup them after; watch me stand smiling as she wells up with tears and says she missed me.

Watch me lean into Robert's side as he puts his arm around me; watch how I don't overreact to him gruffly saying, "Hi, there, Laylapalooza," an old inside joke that became a loving, fatherly nickname.

Watch me say hello to Manon's sister Céline and immediately shower her with compliments on the chunky, over-the-top jewelry she's wearing; watch how she takes the bait and tells me all about it instead of asking how I am. Watch me greet Robert's oldest friend and longtime business partner, and his wife, too; watch as I take a glass of wine from a tray and say how busy I've been, how glad I am to take some time off for this, how much I enjoyed my leisurely walk through the city today.

She was, to put it mildly, crushing it so far.

Out of the corner of her eye, she could see Griffin hanging back, sticking close to the staircase, near one of the sleek high-top tables that dotted the deck, along with artfully arranged potted plants and white club chairs that were probably a total nightmare to keep clean. If he was watching her, he didn't make it obvious, but she pretended he was. She pretended the skin over her knuckles wasn't still faintly buzzy and warm from his touch.

"Has anyone heard from Jamie?" Manon's musical voice called out, and Layla did not even stiffen where she stood with Céline and Rosie. She simply sipped her wine and held out a hand for the sweaty glass of something pink that Rosie was obviously trying to get rid of.

"Thank god for you," Rosie said, handing it over, then immediately using her newly freed fingers to pick up one of the four lemon-rosemary gougères she'd stacked shamelessly onto her appetizer plate pretty much as soon as they'd been set out.

"No problem," said Layla, not really because it was necessary to say but because—with Manon's question lingering in the air—she didn't want to seem as though she'd been rendered uncomfortably silent.

Maybe she couldn't tell for sure if Griffin was watching her, but right this second, she could tell that Céline was.

"He says they're almost here," Robert answered before tucking his phone into his pocket, turning back to the conversation he'd been having with Abram, the friend and business partner with whom—Layla knew by Manon's ensuing eye roll—he was almost certainly discussing business.

"Well!" Manon said, clasping her hands together. "They better hurry; we're launching soon!"

Céline cleared her throat gently.

"How will that be for you, Layla?" she said.

Of all the MacKenzie-associated guests on this boat, Layla probably knew Jamie and Emily's aunt Céline the least well, though having met her when she was still just Jamie's girlfriend, well over a decade ago now, it wasn't as though their acquaintance was casual. She'd spent multiple holidays with Céline at the family table, had once spent two nights sleeping on a pull-out sofa with Jamie in Céline's small Manhattan apartment so they could go see the Macy's Thanksgiving Day Parade ("Banal," Céline had proclaimed, but she'd still trudged out into the damp November cold with them like a chaperone, even though she and Jamie were twenty-two at the time). When Layla and Jamie separated, Céline didn't call, but she did send Layla a short email: I'm sorry to hear about you and my nephew. You were a beautiful couple, and I wish you the best of luck.

So Layla knew her well enough to know that she could have anticipated such a direct question—Céline was blunt and at times impatient, similar in looks to Manon but completely different in personality.

Rosie closed-mouth coughed, a crumb of choux pastry escaping from behind the hand she put in front of her mouth.

"Oh, fine," Layla said, wishing now that she wasn't holding both her own drink and Rosie's. One could not really casually wave a dismissive hand in the air under such circumstances, so she started to add, "You know, it was completely ami—"

But she cut herself off when she saw, out of the corner of her eye, Griffin doing exactly what she'd dared him to do. His eyes on her like hot coals, pressed straight to her middle. *Not like this*, she wanted to shout across the deck at him. *Don't watch me like this.*

She stumbled her way into what sounded, even to her own ears, like a complete lie: "I'm excited to see him."

One of Céline's huge, long earrings got longer as she tipped her head. Layla felt a faint bloom of sweat beneath her breasts, either from Griffin's hot-coal gaze or Céline's obvious curiosity.

Rosie said, her shoulders sagging, her mouth still at least partially full, "I don't really like these, actually. Does anyone want the other three?"

Layla handed Rosie her pink drink and thought seriously about taking the plate and shoving every single one of those gougères into her own mouth, if only to give Céline something else awkward to focus on.

Why had she said *excited*?

But right as she reached a hand out, she heard Emily's voice, a single word, one of those sharp exhalations of frustration that was meant to come out quiet, but that somehow carried.

"Mom."

Layla straightened, her eyes going to to where Manon and Emily stood by one of the boat's railings, closer to where the long dinner table, gorgeously set for a dozen, waited under a canopy of string lights. Already, Manon was speaking back to Emily quietly, leaning in, and Emily had a mulish expression on her face, her thumb bent beneath her first two fingers to rub absently—irritatedly, Layla thought—at the engagement ring on her third.

Quickly, Layla scanned the rest of the sparsely populated deck. Abram and Robert were oblivious, probably talking about brokered CD rates or some other deathly boring financial topic. Abram's wife, Damaris—a relentlessly enthusiastic conversationalist when in any sort of company, probably because she was so grateful not to be talking about brokered CD rates—had cornered Michael near a potted plant, talking animatedly while he stared miserably at Emily.

And Griffin stared at Layla, now with his full *Fix it* face on.

"If you'll excuse me," Layla said, not bothering to risk another glance at Céline. Rosie, Layla could tell, was busy sucking down whatever was in her newly returned glass.

She tried to make her approach seem like a glide, a harmless stop-by only to say hello, another guest keeping the company mingling. But when she was a step or two away, Em's eyes darted to hers and then back to Manon's, a quick and sharp mother-daughter understanding passing between them.

When, a split second later, Manon turned to where Layla now stood, her smile was over-wide and guilty.

Oh god, Layla thought. *They were talking about me.*

"Layla," Manon said, in a real *of course we weren't talking about you!* voice, "did I say how well that dress suits you? It's lovely, really."

Before Layla could answer ("The dress is dead boring, Manon!"), Emily took a step forward and looped her arm through Layla's elbow, linking them close.

"Layla," Em echoed, but she kept her eyes fixed—a little icily, frankly—on Manon's. "My mom was just telling me that Jamie and Samantha were looking into staying in a different hotel while we're all here."

Manon made a noise Layla had heard before: a laugh that was not really a laugh. The kind of noise you make, for example, when one of your husband's drunk work colleagues knocks over the entire bowl of the special cinnamon-spice punch you make every year for your annual holiday party, or when your neighbor's goldendoodle digs up all the newly planted petunias in your yard.

"Oh no, it's not really that, it's—" Manon began.

"And *I* said that was fine," Emily interrupted. "If that's what they want to do."

Layla watched as Manon gallantly fought a full grimace. But Layla had been there for the party where the punch bowl tipped over, onto newly refinished hardwood floors, and she'd been there for that one summer weekend when two hundred fifty dollars of petunias laid, irreparably wilted, across a hot front walkway.

So she still caught the slight twitch at the corners of Manon's eyes, the wobble in her smile.

"Oh," Layla managed. Her and Emily's pressed-together arm skin already felt over-warm and damp. If Layla did not already have an inkling—*more* than an inkling—of what was going on here, Emily's bow-tight posture of obvious frustration would have given it away.

"You know how Jamie is," Manon said, and then turned a soft gaze toward Layla. "He's so tenderhearted; he doesn't want you—"

"She's *not* switching hotels, Mom," Emily snapped. "If *he* wants to move, he can."

"Darling, of course she doesn't have to switch hotels," Manon said, as if Emily was being ridiculous.

As if she wasn't the one who—judging by Emily's sweaty elbow pit tightening on Layla's bicep—had suggested it only a moment ago. As if she wasn't leaving a too-long pause, hoping Layla might go ahead and offer.

But Layla was frozen. Yesterday, crammed into her airplane seat and staring at poor translations of cheerful platitudes, she would have probably been stung but ultimately grateful for a nudge like this—a reason to keep on keeping what distance she could during this event, but this time, at someone else's prompting.

Now, though, with Emily plastered to her side—with the memory of Emily crying and saying, about every other person on this boat, *it's not the same as you*—keeping her distance would at best mean breaking a promise.

At worst, it could mean breaking up this whole entire wedding.

Her brain was whirring through various stalling, noncommittal responses when Emily spoke again.

"I need Layla with me." Her voice had gone worryingly high, and Manon's eyes widened.

For the first time since she'd gotten here, Layla automatically, inexplicably, thought in French.

Non, non, non.

"I need—" Emily said again, but this time, that high pitch in her voice broke.

It sounded ominously like the start to more crying.

And then, to Layla's horror, everything seemed to happen all at once, or at least in such quick succession that there was no time to count the seconds. It was simply a half dozen things that each earned their own special *non* inside Layla's head.

Manon, looking between her and Emily and saying, "Is something going on?"

A uniformed employee ringing an overloud bell, the five-minute warning to the boat's launch.

Robert, cluelessly yelling out his intention to "call my son again before this thing leaves without him!"

Michael, showing up to Emily's other side, looking like a man who fully expected to get broken up with in the next five minutes.

Griffin, appearing behind Layla, bad enough on its own, but then impossibly worse when he set his hand—god *damn* his electric hand—on her arm, curling that rogue thumb over her bicep, leaning in close, way too close, to say, "Can I *borrow* you?" in a way that sent pinpricks of heat through her. She moved—an awkward step away from Emily, their arms still attached at first, and then a slight stumble from them both: Michael there to steady Emily, but Griffin only there to make Layla less stable, less in control of herself.

And then, finally: Jamie, Jamie's dark blond hair and still-boyish smile appearing as he climbed the steps, more of him coming into view as he rushed his way up, pulling someone—Samantha, she was his new someone—behind him, his blue eyes scanning the deck and stopping on Layla's.

Right as she tipped into Griffin Testa's body.

Chapter Ten

Usually, it hurt to have someone touch him.

Not every time, not all the time.

Mostly when he wasn't prepared for it. Like when a TSA agent at Tompkins Airport held out a hand and said, "Hold up a moment, sir," grazing Griff's side, or like when a flight attendant gently knocked into the knee he'd accidentally let drift too far into the aisle, desperate to get comfortable. Like when Michael clapped a heavy hand on his shoulder in a hotel lobby, so happy and surprised that someone had called Griff's behavior *heroic*.

But when Layla Bailey suddenly bumped against him—the blade of her right shoulder against his chest, the curve of her ass against his hip, even the sharp point of her heel pressing into the top of his shoe, against a couple of his toes—absolutely no part of him hurt.

He made a noise, though. A muffled grunt that had nothing to do with the held-breath silence Griff had long ago practiced keeping when he was in pain. It was shock, that was the thing, and pain never really shocked him anymore.

But this did. The feel of her did. Her body against a part of his he hadn't prepared for. Not like a few seconds of holding her soft, cool hand, not even like setting his own to the impossibly smooth skin of her arm. Those were the sort of deadened, rote actions he performed with something else in the front of his mind: get her out of the car, get her away from this pursed-lipped mother-of-the-bride woman who already had a bead on something going on between Michael and Emily. If those actions felt nice or not, he didn't let himself notice.

Or he didn't let himself linger on the noticing.

But this was something else.

This was the sort of feeling you got when you were fully alive, and Griff couldn't remember the last time he'd been that.

"Oh!" she said, lifting her foot from his, taking a step forward, but he had not yet taken his hand from her arm, which was a decision he could not explain except to say that it was not a decision at all. So now, he stood behind her, a narrow slice of air between them, something huge and unfamiliar beating against the sealed-shut coffin of his body, hoping she couldn't hear it.

Still touching her.

That's how he knew, in the end, that the ex had shown up—from touching Layla. Another thing he could not explain: what precisely he felt that told him so. Nothing so simple as a change to her posture, which settled quickly back into the straightness he'd now seen each time he'd been in her presence; nothing so obvious as goose bumps or a flush of heat on her still-smooth, cool skin.

But *something*.

His fingers curled of their own accord, pressing lightly into the soft cords of her bicep, his confused, ticking-time-bomb of a body grasping blindly at trying to figure hers out.

Meanwhile, he *was* still seeing—at a remove, maybe, given the chaos happening throughout the rest of him—but he was seeing. The man who'd just arrived, her ex, tall and tidy and dark blond like Emily, clean-shaven and smooth-skinned, a guy with the kind of blandly handsome face that you might see reading off the news on your local channel, a smile quirking when the story was uplifting, a brow furrowed when the reporting was grim.

Like it was now.

When he looked at Layla.

Griff immediately, irreversibly hated him.

"Jamie," Layla said quietly, which made Griff hate the man even more.

She stepped away then, his fingers curling on nothing now, and something in him—the huge and unfamiliar something, the fully alive something—said, *Wait*.

But with no small effort, he silenced it. Dropped his hand to his side, tucked it back into his pocket, pretending that he was pressing his palm over the mouth of that rogue voice. No time for new voices. He snapped his eyes to Michael, who had a protective arm around Emily, both of them looking between Layla and the new arrival with expressions of barely contained dread.

Fuck.

Before the collision that had momentarily distracted him, Griffin had been doing exactly what Layla Bailey had dared him to do, which meant he'd been watching. At first, her easy smiles and self-assured small talk had impressed and annoyed him in equal measure, but neither feeling had been enough to get him to look away. Instead, he'd been watching when cracks started showing up in the facade: first, when she'd been speaking to the woman who was wearing what looked to Griffin like a triple string of gigantic chestnuts around her neck, and then, a few minutes later, when she'd made her way over to interrupt a tense conversation between Emily and her mother.

Even from where he stood, Griffin had been able to see the way Layla's skin blanched at whatever was being said. By the time he'd heard Emily's voice rising into a near-hysterical pitch, he'd been on the move, an old, flailing anger rising up inside him.

All he wanted was to help Michael, help him get the happiness he deserved, and why couldn't any of these *fucking* people do what they were supposed to do and let it happen?

And now, the ex was here, and he knew that whatever conversation had made Layla turn gray-white had to do with him.

Or him and—as Griffin realized now—his guest.

His *guest*. A young woman, mid-twenties, maybe, surely no older than Emily. Short and scared-looking, in a bright, floral-printed dress and a pair of heels she was teetering in.

He made a fist with the hand in his pocket, controlling an impulse. It didn't make any sense to want to grab Layla's arm again.

He did not grab anything unless he absolutely had to.

Instead, he went back to watching: this time, with the keen awareness that everyone on the deck of this boat seemed to be doing the same, a collective breath-holding that Griffin probably could've registered as being an added cruelty, were he not so focused on what additional mess this was going to cause to an evening that was already going off the rails.

"Jamie," Layla said again as she stepped forward, but this time it sounded different—pleasant and welcoming, as if she herself were the hostess of this whole thing. She extended a single arm—not the one Griffin had been holding—and leaned into the man in a perfectly executed half hug. Shoulders leaned in, hips tilted back, no lingering, not even long enough for Jamie to get a hand all the way around her waist.

Griffin wondered whether it hurt. Whether even that fleeting touch made everything inside her curl and shrivel and scream.

When she pulled back, though, she looked, again, entirely unbothered. She turned toward the wide-eyed woman at Jamie's side, extended a hand, and said, "And you must be Samantha. I've heard so many wonderful things about you," and it was like watching her with the girl on the plane—a real *everything is completely fine* energy that seemed to give everyone—including too-young, teetering Samantha—permission to let out their held breath.

In seconds, most of the party moved forward—Emily and Michael, still entangled, Michael's future mother- and father-in-law, the other older couple whose names Griffin had already forgotten. All of them crowding around the new arrivals and Layla, one big happy family that he didn't trust for a second.

"She's very good, isn't she?" said a voice from beside him, and he looked over and down to see chestnut-necklace lady, her eyes on where Layla stood, still smiling and chatting in an unholy triangle with her ex-husband and the ex-husband's apparent new girlfriend.

"Who?" he said, because he was a lot of things—mean and impatient and reclusive and single-minded—but he wasn't fucking stupid.

The necklace lady didn't answer him. She stood beside him until that tinkling bell rang again and the boat beneath them began to move, and then she slipped a small hand into the crook of his left elbow, shooting a jagged slice of pain all the way to the side of his neck.

It was almost comforting. He did not move a muscle. Didn't make a sound.

She said, "Walk me over to the table?"

And he did, letting it hurt the whole way.

* * *

"So, in a way, Paris has always been our family's second home."

The woman Griffin now knew as Emily's aunt Céline was still, an hour later, at his side—not touching now, but next to him at the table where small plates of a tuna tartare that Griffin didn't eat much of had just been cleared. In that time, she had told him a whole host of things that he had not cared about: her job in New York City as a fabric designer ("upholstery, not that you asked"), her current boyfriend Otto who "dabbled" (*Who says a word like dabbled?* Griffin thought) in music, her recently deceased cat ("A tabby, you know how those are"; Griffin did not), her long-standing cold war with the president of her building's co-op board (related to the recently deceased cat). Through all of it, he had been his usual self, which is to say, he had not encouraged her, in any way, to continue speaking.

Until now.

"Say that again," he said.

She looked up at him, surprised, which he couldn't blame her for. For better or worse, they had settled into a strange norm down here at their end of the table: Céline talked, and Griffin did not.

"I said that Paris has always been—"

"Before that," Griffin interrupted.

"Has anyone ever told you that you have terrible manners?"

He didn't answer. Anyway, the sun was getting lower now: harder and harder to be Daytime Griffin.

She rolled her eyes. "I *said* that Emily spent part of her summers here as a child."

"With her grandmother."

"Terrible manners and a mediocre listener," Céline said. "With *my* grandmother. She was born here, and moved to the States with my grandfather, and then when he passed away, she bought a pied-à-terre here. Manon and I have always been very connected to our French roots, and obviously she's tried to—"

"He came, too?" Griff cut her off again.

Céline blinked. "He—?" she began, but must've followed the flick of Griffin's eyes toward the ex. "Yes. Manon would bring them both."

He nodded, sipped at his glass of room-temperature water, which was not in any way refreshing, but also not as off-putting as the tuna. It had been served in the shape of a firm little disc, and Griffin had thought: *This looks like food you'd give to a tabby cat in a New York City apartment.*

"Why do you ask?" Céline said.

"No reason," he said, not caring now that Céline would know he was lying. What he cared about was that he had at least a partial answer for what he'd been so suspicious about this morning when he was walking with Layla: This city was the sort of place the MacKenzie siblings had a strong enough tie to that they'd want to bring partners here, want to have whole weddings here.

"They honeymooned here," Céline said. "My nephew and Layla. She'd never been able to come before, what with all her schooling, summer internships, and such."

Griffin tried to keep his face completely expressionless, but Céline's next words proved he hadn't managed it.

Maybe he was getting stupider by the second. The collision with Layla like a concussion he was wearing on his face.

"I was also surprised. A bit insensitive to invite her, I thought, but as they say, the split was perfectly amic—"

"I've heard," he ground out.

"Anyway—" She broke off, waved her glass of wine in the direction of where Layla sat, tucked between Emily and Manon, head bent toward her former mother-in-law, a smile on her face. "She's handling it magnificently."

She's a fucking liar, Griffin thought, and this time, he didn't try hiding the way his gaze went to her. A violet sky above, halos of light from the string of white globes draped in a crisscross pattern high above the table, some of the city lights starting to twinkle on behind her. They were stopped now—the boat did that, apparently, at particularly memorable places, and one of the waiters would provide a brief history lesson—and he'd noticed that when it did, Layla was a little more like she'd been this morning: She didn't look around, instead focusing her attention first on whatever the waiter-slash-tour-guide was saying, and then on conversation with Emily, or now Manon, or even Samantha, who sat across the table from Layla, one side of her body always pressed tight to her date's.

Only once had Layla looked up to meet Griffin's eyes: right before the boat had passed under one of the bridges, a dark arch swallowing thickly, the lights over the table like weak candle flames inside the belly of a whale.

For a split second, he thought that look in her eyes was saying something completely different than *Watch me*.

He thought it was saying, *Save me*, and he'd felt the hand that had been on her arm suffuse with a heat that set his teeth on edge.

But by the time the boat emerged again, she'd been back to how she was now: easy conversation, easy smile. The most amicable person in the world.

"So how long have you known the groom?"

Céline again, newly emboldened—as though she thought she'd earned the right to ask him a question, now that she had provided him with information he'd actually requested.

Across the table, Rosie with the piercings perked up, having looked fairly disconsolate since the tuna ("It's cold," she'd said, upon taking her first bite, and the woman beside her—Damaris, Griffin thought it was—had informed her gently that the tuna was, in fact, raw).

"Oh, yeah," Rosie said. "I want to know, too!"

"Forever," Griffin said curtly, another lie, but one that felt close to truth. Griffin and his mother moved next door to Michael's family when Griffin was six years old, and his memories before that were pretty minimal, anyway.

He had the feeling Céline and Rosie were sharing an irritated look, but that was fine. He was grateful for the reminder. He turned his attention toward Michael, who looked decidedly more relaxed now—Layla's amicable magic, apparently, doing the trick. When Emily swallowed a sip of wine and leaned in to press a spontaneous kiss to Michael's cheek, Griffin watched his friend smile and reach out gratefully for his fiancée's hand.

Fine, Griffin thought in Layla's direction. *Lie all you want, then, so long as it's working. So long as Michael can have this.*

As if she heard him, she looked up and met his eyes, her smile flickering at the edges. A little bit belly-of-the-whale again.

He set his warm palm against the leg of his pants, ignoring the memory of her skin. He was not a person she could look to for saving.

The sound of silverware clinking deliberately against glass reset the moment, everyone looking to where Emily's father was rising from his seat, a fast-forwarded version of his son. Griffin supposed it wasn't fair to dislike him on that basis alone, but also he'd heard this man call Layla a ridiculous nickname, so no points in his favor, either.

"Watch," Céline said, presumably to Rosie. "He's going to start by saying he doesn't like public speaking."

"Good evening, everyone," Robert began, his voice pitched deeper than when he'd introduced himself to Griff at the beginning of the night. "It's not my favorite thing to make speeches—"

Rosie snorted quietly.

"—but it's so special for my wife and me to welcome you all here for this week honoring my daughter and Michael."

Griffin took another sip of his tepid water. Women didn't get names in this man's speeches, apparently. Maybe more nicknames would be forthcoming.

"While we're missing Michael's parents tonight, who won't be with us until tomorrow, we do think of this evening as a special occasion—before the party expands as the week goes on and more guests arrive, this is a chance for us to connect with those people who are closest to us."

Griffin couldn't resist another look at Layla, but from here, he saw nothing amiss at this mention of *people who are closest*. Relaxed but still upright posture, one forearm resting lightly on the table, fingers gently set on the stem of her wineglass, face tipped up toward Robert. In the near distance, over her right shoulder, the vast length of the Musée d'Orsay—"in the Beaux-Arts style," the server had said—was bathed in soft, pinkish-gold light, but for its two clock faces. Those looked ruthlessly white, a pair of wide eyes taking in the show.

"As I think all of you know, Paris is a special city to our family. Manon first brought me here in . . ."

Griffin stopped listening, shifting in his chair. What the hell was wrong with these people, anyway, treating this entire city like it was some kind of familial entry test? Michael hadn't told him all this history when he'd let Griffin know about the wedding.

"... and to Layla, who is still like a daughter to us," Robert said, cutting off one annoyed direction of Griff's thoughts and sending them down another, even more annoying path.

Beside him, Céline made a quiet *tsk*, one that seemed like it was for Griffin's ears alone.

"We are so happy you came. Our hearts are so full to have you back with us."

Involuntarily, Griffin let out a noise of his own—not unlike that muffled grunt from earlier, morphing into a half cough, half throat clear. It was loud enough to draw attention: everyone from the opposite side of the table looking his way, this man who actually did seem to like making speeches lifting his eyes from Layla to crane his neck toward where Griffin sat.

Lose your train of thought, he telegraphed to Emily's father. *Stare at my fucked-up face and wonder about it, if it makes you forget what you were talking about. Move on to welcome someone else.*

But before Griffin could really rationalize what he'd done there, distracting everyone from staring at Layla, who was still—no matter what her posture conveyed—sitting inside the stomach of this gigantic MacKenzie family beast, another distraction took hold.

Samantha scooted her chair back from the table. A gritty scrape across the deck that sent a jolt of discomfort down the left side of his neck. When she stood, she teetered again, even though Griffin could see she had a tight grip on Jamie's hand.

"I'm so sorry," she said. "I'm feeling a little—"

She cut herself off, putting her other hand over her mouth.

Déjà vu, Griffin thought, a French phrase he didn't even have to reach for in the recesses of his newly language-app-trained mind. He remembered the girl on the plane, who'd turned the same pallid color as this woman before she'd fainted. Samantha stood still for a second, hand over her mouth, holding everyone at the table in a moment of dreadful suspense before spinning from her chair and bolting clumsily away from the table, pulling her hand from Jamie's.

She shuffle-ran across the deck as far as she could, presumably, before she ran out of time.

And then she reached for a railing, and retched over the side.

Chapter Eleven

At first, there was a long beat of stunned, possibly revolted silence.

And then, everyone seemed to erupt like tiny individual volcanoes, variant in their force. Jamie vaulted from his chair suddenly, but then stood stock-still, as if someone had pressed the pause button. Manon gasped and grabbed up at Robert's arm, rising more slowly and staring after Samantha in the same way she'd looked at those petunias being eaten. Emily's hands jolted up to clap over her own startled gasp, Michael's "Oh no" a bubbling echo, setting off Damaris's quiet "Oh dear," and her husband's gruff "Indeed."

Rosie, as usual, held nothing back, standing from her own seat and saying, "A hundred euros that it was the tuna," which made Céline crack out an inappropriate laugh.

It felt like only Layla sat still, her brain sluggish to process the disaster of the last minute and a half: Her former father-in-law had thanked her for coming, had said she was still like a daughter to him, and then her ex-husband's new girlfriend had *literally* gotten sick.

She didn't see how this didn't ruin a boat cruise.

Let alone a whole entire wedding week.

She blinked, trying to snap out of her stupor, but when her eyes focused again, they went straight to the only other person who'd remained perfectly still and silent.

Griffin Testa.

For once, he wasn't looking right at her.

He was looking beside her, at where Emily and Michael still sat, his face set in barely leashed frustration. She could imagine that his hand—that very same hand he'd touched her with—was back to its white-knuckled *Fix it* fist.

She let her gaze follow his, seeing now that Emily had dropped her hands again, her expression slack. There was a vacant, trance-like look in her eyes, as though a vision of the future was passing before her mind.

A future where this wedding failed.

This cannot possibly get more fucked-up, Layla thought, which, as any doctor knew, was always the thought you had right before things got immeasurably more fucked-up.

"Jamie," Robert said, a scolding note in his voice.

Apparently, no one had yet pressed the play button on Jamie again, because Layla's ex-husband still stood frozen a few steps away from the table. He wasn't *quite* looking toward Samantha, who had most of her front half still hanging over the boat's railing.

"Oh, man," he said. "You know how I get when someone . . . you know, when there's, ah—"

Layla lifted her napkin from her lap and put it on the table. She knew how he would finish that sentence. During her first year of residency she'd gotten norovirus, one of the top five worst experiences of her life, including this boat cruise, and Jamie and his notoriously weak stomach had only ever been able to come as close as the closed bathroom door. Layla had thought it was sweet—endearing, really—the way he sat in the hallway for hours. She'd laughed weakly at him when she finally emerged, finding him asleep with noise-canceling headphones on, the sounds of her sickness so distressing to him.

She pushed back her chair.

"I'll go," said Emily weakly, but Layla could not let that happen. God forbid Samantha had something contagious, and gave it to Emily.

"I'll go," said Layla. "Obviously, I'll go."

"Lay," Em said, concern in her voice, but Layla pretended not to hear it.

Instead, she made her way to the other side of the table, past her in-laws, past Jamie, moving as quickly as she probably should have a minute ago. Behind her, she thought she heard Rosie say, "She's a *doctor*," which was a helpful reminder.

She slowed her steps as she approached the railing, seeing Samantha's back heave, one hand clutching her long hair—gorgeous hair, Layla had noticed upon introducing herself—at the nape of her neck. Layla felt a bracing pang of sympathy. It was awful to be sick, anytime, but this—on a boat, in front of all these people, *god*. She tried not to think too much about the passengers on the deck below: There were windows down there, at least, but what an unpleasant shock to see this go by.

"Samantha?" she said gently, quietly, as though she could restore some of this woman's privacy by pitching her voice a certain way.

Samantha turned her head and looked in Layla's direction.

Then she groaned, closing her eyes.

"I'm just checking on you," Layla said, still quiet. "I'm a doc—"

"I know," Samantha said.

Layla cringed.

Samantha groaned again, but this time, it sounded more rueful. "I'm so sorry," she said, and before Layla could respond, she rushed out, "I know how this must look. But it wasn't because of what Robert said, I promise. I'm—god, this is so embarrassing. The tuna—the smell of it got to me, and I've never been good on boats, like, I get seasick on pool floaties, and—"

Any relief Layla might've felt at this—*it wasn't because of what Robert said*—couldn't really find a foothold under the circumstances, the circumstances being that she was standing next to her ex-husband's barfing girlfriend and probably everyone *else* at this dinner thought it was *exactly* because of what Robert said.

But she spoke reassuringly anyway. "A bad combination, for sure."

Samantha hung her head again, spitting a little, then giving the most despondent nod Layla had ever seen in her life. Layla could tell she was getting anxious now—the shock of getting sick setting in, the waiting confrontation of everything happening behind her. In her periphery, Layla could see the head server speaking in hushed tones to Robert and Manon, probably some decision-making about whether to bring out the remaining small plates.

This poor girl, Layla thought, even though she could register it was patronizing, unfair. Samantha, Layla had learned over the course of the evening so far, was three years older than Emily, but right now, she looked to Layla about as small and scared as Willa. *The saddest déjà vu.*

She took a step forward and set a tentative hand on Samantha's back. "Maybe let's try some deep breaths?"

They did it together, a few inhales and exhales, until Samantha started to uncurl herself from the railing. If Layla had to guess, it was some combination of motion sickness and sensory disgust, though of course, it'd take some time to know for sure if this truly was a one-and-done situation.

Samantha stood up a little straighter, still facing the railing, her breathing evened out.

"Is everyone watching?" she ventured, which was one of those questions no one actually wanted the real answer to.

"No," Layla lied. A quick glance revealed that everyone, in fact, was watching, and no one more intently than Griffin, who Layla was trying desperately not to think too much about at this particular moment, since she knew he probably had déjà vu, too.

Of the *the floor is probably disgusting* variety.

"Just Jamie," she added, lying to herself now. "He's worried."

"He has a sensitive stomach," Samantha said, in explanation, and the comment hung awkwardly in the air, waiting for an *I know* that Layla was absolutely not going to voice aloud.

Samatha winced and said, "This is humiliating."

"I'm sure this is not the first time in the history of these boat cruises that this has happened," Layla said, even though she was reasonably sure that the particular humiliation Samantha was talking about went far beyond the boat cruise.

The woman rubbed a hand over her dewy forehead and finally turned to face Layla. "God, you're as nice as everyone says you are. I am so—"

She broke off, her eyes dropping and slowly widening in horrified realization.

"What?" Layla said, but the question was ultimately unnecessary. Before the syllable was even all the way out of her mouth, she'd followed Samantha's gaze down: first to the wet spot on the skirt of her own dress, and then over to the low wall of the boat, where some of Samantha's sick hadn't quite made its way over the edge. When Layla had stepped forward to pat Samantha's back, her skirt must've blown right into it.

The boat's bell rang, absurdly punctuating the moment. They'd be heading to their next stop soon.

Layla couldn't help it.

She huffed out a disbelieving laugh.

"It's okay," she managed. "I've had much worse stuff on me."

But not at something like this! her overloaded brain howled hysterically. *Not at your former sister-in-law's pre-wedding river cruise in the most elegant city in the world, which you're supposed to be helping her through while your entire former family watches!*

"I'll run downstairs to the bathroom, do a little cleanup. Everything will be totally fine!"

That last bit, she could tell she hadn't managed. It sounded very nearly like a squeak.

"Sam?" Jamie's voice cut in, and Layla turned to find him approaching tentatively, apparently hopeful that the stomach-turning part of this whole disaster had passed. "You okay, babe?"

Babe, Layla's mind echoed, weirdly grateful. That was not a pet name he'd ever used for her.

She thought about warning him off, telling him not to come any closer, lest he get a sense of the skirt-slash-wall situation. But before he could take another step forward, someone else stepped in front of him.

Griffin.

He did not say, *Excuse me*.

But he also did not say, *Your dress is disgusting*.

He simply came straight for Layla, red-hot lava down the side of a trembling mountain, and this time, when he reached out and took her hand, there was nothing tentative or begrudging about it.

His hot palm against hers, his strong fingers curling tight against the edge of her hand.

He said, loud enough for everyone to hear, "We're going."

It was a long time before Layla breathed a word again.

And when she finally did—when she finally could make sense of the streets passing outside the cracked-open back window of a rideshare that she could barely remember being guided into—it was way too late.

"Wait," she said, which is probably what she should have said before she'd let Griffin practically drag her down the steps of the upper deck, and also before he swiped three pristine white cloth napkins off a serving cart and shoved them into her free hand, and also before he stomped down the metal ramp that led them back onto land, and *also* before she simply stood, stunned and silent and desperate not to smell herself, somewhere along the Pont Royal, watching the man who'd brought her there flick determinedly back and forth through a roster of icons.

Rideshare. Maps. Browser. Maps again. And finally, most satisfyingly: a translation app.

Now, he turned his head to her in the car, looking at her as if he'd just remembered she was there.

As if she'd spoken to him in a foreign language.

"This is not the way to the hotel," she said.

"Correct."

Correct? She leaned slightly to the right, trying to get a peek over the driver's shoulder so she could see the address he must've had up on his GPS, but she couldn't get a good angle. She looked at

Griffin again, who now kept his gaze straight ahead: one hand still holding his phone, the other—the one that had held hers so tightly—laid flat on his thigh.

"Where. Are. We. Going," she bit out, insulted by his cool distance, the put-together way he held himself. Meanwhile, she was using one of her hands to awkwardly hold her now napkin-covered dress away from her thigh, while the other one still hummed and heated with the imprint of his.

He'd held it for so *long* this time.

"To get you clothes."

She blinked. "To get me—"

"In case you haven't noticed, your dress is ruined."

Did he not see her doing the weird napkin-holding? "I have noticed that, yes."

"I wasn't sure." He cast his eyes briefly sideways, toward her lap. "The color blends."

She gaped. *Gaped*. He was the rudest person she'd ever met in her entire life. And she'd gone to *medical school*.

In *Boston*!

"I have other clothes at the hotel," she said. "Obviously."

His jaw ticked, his shoulders shifting slightly. She felt as though she'd scored a point, as though—for the first time since he'd taken her off the boat—he was realizing flaws in his plan.

"Too late," he finally said. "We're on our way."

"To where? This is Paris! There's not . . . you know, a Walmart. Stores close early here!"

"Not all stores." He swiped his thumb across his phone screen, tipped it toward her.

It was a good three seconds of stupefied silence as she looked at the name—the images—in front of her.

Then she simply said, "No."

"No?"

"No," she repeated. "We're not going there."

"We are. We are currently almost there." He tipped his phone back toward himself, swiped back to the rideshare app. "Three minutes away. It's open until eight thirty. Plenty of time."

She'd always wondered what it really meant, in books, when someone was described as *sputtering*.

As soon as she tried speaking again, though, she got it.

Two aborted *But*s that came out like *Buh*. An attempt to change course, into something like, *What are you thinking*, which only came out as *You*. A final, limp *I*, which she let drown beneath the too-honest possibilities.

I don't want to. I feel like I might cry. I am pretty sure I ruined that boat cruise.

I think I liked holding your hand?

"It's not that kind of place!" she blurted, finally.

"What kind of place?"

"The kind of place that you go with vomit on your clothes?"

He looked over at her again, assessing. "You've been there?"

"Yes."

A pause, and then: "On your honeymoon?"

She swallowed. The rank mortification of this night continued. "Who told you that?"

"Your ex's aunt. With the—" He broke off, made a casual gesture around his neck.

Layla rolled her eyes, hoping to distract from the heat rising into her cheeks. "Yes," she said. "On my *honeymoon*."

He snorted. "Well. Unless your ex-husband threw up on you there, I doubt this trip will remind you of that."

Under his breath, he muttered something.

Somehow, she knew not to ask for clarification.

"It's a nice place," she continued instead. "You don't go in there and buy a cheap backup outfit."

"I'll pay. For whatever. An expensive backup outfit."

"That's not what I—" The driver blared his horn, cutting Layla off, and then the car slowed to a crawl, packed-tight traffic in the street. She wanted to take her own patience-gathering inhale, but there was still the matter of her lap. Ahead, through the windshield, she could see it: the Galeries Lafayette, the jutting front of its entrance on a corner, making it look deceivingly manageable.

But inside, it was vast. Stunning. So beautiful it'd once made a newlywed Layla clutch at her chest in plain, overwhelmed awe.

"What about the dinner?" she said, quietly now, unsure whether Griffin would even hear her. "I promised Emily I'd be there for her; I said I'd—"

"We could not stay on that boat," Griffin interrupted, as quiet as she had been, but still as effective as any car horn. Grim and final. "We weren't helping."

Suddenly, it cut through her, that *we*.

We, when it had been her.

We're going.

She could not imagine it was a kindness, not from this man. He must mean something else, something harsh and censuring. *We, because you couldn't be left to your own devices. We, because I had to stop you from somehow making it worse.*

"I," she said, a note of defiance in her voice, and didn't let the next thing drown. "*I* wasn't helping."

He turned and looked at her, not a sideways glance this time. Somewhere between the boat and the walk and this car ride, the black hair that had been pushed neatly back from his forehead had gotten mussed, and now a lock of it fell over his brow, like an arrow that directed her right to the dark pools that watched her.

Saw through her.

"*We*," he repeated, and before she could ask him what exactly he meant by that, he said it again.

This time in his halting, careful French.

This time, to the driver.

"Nous descendrons ici."

We'll get out here.

In the dressing room, behind a thick, floor-length velvet curtain, Layla tried to appreciate a moment of relative silence. Outside, the Galeries was still, only thirty minutes from closing, packed with people—tourists, judging by the way they posed for selfies beside luxury brand displays, or crowded along the inner edges of each floor to gape up at the massive dome, to record videos that Layla knew from experience would never quite do it justice.

Experience, as it turned out, had come in handy when she and Griffin had first walked through the building's glass doors. She was still mortified to walk into Paris's most famous luxury department store in a vomit-stained dress, still dreading the fact that this place wasn't one of the Band-Aids she'd thought to rip off during her walk today. But once inside, something had shifted between her and the man who'd basically dragged her here: gone was the frustrated haste from the boat, the purposeful determination of the rideshare.

Gone, too, was any trace of that *we*.

Instead, Layla felt immediately the way he seemed to shrink into himself—hands in his pockets, shoulders hunching against the tide of people on the ground floor, eyes going unfocused in spite of all there was to see. She wasn't even sure if he'd yet registered the dome, despite its near inescapability once you were inside.

"Up," she'd said, and gone for the escalators, instinctively knowing he wouldn't want one of the elevators, no matter that they were a tourist attraction in themselves.

He'd followed her mutely, seeming to relax slightly once they emerged into the less crowded space of the third floor: women's fashion, but the sort that didn't require a second mortgage. When Layla had first come here—her arm linked with Jamie's, three hours of gaping at every level—she'd giggled to see a Levi's display on this floor, a funny American anomaly in a place of such elegance.

If Griffin Testa noticed any familiar brands, he didn't show it. Certainly not with a giggle.

"I'll just . . . pick something," she'd mumbled, and tried not to notice the way he trailed her, an absent presence, a shadow she tried not to keep checking for.

Now, the curtain separated her from him, but there was no real relief. Instead, she stood before the floor-length mirror in her underwear, her ruined dress carefully balled into itself on the floor, tied against an unfurling with its straps, her heels set upright beside it. On the hooks beside her, there hung her two options:

First, a not-all-that-cheap black dress, one that would look fine with her shoes and her purse, fine for slipping on and showing up to the post-boat-cruise restaurant, for waving a hand at the gathered guests and saying, "We took a detour!" and rejoining the party smoothly, maybe even laughingly, as though nothing had happened at all.

And second, a pair of light-wash jeans—Levi's, even, because she knew how they'd fit—and a lightweight gray sweater, neither of which would work with her heels or her clutch, neither of which would do for rejoining the party, neither of which would do for anything other than going back to the hotel, to admitting that tonight was a total wash, a complete failure that she could not hope to fix.

She could not guess how long she'd been standing here, not picking either one. If Griffin was still out there, he was dead silent. Shadow silent.

What do I do? she thought, blinking at her reflection, suddenly feeling as alone as she'd ever felt in her life.

"Layla," came a voice from the other side of the curtain, way too familiar to her already, but brand-new, too.

Because he was saying her *name*. Deep and scratchy. A rasp of rolling thunder, instead of a lightning bolt. It was definitely the first time he'd ever said it.

"Um?" she squeaked back. She was practically *naked* in here.

"I had someone bring shoes," he said, not acknowledging the squeak.

"I . . . Shoes?" She said it like she didn't know the word. She was still hearing her name in Griffin-translation. Something about the way he said that first syllable, a leaning-in. *Lay*-la.

"Madame," came a second voice. "I bring you some athletic shoes. A few sizes, as your friend suggests."

"Oh," she managed, her eyes drifting to the hooks. *Option two*, she thought. *They brought me something for option two.*

She wanted to cry in relief, if only for having the decision made for her. She'd worry about what not going back would mean later.

"Thank you," she said, then added, "Merci."

"The Galeries closes soon, madame," came the woman's reply, which was—with the accent especially—very motivating.

She reached for the jeans, face flushing. While she clumsily unbuttoned and unzipped them, she could hear the low tones of Griffin's voice speaking to the woman before silence descended again. She wondered if Griffin had wandered away like a cloud of smoke, wafting his way through the don't-mortgage-your-house-for-it women's clothing department.

Then, from what sounded like way too close, came his voice again.

"Does this happen to you a lot?"

She paused, one leg in. "Does what happen a lot?"

He cleared his throat. "You go on trips and manage sick people the whole time?"

She couldn't help but laugh. She lifted her other foot, sliding it into the other leg. Jeans felt good at the moment. Comforting and right.

"Sort of," she finally said.

"Sort of?"

She hopped a little, settling the jeans over her hips. A good fit, the kind she liked. Loose in the legs, like she was used to with scrubs.

"I travel for work," she answered. "I do physician leave and shortage replacements at hospitals around the country. So, yeah. Trips. Sick people."

He made a noise, a little *Mm* of understanding that she felt strangely warmed by. It was easier to talk to him through a curtain—those dark eyes off her, that frustration on his face hidden from hers. She thought, maybe, that he'd go quiet again, and was prepared to still count one normal, civil exchange as a victory. But right as she did up the button on the jeans, he spoke again.

"What kind of doctor?"

"A hospitalist," she said, pleasantly surprised by his curiosity. "That's a doctor who—"

"I know what it is."

She closed her eyes, pursed her lips tight, grateful he couldn't see this cringe of embarrassment. Of course he knew what a hospitalist was. Someone with scars like his didn't escape prolonged hospital stays. He'd probably met a half dozen doctors like her, late adds to an already big care team: trauma and critical care, plastic surgeons, infectious disease specialists, probably a couple of psychiatrists. She thought of the burn patients she'd treated—coming on board for Covid infections acquired during their stays, an allergic response to a new medicine, a patch of bedsores on a part of the skin that had escaped the burn injury.

She almost apologized, but he spoke first.

"You shouldn't have helped her."

She froze in the act of reaching for the sweater, back on the boat again: Samantha sick over the side, Emily's panicked, pleading gaze, Jamie hovering uselessly from far away.

"What was I supposed to do?" she said, too quiet, not sure if she was answering him or asking herself.

"Not help her," he said, closer now. Right on the other side of the curtain, if she had to guess. The skin on her arms prickled with goose bumps, and she took the sweater off its hanger.

"Let her boyfriend help her," he added. He said *boyfriend* like the word itself was an embarrassment to his mouth.

She thought of explaining the weak stomach thing—an old instinct to protect Jamie. She wondered if that ever left you, once a marriage ended.

Somehow, though, she didn't think this explanation would be much of a protection from Griffin's poor opinion of her ex. The *boyfriend*, as it were.

"It's my job," she finally said, sliding her arms into the soft sleeves of the sweater, the texture on her still–goose bumped skin pleasantly shivery.

From the other side of the curtain, Griffin snorted derisively. "It's not your job. You're not on the clock here."

She pulled the sweater over her head, heedless of what it would do to her hair. It didn't matter now, if they weren't going back.

Should they go back?

"It's a *moral obligation*," she said as her head popped through the neckhole. "I took an oath."

Do no harm.

I do.

You promised you'd always be my sister.

She tried to sound confident, like all the oaths of her life weren't suddenly colliding uselessly in her brain, but even she knew what was coming next.

Another snort. More scornful this time.

Fine. Mentioning the Hippocratic oath was a long shot. Samantha wasn't having a heart attack. She wasn't even a minor on a transatlantic flight traveling alone. The father of medicine himself would probably snort at Layla right now.

But *still*. Still, he didn't have to be such a *dick* about it.

About everything.

She yanked the sweater over her bare stomach, spun on her heel, and fisted her hand in the curtain, yanking it back. A slice of petty satisfaction went through her as he took a half step of surprise back, and she wanted to keep him there. On the ropes.

So she reached, again, for what little she knew of him.

"At least I *have* a job," she snapped, setting her hands on her hips, readying herself to stare him down with the same sort of judgment he constantly seemed to be leveling at her.

But it . . . did not work.

Because Griffin did not stare back at her with the same sort of judgment, not this time.

Instead, he blinked once, and then . . . *looked*.

His gaze running over her, from the top of her surely messy hair down to her bare toes.

A long look, a leisurely look, and as it was happening—as the practical part of Layla was thinking, *What is he looking at?* another part of her, an insensible part of her, was thinking about a couple of hours ago, about walking into the hotel lobby in her boring but elegant dress, and not having anyone look at her any kind of way at all.

Which was the point. Which was exactly what she wanted.

Or it was, at least until right this second, with Griffin Testa looking at her *this* way, what she *thought* she wanted.

She swallowed at the exact moment she watched his Adam's apple bob along the column of his neck: a synchronicity neither one of them seemed to be able to abide.

She said, "What?" as in, *What are you staring at?* right as he said, "Socks," and then she was caught in his gaze again.

Until she noticed that he was holding a hand out toward her.

Where he held a pair of casual black socks folded into a tidy cardboard sleeve.

"For the shoes you pick," he added.

"Right." She extended her fingers to take them, careful not to brush his. That look on his face plus his hand against hers again—she knew that was not a good idea.

They were interrupted again, then, by the woman who'd brought the shoes, a *We're closing* look on her face that Layla thought must be universal in any language. In her hand, she held a portable card reader, and with only the most minimal instruction—as though it pained her to speak any more English—she took the tags from Layla's newly donned clothes, scanning them first, and then the socks, and then, finally, the one pair of sneakers in Layla's size . . . which she didn't dare try on, for fear of slowing down the process.

"Let me get my purse," she said, turning back toward the dressing room.

But before she could get to it, she heard the *plink* of the card reader's approval, Griffin beating her to it. She tried not to let her shoulders sag in defeat. When she turned around again, the woman was gone.

"I told her we'd hurry," Griffin said.

She nodded, and he turned away, drifting toward the inner ring of the floor—the place from which, she knew, he could stare up into that gorgeous glass dome, if he wanted to see something truly stunning.

With him gone again, it came back—that feeling of utter aloneness, of doubt. The boat cruise had been a disaster, inarguably. She had not helped Emily, not even a little, not even *before* Samantha and Jamie arrived. She had been a distraction, a reason for Manon to be stressed about hotel arrangements, an elephant in the room big enough that Robert couldn't help but acknowledge it in a toast.

She should go, no matter what she promised Emily. A flight out tomorrow.

Tonight, if she could swing it.

When she finished tying the second shoe and stood, she turned back to the open curtain, where an empty Galeries-branded bag sat on the floor, awaiting the clothes she'd come here in. Honestly, what she wouldn't give for a Walmart bag—the plastic ones, terrible for the environment—to tuck the soiled dress into. As it was, she tried to arrange it all carefully: the balled-up dress, the shoes, even her clutch. When she stepped out again, she thought the light was dimmer—displays shutting down, surely, one by one.

Get out, the store was saying.

She picked up the bag, smoothed her new sweater needlessly. Straightened her posture before she walked to where Griffin stood.

Almost right up against the glass balcony now. His head tilted back the slightest amount, but enough to see what was above. A kaleidoscope of color up high, intricate and impossible, a faraway heaven. Ten long legs of glass curving downward from it, blue and green and orange and yellow, the expanses of opaque panels in between like a thick coat of the fluffiest snow blanketing your window. Arch after arch after arch of more color at the bottom, a boisterous bolstering of the whole loudly luxurious affair.

"It didn't go well," she said.

Other than a faint lifting of his shoulders—a deep breath, maybe—Griffin didn't say anything, so she continued.

"As a first outing, I mean. I know you want this wedding to happen—"

She watched as he slowly set his right hand along the top of the balcony railing. Curled his fingers around it.

"And I think it will," she rushed out, even though she wasn't sure of that, not now. "But I'm—I'm a distraction as I am. It doesn't matter what I do. It'll just be the *Is Layla Looking at Jamie?* show."

For a long time, he stayed where he was, saying nothing. Long enough that she heard a soft announcement in French come over some unseen speaker, and another light—somewhere—dimmed.

Long enough that she started to say, "We should—"

"You're right," he interrupted.

She swallowed, unreasonably stung. She *was* right. Still. "About?"

"It will be that. Is Layla looking at Jamie."

Only the second time he said her name. The way he said it—it sounded all wrong, next to Jamie's like that, when Layla had always thought their names sounded so nice together. Perfect together.

"Right," she reconfirmed, weirdly unable to say the rest.

That she would get a flight, go home. Get out of the way of this.

"So," she added limply.

"So," he repeated, and then he dropped his hand. Turned and met her eyes again, took a deep breath before he spoke again.

"So you'll look at me, then."

Chapter Twelve

Griffin had, he hated to admit, always been good at playing a game of pretend.

He could remember it from early on: snippets of memory where he stacked Legos, made worlds for himself while a babysitter or day care provider ignored him, or while his mom fought much-needed sleep on the couch, occasionally rousing herself enough to praise him. Later, when he met Michael, their days of play had been full of pretend: They were baseball heroes, hitting huge home runs; they were generals lining up armies; they were Jedis with lightsabers running on low batteries.

Once he got older—baseball mitts and toy soldiers and plastic swords too small for his grown-up hands, his growing-up brain—pretending had been a secret pathway for him, a way into the kind of problem-solving that would eventually end up changing his life. *What if I'm on the side of the road?* he would think. *I'm on the side of the road, and two of my tires blew, and I only have one spare. There's no such thing as a cell phone on this day where I'm on the side of the road. There's nowhere to walk.*

He didn't tell anyone that's how he got his ideas. He didn't want people—his teachers, his professors—to think everything was a game to him.

Later, when pretending really failed him—when he was lying in bed half-crazy, high and hurting and impossibly alive, telling himself desperately, *Pretend it doesn't hurt, pretend it didn't happen, or pretend that it did and that you're dead, you're dead, you're dead*—it became another thing about his life before that he thought he'd never return to.

But here he was. Five thirty in the morning on a Paris street.

Pretending.

The church, he pretended, was still a burned-out shell of itself, like he'd seen on the news over the last couple of years, still shored up with huge, spidery grafts of scaffolding, still strangely blackened in some places. He imagined it without its great Gothic spire, now newly rebuilt.

He pretended it was still in ruins. That no one would ever come back to fix it.

If that were true, he knew, he wouldn't be able to stand this close to it; he knew it would be surrounded by barricades and warning signs and probably French policemen.

But that little hurdle was no match for his apparently still-skilled pretending brain.

It helped that Paris was so sleepy in the dawn hours. He hadn't passed even one cyclist or runner on his way here, no one trying to frantically squeeze in a half hour of fresh air before going to sit in a cramped cubicle all day. The few people he had seen—a teenager ducking sheepishly through the glass door of a tiny bakery that beamed a U of gold light onto the street, an older woman clucking affectionately at a small dog, a man maybe Griffin's own age blowing out a plume of smoke as he passed—seemed not to notice him, and that helped, too.

Because in this game of pretend, he wasn't meant to be seen at all.

He was meant to be in one of those burned-out bell towers. A monster, hiding from the world below.

A monster who never came down long enough to say something as colossally, shortsightedly stupid as *So you'll look at me, then.*

I live in there, he thought desperately, picturing it now. *I sit on blackened beams of wood. I talk to sooty gargoyles who never talk back. I draw pictures in the ashes. I crouch on stone buttresses and watch Michael get married from way up high.*

Layla Bailey doesn't think to look at me.

"Look at you how?" she'd said to him last night, beneath the dome at that big department store unlike anyplace he'd ever seen, standing there in a sweater that he thought for sure was the right kind of soft, a pair of jeans that hugged her hips and hid the shape of her legs, her feet covered by the socks and shoes he'd thought to get for her.

He thought, *How I feel like I'm always looking at you, ever since I first saw you.*

Like I can't help it.

Like you're the only thing worth looking at.

But he said, "Like we're friends."

As these things went—these things being, he guessed, getting through a destination wedding with more than the usual messy dynamics—it wasn't much of a plan.

But they'd hatched it haltingly on a long walk back to the hotel from the Galeries—two and a half miles, according to his phone, but she'd refused another rideshare, "Now that I have the sneakers," and anyway, walking was good for him, a better alternative to tightening, painful stillness, especially if he was any kind of stressed.

And after that boat ride—after getting Layla Bailey off that boat ride, after he impulsively said, *So you'll look at me, then*—he was fucking stressed.

"It makes sense, if you think about it," he told her as they passed by another huge, ornate building, important enough to draw a well-dressed crowd around its front.

"The opera," she said, by way of brief explanation, not looking twice. Her hand clutched tight around the thin rope of her shopping bag. "What makes sense?"

Did he take you to the opera here? he didn't ask.

"That we'd, you know. Become friends. On a trip like this. Neither of us with dates. Neither of us, you know. Family."

He noticed her jaw tighten at that.

"Rosie doesn't have a date," she finally said. "And she's not family. You're the best man, and she's the maid of honor. If you think about it, *that* makes more sense. For being . . . friends."

The pause there, it was speaking. A stutter over a different sort of idea.

I don't want to play pretend with Rosie, he thought automatically.

"But Rosie isn't the problem," he said instead, and before she could do with that what he knew she'd been doing all night, what she'd been telling herself all night, what she'd tried to say to him back in the Galeries, when he knew, he *knew* she was thinking about leaving, he added, "We are."

"Why do you keep *saying* that?"

He shrugged. "We're the ones who know. About Emily and Michael."

If she clocked that he hadn't *really* answered her—that he wouldn't admit to exploding out of his seat on that boat and dragging her off it, that doing that had felt like a very modest concession to his other idea, which was to throw her ex-husband over the edge of it, hopefully directly into the splash of his new girlfriend's vomit—she didn't say.

She said, "What do you propose?"

So now, here he was, Paris at dawn, pretending he hadn't said any of it: that if Layla stuck close, if she made it seem like she was striking up a friendship with some stranger on this trip, if they paired off on whatever horrible forced-sightseeing outings they went on over the next few days, people would stop wondering if Layla was worrying about the ex.

"You won't seem so alone," he'd said at one point, and she practically exploded at him.

"There's *nothing* wrong with being alone!"

There isn't, he thought now, staring longingly up at one of those bell towers, his mind's eye covering them in smoke damage again, making a home for himself and all his small, monstrous thoughts, the ones he had when he was most alone.

His phone blared a long, shrill ring.

"Fuck," he muttered, shoving a hand into his pocket, pressing the button on the side so it would not, at least, disturb the peace out here any further. His game of pretend disastrously compromised, since he'd have no use for a fucking cell phone in a burned-out bell tower.

He was pretty sure who it was before he pulled it from his pocket. Despite his not actually living in a bell tower, very few people had his number, fewer ever called it. Even Michael usually texted first.

He had, in fact, finally exchanged numbers with Layla last night, what with the plan and all, but he had the feeling a pretend friend wouldn't have cause to use it, at least not at this hour.

"Hey, Mom," he said, when he confirmed his suspicion and swiped his finger across the screen.

"I knew you'd be up," she said, in that way she had, no bullshit, no sugarcoating it.

"Out walking," he said, though he hadn't been walking for a while now. He was only standing here, staring up at this both old and new church, talking into his phone quietly like he was actually inside its sacred walls.

"Early there."

"Late there," he answered.

There was a stretch of silence on the line, or rather, his mother's particular silence, which meant there was always something happening in the background: a gate being closed, a bucket being tossed, dishes being washed, something. Six hours behind, he figured the faint clinking he heard was tea-making.

She still made some every night before bed, same as she had his whole life, even when she'd had to sleep during the days, accommodating whatever punishing shift she happened to be on.

His eyes drifted to the other bell tower, the one he hadn't been looking at, and he pictured his wiry, hardy mother, brown-gray braid down her back, scrubbing its walls clean. Shouting out of one of her stone arches a few times a day, asking whether the monster across the way was up yet.

"You sleeping at all?" she asked eventually.

"A bit," he said, which was not a lie. He'd actually slept last night, four hours at least, which was a good stretch for him. He had a dream, too, but not the sort he'd say anything about to his mother.

It had to do with that sweater Layla got.

That he got for her.

"What's that?" she said.

"What?"

"You made a noise."

"I didn't." Probably a lie. Anyway, if his mother said he made a noise, he'd made a noise. She missed nothing, not now. A monstrous curse he'd put on her without ever meaning to.

Right now, she was probably trying not to ask him a familiar question, the same one he got asked for months and months by doctors and nurses and therapists. She still had to try, even though it'd been years since he'd yelled at her in a fit of frustrated exhaustion. *Please, stop. It's never what you want to hear. It's never going to be what you want to hear, not ever again.*

Still, he gave the answer silently, automatically. *Six out of ten today. Not too bad.*

"How's Leonard?" he asked, to distract her. And himself.

"A stubborn ass," she said, chuckling, because Leonard was, literally, a stubborn ass, the lone donkey on the property that had no purpose other than to eat every other animal's feed and show his weird, too-big teeth to everyone who walked by his enclosure. When Griffin left, Leonard had a sarcoid over his left eye that his mother had been fretting over. "But getting better."

"Good."

"And?" she said.

"And what?" He braced himself for her losing the battle against herself. *What's your pain level today?*

"And how's *your* stubborn ass?" she said instead, and his mouth curved up. "I hope you notice I haven't been calling you. Like you asked."

"I noticed. I'm doing all right, all things considered."

The travel, he meant. The plane, the time change, the hotel, the people. That's what she meant, when she asked—how he was managing all these things that he so determinedly avoided for the last ten years, that he'd had to train for like the most pathetic boxer before he'd left.

"I went on a boat," he said, surprising himself. And then worse, he kept *going*. "Shopped at this famous store. Saw the building where they... have the opera. Looking at Notre-Dame right now."

This was, he knew, a stunning enough recap on its own that his mom would not press for details on any of it, which meant that he would not explain that not a single thing he listed was some kind of sightseeing lark that he'd done of his own accord. Even this morning felt like a strange necessity, a required ritual he needed to perform before doing this new day.

She didn't speak for a long time. Or at least, what felt like a long time, when you were on the phone, thousands of miles away. Griffin could picture her, in the small kitchen of the ranch house where he never really spent much time, stirring her tea until the urge to cry passed.

"That's good," she finally said, her voice perfectly normal.

The light was changing now—pink sky behind streaks of wispy slate-gray clouds, the church changing color along with it, like it was getting dressed for the day.

Probably he should go back. Shower, eat something. Get ready for getting looked at.

"And Michael?" his mother asked, a chippy, nearly undetectable note in her voice.

But the truth was, he didn't miss much about her, either.

He paused, scuffed his shoe across the pavers beneath his feet. "He's good," he lied.

Man, what the fuck, Michael had texted him last night, ten minutes after he'd taken Layla off the boat. Griff had been in the car with her by then, watching her faintly trembling fingers holding her dress away from her body, finally starting to reckon with what he'd done.

Handling it, he'd texted back, as though he had some grand

best man plan. As though he was the crisis manager, and not half the crisis himself.

"Fitz and Paula?" his mother added, which was really what that chippy tone was about. Michael, his mother loved—complicatedly loved, Griff supposed, but still. Loved.

Michael's parents were another story.

"They get here later. This afternoon, I think."

"You won't take any shit from them," she said, but he didn't want to get into this. They wouldn't ever agree on what shit he'd taken—would always take—from them.

So he changed the subject.

"It's the other family that's messy," he said, and as soon as it came out of his mouth, he knew it was the wrong can of worms to open. Knew exactly who it would lead to.

"What kind of messy?"

The chip was out of her voice again. Usually, she was the one telling him mess—some feud in town, drama in the comments of a local animal rescue organization she followed online, a tiff in her book club over whether a main character in the monthly pick was "waiting around for some man to save her!"

Griffin getting anywhere near gossip was about as shocking as the sightseeing.

"Emily invited her brother's ex-wife," he said. "It's—you know. Awkward."

"Weird thing to do," his mother said. "Inviting her, I mean."

A funny thought came into his head: Annie Testa on that boat last night, sitting next to Emily's aunt Céline. Two women with absolutely nothing in common except their not-so-subtle judgment about asking your brother's ex-wife to come to your wedding.

It was that little pretend scenario that somehow got him saying more: not just that the ex-wife was here, but that a new girlfriend was, too. That everyone was acting nice about it—*amicable* about it—but that the whole thing had somehow given Emily the yips. That the ex-wife—he didn't dare say her name, for fear of what his mother would be able to hear in it—was trying to help, but maybe also making things worse.

That Griffin had to try heading it all off.

When he was done, the sky had changed again, rosy gold now, and somewhere along the line, a few stragglers—other early-rising Americans, he guessed—had shown up to get photos in front of the grand lady, newly clad for her morning of being a whole bunch of people's bucket list attraction. He adjusted his hat, tugged the brim down. Imagined himself crawling out of the bell tower, crouching on one of the finials. Later, people would zoom in on their photos. They'd think, *Is that one of those gargoyles? Some weird bird? A ghost, a monster?*

"You're not responsible for Michael," his mother said now, interrupting his thoughts.

The chip was back in her voice.

Something else he wouldn't argue with her about.

Something else they'd never agree on.

"It's something to keep an eye on," he said.

So you'll look at me, then, he heard himself saying again. Saw Layla Bailey's big brown eyes blinking back at him, stained glass sparkling above her as that huge, overwhelming store started shutting down around them. *Supporting them*, he said later, when they'd gotten closer to the hotel, when they both seemed calmer from the fresh air, the walking. *That's a* we *thing now. We stick together. No one looks at you as if you're alone. No one looks at you as if you're only looking at him.*

For a long time, she hadn't responded. She'd kept her head down, one foot in front of the other, studying her new sneakers.

But when he finally heard her quietly say, "Okay," he realized he'd been holding his breath. He realized how badly he'd been wanting her to agree.

And that scared him half to death.

Scared him out of an unexpected sleep, a soft dream he couldn't talk about.

Scared him back into a burned-out bell tower.

His mother made a *hmm*ing noise on the other end of the line. She wouldn't argue, either, especially not when he was this far away. It was too unusual, for them to fight with this much literal distance between them.

"So what's today, then?" she asked instead.

He swallowed, took one last look. Thought about today, and everything about it that would be hard. A train ride, a lot of people, long lines, camera phones everywhere. A six out of ten. A bunch of shit he would probably find pretty disgusting to look at for any length of time.

And Layla Bailey, looking at him, exactly like he'd asked her to.

But since he wasn't going to say all that, he simply turned his back on his pretend house, started walking, and said, "Today, we go to Versailles."

Chapter Thirteen

"Michael, you have to see this part," Emily said, her voice breathless with excitement.

Layla watched, restless but grudgingly pleased, as Emily linked her arm through Michael's and tugged gently, leading him along the thin, delicately draped rope that separated their small, spread-out party from the garish display arrayed before them.

Marie Antoinette's bedroom.

God, there was so much *gold* everywhere.

On the headboard, in the bedspread, all over the canopy. On the curved arms of the fussy chairs flanking the bed, on the wainscoting and wallpapering, in the two gigantic chandeliers that hovered symmetrically down from—you didn't even have to guess it—gold sculptural carvings in the ceiling.

"That's the door," Emily was saying to Michael, "that she escaped through on the night the palace was invaded!"

"Too bad," muttered a low voice from beside Layla, close enough to keep her in the same semi-electrified state she'd been in since this morning.

Since she'd been being *friends* with Griffin.

Looking at him so no one would be looking at her.

They met in the hotel lobby this morning, a few minutes before Michael and Emily's careful itinerary had suggested: That way, when the rest of the party arrived to set off on their grand Versailles adventure, Layla and Griffin could already be carefully arranged on one of those weird sofas, feigning an amiable, casual chat, two friends forged from an unexpected derailment the night before. *We're so sorry we never made it back for the dinner!* they would say—or, rather, Layla would say, since despite this entire ruse being Griffin's idea, he clearly had no meaningful experience at making excuses for himself—*We got caught up trying to find me something different to wear,* and then *one of my shoes broke,* and then *we figured we wouldn't make it in time for the restaurant reservation . . .*

She hadn't really needed the excuses: Their very presence was enough to please Robert and Manon endlessly ("Oh, we were *so* worried!"), to unite Emily and Michael in sagging relief, to even have Jamie and Samantha offering sheepish words of apology to them both ("It was completely fine, I promise," Layla said gently, to a still-wan-looking Samantha, while Griffin had managed a gruff, practically clenched-teeth "No problem").

She would've liked to be able to say, *That won't work, your minimalist* No problem; she would have liked to have been able to tell him that his acting skills were far too subpar—nonexistent, really—for this new plan to support Michael and Emily to ever have a hope of working.

But the problem was, it was, apparently, *No problem.*

Because everyone seemed to be buying it.

Everyone seemed to be doing better.

They sat together on the train out of Paris—forty minutes that

Layla thought she'd have to tick off like acts of torture she'd survived—but it had passed unexpectedly quickly, and not because she'd done a bang-up job of fake chatting with her fake new friend. Instead, it had been Griffin to start the conversation, if it could be called that. First, he asked her bluntly, "Have you been to this place?" nodding in something like smug approval when she answered, truthfully, that she had not.

Then, he had simply turned his phone into a bizarrely effective intermediary—his head tipped down for a few minutes at a time before passing it to her, the screen lit and stopped on some weird, detail-oriented fact about the very place they were about to visit. Twenty miles of pipes for the largest fountain. Twelve hundred fireplaces. Too many flowers and trees for many of its original guests to handle, overwhelmed and sickened by pollen allergies brought on by the sheer excess.

"You know," she'd said at one point, after maybe two back-and-forth passes, the warmth from his phone an oddly intimate transfer from his skin onto hers, "they probably have one of those headset tours. For all these facts."

"Can't wear a headset," he'd said, gesturing vaguely toward one side of his face—the scarred side—and taking his phone again, going right back to scrolling through results. No further explanation on offer.

It had very effectively kept her from asking any more questions about this weird ritual they were doing together, and also, oddly enough—in spite of his refusal to explain—made her feel less like he was faking it as her friend. And while she waited for whatever he'd show her next, she would catch snippets of the pleasant, unstilted conversation from the rest of their party—Rosie chatting with Robert and Manon about wanting to adopt a cat this year,

Jamie telling Abram about work, Céline explaining to Samantha why it was a crime not to have seen the Sofia Coppola *Marie Antoinette*.

Michael and Emily, leaning into each other, looking decidedly less stricken.

Just like they did now.

"They're good," Layla said, keeping her eyes on the pair, even as she spoke to the man beside her, the one she was *supposed* to be looking at. Michael was, of course, not looking at the door through which Marie Antoinette escaped. He was looking at Emily, a soft, adoring smile on his face.

"This is good for them," she added.

Griffin made a noise, something like *Hm*.

Not a note of agreement.

She couldn't help but turn her head to look at him. She'd noticed, over the course of the day so far, that he always stayed next to her on the same side, the unscarred plane of him always facing her, even if it required him to sidestep, to reposition himself. She wanted to say, "It doesn't bother me, you know," which would be a very mild expression of what she actually thought about his face, but also, she figured that the problem was that it bothered him.

That he probably wouldn't believe her, even if she told him what she *did* actually think. That she could probably be doing one of those awestruck faces that Michael was pulling right now, just at the sight of his stern, set brow line.

"You don't think so?" she said.

He shrugged, and she suspected, like on the train again, he wouldn't clarify. But eventually, he spoke, quietly, keeping it a secret between them. "Not the sort of place for honest feeling, is it?"

She blinked at him, instinctively knowing what he meant.

But also not knowing what to say.

"Distracting place," he added. "Mirrors everywhere. Little mysteries, like that door in the wall." He flicked a hand dismissively at the scene in front of them. "All this gold-covered shit."

Yes! she wanted to say. *It's too* much, *right? It's not even pretty to look at!* Part of her felt desperate to recap the range of feelings she'd had over the last hour and a half, since they'd passed through the entry gates: over-warm in the particularly crowded spaces, overwhelmed by the relentless excess, frustrated by the endless *space*, the endless *stuff*. Another painting, another candelabra, another sculpture: everything, eventually, becoming oddly indistinguishable.

But also, she was prickling with annoyance at the way he was bursting her lone bubble of comfort: her feeling that today was going so much better, that the visual assault of Versailles was uniquely suited to stop her from being an *Is she looking at Jamie?* sideshow, that Emily and Michael looked like they were having fun, like they were going to be perfectly fine.

So she said, "Isn't this, like—the decor of your people?"

He slid his eyes toward her, narrowing them slightly.

"Let me guess. Someone told you I'm rich."

She snorted. "Someone told me you're a *billionaire*."

He laughed.

He *laughed*.

A short laugh, but still: a huff of air out, a rasp of the lowest register of his voice escaping through the flash of his straight, white teeth, which Layla had never gotten a good look at. She felt, for a second, like one of the hideous, heavy chandeliers had fallen directly onto her head. Out of the corner of her eye, she saw Michael's face turn toward them—as though even from several steps away, with several sets of people milling between them, he could hear Griffin's laugh, too.

"You're . . ." She trailed off, temporarily stuck on the wrong completion of this sentence.

You're even more handsome when you laugh. You're like a secret door in the wall. You're an electrical storm in my spine.

". . . not?" she eventually got out, hoping she didn't sound too breathlessly curious.

He wasn't smiling anymore, not really. But on that side of his face he let her see, there was still a different set to his mouth, a slight quirk. He'd put his eyes back on the big billionaire bed, but somehow, it still seemed as though he was side-eyeing her.

"That's what all the *at least I have a job* stuff is about, I guess," he said after a few seconds.

Her cheeks warmed. She *had* said that a couple of times. If it wasn't true, she supposed she should be embarrassed. Then again, her threshold for being embarrassed on this trip was now absurdly high. At least he wasn't considering moving hotels because of her. At least he hadn't thrown up on her.

At least she wasn't lying crushed beneath an ugly chandelier.

"So you're not a billionaire," she said.

"No."

That quirk again. A little line in his cheek, as interesting as any one of his scars.

"And you *do* have a job."

He didn't answer. Just kept the quirk, kept staring at every ugly thing in this ugly room inside this ugly palace.

"You know," she said, surprised at the jokey, casual note to her voice. Surprised at how comfortable she sounded. Like they weren't faking anything at all. "A *friend* would tell me."

He made the noise again—the *Hm* from before, but deeper this time, and all sense of jokey, casual comfort fled from her body. Maybe it was only a simple, more contemplative *Hm*, but something about it—Layla thought it sounded, somehow, like a promise.

Like a noise someone would make right against your skin before they kissed it in exactly the right way. Exactly the way you always wanted.

Oh my god. What *was she thinking?*

She swallowed, faced forward again, except of course, the only thing to stare at straight ahead was Marie Antoinette's stupid gigantic bed. She blinked at it, blurring its big, garish florals into a mess of color, waiting for the heat in her face to dissipate, for her breath to go back to normal.

Griffin waited, too. As though he knew.

And when she finally felt like she was ready to move on, he spoke again.

"Maybe I'll tell you," he said, sounding closer to her this time. Warming her up all over again. "When we're somewhere more honest."

More honest, it turned out, was hard to find in Versailles, even once you went outside.

In the vast, carefully cultivated gardens, their party sprawled away from one another—it seemed almost impossible to stay in each other's sights across nearly two thousand acres (conversion from hectares provided, annoyingly, via Griffin's phone), and so Manon had made the declaration: They would wander freely, if they so wanted, and meet again in two and a half hours by the front gates, making their way all together to the train back to Paris.

Initially, Layla felt a rush of relief at this new plan—the thought of how easy it would be for them all to drift naturally away from one another, for her not to have the sideshow sense of herself when Robert and Manon and Jamie and Samantha were all within easy reach. But even though the splits she was hoping for seemed to naturally come to pass—Rosie (who had seen the Coppola *Marie Antoinette* many, many times) and Céline deciding to take the estate train over to Trianon and the Queen's Hamlet, Robert and Manon and Abram and Damaris opting to go to the Gallery of Coaches, Jamie and Samantha lingering longer in the Orangery than anyone else cared to—she still could not relax in the foursome she and Griffin formed with Michael and Emily.

It was stuck in her head, that *Hm*.

Not the second one, thankfully, which she was privately thinking of as the *I must have my rusty horny wires crossed* Hm, but the first one.

The one where Griffin seemed doubtful about Michael and Emily.

She could see it now, unfortunately, in the open air, where the excesses of each garden—huge sculptures, elaborate water features, gigantic shrubs carved into curving, unnatural shapes—at least had to contend with the ill-matching plainness of the now-cloudy sky above. Layla could focus better out here, but unfortunately, that focus was on the way Emily held a huge map of the grounds in her hands, how she seemed to be smilingly but anxiously insistent about matching each grove they walked through with its official name.

Oh, Apollo's Baths. This one is the Ceres Fountain. See, it's called Star Grove because of how the paths are laid out . . .

Yeah, she could see it.

This was not an honest Emily.

This was an Emily Layla could remember from other moments over the course of their long relationship: their very first meeting, when Emily showed Layla her room, trying to make excuses for the Barbie apartment she still had in one corner (*I don't really play with those anymore*, she'd said nervously, apologetically); the night of Emily's junior prom, when Jamie and Layla had come to watch the getting-ready, picture-taking of it all, and Emily had laughed too loud at every joke her date made, had given too big of a gasp at the sight of her (objectively ugly) corsage that did not match her gown; the morning of Layla's small bridal shower brunch, when Emily had pretended to like the taste of coffee to fit in with some of Layla's med school friends.

And while Layla didn't know Michael well—at all, really—she also started to see that soft smile of his in a new way.

A not-horny *Hm* sort of way.

A suspicious-Griffin way.

Was it adoring? Or was there something anxious about it, too?

She thought of Emily in that messy hotel room yesterday morning, her eyes pleading for Layla to somehow *keep her grounded*.

Put down the map! she wanted to call across the Colonnade Grove (fine; thank you, map). *Put down the fucking sometimes-useful map and* look *at him. Talk to him, now that there's no one watching.*

Well. Almost no one.

"Maybe if we left them alone," she said aloud, to the shadow responsible for all these suspicious thoughts she was having.

He was leaning a shoulder against one of the rust-colored columns, the hat he'd taken off inside the palace back on his head now, obscuring his eyes from her. But she could guess he was looking where she was, a dark chaperone for the couple across the way.

"Not sure it'd help," he said. The grim note in his voice unsettled her further.

"Is this—" She broke off, embarrassed at first to ask what she was thinking. She tipped her head up to the sky, the unadorned gray expanse of it, and gathered her courage up.

"Is this their usual dynamic?" she finally finished, hating how plain it made the truth: that she had not been there, at all, for this very important thing in Emily's life. That she was a latecomer to it, completely unprepared for the task of fixing whatever was wrong here.

Griffin cleared his throat. Shifted his shoulder against the column. "I only met her once," he said. "Before this."

She lowered her head again, meeting his eyes. Well, the brim of his hat, at least.

"Really?" She was strangely thrilled by this information. *We really* are *friends!* she felt like shouting, except, obviously, that would be deranged. You weren't friends with someone on account of you both being shitty friends and/or sisters to other people.

"You might have heard," he said, a note of knowing sarcasm in his voice, "I don't get out much."

A smile tugged at her mouth. "On account of your not-job," she said.

A huff of air while he lowered his head, shaking it a little, the brim of that horrible hat hiding his whole handsome face from her. She *bet* he was trying not to laugh.

After a few seconds, he spoke again. "Not to defend"—he lifted the arm not leaning, gestured to where Michael trailed a still-talking Emily—"whatever this is, but I guess if we're being honest, I wouldn't be a good judge of their dynamic. Like I said, I met her once, and it's not as though I'm good at putting people at ease."

"You should've showed her stuff on your phone," Layla deadpanned. "It helps."

"Can't take credit. I picked that tip up from Michael yesterday," he said, the curve back on his lips briefly, before it fell again. "Anyway, that's how I know it's not going right. Not from watching her. But from watching him."

Layla swallowed. "How do you mean?"

Griffin shrugged again. "He's too afraid of losing her to . . . to even try pressing her. To try really talking to her. He's watching her like she might disappear. That's what he's most afraid of."

For a wild, inexplicable second, Layla thought about taking two steps toward him. Close enough to reach out and up, to lift the brim of the hat and take the full measure of him, because she could *hear* something in the way he said this—something honest and hidden and devastating.

"Guys!" Emily's voice called, saving Layla from herself, and Griffin straightened away from the column immediately, as though he was grateful for the interruption.

Layla did not miss the irony—Emily acting as some kind of intermediary, when that was meant to be Layla's job.

When that was the promise Layla made.

So as they wandered through the next few gardens, Layla left Griffin to his more natural silence, instead interrupting Emily's ongoing anxious map-matching—*Oh, the Chestnut Room, I wonder why it's called a room! And this I think is the Saturn Fountain, yes!*—with questions to Michael: about his job, about whether he was excited to see his parents later, about when he knew he would propose to Emily.

And eventually, it did seem to have a grounding effect, Emily letting the map fall to her side in one hand, holding Michael's with her other as he answered Layla, sometimes chiming in with funny asides or additions or loving corrections—*You did* not *know on our second date!* At one point, the four of them standing idly by the almost comically plain-by-comparison Mirror Pool, Michael and Emily effortlessly tag-teamed a story about getting lost on their first trip together, and the huge roadside argument that ensued, and as Layla watched them, both of them laughing their way through the memory of it, she thought, *They'll make it. This is what a good marriage looks like.*

I know, because for a while, I had one.

A sobering thought, but it was easy not to dwell for too long on it, especially when Emily and Michael drifted ahead, his arm draped over her shoulders, his head turning to press a kiss to the top of hers at one point as she laughed in an honest-Emily way.

"Fine," Griffin said grudgingly from beside her. "That was helpful."

She clamped her lips together to keep from smiling. "Your contributions were essential."

He didn't *quite* laugh again. But still. Maybe an indulgent snort at her dig, since his contribution had been complete and total silence during all of it.

"I consider it a moral obligation," he said.

This time, *she* laughed: a crackling *Ha!* emerging right as they crossed into a new space—another circle paved in fine gravel, this one surrounded not by columns, but by risers—two arcs of bright green hedges cut into curved benches, interrupted in the middle by a grand stone-and-shell sculpture that was clearly intended to be a fountain, bone-dry now. There was, of course, some gold—huge urns punctuating the gray stone, but out here, they weren't such an eyesore. Layla thought, for a fleeting second, of Willa from the plane—her book about the fae prince. This looked like the sort of place a fae prince would have, a fairy choir commanded to sing for him, lined up on those lush risers.

"Wow," she said, and for the first time since this outing began, she was not annoyed when Emily lifted her map long enough to look down and say, "This must be the Ballroom Grove!"

Well, fine. An outdoor ballroom made more sense than a fairy choir, but still—still, Layla was happy enough to feel like a moment of whimsy was finally possible, with some of the tension between Emily and Michael now broken. By some magic—*not* the fae prince sort, obviously—this particular grove was comparatively uncrowded, a bored-looking guard in a navy polo standing near one of the urns, and only a couple of other flagging spectators, turning in slow circles with their phones raised in front of their faces, looking like they'd come to the sort of sightseeing saturation point that necessitated video evidence of new things.

"You know what we should do," Layla heard Michael say to Emily, and she looked to see Emily beaming up at him, nodding. A second later, still smiling widely, Emily was shoving her now-crumpled map into her crossbody bag, taking Michael's outstretched hand and stepping into his arms for a music-less dance, like they were in their own little world.

Layla was glad she and Griffin had still been lagging behind, that they hadn't crossed too far into the grove. Without thinking, she stepped back farther, toward one of the risers near the grove's entrance, Griffin following.

"They took lessons," he said quietly, though she doubted it was necessary for him to mind his volume—Emily and Michael had very likely forgotten they were there, and didn't even seem to notice that at least one of the video-taking tourists had turned her phone onto them.

"Cute," Layla replied, also quietly, remembering that she, too, had once taken dance lessons—a gift Manon had given her and Jamie for their engagement, even though they were insistent about wanting a small wedding, with none of the big, fussy traditions.

Every couple should know how to dance! Manon had said, and Layla imagined she said the same to Michael and Emily, who watched only each other, alternating between shared humor and concentration—knowing they weren't very good at the steps, but enjoying the project of doing it together anyway.

They'll make it, she told herself again.

"This way," she heard from somewhere behind her, a voice from another time, a dance lesson a decade ago, and she stiffened, dread pooling in her stomach.

"Oh, Jamie!" came a gasping exclamation, a happy version of the voice that Layla had mostly heard only in a shamed, strangled way up to now. "This is so *pretty*!"

"Goddammit," Griffin muttered from beside her.

"Look who we found!" Jamie's voice again, closer now, probably on the other side of the stone-and-shell wall that flanked the entrance to the grove. Close, but not yet close enough to see her.

Or the shadow beside her.

She watched as Emily and Michael both turned, stilling in their dance.

Emily's smile brightened first at the sight of her brother, then wobbled and dimmed, her eyes darting nervously over toward where Layla stood.

Goddammit, she echoed Griffin silently, this scenario somehow way worse than a simple bonus episode of the *Is Layla Looking at Jamie?* show. Because in this scenario—in that wobble of Emily's smile—Layla saw all the worry from yesterday morning coming back, Layla and Jamie apart here in this garden palace ballroom, a couple Emily had once watched having a perfectly coordinated, devotedly practiced first dance at their beautiful backyard wedding.

"Let's, uh—" she started to say to Griffin, with absolutely no meaningful escape plan in mind, save maybe a fae prince ordering his choir to sing a spell that would make her disappear.

But before she could voice something so desperately ridiculous, a strong arm came around her waist.

Turning her toward the body that had been hovering near hers all day.

One of her hands enveloped in electric warmth. Her arm lifted. And then, suddenly, she was dancing.

Chapter Fourteen

"Look at me," he said to her, for the second time in as many days.

Her eyes snapped up to his, wide and searching, as he stepped to the side, and then backward, his left hand pressed tight to her lower back. That was how she needed it, at least right now, in order to follow him—stiff and startled as she was, as though she'd spent the last couple of hours forgetting that the ex-husband was here.

Or that there was an ex-husband at all.

"Just me," he said, when one of her feet scuffed awkwardly against the gravel as he turned her, further into the circle of the outdoor ballroom's floor, her back toward the ex now, but he couldn't bother himself to see if that guy was watching.

He was very busy being bothered by everything else about this situation, and to him, *everything else* amounted to the fact that he was commanding this woman to look at him from an even more unsafe distance than he would have ever considered possible when he first floated this idea to her last night.

Bell tower! his brain screamed, like an alarm going off. *Bell tower,* not *ballroom!*

One side of his face suffused with heat—the normal side, with the normal, human sort of embarrassed heat, not the prickly, inexplicable kind that sometimes lurked beneath his deadened skin, a trick of his nervous system that he couldn't control, and he prayed it was not too noticeable to her. That the pink flush would be unremarkable, compared to everything else she'd be able to see from this angle.

He felt it then—on the right side, the normal-warm side—a thin wisp of her breath exhaling against his neck. Deliberately steadying as she managed her nerves.

Everything else was now a much more complicated prospect.

Because Jesus *Christ*, that breath against his neck.

Ten out of ten, he thought, for once in his life not thinking of the fucking pain scale.

He flicked his gaze up, over the top of her head, caught sight of the ex, his light-eyed gaze lingering briefly on Layla's back before he turned to the girlfriend with an easy smile, extending a hand but stepping back at the same time.

If he was about to—

Yeah, he was.

What a fucking idiot. A *bow*.

"What?" Layla said, because clearly his face—his *up close* face!—had done something in response.

"Nothing," he said, then shifted his gaze toward Michael and Emily, who were dancing again. For a fleeting second, Michael caught Griffin's eye as he guided Emily into a turn, and mouthed, *Thank you*.

"I don't know if—" Layla whispered, then broke off, swallowing and starting again. "I'm not sure if the solution is turning *ourselves* into the show."

"We aren't," he said, not whispering, but still keeping his voice low. "They aren't watching."

He suspected they both knew that this was at least a partial lie—there was no way that there wasn't some occasional watching, even if it was just from that security guard, who was probably thinking, *Look at these six American assholes*, but at the moment, he did not care.

He cared about that fucking guy showing up and ruining all the good work Layla had been doing.

For Michael, obviously.

"We're two friends," he said, distracting her. "Dancing."

He hadn't had the courage to look back down at her yet, but he could feel her eyes on him, on the normal and not-normal parts of his face, and his jaw ticked in anxious response. So far, at least, his body felt okay. The left hand chafing where it held her, but not too bad. His left leg straining uncomfortably with these unexpected movements, but holding up.

Six out of ten, still.

"How do you know how to dance?" she said.

"All rich people know," he said. "There's a special school we go to when we make our first million."

She didn't laugh this time, and he felt, rather than saw, her eyes drift from his face.

He tightened his hold. Left hand pressing anew against her lower back, damn the chafing. Right hand squeezing her fingers.

Her touching him, too: her small, warm palm on his back, her smooth hand inside his, and nothing, *nothing* about that hurt. Like she put some kind of spell on those parts of him.

They looked at each other now. Up close, her eyes were more than mud-brown. Chocolate-brown, that was probably the better description, with secret flecks of gold, stolen from a palace. The opposite of ostentatious.

"My mom taught me," he said, "when I was a kid."

In their kitchen, first, while a rare dinner she had time to make cooked in the oven. Him standing in his socked feet on her toes. Not so much a dance lesson as a game, which was uncommon in their house. It had been so much fun that he'd always—well, until he got older, bigger, more self-aware—asked her to do it again, anytime she was home and cooking dinner, more relaxed than usual. She would laugh and complain about how big he was getting, counting out a *one, two, three; one, two, three* as they moved.

"I took the lessons, too," she said in answer, an honest confession, and he could tell it cost her something—to admit that something about Michael and Emily had been cut from a cloth she'd already worn, with a guy who was only a few steps away, now doing the dance with someone new.

He nodded once in acknowledgment, thought he could feel the delicate skeleton inside her trembling, despite the way she held herself upright, following his steps smoothly.

So he kept talking. Honestly.

"I suppose most people would say it's a not-job. My . . . job, I mean."

He watched the long line of her pale throat bob in a swallow, her face still tipped up to his.

"I can't work . . . uh. Regularly. I am not reliable. As an employee."

She didn't ask why, but he knew she probably knew. She was a doctor. She was up close to him now. He'd bet she had read papers about people like him.

"My last couple years of college, I made something. Designed something, I guess it's better to say, with the help of a couple of my professors. It's boring—a building material that turned out to have a lot of applications."

"That doesn't sound boring," she said, tilting her head slightly, that little swoop of hair she always had in front moving with her. She was not looking at anything else but him, which was exactly the point of this, but also, he wondered if she could feel his skeleton shaking now.

"I have money from that," he said, overly blunt, as though he could stop the shaking himself if he acted more and more unbothered.

Even though holding her like this was the most bothersome thing he had done in years.

And that counted the plane ride here. The hotel, this whole entire thing.

"Because I hold the patent," he said, briefly stopping to clench his teeth. Somehow, without noticing, he'd moved the hand on her back up, and he thought he felt a brush of her hair on his wrist. But his left wrist was an unreliable place, a mysterious terrain of damage, and he couldn't be sure. It could be a phantom, a figment, a harbinger. His pretend-brain back again.

"And have stake in the manufacturing company that came from the patent," he rushed out, trying to shut it down. "My professors—well, they're not professors anymore—they're the ones who really run it."

"Are *they* billionaires?" she asked, and he sort of wanted to smile. She really had a burr up her ass about billionaires, which was fair enough.

"No."

"Hm," she said, a deliberate imitation, and he liked it—the mocking sincerity of it, the friendship-feeling of it. By now, he doubted there was a need for this—a few brief turns and they would've done what was needed to dispel the tension of that first moment—the ex arriving, Emily's crestfallen face, Michael's back-to-being-nervous one.

But he didn't let her go.

"I also help manage my mom's farm," he added, which was an extremely unnecessary detail, and he realized, as soon as it came out of his mouth, that he was no longer doing this to distract her.

He was doing it to *correct* her.

To let her know that she had the wrong idea about him. That he was not some rich, dissolute asshole who did nothing all day in a gold-paneled house with gold-covered furniture. That he was a person who once had ideas, and good ones, at that. That he still *did* things, mostly small things, but still. *Things*. That he used his money to buy his mother a farm, that he helped her, that he was the sort of person who knew what he owed to other people.

That he'd even—

"Griff," interrupted Michael.

He and Layla stilled—a slowing step into a stop, then both of them backing away from each other. The contact lost piece by excruciating piece: her right hand slipping from his back, his left hand sliding across her back, then her side, until it met the air again, the nerves jangling painfully in the aftermath.

Michael was smiling. He still had Emily in his arms, because that was a very normal thing for a groom and his bride, touching each other casually and constantly. Out of the corner of his eye, Griff saw the ex release Samantha into a spin and heard her giggle, which was also very normal, he supposed, for a boyfriend and girlfriend.

The heat was back in his face again, a shamed sort.

Look at me, that's what he had been doing, telling Layla those things about himself. Not a distraction for her, but an invitation from him. A worse sort of looking than she could do even with her gold-flecked eyes so up close to him.

There was no *point* to that sort of looking.

"Have I ever seen you dance, man?" Michael said. His expression was lit up in a way Griffin hadn't seen in a long time, at least not in relation to him. A clean-slate hopefulness. Like opening his front door and seeing Griff standing there with two old lightsabers that he'd found in a neighbor's trash.

Griffin shifted on his feet. "Not sure you could really call that dancing."

He could feel Layla looking at him. When they stopped, she was on the wrong side of him, and he hated that.

"No but you were actually so good?" chirped Emily. "Did you ever take—"

"Oh gosh," Layla interrupted. "Look what time it is!"

She made a dramatic show of holding up her phone—a noticeably odd move from her, since Griffin had already clocked that she seldom kept the thing in her hand, a rarity among people these days. He could probably count the number of times he'd seen her check it.

Emily made a noise, a squeak of surprise, disentangling herself from Michael. She called across the ballroom to her brother. "Jamie! We gotta head back!"

Griffin did not look over to see if the ex did another one of those stupid fucking bows when his dance was over.

Instead, he watched as Layla stepped toward Emily, linking their arms and walking toward the exit, their heads bent together in conversation. Heard it as Michael moved to stand next to him—right side, of course—and offered another word of gratitude to him, one he didn't deserve.

Felt it, too. Fifteen out of ten.

The feeling of remembering who he truly was.

* * *

As if the universe really wanted to drive the point home, Michael's parents were waiting in the hotel lobby when they returned.

Obviously, Griffin had not been in Paris for any meaningful length of time, but he still felt, upon walking through those glass doors and seeing them hovering near the reception desk, that there were no two people who fit in with this city less than Major Fitzpatrick Plackett and his wife, Paula.

Fitz—that's how Griffin still thought of him, from years and years ago, even though he didn't dare call him that, or really anything, now—stood tall, straight, one hand holding a stiff leather billfold by his side, the other set in a loose fist atop the telescopic handle of his suitcase, which he probably had not allowed anyone else to touch since arriving. He wore a pair of overly crisp khaki pants—medium starch, Griffin knew, from the times he and Michael had to take the major's clothes to the dry cleaner—and a white collared shirt beneath one of those V-necked nylon pullovers, which Griffin thought of as the self-inflicted sensory torture device of all men who played golf.

Paula, for her part, was casting her eyes about the lobby, overawed and smiling, wearing skinny jeans and clunky multicolored sneakers, a bright pink oversize cardigan belted tight and slightly crooked at her waist.

They looked—in completely different ways from each other—like two fish entirely out of their familiar waters.

For the first time since he'd left Versailles, he was grateful to be part of a large party—this crew of people who managed to talk even more on the way back, a round-robin of *Here's what we saw* and picture-sharing. Predictably, Rosie had dominated, with a very thorough recap of the part of the palace grounds that she had renamed "Milkmaid Con," which made Layla lower her head with suppressed laughter.

He did *not* feel jealous about that. At all.

Fresh from their shared storytelling, they all seemed happy enough to let him drop, unnoticed, to the back. He'd been quiet on the train, hat tugged down, Michael beside him this time. "Hurting, man?" he'd asked Griffin quietly, while they'd waited for the train, and Griffin nodded—not lying, not really—gratefully accepting what he knew would come next: Michael making a subtle, discreet bubble of protection around him.

Now, though, back in Paris, Michael had more pressing obligations, and Griffin watched as he led the group—Emily right beside him—toward where his parents waited. For a moment, Fitz and Paula were lost to him in the little crowd of people, but he still heard Paula's gasp of delight, her overloud "Oh, I can't believe we're finally *here*!"

When he could see them all again, Paula had her arms around Emily, rocking a little, her smile huge and warm. Fitz was shaking Robert's hand, probably too hard, because he was that sort of guy, even if you'd already met him a hundred times. Still, he wasn't frowning, which was basically the same as him smiling, and even from only being able to see Michael's back, he could tell that his friend was at ease—his posture not snapping unnaturally into his father's, which sometimes happened when Michael was stressed and around his parents. When Emily pulled away from Paula and waved Rosie over for an introduction, she so naturally stepped next to Michael's body again that Griffin thought that maybe Layla Bailey really *had* fixed everything today.

Obviously, not him.

But everything else that mattered.

Layla was standing with Céline now, her hands clasped loosely in front of her, her smile close-lipped. A perfectly patient posture, waiting her turn for introductions. If she noticed that the ex stood on the other side of Fitz and Paula, his hand cupped protectively on Samantha's hip, she didn't betray even a whisper of awkwardness about it.

Maybe she had managed to fix herself, too.

He eyed the elevator bay. Wondered if he could cross to it, unnoticed, and slip away for a while.

Then he heard Rosie say, "Wait! Where's the best man?"

He suppressed a groan. Stopped hanging back.

Fucking Rosie. Even if that milkmaid story from the train was sort of funny.

When he stepped up to the group, he knew he was braced—his body the polar opposite of a perfectly patient posture. It was how he felt anytime he saw Fitz or Paula. Not as frequently now, but not never, either. Last year, not long after Michael had first called to tell Griffin about meeting Emily, he'd seen Fitz in the produce section of a twenty-five-miles-away Wegmans, ten minutes after store opening. It was his usual haunt, haunted at a not usually busy time. Fitz had stared at him across a display of unnaturally shiny waxed apples and said only, "Griffin," as though a bare acknowledgment was all he could manage.

Then he'd walked away, still holding the empty plastic bag he hadn't filled with apples.

"Griffin," Fitz echoed now, probably choking that leather billfold he held. He flicked his eyes up, and added, "Still with the hat, I see."

Fuck you, Griffin didn't say.

"Nice to see you, Major," he said as quickly as he could, before shifting his eyes to the side, tipping his chin down slightly in respectful but distant greeting. "Hello, Paula."

"Hi, Griffin," she said, and then—because Paula was always a better parent to Michael than Fitz was—she leaned into him, giving him a fleeting, cursory hug that made his whole left side ignite. She kept her face turned fully away.

As compared to the hug she gave Emily, it might as well have been a kick in the nuts.

Griffin could not claim, by any measure, to have a good sense of social cues, even after the last couple of days of being dropped into a deep end of them. But in the aftermath of that half hug, he would have sworn that the temperature in the lobby changed—a chill wind that was impossible to ignore. In the silence that followed—it could only have been a second, though to Griffin it felt like an eternity—he imagined the entire group of guests changed the channel on the little remote controls inside their brains.

No more *Is Layla Looking at Jamie?*

A new show, a surprise drop. The *Why Do Michael's Parents Hate Griffin?* show.

"So!" Emily's dad said, bringing his hands together in a muted *clap*, as though he was about to retune an orchestra. "Two more to our roster! We're so happy to have you here, Fitz and Paula."

Paula practically sagged with relief. "Paris, I can't *believe* it!" she said, turning to Michael. "And this hotel! It's beautiful!"

Is it? he thought idly, a strange and safe dissociation from being stuck here for the moment, doing his best not to make that chilly moment worse for Michael. In his own mind, the hotel—which initially seemed like a comparatively comfortable option, with its larger rooms and more familiar amenities—had started to feel weirdly discordant, its luxury too bare and modern in comparison to the Paris on the other side of the doors. A different Versailles, but a Versailles all the same.

His eyes drifted to Layla's, still with the posture, but now, she watched him, her brow faintly crinkled. Probably, she had clicked over to the new show, too, but also, he wondered—or pretended, maybe, pretended that after seeing that palace, she was thinking the same thing as him.

"Now, I know you might want to rest," Manon was saying to Fitz and Paula, in a teacher-type voice, and Layla's gaze wandered automatically toward it, so he let his own grudgingly follow. "But there's this bistro in the 15th that Robert and I have always loved, very sweet, very Parisian! And we thought you could join us tonight, if you feel up to it?"

Griffin could tell Fitz did not feel up to it. He recognized that thousand-yard stare from probably hundreds of dinners over at the Plackett house, Paula keeping the conversation going while Fitz methodically worked through his plate like he was eating mess hall food and not Paula's consistently good cooking.

A petty satisfaction moved through him, picturing Fitz with that face on in one of the Paris restaurants Griffin had passed on his walks. That first night, he'd seen people stuffed inside each one, spilling onto sidewalks with tables crammed together, sitting so close to strangers by necessity, no one seeming to mind.

Good luck with your thousand-yard stare there, Major, he thought.

Which was not a helpful attitude to have. For Michael's sake.

"Well, we don't want to impose!" said Paula. "If you already had a plan!"

A light rescue effort on behalf of the Major. Something else Griffin could recognize. Fitz never came to school shit, if he could help it—not any of Michael's baseball games, or his honors society stuff. He was there at high school graduation, and that was it. Somewhere in a shoebox Griffin had a picture of it, one his mom took. Him and Michael flanking unsmiling Fitz, both of them gangly-looking in their caps and gowns.

"No, no," Manon countered. "We hoped you'd arrive in time! I booked several tables, actually. I was hoping everyone could come!"

This, she pitched louder—to the whole gathered group, and Griffin's gaze went immediately, again, to Layla. Watched as her full, soft lips rolled inward, her lashes lowering, as though she needed a second to gather her strength. Half of him had a mind to congratulate her: to tell her that this invitation was an obvious indicator of her success today. The disastrous boat cruise not even a full twenty-four hours ago, and already Manon was unbothered about trying again, even if there was something obvious lingering between the best man and the groom's parents.

But the other half of him thought nothing more than a steady refrain of *Fuck, fuck, fuck*, because now, the picture he conjured was of being shoved into one of those small restaurants *with* Fitz and Paula, Fitz not having the option for a thousand-yard stare and instead focusing on Griffin, an even worse sort of *Look at me* than he wanted to imagine. It would absolutely ruin the fucking dinner; it would put Michael on edge; it would make Emily feel worse; it would probably undo every ounce of progress they'd made to the altar today.

Distantly, he heard a mixture of agreements and excuses—Rosie, in, probably because she'd have a new audience for her Marie Antoinette content; Damaris and Abram, out, too tired after Versailles; the ex, out, with another reservation for him and the girlfriend already made. Up close, though, he could see Michael with that straight-up, stressed-out posture. He and Emily were in; they *had* to be in. He wouldn't tell Griffin *not* to go, but also, he would've felt the chill, too. Two days ago, that chill might've been another awkward thing he expected to deal with during his wedding week, but now, with Emily's doubts in the mix, and at an impromptu cozy dinner . . .

I'll pass, he thought to say, but he could not get the words out, could not imagine saying them in a way that didn't sound like a blast of ice-cold wind, directed right at Fitz and Paula. He just stood, a cold column, freezing over slowly, completely unable to help his friend.

"Actually," came Layla Bailey's voice, not distant at all. Right next to him, in fact, though not touching. "I'm taking Griffin to dinner tonight."

Chapter Fifteen

She thought for sure he'd fight her.

Not in the moment—not while everyone was standing there watching, not while she went on to do a bang-up job of making the whole thing sound like a prearranged plan.

"I insisted," she'd said, directing her words to Manon, who'd invited this whole extra charade by deviating from the itinerary (tonight, Layla still remembered from her spreadsheet, was supposed to be *Free Time!* for them all). "A thank-you, you know. For the clothes he bought me last night."

That last part, she tried to say *meaningfully*, the way Manon said things like, *Darling, of course she doesn't have to switch hotels*. She tried to say, *For the clothes he bought me*, like she was saying, *For the way he saved me from Samantha's vomit, and Jamie's cowardice, and for the way he saved today in ways you don't even know about.*

All the while, she stood next to him, oddly relieved to be by his side again, no matter that he was doing his whole smokestack thing, all-black brooding silence with his hat brim lower now. The minutes before—when he'd been ushered over by Rosie, when there had been that awful exchange between him and Griffin's father—had been stomach-droppingly difficult for her, worse than when Jamie and Samantha had shown up on the boat yesterday.

And then, the hug from Michael's mother.

If it could be called that.

She *knew*. Knew from the way he held his body and face—she'd been looking at him all day, after all—that he needed a rescue.

But when the moment passed—when Manon said, "Oh, that's so nice!" as though she was relieved, and when Paula not so subtly took this opportunity to offer an actual agreement to the invitation—Layla thought for sure he'd fight her. That he'd grab her hand again and pull her away, taking advantage of the group's distraction with their meetup plans.

That he'd say, *We're not actually going to dinner.*

He didn't, though.

He turned to her and said, "I'll meet you down here at seven," as though he was a completely normal person and not a smokestack fae prince with a sometimes-job who was also a surprisingly good dancer.

Embarrassingly, until he walked away, she hadn't once meaningfully thought of Emily, only a glancing awareness that she, too, had tensed at the interaction between Griffin and Michael's parents. Only as Layla watched the elevator doors close behind him did it occur to her that making a different dinner plan might feel to Emily like being hung out to dry.

But Emily was on board—more enthusiastic than Griffin's *I'll meet you down here at seven*. In fact, as soon as Griffin was gone, Emily had come over and clasped Layla's hands. "*Thank* you," she'd said. "That was *perfect*. Thank *god* you're here."

"Oh," Layla said, still catching up to what she'd done on impulse, strangely bristled by the way Emily reacted as though this was all part of Layla's plan. Layla's *job*.

"It was no—" she started to add.

"It's like, things are weird there," Emily interrupted. "And with Griffin out of the picture, Michael and I will have an easier time tonight."

Layla said, "That's good, then," but what she was thinking was decidedly less supportive.

She was thinking, *Michael's parents seem pretty lousy, actually.*

And also, *But why are things weird there?*

And maybe, a little bit, *You better get used to weird things, when you marry into someone's family.*

Now, once again standing in front of the mirror in her room, forty-five minutes before she was meant to meet Griffin for this plan that had not at all been offered up for Emily's good, part of her still expected he'd cancel. A brief text from the phone he'd shown her all those interesting things on.

Part of her felt that she'd deserve it, what with what she was *currently* doing on her phone.

What she'd been doing for the last thirty minutes.

What about this? she typed, looking at the photo one more time before pressing send.

Hate it! came the immediate reply. It's a turtleneck

Layla frowned at herself in the mirror, then typed back: It has short sleeves though. It's a summer turtleneck. I thought kind of sophisticated looking

> You look like you're going to someone's wake

> Cara, jeez

> Why is everything you've shown me gray or brown!!

Layla winced, backed up the two steps it took her to sag onto the bed. She did not want to type back, *Because most of what I brought is gray or brown, because I was trying to be aggressively neutral, because I was trying to blend in.*

She saw the typing bubbles pop up again.

> I'm not sitting here on my day off,
> when I SHOULD be napping, to have
> you pick something gray or brown
> for a D A T E!

Immediately, Layla flushed with embarrassment. It had been an impulse to text Cara with this, an uncharacteristic one. No cheery, dishonest flag emojis, not even a more neutral mirror selfie with a quick *Does this look okay?* which would also have been uncharacteristic, but not as immediately un-Layla-like as what she'd *actually* sent, which was:

> I am going out for dinner with the best
> man at this wedding and have no idea
> what to wear.

She had definitely *not* said it was a date.

This was a mistake.

I'm sorry, Layla typed quickly, pressing send. She knew better than anyone that uninterrupted sleep on a day off was the holy grail for ED docs, Cara especially, who worked even more relentlessly than Layla did.

Cara sent back the eye roll emoji.

Then added, Stop being sorry, this is what friends are for! Now tell me what you have that is not Great Depression colors

Layla blew out a breath, tried not to think too hard about the *this is what friends are for* comment and what it really meant, coming from Cara. *You're-allowed-to-hate-him* Cara. *You-can-tell-me* Cara.

You-should-not-go-to-this-wedding Cara.

She typed, Is black a Great Depression color

Sexy black? Or funeral black

Layla stood from the bed again, went to the slim armoire built into the narrow space between the bed and window. Inside, she'd hung her most delicate things, including a black wrap top that she'd brought to wear beneath a—Fine! Fine, *beige!*—blazer. On its own, without a camisole beneath it, it would be low-cut, a deeper V than Layla was used to wearing, its extra short, gauzy, petal-style sleeves decidedly not funerary.

Smokestack black, she thought.

She tugged off the turtleneck. Changed her bra. Ignored her phone pinging once, then twice, Cara probably saying, *I stg, if it's another turtleneck Layla*.

Slipped into the top, wrapping the long ends of it around her waist. She remembered trying it on, liking this part of it—a little secret hug you made for yourself when you got dressed, one that hung on to you for however long you wore it. Beneath the blazer, it was meant to be a private form of comfort.

By itself, it looked different.

She still had on the same straight-cut, ankle-length black pants that had looked business casual with the tucked-in turtleneck— the *sophisticated summer* turtleneck, the *Great Depression* turtleneck. Now, with the top tied, a deep V at her chest, a silky, trailing bow above her hip, they were night-out pants, pants that would show the narrowest slice of skin if Layla moved just so.

She thought of the ballroom garden at Versailles: Griffin's hand on her lower back, over her boring Breton-stripe shirt, no chance of a slice of her unclothed skin in the mix. She thought, too, of opening the curtain of that dressing room at the Galeries, Griffin's eyes all over her even when she was all covered up.

Her phone pinged again.

Before she could stop herself, she picked it up and stood in front of the mirror, snapping another selfie.

Pressed send.

Sexy black! Cara wrote back, immediately.

Followed by the drooling emoji.

Layla used the little eye roll guy back. Smiled down at her phone as she watched the typing bubble come up again, oddly delighted. She realized that it had been a long time since she and Cara had texted this way—light and teasing and not weighted by Cara's gentle prodding after Layla's state of mind, and Layla's practiced answers about how well she was doing, how work was keeping her so busy, how all the travel was so good for her.

How therapy was going great, how she had really started to *make peace* about the divorce.

She started to type, too, her and Cara in their little messaging bubbles on different sides of the same ocean.

I missed this, she wrote, then backspaced. That was too heavy for the moment, too honest. It would make Cara worry, which she still didn't want.

I'm sort of nervous, she tried, but deleted that, too. She didn't want to admit even to herself that she was nervous, nervous in a different way than she had been for every other cursed event of this wedding week so far. She was *date* nervous. Butterflies-in-her-stomach nervous, which had nothing to do with what she was doing tonight. Tonight was a rescue. Two pretend-friends who were both liabilities, staying out of the way for the sake of the wedding's success.

Anyway, he could still cancel.

She watched as Cara's bubble disappeared, too, and for a second, the room felt stunningly, sadly quiet. Layla tapped at the side of her phone, feeling lost in translation. There had been a time, once upon a time, where she told Cara everything.

Put on some heels, Cara finally sent through, and Layla let out her breath, both relieved and disappointed.

She moved back to the armoire, looked down at the tidy row of shoes she'd lined up last night before bed, desperate to do something orderly to distract her from the boat cruise, the Galeries, the deal with Griffin she'd agreed to.

She should probably wear flats. They were beige, but then again, there was all the walking. And also, this was *not* a date.

In her hand, her phone pinged again.

Probably him canceling, she thought, shoring herself up.

But it was Cara again, short and simple.

And Layla?

Yeah?

Have a great fucking time out in Paris tonight.

Luckily, the heels were comfortable.

Not flats comfortable, not clogs-for-the-hospital comfortable, but night-out-in-Paris comfortable. Good-with-her-outfit comfortable. Black velvet, block heel, a little platform. An open toe, and thank god she'd had a (neutral) pedicure before coming. When she got into the mirrored elevator again, she thought of herself two nights ago, dressed in demure blue.

Now, she thought she looked like the better part of a bruise.

He was waiting when she emerged: in the lobby like he had been this morning, but this time, standing. Staring toward the glass doors, hatless, and he'd shaved since she last saw him. Clearly his outfit had not taken any additional planning time, because it was, as usual, all black: shoes, pants, one of those soft-looking long-sleeved shirts again.

But it didn't seem so remote to her now. It didn't seem so rudely lazy.

It seemed like they *matched*.

"Hello," she said, when she got close, trying to close an imaginary fist around every single one of those pesky butterflies in her belly.

At least one—at *least* one—still flapped wildly when he turned to look at her.

He did not return her *hello*, but she felt his roaming eyes like a greeting anyway. Top to open-toe, and then back up, lingering, for the most perfect few seconds.

First at the V.

Then at the bow on her hip.

She was probably pink all over.

"I picked a place," she said, or possibly blurted, but that was better than simply standing there, blushing under his black gaze.

When he didn't say anything, she started to wonder whether there was still time for him to cancel—whether he'd met her here to tell her in person, whether she'd end up watching him walk out those doors alone again.

She shifted in her heels.

Then she saw that little quirk at the corner of his mouth, the one from earlier today.

The Versailles quirk, is how she thought of it. The *Maybe I'll tell you when we're somewhere more honest* quirk.

"That's my favorite color," he said.

The restaurant was on the Boulevard Saint-Germain, cozy and small, with an orange-and-white-striped awning jutting cheerfully out from the building's Haussmann facade, the big-windowed, iron-balconied floors above dotted with planter boxes of trailing ivy and bright flowers, some better maintained than others. Square, wood-topped tables were arranged neatly under the awning, tiny bud vases of wildflowers in the center, or shoved to the side of diners' plates and glasses. On the street, smaller round tables spilled out more haphazardly, some pushed together, surrounded by smoking patrons who leaned back in their woven café chairs, effortless and unbothered and so enviably used to a night like this, in a place like this.

She had not picked somewhere she had been before, because nearly every place in Paris she had been to before was weighted with the memory of Jamie, and their honeymoon, and because this was the first time since she'd arrived on Monday that she had the chance to be truly free of it—no Emily to protect, no ex-husband not to look at, no former family to make feel comfortable—she wanted, at least, to eat somewhere new.

But she *had* picked a place that was on a street she loved, and felt some attachment to as an individual. On her trip here with Jamie, there'd been one afternoon they spent apart—him, completely exhausted by their morning at the Louvre (*I've just been so many times*, he'd said) and desperate for a nap, and her, wired from the newness of it all, absolutely incapable of imagining sleeping during the day when there was so much to see. They'd agreed that he'd get his nap, had kissed goodbye at the Place du Carrousel, and Layla made her way across the bridge that shared its name, a guidebook in her hands that she hadn't had the chance to use much, not when she was with Jamie.

On her own, she'd been comfortable being a cliché. She went to the Café de Flore; she waited too long for a table and ordered a hot chocolate; she snapped a photo of the white cup with its cursive writing; she sat and read her guidebook—specifically, she read her guidebook about the very place where she was sitting. She thought that Saint-Germain *was* Paris: stylish with its luxury shops and uniformly beautiful buildings, but also subversive—coffeehouses where Albert Camus and James Baldwin wrote, where Simone de Beauvoir and Jean-Paul Sartre thought and talked and argued, where Picasso probably stared weirdly at women he'd eventually turn into painted cubist nightmares.

She loved that afternoon she'd spent on this street, all alone. Alive and curious and adult, but with the comfort of knowing she had her new husband to go back to.

With Griffin, she felt it all still.

Well. Minus the comfort, of course.

Once they were seated—outside, under the awning, not that anyone asked their preference—Layla noticed that the symphony of her nervousness, which had quieted somewhat on the walk over, was roaring back in a new key as his eyes tracked around the space: the interior of the restaurant on the other side of the glass, the street across the way, lined with a few flower vendors, the other diners in various stages of their meal.

She realized how much she wanted him to *like* it.

Not because she needed his approval, or his praise for picking something good and interesting and not-too-cliché.

But because she wanted him—after the way he'd helped her today, and after that awful, awkward exchange with Michael's parents—to enjoy himself.

To feel comfortable.

He shifted in his seat. Tapped a finger lightly against the cloth-wrapped roll of his silverware, as though he was wondering whether he should unwrap it, or give up altogether and leave without saying a word.

She almost said, *Are you okay?* but before she could open her mouth to ask a question that she knew now, from a couple of days of experience with him, would not go over well, he blurted—no possibility about it—*definitely* blurted, "Let's talk about something."

Her brow lowered in confusion. "Talk about what?"

"Anything," he answered quickly. "Your favorite food. Where you went to college. Why so many places have these weird Edison bulbs hanging everywhere now. Why you picked this place. What you're going to order."

She blinked at him. In his eyes, there was something wild—like the plane, like the first night on the elevator, maybe a little like the boat last night. *Not* like the walk over here, when he'd been seemingly calm—his steps slowed to match hers, his occasional harmless and sometimes even bluntly amusing commentary (*Honest to fucking god, could they be consistent about where they* put *these street signs?*; *Whose job do you think it is to cut all the trees into this shape?*; *The trash can placement in this town is inexplicable.*).

"Are you having a panic attack?" she asked.

"Not yet," he answered quickly. Starkly.

For a few terrible seconds, her mind went completely blank of everything except all the questions she absolutely couldn't ask in this situation: *How often do you have these, when did they start, does this have to do with your scars, are you agoraphobic, do you take any medication or illicit drugs, does Michael know?* She tried desperately to grab on to the questions he'd posed to her, but it was like she'd never eaten food in her whole life, like college was memory-holed, like *Edison bulb* was a phrase that might as well have been the rarest French slang—

"Because I never came here with him," she said finally, and she watched as his wandering, panicked eyes darted back to hers. She wanted to hold them there. "This restaurant, which—well, I've never been here before, but also . . . this street. This street . . . it feels like it's mine."

"How?" he said, and two days ago, his voice would've sounded cutting to her. A slice through all her halting pauses.

Now, it sounded desperate.

So, she told him. First, about the morning at the Louvre: not the parts where Jamie trailed her, bored but indulgent, but instead about her favorite piece (the *Winged Victory of Samothrace*, not in any way a letdown, even if you'd seen it in pictures a hundred times), her biggest disappointment (the *Mona Lisa*, small and huddled behind a pack of clamoring tourists with selfie sticks), and her biggest surprise (*Death of the Virgin*, Caravaggio, huge and dark and sad, punishingly but beautifully secular). Then, about the Boulevard: the shops she'd passed, the Café and its cursive-branded cups, its intellectual history. She even told him about her dogeared guidebook, the way she'd read it at that café table as though it was a novel, not caring if anyone at all thought it was embarrassing.

At one point—maybe when she was talking about the shops and their careful window displays—she thought dimly about whether she sounded silly, or naive—uncultured and overawed about an experience from a decade ago. But she shoved the doubt away, because the main thing was, this—her talking—was *working*. Griffin was listening, looking at her steadily and a little too intensely at first, until she could sense him settling slowly, the look in his eyes less wild, his head nodding, sometimes, in understanding or encouragement.

When he finally unrolled his napkin and smoothed it over his lap, she had to concentrate on keeping at it, adding detail. On not letting him know what she was noticing.

And when he ordered a drink from the server—only sparkling water, but still, that was something; that was a commitment to this—Layla had to try so hard not to smile in winged victory.

"Thank you," he eventually said, right when she was starting to run out of material about that one afternoon in Paris that felt uniquely hers.

She looked up from the menu she hadn't really started to read yet. She'd been letting her eyes course over the French words she recognized, hoping that any one of them might jog an additional memory that she could offer up for him.

"When I said I don't get out much," he continued, "I was maybe not being completely honest."

She cocked her head slightly. Tried for a Versailles quirk. Something clever and casual to keep him at ease. "You get out a lot, then?"

His mouth curved, but it didn't last. He cleared his throat, reaching for the sparkling water, his hand clutched too tight around the glass as he brought it to his lips. When he set it down again, she suspected that they'd both steeled themselves for what was coming next.

"I haven't left New York in almost twelve years," he said. "Upstate," he added almost immediately. "That's where I'm from, originally. Not the city."

"I didn't think the city," she said, which was not the most sensible response, but somehow, it felt important to say: an acknowledgment of something she had observed about him, *knew* about him without him having to tell her. Griffin Testa had never once struck her as a man who managed himself in New York City, of all places.

"Mostly I stick to my own house. My mother's, sometimes, when she needs something. I do my own errands, but at specific times. To specific places. At night, I go for walks a lot. It used to freak people out, around where I live, which isn't the sort of place you can be anonymous, but they're used to it now. Also I built a gym in my garage. Put a shed out back, heating and cooling and everything. When I do work, I do it from back there."

He paused—another reach for and sip of his water. She could tell he wasn't quite done, so she waited, her menu in her lap, leaning against the table's edge, long forgotten.

"I did twelve weeks of therapy to get ready for this trip. I ate out four times. Four different restaurants. Two in different towns. Once with the fucking therapist, if you can imagine anything more uncomfortable."

Sympathy, she knew instinctively, would be exactly the wrong move here.

"My ex-husband's new girlfriend threw up on me last night," she said.

He smiled. No teeth, but a bigger curve.

"So," he said. "Now you know. That's why the—" He broke off, made a dismissive gesture with his hand that she supposed was meant to account for the almost-panic attack, the need for her to talk. "Because I don't leave my house much. I don't ever travel."

She nodded. Did not look at him for her next question.

"Do you want to tell me about why not?"

She kept her eyes on her menu, making an effort to look in earnest at the dishes now. She hoped his therapist hadn't done this exact thing. She hoped this night felt different to him.

"Do you want to tell me about your divorce?" he eventually responded.

She blinked up at him. *Kind of*, she thought, but she shook her head.

No, she tried to tell him with her eyes. *Not tonight. Not on this street, which was always entirely mine.*

He picked up his menu, put his eyes on it. Not in a disappointed or dismissive way. Somehow, in a way that seemed as though he understood her—her and this street—completely.

"Maybe you'll tell me," he echoed idly, after a few seconds of silence, while they both, she suspected, pretended to peruse the options.

He didn't have to finish the sentence.

The quirk of his mouth finished it for him.

Chapter Sixteen

It was the best food he'd ever had in his fucking life.

A plate of roasted Camembert, drizzled with the darkest, thickest honey he'd ever seen, a different taste entirely from what his mother made on the farm, that he and Layla scooped up with slices of crusty, airy baguette.

A piece of sole so thinly sliced it was almost translucent, soaked in brown butter—*beurre noisette*, the menu said, and he thought it was so good he might write to Rosetta Stone directly; he might tell them that *beurre noisette* should be an essential phrase for all travelers to France.

A dessert—*god*, a dessert; he never ate dessert, not in years and years, and no real reason why—that he let Layla order for him, a chocolate soufflé. Lighter than air, lighter than the color of her eyes. Richer than any gold-covered ceiling.

Despite all that, it had not been a night without incident.

In the first place, there was the moment when they first sat down, when he almost lost his nerve—a thousand eyes on him, it felt like, every person in the restaurant turning to look at the monster come down from the tower.

But even after he recovered from that—after Layla leaned forward in her chair and told him about one perfect afternoon she'd had alone in Paris, and after he'd come around to realizing that probably every person in the restaurant was looking at *her*, her swoop of hair and soft healing hands moving animatedly as she talked, her pale, candlelit V of skin rising and falling with the breaths she took to keep talking—even after that, there were moments of almost-ruination.

A knife cutting across a plate nearby: one of those shrill, unexpected sounds that got Griffin's wires crossed, his left ear vibrating with it, the shock spreading down his neck and across his scapula in a short but still breath-stealing, shooting pain.

The server too close behind him, squeezing by to get to someone else, and the movement he made to tuck his chair further in— too automatic, too careless, a split second forgetting that he had to be diligent about pressing his left hand on textured surfaces like this woven rattan.

Both times, he tried to hide it. But by this point, with Layla Bailey, there was no going back. There was the *Look at me*, after all, and there was also him telling her about never leaving his house, his twelve weeks of trip therapy. There was her dressed head to toe in his favorite color, doing him this favor of getting him away from the Placketts tonight, of giving Michael a reprieve from managing an unexpected outing with both his parents and Griffin in close quarters.

So, she noticed, a darting flick of her eyes over the parts of him that probably showed it most—his knuckles whitening, his jaw clenching, his brow probably shining.

Six out of ten, his mind supplied automatically.

But blessedly, she hadn't asked. She hadn't said a word.

And it made it easier just to *talk* to her—to talk to her about the sorts of things he imagined regular people, not bell tower people, talked about when they went to restaurants. The food here, but also the food elsewhere—*I tried something like this once in Colorado*, or *My mother grows Swiss chard*. The art on the walls, or even the proliferation of Edison bulbs—*Why are they everywhere?* or a joking *What is Big Edison hiding?* The street outside, and how different it was from home—the sidewalks so wide, the corners so splashy with their big awnings and lit-up signs above, the random McDonald's squatting awkwardly in a building that looked like it was made for a prince.

Now, even the squabble they were having over the bill felt normal. Natural.

"I'm the one who invited you," she said, reaching for the portfolio he'd set his hand on top of as soon as the server placed it on the table, his eyes on Layla's triumphant.

"It wasn't so much an invitation. More like a hostage-taking."

He used her moment of stunned—but still good-natured—outrage to pull the portfolio toward him.

"That is such a *lie*," she was saying as he opened it. Good, a QR code for paying. One of his practice restaurants had used these. That night, it'd been helpful for getting off the premises before anyone had the chance to see him go into full-blown, sweating meltdown mode. Tonight, with a couple of taps, he could stop Layla from doing something sneaky like slipping a credit card to the server.

"In *fact*," he heard her say as he finished up, and he was possibly smiling, though he could admit that it was a relatively new sensation. He was eager to hear what she would say. Eager, for some reason, to hear how she would scold him over his teasing truth-bending.

"You were the one—" she began, but then, she abruptly cut herself off.

He looked up from his phone. Saw her lips purse, her eyes widen. She was looking at him, but he had the sense that she'd caught sight of something else. That she'd only just looked back at him in panicky shock.

Oh, what the fuck, he thought, immediately on alert, and because of the last two days—the boat, the ballroom—he was on alert for something, *someone* specific, no matter how unlikely it was in a city of this many people, this many places.

If it's the ex-husband, he thought, turning his warning gaze to the restaurant entrance, *I will tear this entire place to the ground. I'll make it so there's no trace of his infectious presence on this street that belongs only to her. I'll make it so there's no memory of him here that she has to reckon with, even if it means erasing a memory she had with me.*

But there was no one familiar at the entrance, and he was both relieved and disoriented, reckoning with those wild thoughts of defending her that came so quick and easy. When he looked back at her—her still-stricken face, reddened now, he was grounded again. He lowered his brow.

"Wha—"

He stopped.

Because he heard a . . . was that a *slurp*?

He tilted his head, listening through the din of restaurant noise, louder than any one of those practice restaurants he'd been in, but still—he heard it again.

A slurp, and then a sort of . . . smacking noise.

He turned his head, the briefest look over his shoulder that he could manage, but if he was being honest, probably not brief enough. Probably one second past polite, not that he had any real sense of what was polite anymore.

In his defense, this was certainly not part of any of his practice runs.

Two people who'd put themselves on the same side of their small table. Their woven chairs pressed tight together, their plates cleared or perhaps not yet come, their wineglasses empty and clearly long forgotten.

So that they could, apparently, focus fully on sealing their mouths as tightly together as they had their chairs.

Except for those brief, head-slanting half seconds where they...

Holy *shit*, that was so much of a stranger's tongue he was seeing.

He looked back at Layla. This time, her eyes weren't on him—they were over his shoulder, watching the couple kiss.

And kiss, and kiss, and kiss. He could tell by the slurping and smacking that it was still going. It was, admittedly, not the best sound to be party to, but even he could tell when two people were lost to themselves—when the feeling was too good for a thing like an accidental sound to matter.

He maybe heard a moan, and that's when Layla's gaze returned to him, her cheeks pinker now, the whole bare-skinned V made by her black top a delicate, blushing pink.

It was the slowest, softest way he'd ever been made to feel warm.

The first time in forever that he wasn't worrying while someone looked at him.

The first time a phantom sensation in his lips wasn't a pain signal.

Abruptly, she blinked and said, "We should go," shoving back from the table and starting to stand when she was still on the word *go*, clearly not making much of a suggestion. Most times, when he'd seen Layla move, he noticed how *careful* she was, how graceful and deliberate—the two notable exceptions being that one startled moment on the boat last night, and the stuttering step she'd taken into him for their dance today.

Both times, because of the ex showing up.

His eyes followed her as she rose: her head tipped down, her hair swooping forward, as though she'd commanded it to shield her from seeing any more. For a second, her hands fluttered uselessly—like she was looking for a coat she didn't have, like she forgot how to pick up the purse that she did.

He followed her slowly. A punishment he couldn't even admit to himself he was enacting on her—for taking away that warmth, for his lips still tingling pointlessly. When he stood, pivoting slightly to push his chair in, he couldn't help but catch sight of the couple again: still at it. Older than he might have thought, fairly or not: the woman's hair streaked with gray, the man wearing wire-rimmed glasses that didn't have a chance of staying on straight with all that slanting, their clothes bland and casual. Not French, he suspected, but what did he fucking know after only a couple of days. Wedding rings on them both, plain yellow gold.

He thought, *Sorry for staring*, not that they seemed to notice, and turned back to catch up to Layla, to the long line of her back retreating from this restaurant.

The warmth in him was something else now. A familiar, frustrated heat: the way he felt when he saw her kneeling on that airplane floor. The way he felt when she opened her hotel room door to him. When she stood up from a table to save a sick woman she had every reason to stay away from.

Out on the street—*her street*—she turned to the left. Started walking, back the way they'd come, not waiting for him. Not even, maybe, remembering he was fucking there.

Erasing the memory of him from this night.

"Is that what you did?" he said.

Called it to her, practically, since she was steps ahead.

She didn't stop.

So he called to her again. Didn't care who heard. Who saw.

"Did you do that with him?"

That did it. She stilled, her spine straight, but he thought her shoulders rose in a steadying breath.

Don't fucking do that, he thought. *Don't steady yourself for me.*

"Is that how you were," he continued, "when you were here on your honeymoon?"

She whirled on him then, quick enough that he took a step forward, in case she wasn't as steady in those heels as she looked. In case the deep breath hadn't worked.

"*What* are you even saying?" she said, her voice louder than he'd ever heard it, and a thrill went through him.

This was her, the Layla he'd only seen in little glimpses.

The Layla she only showed to him.

"It's just two people," he said, the suspicion in him rising now, the frustration at a fever pitch.

It hadn't embarrassed her to see those people.

It had *hurt* her.

"Two people kissing," he said. "Awkward to be next to, okay. But not a reason to run."

She raised her chin, defiant. But she didn't respond.

"Is that," he repeated, enunciating each word, "how he kissed you?"

He could see her chest rising and falling. He took another step toward her. Behind them, he could still hear the noise of the restaurant, but a half block down, it was so much quieter. If there were people nearby, he didn't notice.

"Layla," he said.

"No."

It wasn't loud enough to be called an exclamation.

Not loud enough, but emphatic enough.

"No, what?"

She closed her eyes briefly, swallowed. When she opened them again, she looked straight at him and said, "No. He never kissed me like that. Like I was—like *we* were the only two people in the . . . in the universe. Not on my honeymoon. Not . . ."

She trailed off.

"Not ever?" He did not mean it to sound so fucking hopeful.

"I don't—" She broke off, bit the inside of her cheek, her lips tightening with the motion. Plumping again when she finally readied herself to speak. "I don't think ever. I don't remember ever."

Obviously, Griffin already hated him. Hated him first for being half a liability to Michael's wedding. Hated him more for getting on that boat with a new girlfriend, for leaving the poor woman to get sick alone over the side of it. Hated him today for bowing gallantly before a dance, and for hearing that he'd left Layla alone, even for a single afternoon, on her honeymoon.

But now—now, hearing this?

He might have hated him more than he'd ever hated anyone.

Including himself.

"He should have," he said.

She shrugged.

Shrugged. It made him so angry he wanted to shake her.

"He's a piece of shit," he said instead.

"He's not," she answered immediately. "You don't even know him. He's a good person. I told you, it was ami—*hey!*"

He'd taken the final step toward her; he'd grabbed her hand. His left hand, that's what he used, because it was most convenient, and he didn't care that it made an inexplicable spot on his thigh radiate with pain. He held her fast anyway, pulled her to the corner. Then to the left, down a different street, darker and less remarkable.

"What are you *doing*?" she said, slightly behind him, but he didn't answer yet. He walked until he didn't feel his pulling hip or his straining knee anymore, maybe another half block. He didn't stop until he saw something he wanted: a deep-set doorway, tucked beneath a stone arch. A gabled overhang above, sturdier than an awning. A dim light tucked into its rafters, flickering slightly.

He steered her into it. Guided her backward with his body, almost until her shoulders met the door. Kept hold of her hand, but loosened his hold as he looked down at her. She could go; he wanted her to know she could go if she wanted to.

But he didn't think she wanted to.

She leaned back, settling herself against the place he'd put her. Looked up at him and said, "What are you doing?" again, but this time, it was a whisper.

"This street is mine," he said, which made less sense out loud than it had in his head, but Layla kept looking at him, her head tipped up, her eyes flashing in understanding.

"I don't know the name of it," she said.

"You don't need to. You only need to know that this is a street where someone once told you something important."

"Okay." A quiet, bewildered consent.

He let go of her hand, and for a second felt the confusion of it: one sensation lost, and his disobedient nerves jangling in response, unsure what price to demand of him. But he was determined: a feeling like he had once in the hospital, when he had to prove he could get out of bed on his own.

He wanted to say this with two hands on her. Right on the shoulders she'd shrugged.

So, he did it—a breath he took in as he lifted his hands, readying himself. Sometimes, like with the chair, both hands at the same time on something new was a problem, the unevenness of feeling too jarring, so the left one reacted like he was touching a hot pan, or an engine only just shut off.

But it didn't happen this time. Layla's magic spell cast over him, even when his hands settled first on a spot different than what he'd intended—her upper arms, bare and smooth and warm, impossibly inviting. He curled his fingers around her triceps, felt the line of them as he moved up, those gauzy, split-open sleeves trailing over his knuckles as he rested his palms on her shoulders.

He thought maybe—*maybe*, through that more reliable right palm of his—he could feel goose bumps rise on her skin in the wake of his movement, but he didn't lower his eyes to look.

He wanted to see her face when he said this.

"You keep saying *amicable*," he started.

"It's *true*," she interrupted, defiant, and the truth was, he believed her. Believed that the man he'd barely met had made it so *nice* for her, whatever had happened between them. Bowed when he said goodbye to her, probably. And he believed, too, that she'd received it gracefully, with those careful movements that hid everything he saw about her.

He slid his thumbs across the caps of her shoulders, leaned in a little farther. He would say this part so fucking *close* to her, no matter that this was closer even than their dance, no matter that she must be able to see every single scar on his face.

He would say it close enough for her to hear it loud and clear.

"There shouldn't be anything amicable about losing you," he said.

There should be a war, he thought. *An army of stone gargoyles, ordered to be alive. All to come get you. All to show you that you should never shrug like that again.*

"He should hurt like hell every time he sees you," he said instead, because this wasn't about him in his imaginary tower. "He should be in a restaurant, watching two people kiss like that, and feel starved to death. Like he never touched a bite of his meal, because he doesn't get to taste you anymore. *He* should feel that way. Not you."

He kept his eyes on hers, but he knew her chest rose and fell even faster now. He could *feel* it, through those curves in her shoulders. He didn't want to hurt her, saying this, but also, it had to hurt worse that no one else ever had.

It had to hurt worse that her husband hadn't.

"You shouldn't—"

"Griffin," she said, cutting him off. Not only with the sound of his name on her lips, but with how she touched him, too: *Griffin*, she said, at the same time she set both of her hands on his sides right above the bones of his hips, and he knew as it happened—as all his damned wires crossed—that for a while, or maybe forever, he would feel those particular bones rattle anytime he heard his name.

He couldn't tell if it truly hurt. He was concentrating too hard on her hands.

"What?" he said, expecting her to push him away. To use those hands to say, *Fine, I heard you; it was a little intense; I've had enough of this now.*

But she didn't do that.

She didn't *say* that.

"It didn't make me think of him," she said, and he frowned down at her. He'd chased her out of a restaurant; he'd dragged her down a dark street she didn't even know the name of. He'd insisted on this, on *saying* all this, so close to her, and she hadn't been thinking of the ex at all.

"Of how he kissed me or didn't," she added.

"Oh," he said, his voice an echo to his own ears, because now he noticed that sometime between her saying his name, her putting her hands at his waist, his own had moved. Over the summit of those shoulder curves, his palms on the faint incline of her trapezius. His thumbs on her collarbone, one upward stroke away from her pale, perfect neck, smooth and unadorned.

Do not, he told himself, trying to reconnect the right wires: the ones that told him he could not touch her like this, he could not *feel* a thing for her like this, not after so many years of hardly feeling anything other than hurt.

It was not *for* him, to feel this way.

But then, Layla Bailey pulled him closer.

Like she needed to tell him something important.

"It made me think of you."

Chapter Seventeen

His mouth on hers might as well have been a brand.

A hard press at first—not really a kiss at all by any standard definition.

But as soon as she felt it . . . as soon as she held the whole lightning bolt of Griffin Testa between her hands, she knew that she did not—right now or maybe ever again—want standard.

She wanted *this*.

Him.

His thick hair under the light of an Edison bulb, his gaze moving over her whole face when she talked, his held-back sounds of satisfaction as he ate.

His bringing her here, to this street and this secret doorway, his body blocking hers from view.

His coal-black eyelashes and how they hung low over his eyes when he was looking down at her, looming over her, to say something as electric as *There shouldn't be anything amicable about losing you.*

And now, this—his impulse, his leaning-in haste, his hands on either side of her neck, holding her with the lightest, most contradictory touch.

His *mouth*.

Moving now that the mark on her had been made: a tilt of his head and a tug of her top lip between his, and then it was as though the kiss broke open for them both, became something else. It wasn't just a bolt of lightning anymore—it was a huge, rolling thunderstorm, the kind that overwhelmed every single one of your senses.

Kissing him *consumed* her.

Her tongue slipped into his mouth first, a desperate initiation she couldn't hold back after his relentless exploration of her lips—a kiss at each corner, gentle suction on the bottom curve, a return to that spot on the top, with a scrape of his teeth this time, like he was testing the texture. She thought, *Me, too, me, too; I want to feel everything, too*, and when she tasted him with the tip of her tongue, the dark, chocolate-soufflé perfection of him, he held her tighter, his fingertips pressing through her hair and against the back of her neck, bringing her into him as he groaned in pleasure, letting her feel the low vibration of it against her mouth.

Letting her feel it *everywhere*.

It would be a lie to say that she thought only of him, because at first—at first, she thought of other kisses, too. The one in the restaurant that started all this. Then, Jamie—of course, Jamie, because Griffin had asked, had *forced* her to think about Jamie. The maybe half dozen men she'd kissed since Jamie, too—matches on an app, all of them, in different cities she'd not really lived in for work.

She thought of them like this: *What was that called, what I saw those people in the restaurant do, what I did myself with Jamie and those other guys whose names I can't remember? What was the word for that?*

Because it wasn't this.

It wasn't anything like this.

It was such a huge, disorienting feeling of having the whole word—the whole *world*—remade, that for a split second while he cupped her face and changed the angle again, she took advantage and started to ask.

"Have you ever—"

But all he said was "*No*," and then he *bit* her—right on the sharpest angle of her jaw, the most erotic correction, before kissing her ear, her cheek, her lips again.

After that, she figured it didn't matter what she was going to ask.

She figured his answer would be *No* no matter what.

After that, she couldn't think of anyone else. She could only think of him, and herself, in matching black and melding into each other. A fae prince and a now immortal-feeling girl.

They kissed for so long that there were stages of it—the storm strengthening, receding, strengthening again. Sometimes, it would turn too close to explosive: a drifting and then clutching hand, a rolling pelvis, a particularly out-of-control moment where one of her legs lifted, her thigh going to the outside of his, basically *climbing* him. Each time, one of them would pull back, only enough to breathe into each other for a calming second before starting again.

Dimly, she realized that it was this way because neither of them were ready to take it to a second location, or maybe both of them were too fearful of breaking this spell. This *kissing*, this conversation, this *tussle*, where their tongues fought for dominance, where one or the other of them used their teeth, where they coaxed with moans and scolded with hisses of breath and soothed with strokes of their hands.

Where they taught each other how to be kissed.

Eventually, new sensations assailed her: her hair catching in a splinter of the door she was pressed flat against, one of her petal sleeves tickling too low on her arm, possibly torn. Her lips swollen-feeling, a little raw, her nipples aching, the space between her legs... *god*, the space between her legs. Hot and wet and pulsing, *hurting*, and it felt so *good*, because that's what he had said—he said it should hurt not to kiss her, and she wanted to stop only long enough to say, *That's how it hurts, not to do more than kiss you right now.*

Then, a voice other than the one in her head cut through the haze. A stream of French, followed by laughter and a few hoots, the sound of it both good-natured and mocking. She could not hope to understand the words, not really, but she thought she caught *embrasser*, which maybe meant embrace, maybe meant embarrassed, but neither one was right for what she and Griffin were doing...

Wait.

What they had been doing.

Now that his mouth wasn't on hers, the noise that intruded was more notable—the laughter, footsteps fairly close. At first, he only turned his face—giving her his right side, the sidewalk his scars, his expression grim and distant. He stood like that, statued in profile, until the footsteps faded, and the truth was, she couldn't think of much—other than how much longer it would take for him to start kissing her again.

So when he started to step away, she reacted. Her hands grabbing his sides, trying to stop him, but he kept going, quicker now.

Away from her. His hands slid from where they'd been on her body—one high up on her rib cage, one in her hair. He held them strangely still for a moment, as though they were frozen in the shape of her, and then shoved them in his pockets as he took another step back.

Not so far that he wasn't still blocking her from sight of the street, but far enough.

Far enough to feel like being hauled out of another world.

He did not look like himself.

Or he did, but not like the Griffin she'd seen tonight.

She tried for something light. Something that would bring him back to how they'd been before, to the memory of what they'd built over the course of today.

"Talk about being the show," she said. The small smile on her lips felt unusual, what with her swollen lips, her chin raw from his stubble.

He didn't smile back. No quirk, no curve.

Nothing.

He said, "Sorry."

Not even an *I'm* preceding it.

A sorry, shorn.

"Sorry?"

His hands shifted in his pockets, curled into fists she knew well now: white-knuckled, impenetrable. Made of stone.

"That was—we got carried away."

"Carried . . . away?"

She knew, in a distant way, that she was only repeating things, her mouth slowly forming around words that made no sense to her. She was thinking in a different language now, the one he'd taught her: *nothing amicable about losing you, starved to death.*

This street is mine.

"It was a mistake," he said, and that one cut through. She couldn't bring herself to repeat it, but it got her to move, at least. A flick of her wrist, her watch lighting. Twenty-five minutes since she'd last looked at it, in her hot, confusing frenzy to leave that restaurant, to stop looking at Griffin Testa's mouth and imagining what it could do.

One kiss was a mistake, maybe.

Nearly *twenty-five* minutes of kissing?

She dropped her hand back to her side, staring at him. He shifted on his feet, looked away from her, and oh, god, it *hurt*. She could hardly understand how it hurt, could only let it gather in her, dark and spiky, and she wanted to get it *out*.

"It was maybe the wine," he said.

"You had *water*," she snapped, and that felt good, getting one of those spikes out and into him, watching his jaw tighten with its impact.

Not enough, though. He took one hand out of his pocket, moved it behind him, and then he had his phone out. The thumb that had stroked her neck, her earlobe, her lower lip—even as he kept kissing her—was now moving with brutal efficiency as he tapped and swiped across the cold, flat screen.

"Getting a car," he said, as though he wanted to answer before she could ask.

But she was not going to ask. She was busy, trying to gather up all her spikes without cutting herself on them.

Because she knew, instinctively, that the car was not for both of them. That he meant for her to take it alone.

This was so . . . She was so *embarrassed*. So out of control and unlike herself: from that moment in the restaurant, maybe even before, all the way to now. Mind under matter, and the matter was him and what he'd managed to do to her in this doorway, on this street that was his.

In this other world.

She stepped out from beneath it. She wanted to wince from the reality check: All she could see now of that kiss was her own desperation during it. Her clutching hands, her rolling hips, her leg hitching over his.

"I'll walk," she said.

"No, you won't."

She started to pass by him, but he reached out—held her at her elbow, and she thought she heard a noise from him—another hiss, an exhalation, something—and it was enough to make her stop.

He dropped his hand immediately. Took a step away.

She should have kept going.

"Look," he said, his voice low, a rasp in it now. "Today was good. We did good, for Michael and Emily."

She absolutely could not look at him for this. She stared straight ahead, back toward the Boulevard Saint-Germain. *Her* street, her safety.

"That worked," he continued. "You know, being friends."

Oh, the *spike* of it. The stake, straight through the heart.

"Amicable," she said, and hoped he would argue.

He did not.

He said, after a beat of silence, as though she hadn't said the word that started all this, "And tomorrow is—the itinerary is full. So we should, you know. Do what we did—"

She started to walk again, even as she heard the sound of an engine pulling up.

"Stop," he said, right on her heels. "Just—the car is here. Just get in the car."

She turned back to him, so angry now. Saying those things to her, kissing her that way, *embarrassing* her with his suggestion of *friendliness*, of all fucking things, and now he wanted to give her *commands*.

Well, she wasn't in his kingdom now. She was halfway back to her own. A place where she'd once been alone, and where she would happily be alone again.

But when she looked at him this time, everything spiky she wanted to say softened on her lips. Her *I said I'll walk*; her *How dare you*; her *I'm not doing what we did today ever again*.

Because now that she was coming back to herself, she could see it: those wild eyes, the restless way his body moved, a dampness at his temples that she hadn't felt when she'd put her hands in his hair. A tension around his eyes and along his neck.

"It isn't a panic attack," he said.

The rideshare driver, idling on the curb, tapped his horn, and Griffin turned his neck slowly. "A minute," he snapped, not even trying it in French this time. She knew now that he usually did—determined, halting efforts, twelve-weeks-of-therapy efforts to prepare for this trip. He always waited until someone spoke back to him in English to concede.

She looked at him. Mind over matter. Her better self said, *It's pain. What you are looking at is pain.*

She'd suspected he had it. Had observed him enough to know that he had the sort of scars that felt alive to him, like a lot of physical medicine and rehabilitation patients who sustained and managed complicated scarring, or nerve injuries beneath burns. But she hadn't been thinking of it. Not tonight. Not in that little world they'd been in. Not in her wounded pride, her embarrassment.

So when he looked back at her, she remembered it all in a new way now: *her* drifting and clutching hands, *her* rolling hips, *her* leg hitching up.

Her grabbing at his sides, when he started to pull away.

"Did I hurt you?" she said.

"No."

But it was the most dishonest *No* she'd ever heard. A violation of every *Maybe I'll tell you* from today.

She could not let it go.

"Did I touch you in some way that—"

"*No*," he said again, desperately emphatic, and still a lie. She thought of his last desperate *No*, the honest one, the one he'd said with his mouth against her. Her mind unspooled with a thousand images of the two of them together. Not just kissing now. Naked and no reason to stop, his *No*s an education for her. She would listen, learn what was okay.

"We could—" she began.

"Layla," he said, his voice different than any way she'd ever heard it. No leaning in to that first syllable this time. He sounded so defeated that she couldn't help but take a step toward him.

He backed away, his eyes flashing a warning.

"I am begging you," he said, his mouth hardly moving as he spoke. Gritted it out. "Get in the car. Please."

It was the *Please* that did it. The tacked-on, broken sound of it. He was somewhere else now, remote and inaccessible to her. Not in the world he'd brought her into for a while, not in the world they'd made together. She could see it in the way he stepped back again as she passed, more distance. He let her open the door herself, his hands never leaving his pockets. He let her close it, too, when she was settled in the black-leather back seat.

He spoke to the driver, and not to her.

"I'll watch the route," he said, flat and menacing, and the driver nodded in understanding.

She thought, *Do you speak fae prince?* which was a very mind-under-matter thing to have in her head.

So when the driver pulled away from the curb, leaving Griffin behind, she brought herself back into the world of real things. Real words. She took out her phone, and opened the translation app.

To hurt, she typed, and got back the must-be-wrong *blesser*.

To starve, she tried, and got *affamer*.

To kiss, she put in, with shaky fingers, and didn't much appreciate the irony of getting *embrasser*.

Embarrassed, she retaliated, and got a boring-sounding *gênée*.

Pain, she wrote, and mouthed the answer to herself: *douleur*.

Friend, she lied, watching it return what looked to her like a little fragment of something horrible: *ami*.

Word after worthless word, all the way back to the hotel.

And not once did she land on one that described how it felt to have had, and then lost, the touch of Griffin Testa.

Chapter Eighteen

Day four dawned too much like day two.

Griffin lying in his all-wrong hotel bed, barely asleep, barely having slept. His body an open wound. Too much pain, too much trying to walk it off.

And Michael, knocking on his door.

Well, talking through his door. That was different.

"Griff," his friend was saying. "You okay in there?"

When he sat up—quick, to get it over with—he let the differences from day two become clearer to him. Yeah, Michael talking, but also the light coming through the sheer curtains he hadn't bothered covering with the heavier drapes, and the muted later-morning noises he could hear through the window.

Two kinds of pain this time.

"Fuck," he muttered, swinging his legs over the edge of the bed and standing. Another difference: He had not been under the covers. He had not even taken off his clothes from last night.

Don't think about it, he told himself, but that was fucking crazy. He was, of course, already thinking about it; he had not stopped thinking about it. Her in the back seat of that car, alone, her lips still swollen from what they'd done in that doorway. Her before that, standing in front of him on the street, slowly working out what had happened.

He'd tried to head it off, her realizing it. He'd said the meanest thing he could think of in the moment.

Calling them *friends*.

He thought of her saying the word *amicable*, and the one kind of pain, the pain that had nothing to do with his body, was almost unbearable.

He wanted to lie back down and die.

"Griff," Michael repeated, muffled through the door, his voice pitched into a different register of concern now. "Open this door or I'm gonna get one of the hotel employees up here."

Griffin blew out a breath and stood.

It figured. Michael had never let him lie down and die, even when he wanted to most.

"I'm coming," he said.

When he opened the door, he was confronted with another difference: Michael looking way less hangdog than he had on day two. Not settled, not easy.

But not damp-eyed and terrified, either.

As soon as he took in Griffin, though, his brow wrinkled in concern.

"Did you sleep in your clothes?"

Griffin shrugged. The lie would be to say he'd slept at all.

"You look like shit," Michael added.

"What's new?" Griffin muttered, backing away from the door, wishing he'd done more to cover up the imprint of his body on the still-made-up bed. He reached up, brushed a hand over the back of his head, felt the hair there, flattened and messy. He must've been lying still for a long time, which probably was not going to help the other kind of pain, the body kind.

"You forget about this morning?" Michael said as the door closed behind him. Griffin's room here was big, the biggest they offered at this hotel, but this morning, his friend's presence felt crowding, overwhelming. He should've gone to the church again, instead of coming back here at dawn. He could've stood in front of his bell tower. He liked it there.

Griffin moved to the nightstand, picked up a bottle of water he should've drank hours ago. Physically, he'd done pretty much every wrong thing since the doorway. Hadn't hydrated enough, hadn't rested when his body was telling him to, hadn't done any of his damned stretches or put on any of his silicone patches, had stayed in the same position for too long, once he was lying down.

He would probably be a wreck today.

And that was so unfair to Michael.

He swallowed, cleared his throat. "No, sorry. Just—uh, had one of those nights."

Michael nodded, brief and knowing: not only about what *one of those nights* meant for Griff, but also about Griff not wanting to say more about it.

Except *one of those nights* was only half-true. *One of those nights* was only one kind of pain.

"Layla sent me up," Michael said.

Oh, Jesus *Christ*. It was so hard not to react to that: the searing, other-pain of it. He chugged more of the water he didn't want, thought of Layla saying, *You had* water, which was exactly what he deserved for the lie. For saying something so cruel and untrue about the reason he'd kissed her.

"We were all in the lobby waiting," Michael continued, settling onto the too-small couch in front of the room's wall of windows. "After a bit she said I might want to check on you."

Griffin winced.

"Discreetly," Michael added. "No one heard."

Holy hell, it hurt to have hurt her. All that, and she'd sent someone up to check on him. She'd done it quietly, unobtrusively. She'd probably managed to distract everyone—Fitz and Paula, to be sure—from noticing he hadn't shown.

"Give me five minutes," Griffin said, because the least he could do now was be good for Michael. "I'll get a shower and get down there."

Michael shook his head, leaned forward to pick up the remote off the side table for the television Griffin never turned on. "Take your time. I told them to go ahead, that we'd catch up."

Griffin frowned. Thought of two-days-ago Michael, terrified of losing Emily.

After a heavy silence, Michael looked up to find Griffin watching him, and must've read his mind.

"Things are good," he said reassuringly. "Yesterday—it was *really* good. Em was so much more herself as the day went on. And the dinner with our parents, that turned out good, too."

Turned out, Griffin repeated to himself. A speaking phrase, he thought, one Michael probably didn't even realize he'd used. *Turned out, once you weren't involved.*

"Everyone got along, though Rosie was halfway to giving my dad a heart attack, talking about her nipple piercing right there at the table." He chuckled, then grew serious again. "And after, Em and I got out for a while on our own. Went to this other little bistro, had wine and dessert. Walked all the way to the Eiffel Tower again, to see it all lit up. *Really* talked, you know?"

Yeah, I fucking know, Griffin thought. The chocolate soufflé, the crème brûlée flavor on Layla's lips when he'd kissed her.

"She slept over," Michael said, a little bashful. He'd always been like that—a gentleman.

I put her in a car alone, Griffin wanted to say. *I hurt her feelings, right before I did.*

"You should thank Layla," he said instead. Tried to make it sound casual by crossing to the armoire, pulling out a fresh set of clothes to take with him into the bathroom.

"She's great, right?" Michael said, which Griffin tried not to hate. She *was* great. It wasn't like he would ever be the sole possessor of that knowledge. He pretended he was looking for a specific shirt, when in fact all of his daytime shirts were pretty much the same: same brand, same soft fabric, same cut, no tags, with seams in places that didn't chafe.

"Em really trusts her," Michael went on. "Last night, she told me that Layla always had a way of putting things into perspective."

I know, he thought again, remembering that moment last night when they first sat down, when he felt cramped and stared-at and strange. Layla telling him everything she knew about the street they sat on, like her whole life depended on talking him through it.

"And she's got a way with people," Michael continued. At some point, he'd flicked on the television and muted it, his eyes on the screen as he flipped channels. The thing was, Michael was good with people, too, but more specifically, he was good with Griffin, which meant he was going to look at other things in case Griff had to get his clothes off before going into the en suite; he was going to talk about things he thought were totally innocuous so Griff wouldn't worry about someone seeing his skin, even if that someone had seen it at its worst.

Griffin grunted, stacking his chosen clothes into a tidy pile he would set on the bathroom counter.

"This morning she was chatting away with Samantha, easy as anything."

She lies, Griffin thought. *I don't know why any of you don't see that she lies.*

He'd told her it was a *mistake*.

"And yesterday, with Mom and Dad, she . . ."

He trailed off, and out of the corner of his eye, while he grabbed a pair of socks, Griff saw Michael cringe. He could finish the sentence for him, way harsher than Michael ever would: *She knew to get you out of the way for the night.*

"Anyway," Michael said, his voice more falsely cheerful now. "It's good you've made friends with her."

"I wouldn't say we're friends," Griffin ground out. God, this day was going to be hell.

Michael looked over at him, expression confused. "Oh yeah? She said you had a lot of fun yesterday. A really good dinner."

Griffin's hands clutched at his little pile of clothes. He could practically *hear* her saying it. So pleasant and calm and false, like how she talked to Robert and Manon, like how she talked to the ex, like how she talked to Samantha, *easy as anything*.

"I'm gonna get a shower," he said, wishing he was alone. The room felt way too small for him and all this fucking *feeling* he had. "You should go ahead. Get a cab, catch up to Emily. I'll be right behind you."

Michael unmuted the TV, resettled himself. "Nah, I'll wait. Fifteen fewer minutes at another museum won't hurt, I'll tell you that."

Griffin clenched his teeth, annoyed, as he went into the en suite and closed the door behind him. At first, he thought it was because Michael hadn't taken his not-so-subtle hint at wanting to be alone. That had been a thing between them sometimes, back when Griffin was in the thick of his recovery, when most days Michael was the absolute last person he wanted to see, or to be seen by.

But as he shucked last night's clothes, waiting for the shower to warm to the temperature he'd spent twenty minutes two days ago learning how to get right, the exact temperature he needed not to want to scream—fucking hotel showers, why were they so *complicated*—he realized he wasn't annoyed about not being left alone.

He was annoyed about that museum comment.

Fifteen fewer minutes.

It made him think of Layla: Layla and that afternoon at the Louvre she'd told him about. She'd left the ex out of it, but Griffin still got the sense that he was there—she slipped and said *We* a few times. *We had a reserved slot*, or *We were there for hours*. But when she talked about the art she liked best, she said *I*, always.

I thought she would be glowing, I guess, she said, when she'd been telling him about that one painting that had surprised her most. *But she wasn't. Her skin was so sallow. Her ankles were swollen. She looked really dead, you know? I've seen that—death, I mean—up close. I thought it was so beautiful, to paint her that way. To let her be human, in the end.*

By then, he'd been well clear of the panic, but maybe he'd lied a little. Fidgeted just enough to keep her talking. He could've listened to her talk about art he'd never seen all night.

You could've kissed her all night, he thought, the memory shifting now. Her mouth, her skin, her scent. Her holding him, and how for a while, he didn't let it matter that it sometimes hurt.

He had to turn the shower to cold to help him remember that Michael was still out there.

To help him remember that, in the end, he *had* let it matter.

He'd let it matter, and he'd hurt her in return.

The rest of his shower was quick, utilitarian, and when he got out, he was in control enough again to remember that *Fifteen fewer minutes* shit. He was clearheaded enough to realize why it bothered him.

He dried off too fast, hitting and scraping against spots he usually babied, tugged on his clothes and tried to ignore that parts of them stuck to him damply. Miserably.

He opened the door, saw Michael more sprawled on the couch now. At the sound of Griffin coming out, Michael said, without taking his eyes from the television, "I don't even know why I have this on. Can't understand anything they're saying."

"Mikey," Griff said, and at that, his friend finally looked over. "Yeah?"

"Emily *is* young," he said, and before Michael could get indignant about it, he added, "I don't mean it to be insulting. I know she's an adult. I know she's mature. Your equal. I mean—lots of things are probably still pretty new to her. Or at least, showing them to *you* is new to her. That's probably why she likes the museums. Going with you to them, I mean. Telling you about what she knows, or what she likes. I bet it's as important to her as the talking. Or the sleeping over."

For a second, Michael stared at Griffin like he'd never seen him before in his life.

And given that everything that had just come out of Griffin's mouth was probably unlike anything he'd ever *said* in his life, that was probably fair.

Then, Michael seemed to move on from the messenger to the message itself.

He stood from the couch, the remote clattering onto the floor from his lap.

"Yeah," he said, nodding once, a look of determination coming over his features. "What am I doing?"

"Getting your asshole friend out of bed," Griffin answered, crossing to the door and shoving his feet into his shoes.

"You're not an asshole," Michael said when they got into the hall, barely a minute later.

Griffin snorted. Stabbed his finger at the elevator button.

"You're not," said Michael. "That was helpful. A good reminder. Thanks."

Thank Layla, he wanted to say, but that would require too much of an explanation. Anyway, Michael didn't need the distraction.

Michael needed Emily, and Emily was—

"Which museum?" Griffin said, when they stepped onto the elevator.

"Rodin," Michael said, and Griffin tried not to be relieved that it wasn't the Louvre.

Still, he might've liked to see that painting Layla loved so much.

"A lot of outside stuff," Michael said. "Sculptures."

"That's good," Griffin said, and meant it. Outside would be good for him today, probably. Fresh air always helped.

When they got into the back of the car that Michael ordered, Griffin took out his phone. He did it to not think about Layla, to look up shit about this museum and these sculptures so he wouldn't have to keep thinking about what it would be like to see her again. What he would say to her once he did.

How he would fix what he'd broken. If he should even try.

But of course, even the phone reminded him of her. Of being next to her on the train, passing it back and forth. She would squint, sometimes, and he wondered if she wore reading glasses ever. He should've asked her that last night, not that it mattered. He shook his head, frustrated with himself. Navigated to a page with a list of the outdoor sculptures, started scrolling.

Stopped and blinked at what he saw.

He couldn't help but let out a huff of ironic laughter.

"Figures," he said to himself, staring down at the little screen.

"What?" Michael said from beside him.

Griffin had to admit: For a second, he'd almost forgotten his friend was there.

"Nothing," Griffin said, pressing the button to black out his screen again. "Just realized we're about to see *The Gates of Hell*."

Chapter Nineteen

"Honestly, I would."

"Ro! Keep your voice down!"

Inside one of the many gorgeous, glossy parquet floor rooms of the Musée Rodin, Emily scolded her best friend gently, with a laugh in her voice—a light and welcome sound after the van ride over here, when Em had been reticent, obviously frustrated with Michael's decision to go get Griffin if it meant separating from the group.

Since Layla had been at least partially responsible for that decision—not that Emily had noticed her quiet suggestion to Michael—she was grateful for Rosie's relentless sense of good humor.

Especially because Layla didn't feel like she had much to spare this morning.

"What's it called?" Rosie said, moving to another side of the pedestal, looking for the sculpture's placard. When she found it, her eyes widened delightedly. "Man! With! The! Broken! Nose!" she whisper-exclaimed.

"Oh my god," Em said to Layla. "I know where she's going with this."

"This is Rodin predicting hockey romance book heroes," Rosie said.

"There it is," Emily muttered knowingly.

"Don't act like you don't read them!" Rosie turned to Layla. "Do *you* read them? I for one am deep in my fantasy era right now, sort of a more magical creatures instead of men situation, but if hockey sounds like something you'd be into, I have some rec—"

"I don't," said Layla, maybe too abruptly. Not because she would not, in fact, take a book recommendation from Rosie—honestly, at this point, she probably would've taken a piercing recommendation from Rosie—but because she did *not* want to think about romance.

In any context.

Layla watched as Emily's eyes drifted ahead into the next room, where Fitz and Paula had advanced to. Even after only a bit of time with them—the lobby, the van, the time they'd spent inside the museum so far—Layla had observed that Fitz treated sightseeing like he was going to be quizzed at the end. He would bend to read the placards, barely looking at the art itself, his mouth moving as though he was committing it to memory. Maybe in someone else she would find that endearing, but she was currently holding a grudge against this man she hardly knew.

On behalf of some other man that she *also* hardly knew.

You're lying, a little voice nudged her. *You do know him now. You know he has panic attacks and he tastes like chocolate soufflé. You know he hurts. You know he hated putting you in that car.*

But she ignored it.

"How'd it go with them last night?" she said to Emily now, giving it her best big-sister voice, taking advantage of Rosie's distraction (posing for a selfie beside *Man with the Broken Nose*).

"*Really* good," said Emily. "It was a smaller group, because Damaris and Abram passed, and Jamie took Sam to the opera last night."

Layla was very proud not to react at all to that. At the moment, she could not even really remember the night Jamie had taken *her* to the opera, all those years ago.

"And I know I already texted you this, but seriously, you taking Griffin to dinner was *so* good."

Layla *did* react to that. A feigned plucking of a nonexistent piece of fuzz off the front of the stupid summer turtleneck she decided to wear today, which had the advantage of hiding the beard-burn she saw on her skin in the mirror this morning.

"It was no big deal," Layla said, about what was possibly the biggest deal of her life in a very, very long time, and noted that it felt as bad to say it out loud as it had to text it last night from her bed, when Emily's all-caps THANK YOU and string of heart emojis came through.

A few minutes later, Emily had sent a selfie of her and Michael, the huge, twinkle-lit Eiffel Tower in the distance behind them, both of them flushed and happy-looking. We're out on our own now, talking and being together.

I'm so glad, she wrote back, but afterward, she'd closed her eyes until she could manage the pressure building there.

"I do *not* understand the deal between them," said Emily now, keeping her voice low. "Michael always says his parents kind of thought Griffin was a bad influence when they were growing up, but like, Mom and Dad know Rosie brought pot brownies to my sweet sixteen, and they're over it." She shrugged. "Fitz *is* kind of inflexible, I guess."

Layla's eyes wandered back to the man—reading another placard, while Paula waited patiently beside him in an oversize T-shirt that said *PARIS* on it, like the whole city was an American university. This was a choice that struck Layla as way more embarrassing than the fact that Rosie was now recording an Instagram Live over by the window.

"And Griffin *is* sort of a jerk," Emily added.

For a split second, she wanted to say, *I think it's more than that; I think there's something else there. I think whatever's between Michael and Griffin and his parents, you might not know the whole story.*

But saying that—she swallowed back a confusing feeling of being tugged in two directions, the middle line of her body stretching uncomfortably. As a sister to Emily, maybe she should. Maybe she should say, *Figure out what that's about before the wedding. If Michael can't tell you everything, you can't trust him to tell you anything.*

But as a . . . *friend* to Griffin, maybe she shouldn't say anything at all. Maybe she shouldn't invite any more speculation on the things he apparently kept private.

The thought alone made her face prickle in remembered embarrassment—his rejection of her, her realization of what that rejection might have been about, him sending her away anyway.

He *was* sort of a jerk.

She didn't *owe* him anything.

"I'm going to go catch up to them," Emily said, preempting Layla from changing course, from resisting that tug in her middle and being the big sister again. "Paula looks bored."

"Paula looks like she needs a jean jacket," Rosie said as she slid back in beside them, linking arms with Layla. "It would match her T-shirt."

Emily giggled. "Hush," she said, and then walked away, catching up to Fitz and Paula as they disappeared from view.

Rosie tugged on Layla's arm, moving them into the next room, as gorgeous as the last—its huge, arched windows casting sunlight over the pedestaled sculptures, the figure sketches hung on the walls.

"Okay, we're alone now," said Rosie. "Tell me *everything*."

Layla blinked down at Rosie, briefly wondered what they must look like from the outside: Layla like a staid chaperone in this beige turtleneck, hair carefully straightened, makeup light other than the (probably) metric ton of concealer under her eyes; Rosie a wayward, charming charge in a top made out of crocheted squares, four small, unsecured braids peeking out randomly in her hair, a smoky eye that (probably) looked so good because it was left over from last night's makeup.

"About?" Layla replied, chaperone-sounding, because she couldn't be sure what Rosie was asking. Had she figured out that things between Emily and Michael were still on unsteady ground? Did she think Layla had some kind of intel on the situation between Michael's parents and Griffin? Did—

Rosie shook Layla's arm, letting out a frustrated groan before whispering, "Did you fuck the billionaire?"

"Oh my *god*," Layla echoed Emily, nothing amusing about Rosie's relentlessness now. Her face was *blazing*. "No! Absolutely not. Why would you even—"

Rosie laughed. "I'm teasing! Well, sort of. The truth is, you two on that train yesterday—pretty cozy! Or as cozy as that guy can look, I guess. He's a bit remote!"

"We were looking at stuff about Versailles," Layla said, feigning interest in a placard. Now *she* felt like the wayward charge.

"And *not* to be a creeper but I was definitely in the lobby when you came down last night. You didn't see me because I was behind one of those big dumb columns! He looked at you like . . ." Rosie did not finish this sentence. Instead, she raised one of her hands and fanned her face.

Like what? she wanted to ask, but she said, "He isn't a billionaire."

Rosie ignored that. Layla had the feeling that Griffin being a billionaire was going to be part of an elaborate lore Rosie was writing about this entire week.

"So nothing happened? You didn't get him drunk and then bang him into the worst hangover of his life, hence him not showing up this morning?"

Layla faked a laugh. She felt like laughing was the right response, the calm-and-in-control response, when the truth was, every joking, flippant thing Rosie said scraped over all of Layla's sensitive spots. Something *had* happened, including him making some asinine, deflecting comment about the wine he hadn't drunk. Something *had* happened, including her absolutely wanting to bang him beneath a doorway.

Something had happened to make him not show up this morning.

And in spite of everything, half of her mind had constantly been on whether he was okay.

"I didn't have anything to do with it," she said, and tried not to think of all the ways she'd touched him. Tried not to think about him backing away from her.

"Ugh, that's disappointing. Although, I slept *alone* in our room last night, so *someone* is still getting it, right?"

Rosie waggled her eyebrows in the direction of Emily, one room ahead, now flanking Fitz on the other side as he read another placard like it was the only antidote in the world for having to speak to people in his current and future family unit.

For a few minutes, she and Rosie drifted together, arm in arm, weaving through pedestals and other museum patrons, and a few students with sketchbooks in their hands, concentrating on some lesser-known piece, or a small cast of something more famous. Rosie kept the conversation going, funny and easy and something Layla should—and *did*—feel grateful for.

But there was so much the *matter*, so much her mind couldn't let go of. She was thinking of Emily, quiet in the van, wondering about what secrets Michael might be keeping from her. She was thinking about Jamie and Samantha at the opera, and why she'd barely been *truly* thinking about it at all. She was thinking about the press of tears behind her eyes last night, and how she wanted to call Cara to talk about it, but she'd shoved her phone under the pillow instead, unable to think of how to even begin.

And she was thinking so, so much about Griffin.

She thought she might get a reprieve when she and Rosie caught up—not just to Em and Fitz and Paula, but to the whole group who'd left together this morning: Céline, the only one of them to get an audio guide, standing elegantly by a window, listening intently ("I don't even need this," she whispered to Layla, when they'd first walked in. "I just need a break from Paula."); Robert and Manon, comfortable in the museum they'd declared "their Parisian favorite!" this morning; Jamie and Samantha beside them, holding hands, Samantha's head resting on Jamie's shoulder.

Great, she thought earnestly, fixing her posture, disentangling herself from Rosie to smooth her still-not-wrinkled shirt. *A distraction from thinking about Griffin. A reason to put a good face on. Maybe someone will even throw up, and give me something to do.*

Of course, then she *really* looked, and realized what made this a room everyone wanted to dwell in.

"Hot," Rosie said.

It was *The Kiss*: big and bone-white in the center of the room, sun and shadow lines cast across two nude figures as they embraced, curling around each other—his huge hand on her hip, her arm curled around his neck, their fused-together mouths hidden by the curve of her shoulder.

Oh no, Layla thought immediately, because there was no way she was hiding her reaction to this. A reaction that was so specific to *today*—to this morning, to seeing something in the light of the sun that she'd done with Griffin in the dark of last night.

That sculpture was . . . it was how it had *felt*, to be kissing Griffin. The two figures looked so beautifully *alone* atop the great slab of marble, the shape of which was nothing specific, really. A chair or a rock or a cloud, it didn't matter, because only their kiss mattered.

In this room, in this world, in this universe.

Layla was . . . she was *bereft*. That's how it felt to look at this sculpture this morning.

That's how it felt to look at it without him.

"Blergh, sorry," Rosie whispered, and Layla looked over at her, still in the thrall of that kiss, confused and then newly embarrassed. Could Rosie *tell*; had Layla's face undone that *No! Absolutely not* from before; if Rosie could tell, could everyone else—

"With your *ex* in the room, very awkward," Rosie said.

Layla blinked. She almost said, *Who?* but it was only a glitch, a second of being too stuck in a memory of someone else. And because she was out of sorts, she didn't think to say anything calm and amicable like, *Oh gosh, it's completely fine!*

She just snapped her eyes up, across the room, to where Jamie stood.

Which was a critical mistake.

He was looking at her, too, Samantha still by his side, but separated from him now—a slice of space between them that was so deliberate, so respectful and *sympathetic*, like the look on his face, an expression she'd gotten so accustomed to in those last few months. In their therapist's office, in the mediator's conference room, across the table from her in their condo during quiet dinners when they both already knew it was over, when it was only the didn't-really-matter details that needed to be worked out.

It didn't make me think of him, she thought frantically, her words from last night that absolutely wouldn't work here—not in this lovely room of elegant treasures, everyone subdued and respectful, this . . . this *monument* right in the middle to what people did in secret, to what she and Griffin had done in secret on that street he claimed for himself last night.

"Do you want to duck out?" Rosie said, and the truth was, even the gentlest note of pity from Rosie—truth-telling but still slightly oblivious Rosie—was worse than sympathy from Jamie, or Samantha, or probably every other person from their party who was looking at her now.

She was about to say no. She'd already, in fact, turned back to Rosie and put the placid smile on her lips.

But then someone said, "Emily," too loud for a museum, and both she and Rosie turned to find Michael striding across the black-and-white tile of the vestibule, crossing beneath the arch into the room where they all stood in this awkward tableau, not even stopping for a second of staring at *The Kiss*.

He went straight to Emily.

Bent to kiss her. Not like *The Kiss*, not secret and sensual. A short but serious *I'm sorry* kiss, which still made Layla ache with longing.

And not for anyone that was in this room with her right now.

"I shouldn't have stayed back," Michael said to a soft-eyed, glowing Emily. "Want to start from the beginning?"

Emily beamed, and big-sister Layla was genuinely happy, but also—also, there was that other half of her body, pulling down that middle line, thinking of Griffin.

Where is he?

Is he okay?

Would he like to see The Kiss*?*

For once, she didn't really care what everyone thought about what she would do next.

She hoped that their collective attention had been turned, at least, to the couple that this week was truly all about—Michael's minor grand gesture, and Emily's clear adoration of it.

But if it wasn't—if it wasn't, and they all thought that she'd stared at that sculpture a little too long, too intensely, too longingly, and thought of Jamie—well.

Well, that was fine for now.

"I'm going to go outside," she whispered to Rosie, and then, without looking at anyone else, she left the room.

She didn't find him at first.

She figured—wrongly—that he would've started toward the beginning, or at least the beginning according to the path most people followed when they entered. The rose garden, lush and fragrant, conical shrubberies at its center, surrounding another famed, pedestaled figure: *The Thinker*. Layla knew that if she stood just so, facing him head on in his curved, contemplative bronze glory, she would see the top of the Eiffel Tower in the blue sky behind him, like it had sprung from his head as another grand, fully formed idea, all in a day's work.

But she didn't stand just so. She kept going, walking too fast for a park this beautiful, for a place dotted with art. She made it all the way to a grand, circular fountain, a bronze sculpture in the center that looked too cruel to contemplate, and turned back, staying on the westward side of the gardens now, growing more determined.

Ignored faces and bodies carved from stone or cast from bronze and looked instead at every real person she passed and thought, *Not Griffin, Not Griffin, Not Griffin.*

Finally, she saw him.

Standing alone, perfectly still, in front of a bronze-cast sculpture, onyx-black: three men, naked and huddled together, heads bent awkwardly in, each of them with an arm extended to a center point between them.

For a few seconds, she didn't move. She thought how odd it was that he stood so alone there, as though everyone milling about—a not insignificant number of people—had looked at him in his all-black, not-bronze glory, and decided to leave him be.

She thought, *Should I leave him be? Like he asked me to last night, like he forced me to last night?*

As though he heard her ask the question of herself, he shifted his eyes away from the sculpture and looked straight at her.

Nothing so cold as sympathy.

Nothing so simple as *I'm sorry.*

He kept his eyes on her, and took one deliberate step to the side.

Making room for her beside him.

When she stood next to him, he was already looking again at the figures: eyes up, expression grave, and she felt unequal to the moment, unsure of whether to speak. She looked in vain for a placard to read, and had a disturbing urge to apologize to Fitz, who maybe was reading, obsessively reading, because he had no idea what to say.

"You're flushed," he said, an opening so unexpected—not the least of which because he wasn't even looking at her—that for a second, she could only stare at his profile.

"It's warm in there," she finally said, but honestly, it wasn't. Not until she'd seen *The Kiss.*

"Hm."

Hm?! Her brain shouted back, that one syllable flushing her anew—this time, with anger. At his reticence and remoteness. At herself for rushing out here, for risking everyone's attention, everyone's *pity*, for thinking there was some reason to come out here and find a person who did not *really* want to be found.

For looking at something like *The Kiss* and thinking it had anything to do with her, and him, and all he had to offer was *Hm*.

"Are you enjoying the gardens?" she said, her voice *dripping* with politeness, distance, because she knew it was the tone that would make him the most mad.

He didn't take the bait.

"I wouldn't say enjoying."

She scoffed. Of course he wouldn't be enjoying it. Of course he'd make Michael late and then only drag himself along; of course he'd make the rest of the day more difficult by being aloof and—

"I'm thinking," he clarified, and there was something so soft in how he said it. It wasn't closed-off, heavy-brow, bronze-cast thinking.

It was an invitation, as sure as that step to the side.

Everything in her softened again, too.

"About what?"

He shrugged, but it wasn't dismissive. Just more of that soft contemplation as he kept his eyes up, coursing over the bodies in front of them. She wondered if this is how she'd looked inside, in front of *The Kiss*. She wondered if she should walk away, and leave him to his thinking.

"Pain," he finally said.

She swallowed at the starkness of it. The honesty of it. It's what she'd wanted him to admit to her last night, on that street where everything had felt so true between them, but now that he'd said it, something inside her turned over.

She didn't *want* him to have pain. She didn't want this to be true for him.

"They look to be in pain, right? This one—" He took a hand from his pocket, gestured to the figure on the far left. "The way he's holding his body. This whole side of him, bent. Like he's trying to get away from himself."

Her heart thudded. She felt as frozen in space and time as one of these sculptures.

"And their hands and feet," he said. "They look so big. That— that looks like pain. To me, it does."

For what felt like a long time, she simply looked: paid attention to what he said he saw in these figures. Let her eyes linger on the long, brutally stretched shoulder of the figure on the left. Let herself study every curled finger and exaggerated knuckle, six separate feet stuck permanently to a hard, crooked ground.

She thought it was what he wanted her—what he was asking her—to do.

"I have neuropathic pain," he said, and she let her eyes go to him again, though he wasn't looking back at her.

"From burns that cover . . . a lot of me. I also have contracture scarring. That's painful, too, though it's not—it's not like the nerve pain. Which is difficult to predict. Confusing. Not well controlled."

She almost said, *I've seen it before*, but thought better of it. Thought better of blurting out something clinical, something that had nothing to do with him, specifically.

"I don't have many pharmaceutical options," he said, making himself sound like the clinician. "Opioids were . . . not well tolerated. Anticonvulsants gave me severe vertigo. I use compression wraps on the worst of the contracture scarring, sometimes. Sometimes silicone patches on other areas. Temporary relief."

Automatically, a flood of information she wished she didn't have access to came to her: images, case studies, drug lists, treatment protocols. A professional hazard.

She turned her face back to the statue. Looked at it like it wasn't any kind of med school slide deck, any kind of textbook.

"When it happens," he continued, quieter now, so she had to strain to hear him, "when I get pain, it feels the way this looks. Twisting, deforming. I'd tear myself in half to get away from it. And it—" He paused, shifted on his feet. "It makes all the parts of me feel out of proportion. Those big hands. This stretched-out neck. I get disoriented. I don't—I don't feel sure of myself, in space."

She closed her eyes briefly, thinking of the way he backed away from her. His hands in his pockets, his unwillingness to touch even the car door.

"How long ago was it?" she finally asked, when she thought she could make her voice sound normal.

He took a breath in, and she thought he might be holding it. Counting.

"A long time," he eventually answered, and she tried to graciously accept the distance he was still keeping. She could tell how hard even this disclosure was for him.

"I'm an unusual case," he continued. "In terms of the neuropathy, at least. They say by now it should be better than it is."

Not necessarily, the physician in her wanted to say.

But she was not standing here as his doctor.

She was standing here as the woman who'd kissed him last night.

Who'd *hurt* him.

"They say some of it is probably psychological. Obviously, as you saw at dinner—I have some struggles in that area, too. But with the pain . . . when the pain hits, I—"

"I'm so sorry," she blurted, because it felt impossible not to—not to think again about all the ways she'd touched him, how many times it had hurt. "I didn't mean to—"

"Please don't apologize," he interrupted gruffly, and once again, the *Please* did it, sealing her lips shut. This one sounded less broken, more determined.

"I wasn't sure what I'd say to you today when I saw you. If I'd say anything, or—try to ignore what I'd done. What I said to you last night. But on the way over here I was looking up this place on my phone. Reading about the sculptures."

Neither of them was looking at the sculpture before them anymore. They'd turned to face each other now, the three figures looming but frozen in disinterest.

"This one, it's called *The Three Shades*," he said. "I don't know much beyond that. But they're also over there." He tipped his head to the side, toward a huge, stone-surrounded bronze door, covered in figures. "At the top. A smaller version. They stand over the entrance to *The Gates of Hell*."

"Griffin," she said, barely a whisper.

"You should call me Griff," he replied. "Considering."

She thought of all the things *Considering* could mean. *Considering that you talked me out of a panic attack. Considering that we had a whole dinner together, alone. Considering I'm the only one on this trip that truly sees you. Considering I had my tongue in your mouth, my hands on your body.*

Considering that I looked at this piece of art, and now I'm using it to tell you something about me.

"Griff," she repeated, and was rewarded with the way his mouth curved, even if it fell again only a second later.

"If that pain hits me . . . *when* it hits me. Because it's always when. I'm—I'm through that doorway. I am in hell. I don't know how else to describe it. I have to find my way out. Over and over again."

"I'm sorry," she said again, but this time, she hoped he knew she wasn't apologizing for herself.

Only for him, and for the pain he was describing.

He acknowledged it. One brief but meaningful nod, and then his gaze left hers, going to the top of that doorway. He was quiet, looking at it for so long that Layla started to think he might finally have finished, that he might've said all he would say. That *now* he would get on with ignoring what he'd done, what *they* had done. That now—with this new knowledge he'd given her—she would understand why last night was a mistake. That they'd silently agree to go find the group and get on with it in the way they had yesterday.

Two new friends who were privately guarding the bride and groom.

She didn't want that, though.

She did not want to ignore it or say it was a mistake; she did not want to go back and find the group of people who saw her all wrong.

She wanted to say, *Griff, I saw a piece of art, too. I saw* The Kiss, *and let me tell you what it made me think about.*

Before she could get up the courage, though, he finally looked back at her.

"I'm sorry, too. For how I acted last night. Once those gates opened for me, I mean."

His eyes dropped to her mouth, to her now-covered neck. A

slow perusal that made her leftover beard-burn tingle anew. He must be closer now; he *felt* closer, though she hadn't noticed him move.

"Because before that," he said, low and quiet, "before that, for me—it was heaven."

Chapter Twenty

He wouldn't say they *abandoned* Michael and Emily.

He wouldn't say they ran.

But the truth was, from the second he admitted to Layla Bailey—to *himself*—what it felt like to kiss her last night, he didn't figure either of them wanted to think all that much about their respective reasons for being in Paris right now.

In the shadow of those three shades, she looked at him, alive and pink-cheeked, her eyes on him interested and hopeful and free of what he feared most from her: disgust or remorse or pity.

She said, "Do you want to get out of here?"

And yeah.

He fucking did.

He wanted her to be the only reason he was here today.

He wanted to find a way to fix what he'd broken in her last night.

As they made their way out of that sculpture garden and back out onto the street, they were quiet—awkwardly so, a sort of *what have we done* quiet that made them stand too far apart, their footsteps sounding too loud beneath them, their eyes on anything but each other.

For him, it had to do with trying to shake off those hulking bronze doors they'd left behind, the gates to the hell he'd described to her. He thought he could feel it biting at his heels, the monstrous voices of those sculptures calling out to him about how he shouldn't have told her all that, shouldn't have opened the door far enough to let her see anything, even only a slice of it, how if she only knew the whole, horrible thing about his pain and why he had it, she would change her mind about him.

For her, he suspected it was something else. On the corner outside of the sculpture garden, she slowed her steps, staring ahead at the huge golden dome he and Michael had passed on the way here, another museum—this one, some old military hospital that was the group's next stop on the itinerary after a lunch break ("Em thought my dad would like it," Michael had said in the car, his voice tinged with regret, his leg bouncing with his restless need to get back to her).

Layla looked at that gold dome like she owed it an apology.

He thought, with a rising sense of dread, that she was about to change her mind.

But she only said, "We should probably text them and let them know."

So, they did. Both of them, separately, sliding out their phones. No coordination of the messaging, which was either risky or genius. Griffin typed to Michael, Turns out, I can't, which was both not true and also not a lie, and because Michael was Michael, he'd written back, No problem, man. Take it easy today.

Layla took longer—her thumbs hovering over her screen for a few seconds, her lower lip tucking in on one side where she must have been nibbling on the inside of her cheek. He almost said, *Don't do that*, almost set his thumb against that plush curve to tug it back to safety . . . to maybe kiss her again.

God, he wanted to kiss her again.

But then she started typing—fast, determined, not particularly brief. By the time she sent it, Griffin could see it was a rectangle of text she was sending along, nothing so short as *I can't*.

He held his breath, waiting for her to put the phone away again, torn between wondering what that long message said and wondering what they'd do next.

"I don't have a plan," she said, her tone almost defiant as she put her phone back in her purse, not waiting for a response from, he assumed, Emily. "I *had* plans, before. For different days. Or . . . different times of days, when I thought I'd be alone. But I don't have a plan for this."

This, she said, a casual wave of her hand between them, but he supposed he was still breathing out the relief of not having to go back into that other place, where that terrible door was.

Because when Layla said *this*, he heard it like it was a whole different door, creaking on its rusty hinges, opening back into heaven—a thin crack of light he wanted to spend his whole day working his way into, at least until the dark took him back again.

He said, "We don't need one."

It was an old confidence that made him say it. Not a *good* confidence, not always, but he couldn't deny that saying things similar to *We don't need one* had, in the past, made for some transformative moments in his life. *We should try this*, to a classmate in a group project at Rensselaer; *I could draw that*, to the professor who eventually became his business partner; *It'll work*, to a team of investors who were all at least twenty years older than him.

He could see now that something about Layla Bailey brought it out in him: her on the airplane floor, her hotel room door. A river cruise, a department store, a garden ballroom.

A kiss on the street, and a sculpture that said too much about him.

She made him want to *do* things.

He was always *doing* things, ever since he first saw her.

But this time—with the whole entire day and the whole entire city open to them, with last night's bad decisions still haunting his body—his confidence pretty quickly abandoned him. Sure, he was pretty good—pretty practiced—at walking without a real plan, like he'd done last night after he'd left her, but that was more . . . that was kind of a stomping and breathing situation. A fully alone situation.

With her by his side, with her hurt from last night still so close to the surface, he'd need to do something different.

It helped that, at first, she struggled, too.

"I had this spreadsheet," she said, still sounding kind of stunned, after only a block or so of him pretending to lead them somewhere specific. "I could pull it up on my phone."

"No phones," he said, which was not really a demand you could meaningfully make of another person in the twenty-first century, especially in a city you didn't live in, but she didn't object.

And so they came to an unspoken agreement. A slower pace, a lack of direction, no real meaningful knowledge of any one thing they looked at. He thought it felt like training, like two puppies on a walk, a long leash letting them wander a little, but no running wild, their bodies always close. *Can we stop here?* one of them would say, and the answer was always *Yes*.

Can I look at this? Do you smell that? Do you want to try one of these? Should we go over there?

Yes

Yes

Yes

Yes

Like that, they were aimless. They got buttery, folded-over crepes from a place with dark red walls and wood crates mounted behind the register, filled with bottles of wine and oils and jars of jam. They took side streets, avoiding thoroughfares, occasionally coming across a perfectly framed view of part of the Eiffel Tower between buildings that neither of them took pictures of. They crossed a mostly nondescript bridge over the Seine, swapping a knowing smile as they both tracked a huge, slow boat filled with people on the top deck. They went into bookstores, English and French, into shops with macarons and pastries and chocolates that might as well have been museums for the way they were filled with edible art; they sat in front of a giant sculpture of a hand holding what looked to Griffin like limp, half-formed balloon animals. They went into a massive domed building with columns and finials and winged figures over an imposing arched doorway, flanked with gold, and Layla laughed at how he said, "This is the *Petit* one?" and then they didn't even look at any of the place's obvious treasures anyway; they just drifted to a courtyard with palm trees that seemed to belong to a whole other world, and Layla made Griffin try the too-sweet hot chocolate she ordered from the café there, more whipped cream than cocoa. She broke the no-phone rule, but only to photograph the floor beneath them—tiny tiles turned into swirls and diagonals.

Later, they walked by a line of people on a pristine street, and Layla—bolder by then, more openly curious by then—asked someone what it was for. Another museum, of course another museum, this one about clothes, and he watched her expression transform with interest, so yeah, he took out his fucking phone for that—two tickets with a few taps, even though they had to wait two and a half hours to come back for their own line-up time.

But there was plenty more wandering to do anyway. Window displays, cheese shops, produce stands, places where you could stop and say, *This is so different from home*, but still feel oddly comforted to see a plain old banana in a city as beautiful as this.

He dreaded it, a little, having an appointment—too close to an itinerary, too close to what they were supposed to be doing today, had they stuck with the wedding party. But once they were ushered through the glass doors at their assigned time, he let it go—Layla's eyes lighting as she looked up at a spiral staircase that rose through a three-story glass display, a rainbow arrangement of dresses and handbags and shoes and hats. Obviously, Griffin himself had no interest in clothes, other than making sure they didn't touch him the wrong way, but he could see right away it was different for Layla. If she noticed the horde of tourists that staged dramatic, social-media-ready photos on the staircase, irritatingly slowing the foot traffic up the steps, she didn't betray any annoyance. She kept her eyes moving over the rainbow, the same way she kept her eyes on every set piece they eventually passed—mannequins in puffy skirts and tight jackets and dramatic, swooping hats, gowns made of what looked like flower petals or the falling parts of the brightest stars. At one point, they entered a two-story room that was clearly meant to be a culmination: music playing, the kind he imagined he should've danced with her to in that grand garden ballroom, light softly changing and projecting images over the ceiling and walls. He looked at gowns he wouldn't ever be able to describe except to say that Layla gazed at them with pure wonder, and all he'd been able to think about was why he'd never seen her in something, *anything* like this, why she wasn't right now wearing that gauzy white dress with the smallest pleats all over the full skirts, like little envelopes waiting to be opened, revealing her secrets.

The best part was after, when she talked and talked about why she liked it, but all in the form of questions to him: *Did you like the way—? Did you see how—? Did you notice that—?*

Mostly, the answer to everything was no, or at least, *I only liked the way you liked it*, but by that point, he was so well settled in to how comfortable it was to be asked. All day, it was asking each other—easier and easier, further and further beyond what was right in front of them for their wandering. She would ask him, *Are you still okay?* or *Should we sit for a while?* and it didn't make him snap in frustration or embarrassment. He would ask her, *Did you go up to the top of the Eiffel Tower before?* or *Have you ever tried one of these?* and it didn't make her look wistful or heartbroken.

The answers, too, were easier and easier to give. He told her about the pain scale, even told her when he got to a six so they could stop, finding a bench in the Jardin du Palais Royal. He rubbed openly at the worst of his contracture scars, the one that tracked from below his left ass cheek all the way to the outside of his knee, while she told him about her family, or rather, her lack of one: her mother, dead in a car accident when Layla was only two, so young that Layla didn't have a single memory of her; her father, distant and ambitious, closer in temperament and appearance to the son he'd already had from his first, failed marriage, and only truly notable as a parent for the way he'd always arranged good nannies and babysitters for Layla; a half brother, Vaughn, almost a decade older and a physician like Layla, but a neurosurgeon, relentlessly busy and obligatory in his contact with her, a brother who "probably" loved her but who never had time for her.

And the MacKenzies, the family she'd come to think of as her own.

If they ran up against a barricade—him, willing to talk about what he did for his pain but not what had caused it; and her, willing to mention her divorce but not who chose it or why—they simply bounced off it, back to safer streets, wandering again.

By dusk, they'd been together for hours, still directionless except for how they kept drifting in the direction of each other, letting those long leashes tangle, their bodies more than keeping close now. His fingers set gently on her spine as she stepped into another shop, her foot moving idly against his when they sat at another bistro, their shoulders and the backs of their hands constantly brushing as they made their way along the river again, where the bouquinistes were closing up their dark green stalls for the day.

Every small touch felt the same as shoving that pretend door he'd imagined this morning further open. Like together, they'd made it so they were both now standing on the threshold of a heaven he could not have possibly imagined three days ago, and all Griffin wanted in the world was to keep pushing through.

He thought of last night—that dark street, that other doorway—and felt the old confidence rise up in him again.

He would be able to do it this time, after this day.

Stay with her, keep kissing her, no touch too much.

He would not mess it up this time. He would not hurt her.

But then, Layla stopped.

Right along one of those gray stone walls that lined the Seine, and somehow—her posture, her eyes not meeting his—he knew not to touch her, accidentally or otherwise. He moved to stand beside her, a slice of space between them, and stared out at the water.

In his periphery, he could see those fucking bell towers again, lit up against a dark lavender sky, another place of pretend coming back to haunt him.

"Tomorrow," she said, and he swallowed, nodded once, though he didn't think she was looking at him. He nodded more for himself, a reminder, a coming-back-to-earth. Scanning his body, he still only felt pain in a mundane way: his feet achy in his shoes from walking, like a regular tourist; four out of ten on the thigh and knee; some itchiness along the ragged terrain of his torso; no weird heat or tingling or electric currents coming from a place he couldn't point to.

That was a victory, he knew.

No crossing into heaven, but no going back to the gates of hell, at least.

"All the other guests arrive," she continued. "It'll really feel like a wedding now. Best-man, big-sister stuff."

He nodded again. But he couldn't say anything, not yet. He was busy packing himself up, a green stall shuttering, vintage postcards from his life that he'd taken out for Layla to see tucked away again.

Bad confidence, he thought, scolding himself. What had his fucking confidence ever gotten him, really, but too close to the sun? He couldn't ever *really* stay with her. He couldn't ever avoid hurting her.

He could never predict what touch would be too much.

He shouldn't have ever let himself wander so far from what he'd come here to do: see Michael settled, finally. See Michael happy.

One hurt he'd always wanted to see healed.

"There's some kind of spa thing in the morning," she was saying, maybe packing herself up, too, in her mind already getting out the spreadsheet that she'd admitted, only an hour or so ago, also had all her carefully chosen outfits listed, the ones that would help her—what a joke, to think it was possible—"blend in to the background."

For the first time in probably a half decade, Griffin thought of this pain management specialist he once went to, a six-foot-five former basketball player who had a wait list a mile long. Griffin had walked into the two-hours-away clinic for his long-awaited appointment and had seen all the state-of-the-art equipment—ergonomic machines, water tanks, massage tables that moved with the press of a button, nerve stimulation kits at every station—and thought, *Give me the works*.

But instead of *the works*, he'd been forced to sit in an uncomfortable chair for thirty minutes while this man talked earnestly to him about meditation, the untapped power of his mind, about how the rest of Griffin's life would be about honoring the days when he felt good, and not allowing himself to forget about them on the days when he felt like he wanted to die.

Fucking fine, he thought, beaming a belated apology to the doctor he'd never gone back to. *I should have kept doing the meditation. I should have learned it all, just so I could eventually remember this one day in Paris with Layla Bailey.*

"Griff," she said, and he let his eyes close, bracing himself for the end of this.

He was pretty sure they were only two bridges from the turnoff toward the hotel. He'd go back to his room, check in with Michael; he'd go back to being a bad best man in the usual aloof Griff way, instead of the entirely-absent-for-an-entire-day way. He'd sit down at that weird little desk in his room and try to remember every single place they'd wandered to today; he'd pretend he was carving it all into the stone wall of his tower.

He opened his eyes, and faced her. He would not put her in a car alone this time. He'd walk with her. Two bridges, a turnoff, the hotel lobby, and an elevator he'd been in with her before. He'd manage.

"Good day," he managed. Then he added, "Thanks," as though she was his paid tour guide.

He would not write this part down, obviously.

Twelve hours ago, she probably would've rolled her eyes at him. She would've scowled and said the sort of cutting thing he'd only ever heard her say to him. That would have been welcome in its own way, he supposed, because at least he would still have the truth of her.

But she didn't do either of those things. She looked at him, calm and steady. She broke bad news like a good doctor did; he'd give her that.

Two bridges, a turnoff—

"The thing is, though," she said, "it's not tomorrow yet."

Chapter Twenty-One

She'd startled him.

She could tell that now, after a whole day of being with him, uninterrupted: Griffin Testa was not, in fact, a column of mysterious smoke that muddled your mind, not a fae prince who stole a part of your soul with a kiss, not a black-bronze statue that broke your heart in half.

Not even, really, *the best man*.

He was just a *man*.

A complicated man. Bold but cautious, demanding but flexible, stubborn but still curious. He would say things like, *No phones*, but then he would—instead of demanding to stop—just slow his steps outside a shop window displaying model trains, waiting for you to say, *You like those?* He'd say, *We're going in here*, when you were halfway to starving but overwhelmed with where to stop and eat, but then he'd wordlessly switch plates with you when it was clear you wished you'd ordered the same as him. He would declare that he had no interest in fashion, and then—like Fitz, not that Layla would ever make the comparison aloud—would read every display text he could in a museum devoted almost exclusively to clothing and accessories, seemingly memorizing every detail so he could mention them to you later.

He had a face you could read, if you really paid attention—if you let yourself stop worrying about what happened on the one side, if you recognized that the tense set of his jaw and the straight line of his mouth were distractions from the dark expressiveness in his eyes. There, you could see all sorts of things. Confusion, and then delight, when he bit into a raspberry macaron. Loving respect when he spoke about his mother; a false, flippant dismissiveness when he talked about his background in product design. Leashed but feral frustration when you told him about your own family: the one you were born to, and the one you married into.

Grudging defeat when something started to hurt. Grim determination when he was trying to ignore it.

Desire when you got close in the right way. When you lingered against him, nothing sudden: light touches on the left side, if at all, more freedom on the right.

Hope when you slowed your steps along the Seine, when the sky was Paris-purple, lights turning on and the city transforming into something else: not a wandering place now, but a destination place—a specific spot, a reservation, a fresh red lip, a set of people you were going to meet.

And then, when you tried to say—clumsily, okay, you've never tried to say something *quite* like this before—what destination *you* might have in mind, before time ran out on the best day you can remember having, maybe ever . . .

Disappointment. Sadness. Loss.

And now, in trying to be *less* clumsy, Layla had startled him—her *it's not tomorrow yet* making him blink and stare in disbelief, in whiplashed surprise.

She took a breath, shifting on her feet, and thought of last night, tucked into that stone archway, into the privacy Griffin had stolen for them. She could try something like that, something stark and stripped down, whatever tonight's version of *It made me think of you* might be.

I wanted to invite you back to my hotel room, or *I think I might die if you don't kiss me again*.

But no. It was more complicated than that now.

And she was desperate to tell him why.

"When I came here before," she said finally, and there—from startled to something else, the frustration again, anytime she got close to something about Jamie, or the MacKenzies.

She liked it. It was complicated.

"When I came here before," she repeated, "I was trying so hard to become something. Some*one*, I guess. Someone who belonged here. Someone's wife. A MacKenzie."

He made a noise, deep in his throat—a rumble that made the *I think I might die* feeling come back, a pulse between her legs that had her wanting to take a step toward him. But even with the rumble, his eyes on hers were still cautious, holding something of himself back.

"I wanted to know Paris like they do," she continued. "I wanted to love it like they do. To make their memories of it mine. Their favorite places would be mine, too. It was another way to be part of their family."

He came closer, his eyes softer. He knew the contours, at least, of this wound now—knew what it meant to her, to feel like she was part of a family, when her own had been so incomplete and fractured and distant. He knew that the Paris of her honeymoon—the Louvre with someone who'd seen it *so many* times, the best restaurants from the MacKenzie family lore, the tempting, clichéd souvenirs she felt too embarrassed to buy—could be full of terrible pressure.

Too much to see, too beautiful, too sophisticated, too delicious. "But today, I just loved it. I love it like *I* do."

They both blinked when she said those last two words: the vow they'd come all this way to witness, and the one she'd once made with someone else. No covenant now, no becoming something other than what she was.

He came even closer. Like this, she had to tilt her head back to hold his gaze; she had to lift her eyes to see everything there. To see how he *understood* her.

"Layla Bailey," he said quietly, his breath drifting across her lips like a sealing kiss, as good as any pronouncement.

She nodded.

Desire, hope: She could see it in him again, or maybe now that he was closer she could *feel* it, warming her straight through. She wanted to say the hotel thing, the *I might die* thing, but there was still the trepidation in him, keeping him slightly apart.

"Tomorrow," she said again, hoping to go back to that moment where he'd turned himself off, to explain better this time. To get rid of that trepidation. "I know I'll need to be Emily's sister again. But for tonight, I was wondering if—"

"I'm afraid," he said, cutting her off. Airplane-aisle sharp. A white-hot blade through the warm night air.

But now she knew that, too, was complicated. The first time she heard him speak, his cutting *Be quiet*. The *Don't tell Michael you saw me* moment in the elevator; the *Let's talk about something* in a candlelit restaurant.

All of it, a version of this. All of it to carve around this truth.

I'm afraid.

Slowly, she extended her left hand—not much distance between them, not much at all to reach him. She set the tip of her index finger against the knob of bone in his right wrist, the easiest place to touch with his hands still in his pockets. She let it linger there, watched his eyelids lower, his nostrils flare gently. This could not be like last night: This could not start with his angry, desperate impulses, could not end with her careless, grabbing hands.

This had to be different.

She moved. The pad of her finger sliding down that knob, to the outside of his hand. She felt that touch all the way up her arm, a delicious, warm tingling that was entirely unrecognizable to her from such a subtle movement.

Then he moved, too: pulling his hand gently from his pocket, as though he wouldn't risk jostling that one point of contact—her finger resting against his skin.

When his fingers were free, he followed her lead—he moved with intention. One slow twist of his wrist to capture her finger, cupping it first against the pad of his warm palm, then catching it, hooking it with his pinky, using it to turn her hand, palm faced up. He curled his pinky around her index finger, dragging it slowly around and into the space between it and her middle finger, then across the faint calluses at the base of each digit.

Her pulse thrummed. In her neck, in her belly, between her legs. *Everywhere*.

When he slid that finger between her pinky and ring finger, her knees wobbled. When he braided the rest of their fingers together—the most careful, erotic handhold she'd ever experienced in her entire life, she had to tip her head down, dizzy and unstable.

And when he took another step forward, she rested her forehead on his sternum, feeling the space beneath throb with the beat of his heart.

He lowered his head to speak, and Layla held her breath as she realized how he'd done it: his left side, his scarred side, against her hair. The crooked part of his lips against her ear.

"You don't know how bad I want to go through this door with you," he said.

What door? she thought, because the thing was, they were close enough now that she could *feel* how bad. Could feel, against her belly, the hard ridge of him, insistent and irresistible.

But then she remembered: the sculpture garden. When he said the word *heaven*. How it felt for him to be with her.

"But if I hurt you again—" He broke off, and she lifted her head—slowly, she knew she had to move slowly—to meet his eyes. She'd thought his fear was for himself: the pain, *The Three Shades*, *The Gates of Hell*.

But those dark eyes on her, the knife-edge of his voice like a caress now . . .

The fear was for her.

She thought it was almost all for her now.

"I can't ruin this day for you," he finished. "Not after everything you just told me about what it means to you. If I get—if what happens last night happens again . . ."

He trailed off, his throat bobbing, his eyes closing as his length pulsed desperately against her. She was, without realizing it, stroking her thumb up and back along his. She was thinking a thousand complicated things as she watched him struggle through this: that it *would* hurt if it happened again, but also it would somehow hurt worse if nothing happened at all; that he was right that it would be horrible to have the day end with his pain, but also the truth was, he *was* what this day meant to her, he *was* the day; that she'd told him *it's not tomorrow yet*, but also she thought that when tomorrow dawned she would still feel this exact way, forever snapped out of the post-divorce fog of dully moving through her days according to a schedule—

"What if," she said, an idea cutting through the complication, simple and beautiful and inevitable, "we do what we did today?"

He furrowed his brow, frowned down at her.

"Keep . . . walking?" he said, so disbelieving that she had to bite her lip to keep from smiling.

He lifted the hand that wasn't still holding hers, set the pad of his thumb on her chin and pulled gently, watching intently as he freed her lip, as she ran her tongue quickly across it.

"Wandering," she whispered. "Like we did today. We go back to my room and we . . . wander."

She held her breath as she waited, hoping he would understand—that he would play back the day and know what she meant.

Do you like—?

Can we stop—?

Want to try—?

He moved his thumb again. Across her cheek, behind her earlobe, along a cord of her neck until he reached the edge of her summer turtleneck, which she absolutely hated right now, and so did he, judging by his huff of frustration, his redirection—across the line of her jaw, back to her bottom lip. He pressed lightly, right in the center, and watched, transfixed, as it plumped back into its natural shape.

She *would* die if he didn't kiss her again.

If he didn't say yes.

He said, "No."

But also, he kissed her. A soft brush of his mouth against hers, a slip of his tongue against her lip. He whispered his real answer against her mouth.

"My room," he said.

* * *

When they got there, he got her against the door again.

Not pressing against her, not yet, but only caging her in: one hand on either side of her tipped-back head, a papery crinkle on one side as the small bag he carried pressed against the wood. Both of them were breathing heavily—not from the trek back, but from the exertion of this interminable wait, as though all the hours between their kiss last night and this hotel room tonight had squeezed together and settled into their lungs as they walked the remaining way, as they stopped to duck through a set of glass doors beneath a lit-up green cross, as they moved quickly through the aisles to find what they needed, as they finally made it through the threshold of the hotel and crossed the lobby to the elevators.

As they rode up, side by side, staring at each other in the mirrored surface.

Her cheeks pink, her lips restless for the pressure of his mouth.

His eyes dark and roaming, as if he was making a plan.

Now that they were finally, truly alone, he leaned into her, set the right side of his face against her cheek, scraped her deliciously with his stubble, and breathed her in. He said, "I hate this shirt," and dropped his head to catch at the high collar with his teeth, pulling it off her neck and stretching the cloth away from her skin for a cooling, freeing second before letting it snap back against her.

She thought she might slide down the door.

"I'll take it off," she said, but he shook his head, his forehead against her shoulder, his warm breath pulsing through the fabric of her shirt, making her nipples peak and ache. She felt strangely, unfamiliarly sensitized, like she knew now what the lightning bolt effect of him was for—to turn her into this, to change the way her skin experienced every touch, even the indirect ones. His eyes on her, his breath on her, his mouth moving while he spoke.

"*I'll* take it off," he said. "In a minute."

Then he lifted his head and kissed her. Not soft this time: all the pressure she'd been desperate for, his tongue licking into her, his teeth back on that bottom lip sometimes in a way that told her, without words, that he loved that part of her, that he could not get enough of that part of her, that he was not yet ready to move on to all the other parts that had always seemed, before, to be the end goal of sex.

Layla Bailey, she thought as she kissed him back, triumphant and happy and more aroused than she could ever remember being in her life.

She lifted her hands, desperate to touch him—*Griffin Testa*, his name like an overlay of her own—but caught herself, her fingers curling into her palms. He would have to stop kissing her if he wanted this wandering to be mutual; he would have to give her enough air to ask *if he liked, if he wanted to try*; he would need to be able to say if he needed to stop.

He noticed, even through the kiss, dropping his hands from the door, the bag from the pharmacy hitting the floor. With his right hand—was it shaking, maybe?—he circled one of her wrists, more slowly bringing up his left to take the other. She knew that now—his right hand always first to touch something, his left tentative. She wanted to say, *I noticed that; you can trust me; you can tell me; I'll make this wandering work for us both.*

But he spoke first—against her lips, a soft secret.

"I need to build up my confidence first."

She leaned her head back against the door, looked long at him. He let her do that more now—no ball cap, no turning one side of his face away, and while she wouldn't interrupt him in this moment, she made a promise to herself to tell him later: *You're so handsome. I've always thought so. From the very first second I saw the whole of you.*

"If you'll let me see you. Touch you. Find out what makes you feel good, first. That's what I need, before I—" He broke off, dropped his left hand from her to curl around the hem of his untucked shirt.

Before he let *her* see him, he meant.

She searched his eyes. His gaze on her was the perfect mixture—pleading and honest, but hot and hungry, too.

"Can I touch you?" she whispered back.

"Right side, for now," he said, against her mouth. Another kiss. A press of his hips into her, their joined hands trapped between his hardness and her stomach.

"Not too much touching this yet," he added gruffly, pressing his length once against her hand, but when she snaked her tongue out, she could taste the shape of that Versailles quirk on one side of his mouth. "I gotta be able to focus."

He lifted his head, looking at her again, waiting for her answer. One hand gripping hers, the other still fisted in his shirt. Intense and beautiful. A column of smoke clearing her mind, a prince bargaining for a piece of her soul, a sculpture holding out his own broken heart.

A man who'd helped her get herself back today.

"Okay," she said.

He moved fast then—breaking his hold on her hand to grab her hip, to pull her off the door and onto his mouth. He spun her, still kissing her, backing her into the darkened room, a pale glow coming from one side, but Layla didn't bother looking around. She had her hand on him now: right side, like he'd asked, beneath his shirt, on the warm skin of his ribs, her fingers fitting into each space, his pulse drumming insistently there, too. She had the dim sense of the room's hugeness, of how long it took for her calves to hit the edge of a mattress, of how the sound of their breathing echoed, of how, when he gently nudged her to sit, there was an expanse on either side of her, so much larger than the bed in her room.

But dim was the extent of it, because he had his fingers curled into the hem of her shirt; he was tugging it up, her arms lifting wordlessly, her neck stretching as he pulled it over her head, her hair lifting and then falling in what was probably a disastrous, staticky tangle around her shoulders.

Except Griffin didn't look at her like she was disastrous or tangled. He looked at her like she was the only thing worth looking at in this whole city, his eyes tracking over her collarbones, her flushed chest, her simple, beige bra that was, at the moment, no match for her tight nipples. He held the summer turtleneck between his hands like he was about to tear it in half, and honestly, she wouldn't have minded. She hated it, too, for all the hours it'd kept him from seeing her like this.

He dropped to his knees, the shirt falling to his side, and she could admit, there was a hiccup there—her hand reaching out automatically, her voice saying *"Griff,"* in a sort of scolding way, her mind on the contracture scarring he told her about, his limp late in the day before they rested, his hand rubbing methodically up and down his leg as they sat on a park bench.

He said, as he gripped her waist, fingers flexing, "I'll tell you if I need to stop," and she nodded, murmured "Me, too," and that was good; that was true and also more mutual.

They were on equal footing here, the way they had been all day.

She toed off her shoes and her socks as he hooked his thumbs into her waistband, as he lifted her enough to slide her pants down her legs, his head bending as he kissed along the top of her thigh, her knee, and oh, *god*, his hair, the way the ends of his hair trailed along her—

"You're so soft," he said against her skin, and she set a hand on his head, right side, her fingers running through the silky, dark strands.

She said, "You are, too," and he curved his mouth against her, dragged his teeth against her inner thigh, which made her jolt with pleasure. She could somehow sense him filing that away, keeping track, getting answers to the questions he didn't need to ask out loud.

He came back to her mouth, his lips on hers harder, one hand on the side of her neck as he led her farther back onto the bed, rising up and over her in all his dark, soft, sinuous heat. Once he had her there—in the middle of this huge bed she didn't think she could find either edge of, the crisp white duvet beneath her, her skin bared to him and her limbs restless with wanting to be covered in him—that was when he *truly* started to wander.

Her body a map he was making only in his mind, his mouth and hands surveying her—stopping, *staying*, when she gasped, when she arched, when she whispered his name. He said *I like this* at the join of her neck and shoulder, told her how good she smelled there, told her he could *live* there, except there were other places he wanted to see, too. He turned her when he wanted to unhook her bra, got distracted by the line of her spine, showed her a new place there halfway down—she could not remember a single thing she knew, no matter that she had never been anything other than top of her med school class in anatomy—that sparked with feeling when his tongue licked across it, her whole body still buzzing from it when he turned her over again, when he stared down at her breasts and groaned desperately, lowering his head and letting his damp forehead rest against her sternum for a few perfect seconds, his breaths deliberate and determined while he got himself back under control, readying himself to wander again.

New paths, then: her hand back in his hair, down the back of his neck, along the ropy, strong shoulder covered by his shirt while he explored. The outer curve of her breast, the highest crest of her hip bone, the crease above her thigh where the elastic of her underwear rested, apparently waiting all day, all her *life*, to be soothed by the breath he blew across it. She thought vaguely, indistinctly of another night in a Paris hotel room; she thought not of Jamie but of herself, of how badly she wanted to be *claimed*—a youthful desire, a lonely one, nothing Jamie ever could really understand anyway.

She thought of how this was nothing like that. She thought of being discovered, not claimed; she thought of being *Layla Bailey*, of lying beneath a man who could say he was afraid, who could build his confidence not by possessing her body but by visiting it, *learning* it, *liking* it, wanting to wander all night in it . . .

He licked her—right at the wet seam between her legs, and she couldn't think of anything, *anything* else. A groaning, famished licking, and then sucking, like he hadn't spent half his day tasting some of the best, sweetest things in the world, like he had never tasted anything else at all. She nearly came off the bed from it, the single-mindedness of it, the whole-bodyness of it—hers, but also his; she could *feel* that it was also his, and she could see the way he'd let go of something within him, both his hands hard against her now, holding her open, both his shoulders tight against her thighs, his hips pressed tight to the mattress, moving in time with her own.

At some point, probably right about the time he slid two fingers inside her, right around the time she cried out his name—stretching it and transforming it into a swear word she could not ever remember saying out loud at a time like this—she realized she'd lost track of one of her hands. One was still in his hair, but the other was on what she could reach of his shoulder—over his shirt on that forbidden left side. She jerked it away, her curse turning into a gasping, "I'm sorry!" but he didn't stop—he only lifted his left hand and gripped hers with it, no caution now, and guided it back to his body.

This time, to his skin. To the side he worried so much about. His jaw, his neck—the whorls of scarring beneath her palm and fingers meaning nothing to her beyond trust, beyond permission, an invitation to start making a map of her own. The thought of it, of this first indication that his confidence was building, that he would be able to get to that promised next step with her, made her pleasure ratchet higher. Soon she would be able to touch him, to explore him, to make him feel good the way he was making her feel right now...

She whimpered and squirmed beneath him, desperate to get there, because oh, *god*, he was so good at wandering, so good that he couldn't *help* but find the very best destination, and he knew exactly where—

He curled his fingers.

He sucked harder.

And oh—

Oh, he got her there.

Chapter Twenty-Two

She came like a city of light, like a tower of sparkling gold.

From his spot between her legs—a heaven he would not have ever been able to fathom—he watched it happen, looked up at the rolling crest of her body, her chest heaving, her head tipping back to expose the long line of her neck, her hair spread beneath her. Something that made you stop and stare, awestruck and also somehow relieved—this big, beautiful thing you always wanted to see was as good as, better than, you ever imagined it could be.

He could *feel* it, of course—the way she pulsed rhythmically around his fingers, how that pulse echoed at the base of his cock, even though that part of him wasn't anywhere near her. And he could taste it, too—a rush of that same tangy sweetness he'd been trying to get his fill of for the last few best fucking minutes of his life.

But watching it was something else.

He waited while she came down from it, his fingers eventually sliding from her but his mouth resting on her mound where she held him, a hand in his hair, like she needed the pressure—like holding him there prolonged the light that flashed and flickered out of her. He could not help it—he licked at her again, seeing if he could spark her like this another time, but she curled her fingers, catching at his hair tightly, a scolding that had him shoving his hips against the mattress again, his own need asserting itself in a way he'd been able to hold off while he'd been memorizing her, meditating on her.

"Griffin," she said, breathlessly full-naming him, which had the same effect as the hair-holding, so he lifted his mouth, raised himself up and over her, bending his head to kiss her again—a filthy, wet kiss that she moaned into, and he thought, *Layla Bailey, Layla Bailey, this is what you taste like, this is you without being fucking* amicable; *this is you when you let yourself feel something real.*

She tipped her head back as though she heard him, arching again, her now-freed lips pressing together, a moan of what sounded like frustration rumbling behind them. He thought she might say, *Fuck me*, which would have been good, would have set him on some kind of autopilot mode. He could get up, grab the bag he'd left on the floor. One flick of his fingers over the button on his pants, his zipper lowered. Shoving down the cloth just enough to get inside her. He'd been with women that way since the fire—fast and focused once they were past foreplay.

Good for them, but at best narrow for him.

But of course, Layla didn't say *Fuck me*. Not after everything that had been between them before this.

She said, "How's your confidence now?" and curled her free hand into his shirt, telling him without words what she wanted.

Not fast, not so focused.

Wandering and *real-feeling*, exactly what she'd let him have of her.

"Pretty good," he said, shocked to realize it wasn't really a lie, not after all that light she'd let pour all over him. "Especially if I can get you to come like that again."

She had her eyes on him, all over him—his hair probably a mess from her fingers, his mouth wet, his pulse a hammer at the side of his neck. If he took off his shirt, his pants, she would see it all, parts of him that didn't look different with sex: skin that didn't sweat or flush with pleasure, skin that might respond all wrong to her touch or not respond at all, skin that he knew would feel strange to her, inelastic and alien.

"You probably can," she said. "I'm—I can do that. I'm lucky. I have this toy—"

"Oh, *Christ*," he said, his whole brain scrambling away from his scars with the thought of it—Layla with a sex toy between her legs, lighting up a room all on her own, multiple times—and he pushed off her to stand at the foot of the bed, lifting his right arm to grab at the back of his shirt and pull it off, tossing it somewhere to the side.

But even an image of Layla getting herself off couldn't quite stop the flood of panic he felt when the air hit him. First, there was the familiar sensation of unevenness, that desperation to do a scan. *What hurts, what's starting to hurt. What kind of pain, what number out of ten.*

(Shoulder, knee, ass cheek, maybe also shin. Dull pain, one buzzing spot at the back of the thigh, four out of ten now.)

Second, there was the not-very-familiar sensation of letting someone see. Scars but not the kind most people pictured, not even really like the kind you saw in the movies, the ones with heroic combat veterans or comic book villains dipped in acid or whatever. Griff's scars were worse than that, more confusing than that. There was the part of his arm—his whole bicep, really—that almost looked decorative, an inexplicable pattern baked in when you got close. There was a strangely untouched patch on his elbow, one of his most pain-reactive spots, and then the shock of his forearm, bald and gnarled and multicolored, mostly dead-feeling. There was the place on his pectoral deformed by a skin graft that hadn't gone well, a bad infection after, an ugly, unignorable dent where the muscle gave way to his armpit. There was his abdomen, his side, part of his back. Nothing to be said about it, really, nothing to describe it. It was a city destroyed, not quite flattened but reduced to rubble.

But Layla Bailey wasn't any someone.

She pushed herself up, one elbow, then two, one of her bent legs falling open to the bed, and if she meant to distract him it fucking worked, at least for a second. God, he could *smell* her, what he'd done to her. He wanted that smell all over him, and soon.

She didn't pretend not to see it all, but also, she didn't make any of the faces he dreaded most, not a furrowed-brow doctor face or a wet-eyed pity face, not even one of those *oh, sorry, I looked by accident* ashamed faces. She looked at him whole, both sides, and she let herself be both sides, too. A person who'd come all over his face, her eyes hungry and her chest and face all pink, but also a person who could look straight at him, who could reckon with the ways he was different.

"You're like—*fit*," she said, and he breathed out a laugh, relieved at what she'd decided to comment on directly. A good confidence builder, even if she did sound surprised by it. He reached for the button on his pants.

"I do a lot of fucking yoga," he said, which was true, but also he didn't want to talk about it. "What kind of toy?"

She smiled and sat all the way up as he lowered his zipper. Set her hand on his stomach, right side, running her soft hand over the ridges of muscle there, her lashes lowered.

"Just a toy," she said, a teasing, false sheepishness in her voice. She waited until he hooked his thumbs into his waistbands—pants and boxer briefs, both, might as well do it all at once—to add, "It goes inside."

He practically tripped over himself to get naked. Shoes, socks, pants, briefs, all of it came off in a balled-together bundle. He did not care about his hip, his leg. Wasn't any worse than what she'd already seen. If she had that toy in her hotel room they should've stopped there first. The picture in his mind now, with her legs open like that . . .

"What's it made of?" he growled, not waiting for her answer as he turned back toward the door, strode over to get the pharmacy bag. He was pulling it open as he stalked back to her, stopping at the foot of the bed and tossing the box up by the pillows. If he thought of it, he wouldn't have stopped; he would've kept moving, climbing back over her right away so there couldn't be too much looking.

But he didn't think of it. He thought of how she hadn't answered. How bad he wanted to know.

And how she was doing a different sort of looking now.

"What's it—?" she repeated, obviously distracted.

"Made of," he finished for her, setting his hand beneath her chin. Tipping her face up.

She licked her lips. He tried to make the breath he blew out discreet, but honest to fucking god, that mouth being so close to his—

"It's not that big," she said.

He looked down at her. Tried not to laugh.

About this one thing, he did not lack confidence.

"Um, my toy, I mean!" she yelped. "It's . . . I mean, what I was trying to say was, you are much . . . well! You're very—"

He pulled her up, one hand under her chin, the other beneath her elbow. Kneeling on the bed like this, with him standing, they were almost eye to eye. She shuffled closer, pressed all her bare skin along his, and if it hurt anywhere, it wasn't too much. He kissed her, moved one of his hands to the outer edge of her breast, which he'd already learned was sensitive.

"Big," she whispered, when he gave her enough space, and he bit her lip.

"What'll work?" he asked her, between kisses that were growing messier, wetter, hotter. "To get you there again?"

She *hmm*ed against the edge of his mouth, and he clutched her, shaking his head slightly—that was risky, that kind of vibration; that got his wires crossed. But now, she wasn't so tentative with him—she just backed off, moved over to his right side, kissed along his neck.

"If it's deep," she finally said, which made all the remaining blood leave his brain. "And if I—can I be on top?"

Fucking yes, he thought, but instead of saying it he moved, taking hold of her hand as he shifted to one side of the bed, liking the way she half crawled to keep up. He was so hard now, his head so full of pictures of her, that he didn't notice how the bedcovers felt beneath his bare skin, didn't notice the pillows beneath his back when he leaned onto them. He patted his right thigh and watched her straddle him slowly, her body already so knowing even though he hadn't noticed her doing the same study of him as he'd done of her. Left wrist on his right shoulder to steady herself, more weight on her left leg as she lowered onto his lap.

"It's all right," he said, gripping her hips, evening her out, groaning when that wet, soft part of her slid along his shaft. She moved once, up and back, her breath hitching, and he yanked her closer, getting his mouth on one of her breasts, criminally neglected so far.

"Oh," she breathed, leaning into his mouth, wetter again already, and he grabbed for the box of condoms.

He'd barely dragged it toward them when she took it from him, backing up so that his lips and tongue lost contact with her, which made him press his fingertips into her hips in frustration. But that was nothing compared to her, the way she tore at that box—no patience Layla Bailey, no *pleasantness* Layla Bailey—desperate and direct and fully herself when she got one free, tearing the package and taking his cock in hand, her tongue peeking out as she rolled it on.

He sucked in a breath through his teeth. He thought, *Her hand on me is electric, not hell electric but heaven electric; every gate here is to heaven.* Until now, what kept him from coming—in his pants while he ate at her, while she came on his face, on her skin when she talked about that toy, when she looked at his cock—was an iron will he'd forged inside hell, a vigilance he exercised over his body at all times for all these years.

But here, in this hot heaven, it all melted away.

He said, "Layla, please. Let me in there. Put your hand back in my hair and take—"

She did. One hand in his hair, the other guiding him to her entrance. Just the tip, at first, while she gasped and got used to his size, and he could not describe what happened inside him as she lowered herself: an awareness of his body that was so different from what he was used to that he had to tip his head back to rest on the headboard, to watch her through slitted, watering eyes he didn't want her to see—because it wasn't pain, he did not want her to think it was pain.

But with her moving like that—her tight heat around him, her weight on his lap, her eyes lowered to where they were joined, he would never be able to say all the things it was. Relief but with desperation at the edges—to get deeper, to go harder, whenever she was ready. Pride pleasantly blunted by gratitude, by the knowledge that it wasn't really him, it was *her*; she was the key to this working, everything about her from the first time he saw her. Insane pleasure, pleasure like he'd never felt, sitting alongside familiar hurt—that fucking left leg, that vibrating elbow that had reacted to him squeezing at her—but it didn't make him feel even a little afraid.

He was a tower now. Burned out once but getting rebuilt.

He pulled her closer, shoved her down harder onto him as he did, telling her without words he was okay, he was done with anything tentative. She moaned, her hips rolling with intention now, her breasts rubbing against his chest, and *holy shit*, if she didn't come soon—

Well. If she didn't come soon, he would, and then he'd get this condom off and go back to licking her, getting his hands on her, making her come another way until they could do this again. He would do anything she wanted; he would not rest until he got to feel her clench around his cock the way she had around his fingers.

But he did want it this way, this time.

She gasped out his name, her hand going even tighter in his hair, and he realized he'd punched his hips and thrust up into her deeper. He murmured an apologetic, "Okay?" and she huffed out a shocked-sounding laugh, then moved her mouth over to his ear, right side. She didn't whisper, didn't say it right against his skin, which was good, which was perfect.

"You feel—I'm so close, Griff. I've never—"

He set a hand between them then, not on her clit but on her sternum, his palm flat where her heart pounded, because whatever the end of that sentence was—*I've never had it better, I've never come like this, I've never felt so good*—he knew it would break him open. So he pushed her back with that palm, changing the angle, going impossibly deeper, so deep he had to clench his teeth, grunt with effort and frustration and the little control he had left.

Still, he watched it happen, this final thing he needed to set him over the edge—*there*, there it was. That glazed look, that arched back, that different kind of gasp, the lights in her coming on bright again as she rode him, crying out and clenching her muscles—*Layla*, he thought, or maybe he said, maybe he shouted, but he didn't know for sure.

Because he was coming then, too—following her, his whole being getting scrubbed out and clear of soot, his body scaffolded first by her pleasure and now, for now—

He was something entirely new.

It lasted through the second time.

The newness, that was.

He'd brought it on himself, that second time. Her beneath him, no care for how much weight he put on his left side, his cock in charge of everything once she'd put her mouth on it for a while and, as she put it, *wandered*.

He thought she might kill him with that wandering.

Now, though, he felt it. Not enough to make him regret it; he could've literally died during it and not regretted it. He'd have found a way to haunt Michael long enough to apologize for missing the wedding, then he would've happily returned to the world of the shades with this one memory, this one night with Layla.

In the bathroom, moving quietly, he wrapped part of his leg, slid a pair of sleep pants on, hating the feeling of the bandage and fabric meeting, but he didn't want to go back out there with the wrap showing. After that, a silicone patch on his side, where itching often got to him, then a T-shirt. He stood still for a long moment, waiting—trying to tell if it was going to get worse, but maybe the orgasms had fucked up his senses more than usual, too much oxytocin or whatever the hormone was, because he couldn't determine yet the kind of night he was going to have.

Or rest of the night, early morning, whatever time it was now. After the first time with Layla, when she'd come out of this bathroom wrapped in the same kind of robe he'd seen her in only a couple of mornings ago, she'd gone to the windows—an L-shape of them, floor-to-ceiling—and taken in the view a room like this offered. Way in the distance, there it was—the huge iron tower, not sparkling but still glowing, and he stood behind her, nuzzling her hair to the side to get to her neck, listening to her tease him about his big billionaire room ("Not a billionaire," he'd said, biting at her skin), his view he should've told her about before ("Didn't think you'd have a reason to see it," he told her, his tongue curling around her earlobe), his booking the best corner of the whole hotel when it wasn't even his wedding ("Selfish," he murmured, ignoring his hard cock, flicking her nipple).

She said, through panting breaths, that the tower sparkled every hour until eleven, and he slid a hand inside the robe and said, "Or earlier," which she did not understand and he did not explain. He walked her into the window until her forehead tipped against it, until she drove her hips back into him and he touched her until she came again.

Now, when he emerged from the bathroom, the room was darker, the lights outside dimmed, the tower off for the night. Layla, too, was off—a barely visible lump between the wrecked white covers, a ribbon of her hair curling over one of the pillows.

He stood still, unsure how to handle this next part. He could go lie on that little couch Michael had sat on earlier, try to get some rest there, but it'd be bad news for tomorrow, worse than whatever he already had coming for him. He could get in the bed, but with the pants on, he'd probably go crazy, and anyway, in all likelihood, he wouldn't sleep. He'd be restless, annoying to someone else, even in a king-size.

He didn't want her not to sleep.

He knew tomorrow—today, he guessed—was important.

But also.

Important not to hurt her.

Not ever again.

He took a breath and stepped beside the bed. Listened to her deep, even breathing.

He'd say it nice. He'd say—

"Layla," he murmured softly, before he'd worked it out.

Her name sounded like a prayer to him.

"Mmf," came the reply, from beneath the blanket. He almost smiled. That was about the extent of the response he felt like he'd gotten to prayers, anytime he'd ever tried them.

But his smile faded when he remembered what he was trying to wake her for. Some nice way to say, *You'd be better off in your own room*.

He leaned an arm across her, gently pushed a hank of hair that had fallen over her eyes out of the way.

She repeated her muffled acknowledgment of his presence, but otherwise didn't move.

"Layla," he said again, trying to make it sound less like a whispered devotional. More like an actual attempt to wake her.

Her eyelids slitted open, her long black lashes looking weighted. He should've gone to the fucking couch. This was a dumb move.

Now he had to face it head on.

"I don't want to bother you," he said, which wasn't much of an explanation.

Her lips lifted into a sleepy smile. "Not bothering."

Like that, she was out again.

He furrowed his brow, a pang of worry needling him. All right, they'd had a long day, and then he'd fucked her hard, twice, plus made her come a couple other times. But should she be this conked out already? He hadn't been in the bathroom *that* long.

He lifted his hand, stroked the back of his fingers down her cheek. Smooth and perfect. She turned into the touch.

He should not start this, touching her again.

"Don't," she said, confirming it, and he pulled his hand away.

But she reached up, took his wrist in a grip that belied her sleepy state. Put his palm back on her face.

"Don't *go*," she said grumpily. It was fucking cute.

"You're in my room," he said, smiling.

She stirred in earnest then, her lashes lifting more determinedly, her body moving in a sinuous stretch beneath the covers. His cock twitched.

Not helpful.

She lifted her head like it weighed a thousand pounds, then propped herself on her elbow, both movements looking like they were the most challenging thing in the world.

Well, fuck it. He'd go to the couch.

He leaned down, kissed her forehead. "Go to sleep."

She took his wrist again. "I *was*," she said, in a pouty voice.

He liked it, that whiny note. He could imagine doing things to her that would make her whine, not sleepily. Keeping her right on the edge for hours, keeping her—

"Oh," she said, sitting up straighter, getting a sense of it now. Remembering where she was. "Oh, I see."

"No," he said, hating the look on her face. "No, you don't."

"I'll go," she said, getting her hands in the covers, starting to push them away. "Give me a second to—"

"It's that I don't sleep well," he said, talking over her, too loud, too sharp. He tried to soften his voice when he spoke again. "I move around a lot. Or I get up, do stretches. Sometimes I have to—be up, to keep my mind off it. It'll keep you up."

She'd stopped trying to get up, at least. She looked at him straight in his eyes, a real doctor-about-to-be-in-your-business face if he ever saw one. "Do you want me to go?"

He shook his head. "But I—"

She slumped back against the bed, pulled the covers up again. Arranged the pillow.

Huffily.

"You do whatever." Her eyes were already closed again.

"What . . . ever?" he repeated slowly, dumbly.

He had never seen this Layla. Selfish, dismissive. A little rude, actually.

He fucking loved it. He hoped he was somehow responsible for it.

She could stand to be more rude.

"I won't wake up," she said. "Not unless you nudge me hard. Or I guess unless you make the exact same noise my pager app makes."

He snorted in disbelief. He couldn't imagine anyone sleeping through his nights. Still, he lingered. Stayed quiet, stayed positioned over her. He wanted her to sell it to him, convince him.

He did not want her to go. He did not want it to be tomorrow yet.

"Griff."

It was a good start to convincing.

He put a knee on the bed.

"I sleep like the dead," she added, scooting over, making space for him, dragging the pillow she'd apparently claimed as her own with her. "In whatever apartment I'm in. Hotel rooms. On-call rooms at whatever hospital I'm working in. Lying down, sitting up. I can *sleep*."

"You don't have to brag."

She laughed softly. How'd all of him get on the bed?

"Anyway, you're a doctor. You know your sleep can be disrupted even if you don't wake up."

"Not mine," she said, wriggling beneath the covers. She pushed herself back against him. Spooning, that's what this was. Not that he'd ever done it.

His fucking leg hurt. Also, his dick was fully hard again.

And no telling what he'd feel like tomorrow.

Still, he closed his eyes.

He'd get up in a second. Once she was back to sleep again.

He didn't notice that she already was.

Chapter Twenty-Three

In theory, a spa morning was the perfect idea.

Because Layla woke up sore.

Two kinds.

First, from walking: her feet, her calves, her hip flexors.

Second, from Griffin: the space between her legs, her lower abdominals, her heart.

God, her heart. Too hardworking, the whole night, no matter that she kept scolding it. *You stay out of this*, she told it, countless times, when whatever wave of pleasure he put her through ebbed for a moment, until the next one; when she saw him fighting a sheen of wetness in his eyes at their first joining; when she woke early this morning to find him asleep next to her, his hair a mess and his face finally, fully placid, an expression she had not—never once—seen on him since they'd met.

But in practice, there was no massage on the list for that.

"I picked the one for lymphatic draining," Manon was saying from across the way, lounging elegantly beside Céline on one of the cream bouclé chairs arranged artfully around this calmingly dim, teak-walled lobby, the scent of eucalyptus wafting from places unseen.

Layla breathed in, trying to enjoy it. To be in the moment.

But even setting aside her heart, her body, too, seemed to be fighting her presence here, unwilling to take in the luxury of the space. It wanted back into Griffin's bed, the soft, rumpled warmth of it. It wanted to stretch out, feel the twinges left behind by him, not have them rubbed away by someone else, let alone a stranger. It wanted to be next to his, to notice more deliberately the new sensations that collected within her throughout the night. It wanted to flex, to brag, to practice all its newest movements, the ones that felt native to the place of him, already attuned to where not to touch, and where to wander freely.

"It's slimming!" Manon added, and then repeated the name of her selected massage-menu-item in her perfectly accented French.

At that, Layla's body finally gave her a break, bringing her back to the moment.

Beside her, she felt Emily tense.

Emily, Layla reminded herself now, the same way she had when she finally forced herself out of Griffin's bed this morning. *It's tomorrow*, she'd told herself, trying not to curl back into him. *It's tomorrow, and you promised you'd be there for Em.*

"Even in French, it's still pseudoscience!" Layla said, and then snapped her mouth closed, widening her eyes down at her lap.

What the hell was that? she thought frantically, even as she tried to recover with a light, polite laugh.

"I'm kidding, of course!" she finally managed, smiling across the way at Manon. "Physician humor. You know me."

You know me not to ever say anything like that, she thought. *You know me not to blithely walk out of a museum and disappear for a whole entire day. You know me to show up on time to spa morning, and not ten minutes late to the lobby because I couldn't get out of the best man's bed, because I had to go back to my own room so you wouldn't see me in the clothes you saw me in yesterday.*

But if Manon was thinking of any of that, too, she didn't say it. She laughed, right at the same time Emily snort-gasped, and then said, "Pseudoscience started to look *much* more appealing when I hit sixty, chérie, I'll tell you that!"

She clinked her cucumber water glass with the one held by Céline, who was maybe looking slightly askance at Layla, but thankfully, the conversation moved on. The rest of their party this morning—Damaris and Paula, who both seemed a little put off ever since being coaxed into the wispy spa robes they'd been given upon arrival; Rosie, who gave Layla a dramatically unsubtle wink in the lobby and then promptly linked arms with Samantha, as though she were sparing Layla from what she'd clearly assumed, after yesterday, were jealous feelings over Jamie—started chiming in with their own selected menu items.

"Oh my god," Emily whispered, leaning into Layla's shoulder. They were huddled on a love seat upholstered in the same bouclé, which had struck Layla in exactly one way when she'd first sat down: *Griff would hate the texture of this.* But then, Emily had come to sit beside her, and once again, Layla had tried to reset her mind.

Bride, not best man.

"That was hilarious," Emily continued. "You know she told me to get Botox before the engagement photos?"

Layla pressed her lips together, fearful of another uncharacteristic outburst. But she set a hand on Emily's knee, squeezing lightly in understanding. It was centering, this touch, flooding her with a rush of affection and tenderness. As much as she genuinely loved Manon—her generosity, her openness, even her vanity, which could be charming in its own way, especially since she was so self-aware about it—this moment of commiseration with Em over Manon felt *sisterly*. Layla, too, had once been party to Manon's gentle brand of suggestion, on everything from Layla's engagement ring ("Oh, a sapphire, I wonder what made him pick *that*?") to the way she and Jamie decorated their first apartment ("I've always admired bold colors in a home, even if they're not for me!"). For the most part, Layla—who had lived without a mom for her whole life—had been weirdly grateful for these maternal intrusions.

But even she could see the way it grated.

And who else could truly understand that but someone in the family?

Who else could get it but a sister?

She turned fully to Em now, crossing her legs and valiantly ignoring the slight chafing sting on her inner thighs where Griffin's stubble had reddened her skin. She kept her voice low, glad for the love seat's relative separateness from the rest of the lobby.

"How are you doing today?" she said, trying to inject some extra meaning into it. She sounded more like herself now—calmer, more in control.

Emily's eyes dropped to her glass of fruit-infused water, one shoulder lifting listlessly, and Layla's stomach sank with this confirmation of something she'd suspected since she first saw Emily this morning, anxious and tired-looking as she tried to nod along to something Paula was telling her in the lobby. Maybe it wasn't full meltdown mode, like it had been on the morning after their first dinner here, but it also was a marked change from yesterday morning at the museum, when Emily's expression had lit with joy and certainty as soon as Michael arrived.

"Em," Layla coaxed.

Thankfully, when Emily raised her eyes, they weren't wet with tears. But they *were* worried, and Layla felt a guilty, nervous pang.

"Yesterday started so well, honestly, especially after Michael showed up. We had a really nice lunch before we went over to Les Invalides, and that was pretty good, too. There was a *ton* of medical stuff; you probably would've loved it."

There was that pang again. Layla opened her mouth to apologize, an automatic instinct, but before she could, Emily kept going.

"But, I don't know." Here, she raised her eyes, made sure Paula was still on the other side of the room. Lowered her voice even more as she continued. "Michael's parents—it's difficult there, and I don't fully get it? Fitz is hard on Michael about the smallest, stupidest things, and then Michael gets in a bad mood."

"That's tough," Layla said, meaning it, but she also knew her job here wasn't really to care about Michael and his dad; it was to care about Emily. "But does he get in a bad mood with *you*?"

"Not really, but—"

Layla did not like the way Emily was running her finger around the lip of her glass. Over and over.

"But what?"

Em shrugged again, blew out a breath. "Well, it's like—Fitz makes these little comments to Michael, and then Michael gets quiet. And Paula"—another darting look across the room, an even softer whisper—"she doesn't want Fitz going at Michael; she doesn't want them at odds. So she sort of . . . I don't know. She redirected, I guess. She blamed Griffin."

Layla's sore heart stuttered, her face heating.

"Blamed him for what?"

"She said that's why Michael was quiet. Because Griffin didn't come to anything yesterday."

Layla wanted to feign surprise at this. To say something casually unaware like, *He didn't?* But the pang of guilt was now more like a stake through the stomach. It wasn't *just* that she'd abandoned her sisterly post yesterday; it was that she'd lied about it, too, or at least lied by omission. When she'd texted Em yesterday from outside the Rodin museum, she'd been standing right beside Griffin, but she hadn't mentioned him at all. Instead, she'd typed out a too-long and strategically vague explanation, the main gist of which was: *I'm a little overwhelmed this morning.* Then, she'd made a few bland, nonspecific assurances.

I'm really okay and Don't worry about anything and I'll text in a bit to check in and I'll be back if you need me.

In that moment, she hadn't cared if everyone thought she was overwhelmed about Jamie—about the end of her and Jamie, about Jamie and Sam, whatever.

In fact, as she'd stood there beside Griffin, knowing he was making his own excuse to Michael, there was a not-insignificant part of her that thought—about her own divorce!—*That's convenient.*

Now, face-to-face with more of Emily's doubt, the responsibility she should've felt yesterday roared loudly back. She was supposed to be making sure this wedding happened. She was supposed to be *here* for Emily, making it up to Emily—all those months of absence when being amicable felt impossible.

"*Was* Michael upset that he didn't come to anything yesterday?"

"I think he was worried, initially, but not overly so. Like, obviously, Griffin has"—she lifted a hand, waved it in a dismissive gesture that was so like one of Manon's, Layla almost wanted to grab Em's wrist in censure—"*problems.*"

Layla's back teeth ground together.

"But it was more like, once Paula brought up Griffin, that got Fitz going—a couple asides about how Griffin has always been unreliable, how Michael would've been better off making his cousin Bryan the best man. Which is *rude*, I'm definitely not on Fitz's side about that, but . . ."

"But what?"

It sounded sharper than Layla intended, though Em didn't seem to notice.

"But honestly? Michael is *so* defensive about Griffin. And if I press him about it—god forbid I try to actually find out why my fiancé's parents are so weird about the *best friend* he's had since *literal* childhood—Michael gets quiet with *me*. But shouldn't I know? Shouldn't I know what all this secrecy with Griffin is about?"

Layla swallowed, the question—with a slightly different inflection—ringing through her ominously.

Shouldn't I know?

Suddenly, the parts of her that had been so fully in charge for the last twenty-four hours—her overinvested heart, her disobedient body—seemed to quiet. Now, it was her brain turning back on, back up to full volume.

Shouldn't I know?

"You . . . you don't?" Layla said. She was already calling to her mind everything she *had* learned about Griffin yesterday: his absent dad, his ultrareligious grandparents who'd functionally abandoned his mother when she got pregnant at nineteen. His lonely youngest years, his mom working multiple jobs, and then, moving to a new neighborhood and meeting Michael. His good grades, a gifted program, a scholarship to Rensselaer. His current house—"Small. Simple," per his description—and how he could walk to the farm his mother lived on. Her ranch home, her boyfriend named Peter who was a large-animal vet and who was only allowed—his mother's rules, not so fully freed of her parents' attitudes, as it turned out—to stay over twice a week. His work and how he missed it, but how he couldn't see himself going back to it full-time, not really.

Of course, she noticed what he hadn't said. She noticed that there seemed to be a gap of several years he simply did not acknowledge to her. A big skip between those years after college, to now.

But yesterday, that had felt fine. Comforting, even. A signed permission slip for a field trip where she didn't have to say a single word about her marriage, or her divorce.

Em shook her head, her lips pursed. "I know there was a house fire. I know that's how he got hurt."

Layla's body was back in it now: her stomach clenching uncomfortably at this new knowledge—*a house fire*—combined with such an inadequate phrase for what had happened to Griffin as a result. It felt like breaking an unmade promise, to hear it this way.

A house fire.

He got hurt.

"And one of their friends from high school died during it," Emily added. "Which is horrible."

Layla blinked, unaccountably stunned. She *shouldn't* be; she knew she shouldn't be. She had seen Griff's body, had seen those scars up close, even had her fingers against more than one of them at various moments over the course of last night. She knew you didn't get scars like his without something catastrophic happening, something that could kill.

Thank god he didn't die, she thought automatically, even as her heart twisted with the knowledge that he and Michael lost someone in such a tragic way.

Emily sighed gustily. "Last night when we got back from dinner, I tried to talk to him about it again, but it's really the only thing he'll shut down with me about. He said that fire was the worst thing to ever happen to Griffin, and he deserves his privacy about it. That I need to *leave it alone*. That's what he said! Leave. It. Alone."

Everything that had felt separate within Layla—heart, body, brain—now seemed to coalesce into a churning, strengthening whirlwind. In the midst of it, she couldn't grab on to any one thing: her forged-in-family concern for Emily, her brand-new protectiveness over Griffin, her own pressing but possibly inappropriate curiosity.

She wanted to know so much about Griffin—about all those years he hadn't told her about. About the house fire, about whoever he lost, about everything after.

But also, should she even *want* to know?

Hadn't *she* been the one to say that yesterday was temporary, that today would have to be back to normal, that after last night, it could only be about Michael and Emily from here on out?

After this week, she probably wouldn't have reason to see Griffin Testa ever again.

Would she?

"I mean, do you think he should tell me?"

Emily's whispered question was a reminder that Layla had, in the midst of her whirlwind, gone awkwardly silent. She inhaled, repeated Emily's question back to herself silently to drown out all the other ones she wasn't going to get answers to right now.

She had to answer this for Emily, and not make it about Griffin.

"I think he shouldn't be putting you in situations where you're in the dark," Layla said. "Griffin"—she hoped Em couldn't hear the catch in her throat when she said his name—"deserves privacy, of course. But also, when it comes to Michael, you shouldn't have to feel like you're walking around land mines you don't know the location of all the time."

"Yes!" Emily said, relief in her tone at being understood.

It came out loud enough that a few others looked over, so Layla smoothed her expression into a smile, made it look, she hoped, like she and Em were whispering over something like wedding night lingerie, or why men could never find the ketchup without help, even when it was always in the exact same place in the refrigerator.

Em lowered her voice again. "Remember when you came for Christmas the first time, and Jamie explained to you in the car on the way over why Dad and Uncle Steve don't talk about Gramma MacKenzie? It's like, *that* is what I want, you know? *That's* marriage!"

Layla was thinking, *Your dad and your Uncle Steve had a stupid fight over Gramma MacKenzie's ugly dining room set. It wasn't a house fire where someone* died, *Em.*

But before she could find a better alternative for that bit of sharpness, Emily groaned and shook her head.

"Ugh," she said. "Sorry to bring it up. After yesterday and everything." She grabbed one of Layla's hands, a look of soft apology—pity?—in her eyes. "How are *you*, Lay?"

It was a few seconds before Layla put the pieces of this together. The *it* Em was sorry for bringing up was Layla's marriage. The *After yesterday* was about the museum, about Layla leaving under the weighted reminder of *The Kiss*, under the watchful gaze of her ex-husband. And probably everyone else.

"Oh," she said, no *That's convenient!* sense of things in sight now. She was either going to have to come clean about her day with Griffin—a terrible idea, given what they'd just been talking about—or continue to let everyone think she'd left yesterday because of Jamie.

"I'm really okay," she added, trying to talk over the still-churning whirlwind.

I slept with Griffin and got my heart involved. I'm sore all over this morning, because he explored my body so fully, so perfectly. I want to get up and leave this spa; I want to go find him and ask him about the house fire, the friend he lost, the lazy judgments of people like Fitz and Paula, and maybe even you.

I want to know if he'd ever want to see me again, after all this.

"It was . . . you know." She clutched for a word, any word, and landed on: "Memories."

Em clucked in sympathy, a noise that made Layla shift in her seat with . . . well. More guilt, surely.

But also, maybe annoyance.

Not those *memories*, Layla wanted to clarify.

Not memories with your brother.

But she couldn't very well go on explaining it. She couldn't say, *Actually, the memory that sent me out of that museum yesterday was with Griffin. A cozy dinner, a fight in the street, a kiss you could carve a sculpture of.*

She couldn't say, *And then we made a bunch more. All day, all over the city. All night, in his bed.*

So she squeezed Em's hand back and said, "I'm good today. Promise."

"Good." Em took a breath, leaned back. "Because after these massages . . ."

Emily trailed off, looked toward where Manon and Céline sat, to where Paula and Damaris stayed huddled in conversation, to where Rosie and Sam had wandered farther down the spa's cavernous hall, where the Turkish bath—the place they were all to regather after their treatments—was located. Layla could tell Em was thinking about how this small group of guests was set to expand over the next few hours. Most of them, Layla had already discerned, were from the bride's side of things—Uncle Steve and his third wife, despite the dining room table theft, two of Manon and Céline's French cousins and their spouses, coming in from Nantes, a couple more of Em's close friends. Tonight, they'd gather at the rental property nearby that Manon and Robert had booked for the next three days of formal events in honor of the bride and groom: cocktails and music this evening, an informal rehearsal tomorrow morning followed by tomorrow night's ceremony, and brunch the morning after.

In other words, after these massages, this destination wedding became a lot less *destination*.

A lot more *wedding*.

And Emily still had that fretful, anxious look on her face.

"Can I do anything?" Layla asked.

Em blew out a breath, shoulders sagging. Across the room, one of the frosted-glass doors opened, and a tight-ponytailed woman all in white emerged, announcing readiness for "the MacKenzie party."

Manon stood and said, "Enfin!" and Céline leaned in to chide her for the expression of impatience.

"Probably not," Em answered, rising slowly and smoothing her robe. "Unless you can somehow teleport across this city to wherever the guys are, and make it so Griffin somehow doesn't make anything worse today."

For a few seconds, Layla stayed sitting—staring—as Em made her way toward Manon, trying to decide which part of this whirlwind waiting room had blown her off course the most.

Was it the reckoning with the depth of her feelings for Griffin, after only a single day and night spent alone with him, fully in his company?

Was it what she'd learned about him, and how he was hurt?

Was it this sharp, sudden feeling of frustration she had toward Emily—Emily, her *family*!—for saying his name in that uncharacteristically unkind way?

Or was it the slow, dawning realization that didn't turn out to be much of a relief at all: that Layla—pitied, brokenhearted Layla, brave-facing it for the ex-in-laws in the city they'd claimed as their own, accidentally reminding the bride that marriage was not forever on the very first night she was here—was not, in fact, the biggest threat to this wedding happening?

She swallowed and stood, her legs wobbly, her mind racing.

Her heart somewhere across the city.

With the man who'd once accused her of ruining this whole week.

With the man whose secrets might have been just as responsible all along.

Chapter Twenty-Four

At first, Griffin thought Montmartre seemed designed for one thing.

Pain.

He could appreciate that he was operating at a significant disadvantage. The regular ones for him, but also—more so—the morning-after ones. It was his legs and feet, sore from all the walking, but it was also the sleepy fatigue, a sort he wasn't used to. Usually, when Griffin's body got overtired, his brain got wired—hyperfocused on whatever hurt, hyper-alert to every sensation, so much so that he would sometimes avoid simple, necessary things. He'd think, *If I eat, I'll have to chew, and there's that one spot on my jaw sometimes.* All the thinking, all the vigilance—it would make him more tired, but still not sleepy tired, and the day would go on like that until the whole system shut down, and he'd sleep in a deadened, unsatisfying way, waking up with a feeling like a hangover.

This morning, though, Griffin was tired like someone had dropped a veil over him, like he'd never been hyper-anything. He'd woken—woken!—on his side, with a note beside him, Layla's writing. A messy scrawl, same as every doctor whose writing he'd ever seen, but he liked it. It didn't say anything like *hypertrophic* or *escharotomy* or *nerve compression* or *autologous fat grafting*.

It said, *I had to go for the spa morning. I set your alarm for you.*

Then, a small, uneven heart—as if, halfway through, she'd doubted the sanity of putting it there. He stared at that heart until his lids drooped, and then, who knew how long after, he'd woken again to a sound he didn't think he'd ever heard his phone make.

He moved through getting dressed with the veil, made his way to the lobby with the veil, answered Michael's quiet, concerned queries with the veil. The veil was made of that bed upstairs, of Layla's scent lingering in it, of everything he kept remembering from the day and night before.

He did not want to take the veil off.

But then, everyone else finally made it to the lobby: Fitz, looking upright and already annoyed; Robert, bright-eyed and cheerful; Abram, talking into a Bluetooth headset; then, of course, Jamie, who also looked tired, which made Griffin think—smugly, immaturely, disrespectfully—*You're not tired like I am. You're not tired from her.* Robert announced a "special arrangement" he'd made for "just us guys," and that's when Griffin found out that they'd be going to Montmartre for the morning, though Robert was still keeping it a secret, what they'd be doing there.

The first thing was, they had to take the Metro: Griff's first time, since every other day he'd been here, he'd either used his feet or a rideshare. It wasn't as though he was philosophically opposed to public transportation, and he could tell, as these things went, that Paris's version of it was special: easy, elegant, clean. But holy fuck, the fucking stairs. He was not in good shape for the stairs, and it embarrassed him to lag behind, to have Michael lag, too, to see Fitz flex his jaw in annoyance and have Robert pat his shoulder encouragingly when he finally caught up.

Then, after the Metro, Montmartre itself: one giant hill, that's how it felt to him, and not a gentle, rolling situation, either. Streets that went straight up, a huge church at the height of the whole thing, white and glaring. He thought, *Fuck you, you fucking show-off church*; he thought of Notre-Dame and how he liked it much better. At one point, when he caught a snippet of conversation that he largely couldn't process through the effort of making this slanted-walking look easy, he heard Robert say, "Moulin Rouge," and he had a memory of that—a movie he watched with his mom a long time ago, strange and color-saturated and extremely boring. He thought, *If this man is taking us to some place where people are going to cancan dance in front of me before noon, I'll probably die of hating it.*

He also thought, *But I'll die having been with Layla Bailey.*

And then—and then! They finally made it to their *actual* destination, a glass-fronted shop halfway up one of the murder hills, the sign above it covered in blooming, trailing pink flowers, which to be honest looked very nice, very like postcard-photograph-Paris, except for the fact that when you stood right under them and looked up, you saw that they were not real. They were polyester, like the kind that were stuck into the various seasonal wreaths his mom kept on the front door of her house.

Griffin hated the feel of polyester.

"So, as soon as this group finishes up," Robert said, gesturing to the glass, "it'll be our turn in there," and that's when Griffin realized he'd be hating the feel of at least two other things this morning: First, whatever he'd have to touch to get through Robert's "big surprise," a fucking *baking* class, a bachelor party for assholes, because "knowing how to make a good pastry has saved me many a time in my marriage!"; and second, the feeling of doing the whole thing in a glass room, so that anyone walking by on the street could see him.

I should've slept through the alarm, he'd thought. *In case she wanted to come back to me. In case she wanted to look, since I don't seem to mind that at all.*

So.

So at first, Montmartre was mostly morning-after pain.

But once they finally got inside the Maison-Something-or-Other—the other part of the name obscured by the fake flowers—Griffin was surprised to find that things improved considerably.

One thing was the smell—warm butter, sugar, cinnamon, chocolate—maybe the only combination of smells that could make him miss Layla's scent slightly less. There was also the tiny cup of espresso each of them was served as they were introduced to their instructor, a Black American woman who'd trained as a pastry chef here in Paris and who'd lived here for the last thirty-five years, the last ten teaching classes like this to tourists. She wore a tidy white coat and hat and she did not laugh at any of Robert's little attention-stealing asides, and as Griffin sipped at the cup of jolting caffeine, which he did not typically allow himself, he started to feel okay enough to lift the veil himself, to pay attention to what Chef Williams was telling them about what they'd be learning.

When they got started, Griff and Michael stood together at one of the butcher-block tables, like they had when they were lab partners in tenth-grade AP Bio. Croissant-making was, as it turned out, not hugely unlike some of the lengthier, more complicated labs Griffin had done in school, so some parts of the process had been prepped for them in advance, with Chef Williams still explaining every step carefully. Griffin thought that all the touching of things he'd have to do—appliances, ingredients, dough, utensils, whatever—would cause a problem, but on the whole, he escaped with minimal disruption.

He concentrated. He learned things. He showed off his superior lamination skills to Michael, and he even once laughed at an exchange between Abram and Chef Williams, who said Abram rolled his croissants like he was pushing a boulder over a speed bump.

He couldn't believe it, but he was fucking *enjoying* himself.

"You dickhead," said Michael. "Of course your croissants look like that."

Griff smiled down at his six fairly perfect-looking, still-unbaked croissants, then he let his eyes drift over to Michael's less-than-impressive efforts. He only had five, because Chef Williams had already thrown one away wordlessly, clucking her tongue in disgust.

"Yours aren't bad," he said, which is also the kind of thing he used to say in AP Bio, before he took over and redid most of Michael's work for him.

Michael sighed. "Let me have your tray. I'm going to go show it to Robert and say it's mine."

Griff shrugged, noting that there was still enough pastry on the corner of their table to maybe try rolling another small croissant.

"Whatever, man," he said, and Michael took the tray, muttering, "Dickhead," again, which made them both laugh. Griff watched him cross the room, to where Fitz and Robert looked as though they didn't have a single thing to talk about comfortably, and then set his attention on the leftover pastry dough.

Or partly on the pastry dough, and partly on Layla.

Whether she'd like a class like this. Whether she took AP Bio. Whether making her a croissant would save a marriage with her, which was really an insane thing to think, as if it made sense for him to ever imagine himself waking up early the night after some dumb fight with Layla, Layla if she was his *wife*, to make croissants good enough to make him worthy of her again. Whether she—

"Hey," interrupted a voice.

Griffin, unfortunately, recognized it by now.

He looked up to meet the eyes of the man who had once actually called the woman he'd just been thinking of his wife.

Griffin did not say *Hey* back.

Jamie looked away—after one of those *I didn't mean to look* scans of Griff's left side—and down at Michael's tray of sad, misshapen croissants.

Those aren't mine, Griffin wanted to say. *Mine could save a marriage, probably.*

Obviously, yours couldn't.

"So," Jamie said, his voice low, his eyes still darting around, avoiding any additional accidents of looking at Griffin's face, and Griffin realized that he was working up to something. In the days since he'd first been introduced to Jamie MacKenzie, he'd had exactly nothing to say to the man, and the feeling seemed mutual. And up to now, one of the many reasons Griffin had for liking this workshop was that it hadn't really invited much mingling.

If Jamie came over here, it wasn't because he suddenly wanted to be polite.

"So," Griffin repeated.

"Look, I debated on whether I should say anything to you about this."

Oh, what the fuck, thought Griffin, and what he assumed was that Jamie was about to say some bullshit about Griffin's best man performance so far. He'd have to bite his tongue hard for that, keep things fine for Michael—

"I saw you and Layla," Jamie said.

Griffin blinked. He had his right hand resting on the edge of the counter, and he curled his fingers inward.

"I was in the hotel lobby when you"—he paused, cleared his throat—"when you and she came back last night."

Griffin had been touching her in the hotel lobby. His hand low on her back, his pinky and his ring finger along the upper curve of her ass. In front of the elevators, she'd leaned into him, a lot like she had that night on the boat cruise, but this time, she meant it. He'd pressed his face into her hair.

"And?" Griffin said, but he did not like this one fucking bit. He did not like that neither he nor Layla had noticed anyone in that lobby, and they'd looked, too—right as they crossed through the glass doors, him staying a few steps behind her then, both of them scanning the expanse of it. He did not like to think of this guy, her fucking ex-husband, her ex-husband who brought a *date* to this thing, skulking behind one of those weird lobby columns, seeing him and Layla at the end of their perfect, private Paris day.

"And you looked . . . You were touching her."

You have no idea, he thought. *You have no idea, and you never will.*

But Griffin said nothing. It was the only keeping-things-fine version of *It is none of your fucking business* he could think of.

Despite the silence, Jamie held up both of his hands, as though he was surrendering to something, a real *I'm just saying, bro!* posture if Griff ever saw one. The thing was, he had known guys like Jamie. Nice guys, guys from good, loving families who were tall and golden-boy good-looking but also not complete assholes about it. In school, Jamie would probably invite someone eating alone to join his table, introduce them around to his buddies, earnestly say, "That's cool" when the kid admitted, sheepishly, to being in Math Club. At work, Jamie would bring in a box of donuts, one for everyone, even a couple of the weird vegan and gluten-free ones, because he didn't want anyone to feel left out. On the way home, he'd have no problem pulling over to help someone change a tire, unless, Griff guessed, that someone was also throwing up.

So, by and large, Jamie was, probably, a nice guy. A guy more like Michael than Griffin. A guy nice enough that Layla Bailey had once—possibly still—loved him, and as far as Griffin was concerned, that should be a point in any man's favor.

But Griffin still hated him.

"Okay," Griffin said blandly. Quietly. "You saw what you saw."

Jamie shifted, leaned his own hand on the counter, so now he was mimicking Griffin's posture. Griffin immediately, desperately wanted to move, but didn't want to give Jamie the satisfaction.

"I haven't said anything to anyone," he said, as though basic discretion was deserving of praise.

This was sometimes the thing about nice guys. The way they wanted praise.

"It's only that I'm concerned. About Layla."

Well. Griffin hated that, the way the man said her name. The way he said he was *concerned*.

"This is a difficult week for her," Jamie continued. "We all can see that. And I'm worried that she's not herself, you know? Layla's not really the type to—"

"I wouldn't finish that sentence," Griffin said, through clenched teeth.

Jamie's eyes widened, but Griff was too busy dealing with his own surprise at the gall of every single thing this guy just said, and what he was obviously getting ready to say before Griff stopped him.

This is a difficult week for her because you all invited her, when anyone with good sense and a brand-new girlfriend wouldn't have. You all can see it because you watch her like she's a glued-together glass, and you're waiting for her to crack. She only seems not like herself because she's not doing your weird MacKenzie Paris gauntlet anymore.

Layla's not the type of anything.

Layla Bailey is herself.

Jamie cleared his throat nervously. The man could still not fully settle his eyes on Griffin's face, which was probably a good thing, because now, in addition to the scars, there was likely a full-on murderous expression there.

But if Griffin could give this guy anything, it was that he didn't quit.

At least at this.

"I don't mean to offend you," Jamie said, so, naturally, Griffin braced himself to be offended. "But it isn't as though your behavior over the last couple of days . . ." He trailed off, shifted on his feet again. "Look. Layla deserves someone good. Someone reliable."

Unfortunately, Griffin could not call himself offended.

Someone good. Someone reliable.

He was neither of those things.

And he knew that.

He'd known that for years.

But maybe he had forgotten it for a few hours.

At some point, he'd moved his right hand again, a full fist, set upright on the counter. He did not like the way he could feel the flour on his skin now, gritty and dry.

He knew he had gone still—too still, too quiet, half of his brain running *Someone good* and *Someone reliable* on a drumming, crushing, repetitive loop, the other half retreating into a familiar scan of his body. He looked at Jamie MacKenzie's nice-guy face and felt every fucking step to the Metro, every steep street incline.

He thought, *I bet you don't feel a thing.*

Jamie was clearly not the sort of man to be comfortable with silence, because he spoke again, quieter now, and the worst thing about it was the pity Griffin could hear as soon as the man opened his mouth.

"I can see that you've had a diffic—"

Griffin could not let him finish that sentence. He could *not*.

"Layla isn't your concern anymore," he said, leaving himself out of it.

Now, Jamie went quiet. Stunned and blinking, as though he could not conceive of what Griffin said. When he finally gathered himself, he stood straighter, the first sign that he had some real fight in him.

"She's family," he said.

Griffin forgot all about *Someone good* and *Someone reliable*. He even forgot the pity, the fact that golden boy Jamie MacKenzie was going to say that Griffin had a *difficult* time, life, whatever the fuck.

He only remembered Layla on the Paris streets, talking about her life. About her mother gone, her father useless, her half brother distant. He remembered how much the MacKenzies meant to her, how they were the family she'd always wanted, and right now, this fucking guy was nothing to Griffin besides the guy who'd taken it away.

"You're not her family," he said.

That shocked look again, more indignant this time. "I am. I was mar—"

"If you were her family, you wouldn't have left her."

He could see he'd done it now—the nice guy gone, and that was good for Griff. He wanted that guy gone. He wanted an excuse; he was *waiting* for one. Jamie's face flushed, his stance going more rigid, his jaw tightening.

Griffin wondered whether the flour on his hands would make throwing a punch feel more or less weird.

What he expected was Jamie to go after him again: to say, *You hardly know her*, which was, on the face of it, true. He knew now that Jamie and Layla met at freshman orientation at college, knew they'd been together for years before they got married, while Griffin hadn't even known her *name* for a full week.

But he felt ready for that; he somehow felt confident about that. *I do know her. I may not be good or reliable, but I know her.*

He did not feel ready for what Jamie actually said, though. A snappish, spontaneous response. The man practically bit it out.

"If Layla wanted family, she wouldn't have left *me*."

It wasn't that Griffin didn't believe it. He *could* believe it. He knew she might have had any number of reasons for walking away from a marriage, and she would have.

But in all the times she'd gotten close to speaking about the end of her marriage to this guy—all her *It was amicable* bullshit—Griffin had always, always had the feeling that it hadn't been up to her.

That *amicable* is what she settled for in a situation not of her choosing.

That she had come to this wedding as an exile, missing this family she'd desperately wanted to keep, that she would've done anything to keep.

"What the fuck does that mean?" Griffin said, but as soon as he did, he knew it was the wrong question, or at least he knew he didn't want the answer to it from this guy.

He also knew he'd said it too loud.

"Griff," said Michael, rushing up behind Jamie, setting his hand on his almost-brother's shoulder, and Griffin hated that. In his periphery, he could see Fitz, turned toward them, and everything in him clenched.

This was not good for Michael.

He was fucking this up for Michael.

He held up his hands, a ridiculous mirror of Jamie from only a minute ago, knowing the posture didn't look natural on him, knowing it showed off his gnarled left hand.

"Sorry," he said. "We were talking about . . ." He trailed off. He could not come up with any meaningful lie related to pastry dough that would've gotten him—let alone Jamie—this mad.

Jamie did not supply an alternative, and the three of them lapsed into strained silence until Michael squeezed Jamie's shoulder and said, "All right?"

"I'm good," Jamie said, stepping away. "Gonna go check on my croissants."

Michael looked at Griffin. Long and disappointed.

Then he tipped his head toward the door, and turned to walk away.

Griffin wordlessly followed.

Outside, Michael stopped—arrested on the street, one look up the hill, one look down, his face setting into an even deeper expression of frustration: the endless, exhausting awareness of knowing Griffin so well.

"It's fine," Griffin ground out, going to the right, going *up*, ignoring the hitch in his leg. Only a few steps to a corner, where they could turn and duck out of sight from the pâtisserie. They didn't go any farther: enough for privacy, for quick access back to where they'd been. Griffin set his shoulder against a freestone building, getting the weight off his leg.

"Man," Michael said, not leaning against anything. "What are you doing, getting into it with my brother-in-law?"

Griffin clenched his teeth, unsure how to answer. He had not planned to tell Michael about Layla, maybe not ever and definitely not yet, not because it wasn't important but because he knew it was *too* important. Certainly too important for this week, especially now, when Michael was under additional pressure.

He said, "He was rude about your croissants."

Michael blew out a breath, rubbed a hand over his face. More frustration, but also, Griffin knew him well enough to hear something else in that huff of air—grudging laughter.

But when he lowered his hand again and looked at Griffin—right at him, Michael always looked right at him—his expression was fully serious.

"I heard him say something about Layla."

Griffin lowered his head.

"Oh, Jesus," Michael said. "I *knew* it."

"How'd you know it?" Griffin said, his eyes snapping up.

"As soon as you said *I wouldn't say we're friends*. Yesterday morning. I knew it by the look on your face."

"I don't get looks on my face."

Michael rolled his eyes. "You sure had a look on your face with Jamie. Like you'd shove him in one of those ovens just for saying her name."

Griffin said nothing. Michael rubbed his face again. He so rarely got mad. When he did, he was like this—fidgety, slow to speak.

"*Years*," Michael said finally. "I wait for years for you to show genuine interest in literally anything again. Work. A hobby. That fucking farm you bought."

"The farm was for my mom," he interrupted uselessly.

"A woman," Michael went on. "*Anything*. And it's my future brother-in-law's ex-*wife*?"

Don't call her that, Griffin thought.

"During the week of my wedding? When Em's already . . . how she is right now?"

"It's not—" Griffin broke off. He was not going to say *It's not serious*.

Michael stared at him. "Did you sleep with her?"

Griffin's only answer was a request. "Do not tell anyone."

Michael blinked. "Well *clearly* the cat is out of the bag!" he almost-shouted, gesturing back toward the pâtisserie.

Griffin shook his head, knowing instinctively that Jamie MacKenzie was not going to spread this information around. Out of respect for his ex-wife or out of jealousy over her, or some combination of both. Griffin didn't care. All he cared about was that Layla would not want this to become the story, especially if everyone took it the same way Jamie had.

Layla broken and lost, falling into bed with someone *not good*. Someone *not reliable*.

"He's not going to tell anyone," he said. "Mikey, listen, I'm sorry. I—"

Michael spun away, took two stomping steps, hands set low on his hips, before turning around and stomping back.

"Don't be sorry!" he said, still in that almost-shout. He added, "I'm happy for you!" in a way that sounded like, *I'm so fucking pissed at you*, and Griffin knew it was both.

And if he was honest with himself, both were upsetting.

He didn't want Michael pissed at him, but also—

He didn't want Michael thinking this was something other than what it was.

He didn't want *himself* thinking it was something other than what it was.

He was not good. He was not reliable. And he and Layla had both known that last night was not today.

That today, they had to go back to this.

He still couldn't bring himself to say something like *It's nothing* or *It was one night* or *There's nothing to be happy for me about*, so he focused on what mattered most about this, and that was protecting Layla. He was already thinking about going back into the pâtisserie and quietly threatening Jamie MacKenzie with grievous bodily harm if he even attempted to express his "worry" to her.

She would hate that.

"You can't tell anyone," he repeated. "No one. She would not want that. She would not want to . . . to become the focus of this. You can't tell Emily."

Michael huffed out another breath, no amusement in this one. Only exasperation.

"Just what I fucking need," Michael said, turning away.

But then Griffin caught it—the addition of something else. A muttered exhalation. Griffin thought maybe he wasn't supposed to hear it, but at the same time, Michael wasn't stupid. Wasn't reckless with his words. If he said it, some part of him wanted Griffin to hear it.

"Another secret to keep from her."

An ominous prickle went through Griffin's skin. Left side.

What the fuck does that mean? he wanted to say, but those words were still too fresh in his mouth from talking to Jamie, from some other held-back piece of knowledge about someone else he—

Well. He couldn't think about that now. His skin was getting pricklier, warmer. The flour on his hands felt itchy.

"Mikey," he said to his friend's back. Sharp, even with the nickname. "What secret?"

It was a long wait. Griffin watched his friend's shoulders move up and down, fists clenching and unclenching at his sides.

"What secret?" Griffin repeated. Needles now. Hot.

Michael turned around. Did not look at Griffin's face.

He said, "She doesn't know about Sara Beth."

For long seconds, Griffin could not think, just from the sound of her name, which he tried to never hear, even after all this time. Because for so long, for years and years, that name had only been a scream to him: his own, first, desperate and searching and panicking, and then, later—after—Michael's.

A sobbing howl, broken and disbelieving.

"You said you told her," Griffin said eventually, his voice quaking. He thought distantly about how they were out on the street. Not a busy street, but not a desolate one, either. This was a different city than the one he'd been in yesterday. Steep and crooked and wrong.

"I did tell her," Michael said. "I told her there was a house fire. That—that it's how you got hurt. I told her a . . . a friend of ours died."

"A friend of ours?" Griffin repeated. He could still feel the scalding pain along his skin, but also, he was strangely numb to it, his brain on fire now.

Michael looked devastated. Ashamed.

"You were going to *marry* her," Griffin said.

He felt ashamed, too, saying that. It was too simple, really, for what Sara Beth had been. Michael *was* going to marry her. He'd bought the ring the week before his graduation from the Air Force Academy. He'd sent Griffin a picture of it. He'd already asked Sara Beth's father, who was an absolute deadbeat, but still. He'd known she would say yes. Everyone knew.

Because Michael and Sara Beth had loved each other for years.

Since ninth grade. High school sweethearts. Kept it together long distance, all through college, a rarity. Sara Beth practically lived at the Plackett house, from the time she turned seventeen. Had chosen Paula to be her sponsor at her community college graduation, had been the only person that could ever get Fitz to laugh.

Had called Griffin "Griffy."

She was sweet and sometimes annoying and Griffin had loved her because she was Michael's girlfriend, Michael's forever, but he had also loved her because she was herself. A good friend, a good person.

"How could you not tell her?" he said, and Michael winced.

"I wanted to," Michael said. "I've tried. But Emily is . . ." He trailed off, and Griffin thought, *He is not actually going to say it, is he?*

"Young," his friend finished, sounding utterly defeated.

Now Griffin turned away, a wild, short-stepped pacing that sent a shaft of pain through his leg. He had never wanted to lay hands on Michael in his life, but he did now, and he had to get far away enough—only a couple of steps, fine—for the feeling to pass.

When he turned back around, Michael was pressing the heels of his hands to his eyes.

"Your parents never said anything to her?" Griffin asked, astonished.

Michael shook his head. "I asked them not to. I told them I would, eventually. I just wanted . . . a fresh start."

Griffin tried not to wince. It wasn't his place; he knew it wasn't his place. *Griffin* had not lost his first love that night.

But he didn't like thinking of Sara Beth as a person you tried to get a *fresh start* from.

Another thought struck him then. "What if *I* had said something?"

Michael stared at Griff like it was a stupid question.

"You don't ever talk about it," said Michael, and that was true. Griffin never, ever did.

So why did it feel like *he* had done something terrible to Emily?

Why did he feel he'd done something terrible to *Layla*?

He flashed back to himself, that first morning. *You said something to her*, he'd said, standing at the threshold of Layla's hotel room door, *accusing* her. *You need to fix this*, he'd demanded in that shitty little courtyard, so separate from the reality of Paris he didn't think he ever wanted to see it again.

The wedding has to happen, he'd said, and he was swamped with a sick, guilty feeling. How had that been any different than wanting a *fresh start*?

Had he ever even made an effort to see Emily as anything other than the just reward for Michael, for his friend who'd lost so much?

"You have to tell her," Griffin said, his voice flat and unyielding. "You cannot keep this from her. You can't marry her if—"

For the second time that morning, Griffin watched as someone's leashed anger broke free. But this time, on the face of his very best friend, Griffin didn't feel anything close to victory.

"Why don't you tell me, Griff," Michael said, taking a step forward, speaking through gritted teeth. "Why don't you tell me about the last time *you* told the story of that night to someone?"

Griffin swallowed. He hurt all over now. The left side was nothing.

"No answer for that? No answer from a guy who's spent *years* hiding himself away so he never has to tell anyone it happened? Me, your mom, that's it, and your mom probably only because she was your emergency fucking contact. Otherwise you probably would've tried to get someone to convince her you were dead. You think it's easy?"

Michael's voice was raised now, his face reddened, his hands at his sides curled into fists.

"You think it's easy to say, *A girl I loved once died. My best friend almost died, too. Sometimes I think he* did *die, for all the ways he changed after?*"

"Jesus," Griffin said.

"You think it's real easy, I bet, to explain to someone like Emily—Emily! Who thinks people are fair and good and forgiving and flexible—that my fucking parents blame that same best friend for the fire that killed a girl they thought of as a daughter? That they probably blame me a little, too, just for sticking by you?"

"Mikey."

"No!" Michael said, slicing an arm through the air, drawing a line as real and sharp and uncrossable as Griffin had ever seen. "You don't judge me for this. You *don't*. You, never leaving your house. Never getting out there again, in all these years. And even if you did—" Michael broke off, something dawning on him now. "Even now that you *have*—you still haven't said, have you? You didn't tell Layla? You didn't break up the best feeling you've had in forever to say, *Let me tell you about the worst thing that ever happened to me?*"

He didn't know how Michael was managing to make this a searing indictment—not when telling Layla would have been disastrous for this wedding, for Michael and Emily.

But damn if he didn't succeed.

Damn if Griffin didn't feel like the worst, most dishonest person in the world.

He shook his head. A minute movement. Barely an admission, and Michael's expression shifted into something Griffin hadn't ever seen on his friend's face. A curl of his lips like a sneer, even though his eyes were wet. Griffin thought of Sara Beth, of Michael's grief. Of all the days Michael sat by Griffin's hospital bed, never once blaming him for what happened. Clinging to the person he had left.

You should have been looking at me like this all along, Griffin thought.

You should have never let me be your best man.

And maybe, for once, Michael thought it, too. Because before he turned to go, he pointed a warning finger at Griffin and spoke, even though his voice shook.

"I'll keep your secret, Griffin," he said. "And you'll keep on keeping mine."

Chapter Twenty-Five

The text came when Layla was getting out of the shower.

She was not *supposed* to shower, the masseuse said; she was supposed to let the oils or whatever else *soak in*; she was supposed to give the *energy* from the massage time to *settle throughout her body*. Manon said, "Layla, you can't go *shower*!" and Layla lied and feigned a need to scratch at her neck, saying she thought she might be allergic to something.

But really, the massage made Layla feel restless and uncomfortable: the troubling conversation with Em too fresh in her mind, the traces of Griffin too fresh on her body. She felt as though she spent the whole ninety minutes clinging to both—worrying over whether to tell Griffin what she'd heard, and resenting every touch that covered over one of his.

When the massage finally ended, Layla dressed hastily, relieved that the rest of today was intended as "free time" for the guests to rest before tonight. She took out her phone before even clearing the spa's doors.

Text me when you're back, she wrote to Griffin, which, on reflection, might have read as overeager in a vague but still somehow too-specific way: a real *Please let me into that hotel room again* plea.

That he hadn't replied right away had perhaps driven her more quickly into the blazing-hot shower. A new reason to rinse—the shame of accidentally coming off as desperate.

So when she heard the pinging notification at the same time she shut the water off, she purposefully did not rush over to read the screen. She wrapped up her hair carefully, toweled off completely, tied herself into the room's now-familiar white robe. She tried to ignore the hope that his reply would be a simple *Come up*, that she would follow his instructions, that he would draw her into the faerie kingdom of his room, that he would make it so she wouldn't have to think about any of his secrets and what they might mean for Em and Michael's wedding.

But when she finally checked, she had a sinking feeling.

We need to talk, his text said. Then, an address for a café a few blocks away.

Much like her own text, it was vague but still too specific.

A prologue to *We made a mistake* if she'd ever seen one.

She sent back a curt OK, which was how *Doctor* Layla Bailey replied to texts that annoyed her, and this felt good to do—armoring and appropriately defensive. When she dressed, she did so without a care for all the concerns she'd had earlier in the week about the chicness of Parisian café culture; probably if she'd had access to Rosie's neon-green crop top, she would've put that on in some kind of petty defiance.

As it stood, she still only had neutrals, but she picked her slouchiest ones to wear. She left her hair wet and slicked it back into a bun, put on her sunscreen and her lip balm and nothing else, shoved her feet into her sneakers. She put on her sunglasses in the elevator and didn't smile once as she crossed the lobby. She thought, *I'm not even going to let him say it was a mistake. I'm going to make it about Michael and Emily, because that's what I said today would go back to being.*

It took her ten minutes to walk to the café, a nondescript corner spot with a faded awning and tables and chairs that were a little shabbier than she was used to seeing. It was crowded—not with tourists, she could tell, but with people who looked as comfortable as if they were sitting in their own homes, with family or friends they had over.

So it took her a few seconds to spot Griffin.

Obviously, he was alone. All-black, his hat on and his hands clasped loosely on his lap. Remote and magnetic, his own whole universe. He did not have his phone out; he was not reading. There was a bottle of Perrier on the table, two empty glasses, and another tiny cup of what was probably decaf in front of him. Layla thought he looked so strangely like he belonged there. Like he had somehow nailed Parisian café culture, no cigarette necessary.

"Annoying," she muttered to herself, shoving down the unruly twist of desire in her stomach, striding gamely toward him and thinking about how she was going to start by saying, *Actually, I think* you *need to fix this wedding now.*

But before she even got to his table, he stood. A column of smoke himself, and when she reached him—when his gravity had succeeded in *pulling* her to him—he set his right hand beneath her elbow, cupping it in the softest touch.

And he leaned in and kissed her. Right at the corner of her mouth. A Parisian kiss, but more possessive. He smelled like *butter*, butter and sugar and cinnamon, and he said, "You look pretty," in a voice so low she could not be sure whether she'd dreamed it.

She practically slid into the chair he held out for her.

Emily and Michael, she said to herself desperately, not wanting one single kiss, one simple compliment—*You look pretty*—to stop her from preempting this gently delivered *We made a mistake* business.

"Jamie knows," Griffin said—not gently—as soon as he sat down across from her.

She blinked.

She was so startled that it almost felt as though she had no idea who Jamie was.

"About Michael and Emily?" she finally said.

Griffin shook his head. "About us."

For what felt like a long time, Layla didn't say anything at all. She was thinking about something Griffin had told her yesterday as they'd searched for a comfortable place to sit in the elegant, secret-seeming Jardin du Palais Royal. He'd said, *Usually, I'm scanning for a feeling. I'm making sure I'm not too far gone.*

That was what she felt like now. Like she was scanning for a feeling. Something that would tell her whether it mattered to her that Jamie knew.

She could not, for the life of her, find one.

"Michael knows, too."

Oh. There was a feeling. A nervous one, an uncomfortable one. She'd come here to talk about Michael, about trouble between Michael and Emily, and whether or not she cared about Jamie knowing, she still didn't want what had happened with Griffin to become a sideshow when things were already strained.

Griffin said—as though he was reading the scan himself—"He won't tell anyone."

She reached for the Perrier, poured herself a glass, and sipped. Steadying herself, even though the water sparkled joyfully in her mouth. The bubbles tasted better in France; she didn't know how to explain it. She licked her bottom lip, liking the tingly feeling.

When she looked up again, Griffin's gaze was there. On her mouth. Dazed and hungry.

I'm too far gone, she thought.

She straightened, cleared her throat. "How did he find out?"

Even as she said it, she realized she wasn't sure which of the men she was talking about. Jamie, Michael, it didn't really matter. But as soon as she asked, Griffin blinked out of his haze, shifting in his seat. Arranging himself so his left leg was straight. He looked uncomfortable, but she got the sense it had, for once, nothing to do with his body.

"He overheard a part of the conversation. With"—a long pause, like he was about to swallow something bad—"your ex."

Layla almost laughed. *Laughed!* Instead, she smiled, hoped it looked sardonic. "You can say his name, you know. It doesn't bother me."

Griffin looked to the side briefly, his jaw flexing. "Well. It fucking bothers me," he said bluntly.

She took another sip of her joy water. Waited for the bubbles to *ping* their way through her before speaking again. Wondered why she felt so . . . so *effervescent* about this.

"Did you argue?" she finally asked.

"We . . . had words." Another shift in his seat. "Guess he was in the hotel lobby when we came back last night."

Here, he paused. Took a sip of his dark black drink and set it down with a *clink*.

"He's worried about you," he bit out.

Later, she would think so much—over and over—about this simple, specific thing Griffin said to her. Not even his own words, but someone else's. Not even something *new*, because hadn't she heard it, some version of it, a hundred different ways, from all of the MacKenzies, since the separation?

And yet in that moment, in that shabby corner café, said to her by *this* man—

It suddenly sounded so *insulting*.

It was the beginning of having a curse broken.

Her dark, cruel-seeming fae prince, jolting her into a different reality than the one she'd been trapped in for the last two years.

"It's not his job to worry about me," she said. She sort of wanted to take out her phone and type it into the translation app so all these French people could hear her say it in their language, too.

Griff's face softened, one side of his mouth tipping up. "That's what I said, too."

For a second, they looked at each other, as though both of them had just taken a big gulp of bubbly water. As though they were both thinking, *This is simply delightful!*

Then, wanting another hit, she said, "And what did he say to that?"

Griffin's smile faded, his body shifting again, his eyes lowering. She thought, at first, that she might've miscalculated—showing too much interest in Jamie himself, when really what this was about was how little it mattered to her that Jamie was *worried*, how she so thoroughly felt that she did not want that from him, not in any area of her life. Not anymore.

But after a few more seconds of silence, she could tell it wasn't that. She could tell there was something Griffin did not want to say to her.

"It doesn't matter," he said.

"It does. Tell me."

Griffin cleared his throat, made a flicking gesture with his right hand, as though he was trying to preemptively swat away what came next. "He said you were family."

Layla shrugged, unbothered. That was no big reveal. After all, she'd explained this to Griffin yesterday—what being a MacKenzie had meant to her. What it had felt like, to finally feel part of a family, and why it had felt like a failure to need distance from them after the divorce.

Why it had been so important to her, to be here this week for Emily.

"I may have—I may have had a reaction to that," Griffin said.

"You *may* have?"

He lifted his left hand and took off his cap, shoving his right hand through his hair before putting it back on. Lower this time.

"I said that if he was your family, he wouldn't have left you."

Layla swallowed. Every bubble in her body went flat.

"And he said?" she asked, but she knew. She knew what she was about to hear.

He did not want to say it. She could tell, he did not want to say it.

So he rushed it out. "He said if you wanted family, you wouldn't have left him."

In all the months it had taken for Layla and Jamie to split—to really, committedly call it quits—she had never once felt truly betrayed by him. She felt that he'd changed, and that he'd hurt her in the changing. She had told Cara, over a lunch where she didn't cry even once, that she and Jamie both had come to think of their vows as more metaphorical than literal. That *til death do us part* only meant that they had an obligation to stay connected. To be there for each other.

Cara *hated* that.

But this—this thing that Jamie said. It *was* a betrayal. A violation, a vow-breaking. He may have kept it vague, but to Layla, it was not vague *enough*. It was not honoring the promise that *Jamie*, after all, had been the one to suggest.

That they keep it true, but unspecific.

We grew apart. We had different priorities. We wanted different things.

She could not help but think that him telling Griffin—the first man Jamie had seen her with since they split—was somehow the worst part of all.

So she sat up straighter in her chair, and for the first time, she said it to someone plainly.

Proudly.

"We got a divorce because I don't want children."

It was easy to tell him.

Shockingly easy, after so long of not really telling anyone, or of always protecting Jamie—protecting what they'd had for so long—in whatever telling.

It hadn't ever been a secret, before the divorce, that Layla did not want children. Any woman who felt the way she did knew that you didn't really get away with *not* talking about it, whether you wanted to or not. People would casually say things like, *When you have one of your own* or *You don't really know sleep deprivation until* or *The best timing in terms of your career is*. People would say, *You would be such a good mom* or *Of course you could afford a great day care*.

And when they did, you could maybe smile politely and say nothing. Or you could say, *Oh, that's not really in the cards for me*, but then sometimes there would be these *looks*—pitying looks, looks like you meant that you wanted to and couldn't, looks that preceded something whispered and well-meaning like *My niece did IVF* or *Have you ever considered adoption?*

So, you would eventually say the truth of it. *Actually, I don't want to have children*, you would say, and then a lot of times you would have someone tell you that you would change your mind, or that losing your own mother must've been traumatic for you, *Have you seen anyone about that?* or that you would regret it, eventually, or—everyone's seeming favorite, a cutting last resort to kick up your existential dread—that you would not have anyone to care for you when you were old.

Layla had long felt that she'd gotten very good at those particular types of conversations.

But since the divorce, this certainty of hers—this thing she had never once doubted about herself, not in all the years since she was capable of really thinking about it—became shrouded by the painful memories she carried with her about the way it all fell apart with Jamie.

And it felt so *good* to finally tell someone.

To tell Griffin.

"He'd always said the same," she told him. "Since we first met in college, he'd said the same. What we wanted out of life—our work, our hopes for traveling, the way we felt about the future, the lifestyle we wanted—we didn't want to bring kids into that. We felt the same."

She told him, too, that she never took it for granted. That she had always felt this pressure, this *obligation*, to make sure he was truly certain. It must have been hundreds of times, she asked him. When they were dating, on the day they got engaged. All the way up to the wedding.

And Jamie had always reassured her.

He was certain, too.

But then he wasn't so certain anymore.

It started slow, but not so slow that it hadn't made her feel dread right from the start.

A birthday party for one of her attendings, where Layla had

helped out a fellow resident for maybe a grand total of half a minute by holding their three-month-old, and how Jamie had said, on the way home, that it "surprised" him to see it. To feel "some kind of way" about it.

A holiday card sent by a friend from college, a collage of photos featuring a three- and five-year-old, and Jamie's wistful, *They are cute, aren't they?*

Then, more serious moments. *Sometimes I do think about it. Lately, I wonder what a kid of ours would be like. Don't you think we could make it work? Don't you think for us, it'd be different? What if we agreed to a timeline for revisiting it? What about when you've had five years as an attending?*

Eventually, it became crushing: a vise around her middle, tightening and tightening as it was increasingly clear that Jamie had become certain about something else. Counseling, which she agreed to, even though it was evident from the start that Jamie saw it as counseling for *her*, that Jamie had somehow become one of those people who thought Layla's decision must have a deeper seed, a motherless child who could not imagine herself as a mother. Special "date nights" that felt weighted with expectation, never more than when Jamie once said, *What if we leave it in the hands of the universe?* and she'd thought, *We're the universe, remember? We make our own gravity.*

But instead, she'd said, *I'm not taking out my fucking IUD, Jamie*, and it had been that—that moment of pure, undiluted frustration, so rare from her—that had seemed to spell the end of it.

So, finally, it was softer, quieter conversations. Tearful ones, brokenhearted ones, heavy with their long history together, all the ways their lives were intertwined. Jamie would sometimes say, *It doesn't matter; I'll get over it; I love you and I love our life*, but Layla knew he was lying to himself.

She knew that part of him was waiting—would always be waiting, until it was too late—for her to say that she'd changed her mind.

"But I won't," she said now to Griffin, who sat across from her almost perfectly still, a statue, a shade from the underworld readying himself to throw open the gates, to shove a new sinner through the fiery doors.

She knew that she was not that sinner, and it felt so *good*.

"Remember yesterday?" she said, watching as the hellfire in his eyes immediately banked, transforming into something else—warm with memory. "When I said what it had been like for me to come to Paris the first time?"

He nodded. At some point, he'd taken off his hat, tucking it behind him on the chair to make room for the food they'd eventually ordered. A few minutes ago, a new pair of people had taken seats at the table beside them, and Layla had noticed—in her periphery—the way one of the men stared openly at Griffin's profile.

She wanted to hiss at him. Like a little hell-creature.

But Griffin hadn't seemed to notice at all.

"You said you were trying to become someone," he said.

She nodded, too, pressing her lips together as though it would keep her from speaking this complicated thought too soon. It'd been living inside her for a long, long time. Since that first moment, that first *It made me feel some kind of way, seeing you hold a baby*. It'd gathered speed and mass, like a rock rolling down a muddy hill, picking up dirt and moss and whatever else, faster and faster the heavier it became. Every sly, and then direct, comment, every counseling session. Every conversation about ending it.

"I *did* become someone," she finally said. "For him, I did. When I met him, I was so in love with him—with who he was, and also . . . how he'd become who he was. His traditions, his favorite things, his family who loved him so much, and I didn't have many of those on my own. I wanted so badly to have them, but I . . . I didn't have many people to *show* me when I was young."

Griffin did something then—something she knew mattered, when it came to him.

He reached across the table, not pausing, not calculating, not worrying, and touched her. His right hand on her left wrist, curling his warm, strong fingers around her. He didn't say anything at all.

"But I did have some things of my own, and this was one of them. This knowledge of myself, of what I didn't want for my life, and never had wanted, the same way other people know that they *do* want it. And I look back and think—this was my one thing. My *one* thing I brought to that marriage that I couldn't—that I wouldn't let become something else. I wouldn't do it to myself, and I certainly wouldn't do it to a kid."

He was stroking that soft, vulnerable skin on the inside of her wrist now, and it felt perfect. Comforting and courage-giving, so she could say this thing she'd never felt ready to say to anyone.

"And for all Jamie ever said to me about us being family, it feels funny. It feels funny that it only took one thing for us not to be one anymore."

There, she thought, triumph moving through her—like one of those great, gold-winged horses they'd passed on the Pont Alexandre yesterday, rearing up in what looked to her like celebration. *There, I finally said it.*

We aren't *family anymore.*

For her, it was a huge admission. A painful secret she'd hidden from herself, in the deepest, most broken parts of her heart.

She must have been quiet for a while, letting it sink in, because eventually she realized that Griffin had moved his hand again to take hers, intertwining their fingers on top of the table.

He said, "I fucking *hate* him."

This time, she did laugh. A little release, a sip of bubbles popping deliciously inside her.

She shrugged and said, "I guess I hate him a little, too."

At that, Griffin looked a bit like a gold-winged horse himself, which was maybe fair enough, but also, she didn't want it to be too simple.

She was glad to have said all this, glad to have admitted it.

But the truth was, she knew that hating Jamie, even a little, was because she had loved him. Because she had not wanted, ultimately, for him to live his life without something he had started to want so badly. Not acknowledging that felt strangely like taking away something from herself. A strength she had that no one truly seemed to understand.

Giving in to him—having a kid with him, even though she didn't want to be a parent—*that* would have been weakness.

Saying no was strength.

"Him wanting kids—that's okay," she said. "I don't dislike kids; I don't dislike anyone else who wants them. I think he would be a good dad."

Griffin snorted. "Except he's a *liar*," he said, and it was such a petty-sounding thing to say that she laughed again.

"I don't think he lied. I think he changed his mind." She shrugged. "Who wouldn't want to be amicable about that?"

"Me," Griffin said flatly. But his mouth quirked on one side, and for a minute, they sat together—holding hands across the table, Griffin having given up his post at the gates of hell for the time being, and Layla feeling lighter than she had in almost two years.

Eventually, though, she realized something—that the light had changed on the buildings around them, that the café crowd had thinned dramatically, that the rhythm of pedestrian traffic had changed. She sat up straighter in her chair, pulling her hand away from Griffin's. She reached for her phone in her purse, then blew out a breath when she saw the time. In less than three hours, the open house was starting.

The wedding well and truly on.

A different reality rushed back in. The spa this morning, that conversation with Emily. Everything Layla had learned—*a house fire, how he got hurt, a friend who died*—and how all of it was the *actual* risk to this wedding.

That is what she'd *really* come to this café to talk to Griffin about.

The secrets Michael was keeping from Emily.

She felt a pang of loss for how drastically she was about to change the tone.

"So, this morning, when I was with Emily," she began, and she could see how his gaze immediately turned wary. Not quite like it was that first time he'd confronted her about this—*something you said*—but wary nonetheless.

"She's still having doubts. About Michael. And I don't think—"

"Layla," he interrupted, and the *way* he said her name.

Low, like a plea, like sometime last night in the dark, with their skin pressed together, with his mouth close to hers.

"Y—yeah?" she managed.

"I know it matters. And you can tell me. But after everything you just said—I want a little more time where it's not you worrying about this fucking family for once. I want you to leave Emily and Michael to themselves for a minute."

She blinked at him, relieved and surprised, and also pulsing with arousal at how he'd said her name.

But it was the relief and surprise that were overwhelming her.

Relief because Griffin was right—at the moment, after everything she'd admitted about her and Jamie, after saying out loud that he wasn't her family anymore—there was a new weight to what Emily was or wasn't to her, a new weight to what had driven her to come all this way, and she wasn't ready to think about it yet.

Surprise because in all the time she'd known Griffin, she'd known that Michael—Michael's happiness, Michael getting *married*—was never far from his mind.

"Well, I—"

"One hour," he said, but he was already pushing back from the table. Already holding out his hand. "Just give me one hour."

"That's longer than a minute," she said.

He was standing now. Smiling down at her. He said, "I lied."

Chapter Twenty-Six

He took her to a perfume shop.

A *parfumerie*, he thought the French word was, which was better for the place he'd seen on his walk over to the café: a tiny space, deserving of that *-ie* ending that *sounded* small to him, tucked neatly and cozily into a row of stores in the shopping district of the Marais.

What made him notice it first was not its smallness but its color—his favorite color, which formed the shop's facade, a striking matte black contrast to the pale stone above and around it. The lettering above the door was small, simple, no showy script or fancy logo. Through the glass, he saw a wild display of boldly colored flowers, deep reds and magentas and jewel greens, and because he'd been with her all day yesterday, because he'd walked by and in countless shops with her, he immediately thought—a relief from what had otherwise been pounding through him with each step—*Layla would like that*.

But he'd forgotten about it once he got to the café, once he sat and fully took stock of the smoldering remains of the morning. He waited and thought about how to tell her that Jamie knew, that Michael knew.

About *whether* to tell her that there was something else, too.

A secret Michael was keeping, something that would matter so much to Emily.

The woman who was about to marry his best friend. The woman Layla thought of as a sister.

He'd forgotten about the shop even more once his conversation with Layla took a different turn. For a while, he'd forgotten everything, ever; he listened to her and lived only inside the cocoon of hate he seemed to be constructing around himself, the whole thing made up of every detail Layla told him about her ex-husband.

What a fucking idiot, to lose her. To lose the reality of Layla, all for some imaginary kid.

What an asshole, to try to convince her. To make family a bargaining chip. To use the thing she wanted most in the world against her. To change the meaning of it after you'd made your vows.

But the memory of the shop came back to him almost as soon as Layla brought Emily up again—her doubts, her doubts about *Michael*, Michael who'd shouted at him on the street, Michael who'd not spoken to him for the rest of the morning, Michael who'd left the pâtisserie with a basket of croissants that Griffin had made and a look on his face like he barely knew where he was anymore.

He did not know what to do about Michael. About Emily.

Not yet.

But when he thought about that perfume shop, he knew something he could do for Layla.

He walked her back there, holding her hand the whole way, even though he could genuinely not remember the last time he'd held hands with someone outside of a nurse in a hospital hallway, clutching and desperate during weight-bearing exercises that made him feel subhuman, gawked at, pitied.

He kept Layla close on his right side, like a bulwark against what was still hurting on his left—seven out of ten, he was pretty sure—ever since this morning in Montmartre. He didn't mention it to her, because mentioning it to her meant explaining what'd happened with Michael, and in the end this detour was for him, too: *a little more time*, like he'd told her, even if what he was letting himself forget for a while was his best friend.

When they got close, she looked up at him, said, "Perfume?" and he was nervous for a minute, worried it had been a bad idea. He knew some women didn't wear it, didn't like it, and maybe she was one of them.

Except he had a sense that she wasn't. He had a sense this was right.

So he took her inside the shop: dimly lit and den-like, the flowers on display highlighted with some hidden glow coming from somewhere tucked away. He said, "Bonjour," to the woman dressed in all black who stood inside behind a long marble counter, because Layla told him yesterday that you always had to say *Bonjour* when you walked into a shop here, *always*.

She said *Bonjour* back, but also asked in English whether she might help them, so clearly he had not mastered his pronunciation.

He took out his wallet, slid out a credit card, and handed it to the woman, whom he trusted instinctively, what with her outfit and all. He said, "For her," gesturing at Layla. "For whatever she picks."

"Griff," Layla whispered, like she was absolutely *scandalized*, and he could not help but smile, especially given what he'd done to her last night.

"I can't stay in here," he said, which was true—the aroma was overwhelming, the kind of sensory overload that would get his wires crossed, especially at a seven out of ten. It was more than that, though: It was that he wanted her to pick something only for herself. He wanted her to go to that open house tonight wearing something she'd picked because she *liked* it, and not because it looked a certain way for the MacKenzies, not because she wanted to blend in or be appropriate or fucking *amicable*.

"But I—" She broke off, at a loss for words, as though no one had ever done something like this for her before, which added a layer to that cocoon of hate he'd been working on.

"I can pay for it myself," she finally finished.

"I know," he said.

It struck him that knowing it—knowing that he was buying her something comparatively small, something she could buy for herself—was part of why this mattered to him. He'd had his money for a long time now, a complete fluke after all these years, the kind of money that grew without him doing a damn thing worthwhile with himself, and the only way it'd ever felt okay to him was when he was buying his mother a farm or paying for most of this insane, over-the-top wedding. If he wanted that sort of feeling, he would've found a way to get back to that clothes museum Layla loved from yesterday; he would've tried to get someone to sell him one of those starlight dresses, straight off the mannequin, or he would've leaned into his hate-cocoon-driven urge to buy her some hulking, unmissable piece of jewelry, just to stick it to Jamie MacKenzie.

He might not be good; he might not be reliable. But he *was* rich.

This, though. This was different.

So he leaned down quickly, set his lips against her for one of those corner-mouth kisses he liked to give her, and ducked out of the store before she could object again.

Back outside, he tucked himself off to the side of the building, and almost immediately—as soon as he was out of sight of the shop's window, no longer able to see Layla—the forgetting part was over. In his mind, he was away from the Marais, back on the hill in Montmartre with Michael. He was staring down at a heap of debris and ash; he was thinking, *What happened here?*; he was sorting through the answers that were too numerous and too quick in coming.

He realized now that he'd been wrong about this wedding—about the *risk* to this wedding—from the beginning. He had not known how far Michael had already gone to ensure it would happen, and in the not knowing, he had simply blamed Layla. And then he had grown close to Layla, closer than he'd let himself be with anyone in years, only to be reminded—first by her ex-husband, and then by Michael, too—that he was not good enough for her, that he was unreliable, a hermit who never left his house, a man who had no room to judge.

It rang in his ears, that *You don't judge me for this*, that broken note in Michael's voice as he said it, and the worst part was how much he *understood* it. He understood how long Michael had grieved for Sara Beth, how much harder and heavier the grief had been for how close Griffin had come to dying, too, how challenging Fitz and Paula had been in the aftermath.

He understood, too, that Emily was a miracle to Michael, a balm to him. He understood that Michael genuinely loved her, and that's why he was so afraid to lose her.

And he supposed he also understood—now that he'd been with Layla—why the whole truth was sometimes so hard to say.

You didn't break up the best feeling you've had in forever to say, Let me tell you about the worst thing that ever happened to me?

He hadn't. In all the time he was with Layla, yesterday and last night, he hadn't.

Except . . . except it *wasn't* the same.

He knew it wasn't the same, no matter if now, he thought maybe he could tell Layla about the fire, about Sara Beth and how he hadn't been able to save her. It wasn't the same because he hadn't been with Layla for over a year, hadn't proposed to her, wasn't going to *marry her* tomorrow night.

That thought—*marry her*—sent a shock through him, an unfamiliar sensation that didn't show up on the pain scale.

He shoved it aside.

He thought of Emily finding out about Sara Beth later. After the wedding.

What it would do to her, to find out later.

And then he thought of Layla again, across from him at that café table, telling him about her divorce.

That's not the same, either, part of him thought. *All right, I still fucking hate him, but I can see that he didn't really* lie. *Not like Michael's lying. He changed his mind, like Layla said.*

But a bigger part of him—a better part of him, maybe— thought, *It's the same. Emily could get hurt the same.*

And when she did—when she got hurt from finding this out, after she'd already married him—Michael would lose her.

From his spot against the coal-black building facade, Griffin raised a hand to his forehead, pressing his fingers beneath the brim of his hat, rubbing at the tension there. Distantly, he thought, *Do I have a goddamn headache, a regular-person headache? How strange*.

It was more complexity than he had allowed into his life in ages. For years, he had been guided by only a few things. Managing his pain, making sure his mother was taken care of.

And Michael. Seeing Michael happy, and settled.

The way he would've been, if it hadn't been for the fire.

Now, though, it was different.

He thought of Michael looking at him, hard-eyed but scared, Michael saying, *You, never leaving your house*, and he wished Michael was here right now. He wished he could say back what had just come to him, bright and blinding and so terrible that there was no one he wanted to tell except for his best friend.

But I did leave the house. I left the house; I crawled out of the bell tower, out of hell itself, and it hurt almost the whole fucking way.

And that's how I know what you're doing isn't right.

"Hi," Layla said, and he straightened up, turned to face her—the warm, smiling aliveness of her, something pleased and sheepish in her eyes.

He did not forget about Emily, about Sara Beth, about Michael. But he did focus.

"You get something?" he asked, and she nodded, the sheepishness in her expression turned more teasing.

More tempting.

She had a small bag dangling from her fingers, swinging gently, but she said, "I'm wearing it."

He took her elbow, drawing her to him and spinning her so her back was pressed to the building, so he could crowd her again like that first time he kissed her.

He dropped his face, tucked it against her neck, and took a deep inhale.

The best breath of his life.

She sighed with pleasure. He recognized the sound of her pleasure now, and it sent blood straight to his groin, but he didn't press that part of himself hard into her, like he wanted to.

"Lily," she said, not too close to his ear. "White musk, and—"

He pressed his lips against her neck.

"I forget," she breathed.

"Doesn't matter," he said, because it didn't. He thought she would smell good to him no matter what. She could've said, *lily and ash heap*, and he would've thought, *It works on you*.

"Do y—" She broke off when she felt his tongue touch gently, quickly, against her neck, then tried again. "Do you like it?"

He had an answer. Of course he had an answer. But he thought maybe it was the wrong question, the amicable question, and after everything she'd told him, Griffin didn't want Layla to ever feel like she had to ask him any of those.

"No," he lied, but he kept his face right there. He breathed it in again.

He felt her smile. She said, "Well, I don't care. I do."

He lifted his head and kissed her once, hard.

"Good," he said, and then kissed her again, and again and again, too much for the street, no nighttime, no doorway to protect them now, but neither of them seemed to care.

When they finally stopped, both of them out of breath, Layla glassy-eyed with her head tipped back against the black facade, he knew their hour was up—they had to get back to the hotel, get changed, get over to the open house. He sensed that she knew it, too; he watched awareness gather back into her eyes.

He felt as though they were standing still against some threshold, a gate he didn't want to give a name to: on the other side, Emily and Michael, the ghost of Sara Beth. Jamie and what he'd seen last night, Jamie and the rest of the MacKenzies and the way they looked at Layla. The way she looked at all of them, too.

The column of her throat moved in a swallow.

She said, a slight catch in her voice, "You do like it, though, don't you?"

He looked at her, long and searching. He thought something he had not thought in years and years, or maybe ever.

He thought, *You need me*, but for once, it didn't have anything to do with his money. It had to do with how he would answer this question. It had to do with his shrewdness, his ability to see her, his opposite-of-amicability way of moving through the world, which had only ever been a survival tactic until now, him *I don't care*-ing himself through the half-life he'd been clinging to. It had to do with the way she needed to be reminded of what she didn't owe—what she would *never* owe—to anyone else.

It had to do with how Layla, for too long, had been telling people what they wanted to hear: *It's okay that you changed your mind; of course we'll still be family; yes, I'll come to the wedding.*

He thought, *I am needed*, and for all the scanning of his body he'd spent all these years doing, he couldn't decide, in the moment, whether it made him feel heavy or light.

So he just smiled at her, for once not thinking of what it did to his face.

"I hate it," he said.

He watched as she smiled back, slow and revelatory and satisfied, the *I don't care* written all over her face. He watched as she realized his answer was the most beautiful, loving lie she'd ever been told.

And he wondered, as he walked back to the hotel with her, how hard it would be—how heavy it would be—to tell someone else he loved exactly what they needed to hear.

Chapter Twenty-Seven

Something had happened since she left Griffin.

Layla stood in the large, open-plan living area of the huge ground-floor apartment that the MacKenzies had booked for the weekend, the culminating site of the week's events. Behind her, a set of wide glass doors opened out onto a gorgeous, private courtyard. Tomorrow afternoon, it would be transformed for Emily and Michael's ceremony. A flowered arch she'd seen pictures of on that first night at dinner would be arriving tomorrow, set up for them to stand under as they exchanged their vows.

For now, though, all the guests—and now, it was truly *all* of the guests, not just those who'd been able to come early for the Paris-tourism part of it all—were mingling indoors, driven inside by gray skies and a chill in the air.

It was, Layla could admit, a gorgeous apartment, if a little cream-and-white sterile, but she figured that was part of its appeal for a weekend like this: more of a staging space than a settling space. When she arrived a half hour ago, Manon and Céline had taken her through the three bedrooms, which they'd taken to calling "the bridal suite," "the groom's retreat," and "the honeymoon sanctuary." Tomorrow, Michael and Emily would have their separate "getting-ready" quarters, but then after the wedding, they would have this whole apartment to themselves for a few days, moving into the primary, balconied bedroom that overlooked the courtyard.

But once the tour was over, a sense of foreboding slowly crept over Layla as more guests arrived, as the catering servers started making their rounds, as the quartet of musicians set up in the loft above started their muted-sounding performance.

It shouldn't have been a surprise, that foreboding feeling—not after this morning's conversation with Emily, not after what had happened between Jamie and Griffin, not even after Layla realized, once she was back in her hotel room post-parfumerie-detour, that she'd run out of time to tell Griffin what Emily had said about the fire.

Somehow, though, it still was: Somehow, Layla had arrived to this open house feeling *genuinely* calmer than she had in ages, no mind-over-matter affirmations necessary. She had chosen the black top again, the one Griffin first kissed her in, no blazer over it; she had dabbed her new fragrance behind her ears like a secret she was keeping from everyone but him; she had made her way across the cobblestone streets between the hotel and here and thought, *Who cares if they hate it?* even though she couldn't even have said, in the moment, who *they* or what *it* was.

So when that calmness started to slip from her grip—when she saw Em, hovering nervously around the caterer in the kitchen, checking and rechecking things like a mini-Manon; when she saw Fitz and Paula, tense and unspeaking in a corner, looking suspiciously at the Nantes cousins; when she saw Jamie and Sam, whispering to each other near the bathroom—she was rattled by the shift. She started to think, *Where's Griff?* in a way that felt overly needy for how not-long she had known him, and then, when she connected the obvious dot and thought, *Wait, where's* Michael? she did not feel any better to realize that they *both* hadn't yet shown.

"Vibes are off," a familiar voice said, interrupting her thoughts. "Am I right?"

Layla turned to look at Rosie, whom she had last seen slapping Emily's hand away as the bride-to-be reached for a glass of champagne off one of the server's trays. Tonight, Rosie was not beating any *don't steal the bride's limelight* allegations, because she was wearing a hot pink tiered tulle skirt with a black bodysuit beneath it, a peek of bright yellow lace sticking out from the neckline, presumably part of her bra. Layla thought she looked simultaneously amazing and ridiculous.

"You're not wrong," Layla said, sipping her own champagne. She decided it was no longer off-limits, it being completely clear now that she'd never drank enough of it to say anything to mess up this already-messed-up situation.

"I texted Michael," Rosie said, "but no reply yet."

Layla feigned mild interest—a quiet *Hm*—when really, the foreboding was pounding through her now. She thought of leaving Griffin in the hotel lobby, how he'd said, with a grim set to his mouth, *I'll see you there. I'm going to try to catch Michael before we go.*

Both she and Rosie turned their gazes to Em, who'd stopped haranguing the caterers and was now laughing too loud with one of the new arrivals, an old high school friend Layla recognized from past MacKenzie gatherings but couldn't quite remember the name of. She'd come with her new husband, who looked like a paper doll cut out of a book called *Finance Guys*.

"Five more minutes and I go find him," Rosie said. "She cannot laugh like that all night. It's so fake! I mean yes, Michaela—

Madison? Miranda! Yes, Miranda the field hockey girl!—brings it out in her, but come on. This is about Michael, right?"

Layla looked over at Rosie, who now had a furrowed-brow expression that was somehow more concerning than her panicky *Thank god you're here* from the first morning, when the initial crack in this week's facade had shown itself.

"If he has cold feet, I'll kill him," Rosie said. "No. I'll cut the cold feet off. And he can stand up there on his new bloody stumps and say *I do*."

Layla cringed, though she was grudgingly impressed. Rosie had so much fierce heart in her. Slow on the uptake, maybe, given the week's events, but still, fierce. Like Cara had been—had tried to be—for Layla.

She would need to tell Cara that soon. When she got back from this trip, she would need to tell Cara so many things.

"I don't think he has cold feet," Layla said, looking back toward Emily. *I think he's keeping a secret.*

In that moment, the foreboding felt almost overwhelming—a weighted cloak settling over her shoulders, one that she'd managed to set down for a while. She had wanted to tell Griffin that she knew about this secret—not what it was but *that* it was; she had wanted to warn him that it was getting in the way of Em's certainty about this wedding. But now, looking at her former sister-in-law—that fake smile, that fake laugh, so *amicable*—she wondered whether warning him was even the right thing to do.

She wondered whether she should walk right up to Emily—sweet Emily, still family, no matter what—and say, *Don't marry him until you know. Don't let him lock you out of this.*

Everyone would blame her, of course. Manon, Robert, Jamie. The Placketts, probably, who looked like they'd blame a napkin for not staying clean. God, *Griffin* would surely blame her, wouldn't he? No matter what had happened between them? He would still get that implacable face, that *The wedding has to happen* fist. It wasn't as though she mattered to him more than his best friend; it wasn't as though she *should*.

It would make a mess of everything.

But maybe she shouldn't care.

Maybe she *didn't* care, at least not about everyone on that list. Not anymore.

"—if he *actually* comes, though, I'll probably die."

Layla blinked, focusing back on Rosie, who clearly had been in the middle of something that Layla had entirely tuned out.

"What?" Layla said. "We *want* him to come. It's the night before their wedding."

Rosie rolled her eyes. "Catch up, Grandma. I'm not talking about Michael now. I'm talking about Matthieu."

"Matthieu?"

"The hot driver? From the night we went on the boat? Were you listening?"

"Oh," Layla said, obviously having not been listening. Still, rude to get called a grandma, especially when she was wearing this top. She wasn't *that* much older than Rosie. "Yeah, I—"

"I mean, look, getting finger-fucked in the back of his work vehicle was honestly a top-three experience of this trip, but also, it's not like it's the start of a *relationship*. When he talks I don't even understand what he's say—" She broke off, digging her elbow sharply into Layla. "Oh my god, Michael's here, fucking *finally*."

Layla's eyes snapped to the entrance, shaking off her momentary curiosity—Matthieu the driver! Rosie was really a dark horse—to see Michael coming through the door, head down. He was in a suit—navy, well-tailored, a purple flower tucked into his lapel, probably a Manon MacKenzie production. But Layla had never seen anyone look less put together while wearing something so nice. Even with his head lowered she could see his skin was red along his neck, a stark contrast to the bright white of his pressed collar. His hair, which he usually had meticulously combed, looked haphazardly done, uneven on one side. When he took a step, Layla saw that one of his shoes was untied, a string flapping against the parquet.

All that, she maybe could have ignored. A harried groom, a big night, a forgotten final look in the mirror before getting out the door.

But two things made it impossible.

First: When he lifted his eyes, he did not, for once, look for Emily immediately. Instead, his gaze seemed unseeing, drifting over the room as though he didn't recognize anyone here at all.

Second: Griffin was not with him.

"Why the long face!" Rosie whisper-shouted, referring to Michael, but at this point, Layla was well past foreboding. She wasn't anticipating something going wrong anymore; she was watching it happen.

"Rosie, can you—" she started to say, hoping to ask her to . . . she didn't exactly know what. Designing some sort of distraction in that skirt seemed possible, or maybe announcing to the room the thing about the top three events from this trip. If she could get Rosie to pull focus, she could go over to Michael. Find out where Griffin was, find out how to help.

But Robert had already noticed Michael, crossing the room to pat his shoulder and say something jovially scolding about his tardiness, immediately drawing him over to the Nantes cousins, who were probably still getting the stink eye from the Placketts for being so foreign, so *French*.

Layla felt a pang of sympathy for Michael, of genuine understanding. She remembered her own rehearsal dinner, her and her father's distance from each other impossible for anyone to miss, the tongue-clicks of pity over Vaughn ("Oh, your only brother!") being unable to make it, all of it contrasted with the MacKenzies' gregariousness and warmth and abundance.

She'd loved that about them.

But it had been so much pressure sometimes. Especially early on.

Michael was smiling in a strained way, shaking hands, leaning in to say what Layla thought was, "Again, I'm sorry?" to one of the cousins who was speaking quickly, probably in her thickly accented English. For the first time since arriving in Paris, since that first morning after the dinner where she *thought* it had all gone wrong, she thought she could probably be more useful to Michael than to Emily.

"Can you distract Emily for a few minutes?" she said to Rosie. "I'm going to grab Michael real quick. He looks a little overwhelmed."

Rosie said, "Uh, *yep*," as though this was the only plan that made any sort of sense, and then she was flouncing off, probably to call Miranda's husband "Finance Guy" to his face.

Layla did not hesitate. She breathed in through her nose and put on a placid expression, a real *walking up the airplane aisle* expression, holding her champagne lightly and weaving her way toward where Robert and Michael and the cousins stood, Céline a new and sharp-eyed addition, judging by how keenly she was watching Michael.

"Laylapalooza!" Robert said in welcome, extending an arm as though she might automatically tuck herself right there, the way she had so many times in the past, when she was like a daughter to him. But she dodged it, worried it would delay her. She smiled at the cousins, who had already given her double-kisses in greeting when they first arrived, one of them—her favorite, Anne—leaning in to *tsk* dramatically and say that Jamie must be *bête comme ses pieds*.

"I've been sent with a message for the groom," she lied, a light, conspiratorial tone in her voice, the kind of *I'm doing one of those secret errands!* codes that no one ever questioned at a special event.

Anne said, "Oh! We beg your pardon!" in her lovely accent, and drew everyone away, including Robert, who looked like he was going to attempt—probably not for the first time—to pry the Placketts out of their corner.

Layla was waiting, wanting everyone well out of earshot first, when Michael said, "A message."

No inflection in it—no question mark at the end, and when she turned to look up at him, he was already looking down at her with that strange blankness in his eyes, unlike anything she'd ever seen since she'd first met him.

He looked hollow.

"Michael," she said, nervous now, that brief *I don't care* boldness absolutely abandoning her. "I was wondering if I could talk to you about—"

"Are you over Jamie?" he interrupted.

She stared at him. No doubt her own expression was blank now, wiped clean at such an unexpected question, so bluntly asked. What in god's name did he care about her and Jamie for?

"Am I—what?"

"Over. Him," Michael asked, suspicion in his eyes now.

"Yes?" she said, the inflection in her own voice more about her ongoing surprise to be asked rather than any doubt. Strangely, when she said it—when she heard the question in her voice—she knew that there wasn't any question. Not anymore. She didn't suppose she would *really* ever get over the whole thing of it—the feeling of family, of losing it, of losing herself in the aftermath of it. She didn't suppose that was the sort of thing you ever did fully *get over*. She didn't suppose it would be right to.

But she had gotten over Jamie.

She'd let go of him, maybe longer ago than she'd ever realized.

"You don't sound sure," Michael said.

"Well, I am," she said, snappishness in her tone now. They were in the middle of a *party*, for god's sake; it wasn't like they could drag out this conversation. She had a *purpose* here, and Jamie didn't have anything to do with it.

"I don't see how it's any of your . . ."

She trailed off, an idea nudging at her—something about the way Michael was looking at her, the way he was asking her this. It reminded her of those first couple of days with Griffin, the way he thought that what was going wrong with the wedding—with Emily—had to do with *her*, something she *said*, her and her fallen-apart marriage, and how it might somehow infect this whole week for everyone.

"Look, this isn't about that, I swear to you," she said. "Emily doesn't care about me and Jamie. She's worried about . . ."

This time, when she trailed off, it was because Michael had so clearly stopped listening. His gaze had gone over her shoulder, wholly hollow again, even bleaker this time. Layla hardly knew Michael, and still, it hurt to see him look this way, no matter that he'd just been sort of rude to her.

So she turned, too, and that's when she saw him.

A column of smoke moving through the room, dressed in the same clothes he'd been wearing earlier, no change for the sake of this party. No intention to *be* at this party, at least not for long. She had not heard him come in; she suspected that no one had heard him come in; she wondered if maybe he had simply slipped, sinuous and untouchable, through the cracks in the door. If he looked around, she couldn't tell, because he had his hat brim pulled low, like when she'd first met him.

But one thing was clear.

He had not come to this party looking for her.

Oh no, she thought as she watched him make his way to where Em stood, Rosie beside her, the Finance Guy and his field hockey wife having moved on at some point, and Layla had the sense it was good that Rosie was there in her big pink skirt, her yellow bra showing, a fierce faerie sprite that wasn't afraid of this dark prince who Layla knew was the culmination of all this gathering foreboding, all this *inevitability*.

Behind her, Michael did not move.

He did not move when Griffin reached Emily, and he did not move when Griffin bent his head, leaning in to speak beside Emily's ear.

He did not move when Emily's eyes shot up, surely catching Michael's gaze, and he did not move when her face drained of color.

And he still did not move when the column of smoke straightened again, and turned to leave.

Out the very door no one had even seen him enter.

Chapter Twenty-Eight

He knew she would come.

He could tell himself that he wasn't waiting for her, that he was only taking a little time to breathe through the reality of what he'd done, and then he would get up and move. A silicone patch would be good, staying limber would be good, because he felt a bad night coming on.

But he knew he wouldn't do any of that.

Not until she came.

So he sat on the small couch, more uncomfortable than he could have conceived of, his back curved, his left leg stretched as long as he could manage. He thought of Michael sitting right here. Only yesterday. Stalling on going to the museum, floating on a brief balloon of confidence about Emily that Griffin had let the air out of.

Now, he had done more than let the air out.

He had basically shot his best friend out of the sky.

When the knock finally came, he stood slowly, creaking and screaming and shivering on the inside, waiting for his left leg to get right beneath him. He thought of how familiar this was: being on one side of the door, knowing she was on the other. He thought of how his mind was racing and his heart was pounding.

Déjà vu.

He thought of the big difference.

He thought of how—unlike that morning—this time, it was something *he* said.

"Griff?"

Her voice was muffled through the door, but he still tried to read something from it. *Griff* was a good sign, but he couldn't tell anything else. Whether what he'd said to Emily was something she already knew. Whether she knew more than that by now.

It didn't matter. He was going to tell her himself; he'd already decided that.

He just needed to tell the person who most deserved—most needed—to know, first.

He opened the door.

She looked beautiful. The shirt she'd been wearing the night he first kissed her, the skin of her neck and chest showing, no adornment except for the perfume he knew she was wearing. Her hair was down, curled softly; her makeup light and lovely, her lips done with something that made them berry pink and full. When he had come to her room that first morning, she'd been so disheveled—mascara in the crescent moons beneath her eyes, her hair a wild tangle, her hotel robe haphazardly belted.

Beautiful, both ways.

"Hi," she said, and he didn't bother replying. He stepped back from the door, holding it open for her as she crossed the threshold. He should've used the time to think of exactly how to start this.

But he also probably should've known by now that she would: that she was calm in a crisis, efficient in her movements, good at asking good questions and giving necessary information.

She went straight to the terrible couch and sat. It seemed the perfect size for her. She looked up at him and said, "Michael and Emily left the open house."

He stood, still near the door, his hands shoved in his pockets. He nodded.

"Rosie's handling it," she added. "She said she'd distract everyone for as long as she could."

Another nod. He had been distantly aware of Rosie standing there, when he'd gone to Emily, but only distantly. He did not want to see anyone else when he did it, for fear of losing his nerve. Not Michael, not Fitz or Paula, not even Layla. Especially not Layla, maybe.

He kept his gaze tight. At one point, making his way across what felt like an endless room, he'd thought: *I'm moving like a monster. I'm moving like I'm stalking prey.*

"Can you tell me what you said to her?"

It was a few seconds before he could make himself move. He did not go to the bed, because sitting on that bed, right now, in Layla's presence, when he was about to tell her this, felt sacrilegious. Like watching a church burn.

So he went to the weird little desk. Took off his hat, tossed it on top of the hotel-branded notepad. Pulled out the chair, turned it toward her. Then he sat, comforted somewhat by the hard, unforgiving surface beneath him. An upholding surface, if not a comfortable one.

He looked straight at her.

"I told her that she needed to ask Michael about Sara Beth."

She didn't speak right away, but he could see her mind working. Deciding what to say, what to ask next, like a good doctor does. With difficult patients, patients with multiple injuries—patients like him—you sometimes had to be strategic.

"That's your friend from high school," Layla said. "Who also died in the fire?"

He tipped his head down. A *yes*.

"Emily knew that," she said. "She knew there had been a fire, and that someone close to you both died."

"She was Michael's girlfriend," Griffin said abruptly, cracking open the gates. "Since ninth grade, his girlfriend. It's not really the right word. He was going to propose to her. They would've—" He broke off, back then and right now colliding in his mind, two unfulfilled futures for Michael. Him involved in both.

"They would've gotten married," he finally said. "They definitely would have gotten married."

"Why didn't Michael tell her?"

A bad question, he thought. A rare miss. You could only really ever ask a patient to explain themselves: their own pain, their own side effects.

"It's hard to talk about," he answered. For himself. But probably for Michael, too.

He could tell that answer was unsatisfying for her—that there was a part of her that was angry at Michael, wanting answers from Michael for what he had done or not done when it came to Emily. But Griffin could not answer for Michael. He wouldn't even try. He had spoken enough for Michael tonight, one sentence said to Emily that would probably lose him his best friend, and he could not bring himself to say more about whatever Michael's motivations were. Whatever his demons and fears were.

His own were enough.

"She was my friend, too," he said, loath to give Layla enough time to formulate another question. He wanted it over with. "Sara Beth. When Michael met her, we were fourteen years old. Of course I was a little prick about it at first, ragging on him for how he mooned over her. Rushed off after classes so he could wait outside of whatever room she was in, bought her a carnation for every class period on the Valentine's Day fundraiser. I was jealous, I can admit it. Because before that, it'd been me and Michael, for a lot of years. He's . . ." He trailed off, inhaled.

"Your family," Layla finished for him, and he blew out his breath. Of course she would get that.

"But Sara Beth, she didn't have any time for me being like that. She was like me. Only lived with her mom, not much money, spent a lot of time alone growing up. Her mom was . . . I guess you'd say, a little more troubled than mine. So she was going to make her own family, and if I was a part of Michael's, then I was a part of hers. She was like that."

Scrappy, he had called her once: eleventh grade, homecoming photos, Paula holding the phone, Fitz looking typically frustrated. *Posture*, Fitz'd snapped at Michael, and she'd called back to him immediately.

I don't want him looking like he has a stick up his butt in this picture, Sarge!

"Fitz and Paula really loved her. She could say things to them—Fitz especially—that no one else could get away with. She was good for them. They were a happier family with Sara Beth. Like they needed her. Like she completed them."

He watched Layla close when he said this, knowing it would probably hit her forcefully, given her own history. And it was hard not to think now of Sara Beth, still alive. It was hard not to think of what she and Layla would make of each other.

Don't, he scolded himself. *Don't think about things that can't happen. Focus on the things that did.*

"Fitz and Paula got married young. Fitz was nineteen, Paula eighteen. So that was . . . it was almost like they thought Michael waited too long to ask her. They probably would've liked it if Michael and Sara Beth got married before he went off to the Air Force Academy, and she could live with them while he was there."

Layla did not like that. He could tell by the way she shifted on the couch.

"But Sara Beth wouldn't have said yes to a proposal then. She didn't have any insecurities about Michael. About whether they'd make it. She was going to work, go to community college part-time, save up money. She knew when he came back, her life would be a little more tied to his. Five years of active duty after he graduated, that was his commitment. She would eventually be moving wherever, to be a part of that. They had time."

It hurt to say that part. He felt it, a slicing shock along his left side that made him jerk in his chair, Layla startling in response, half standing from the couch immediately.

He held up a hand. "I'm okay."

But his own time was running out, he could feel it: ten minutes, maybe twenty, until he would have to get up and move. Until this got bad enough that he probably wouldn't be able to say much at all for a while.

"You know I went to Rensselaer for school. Pretty lucky, it not being too far from where we grew up, and I had a good scholarship. My first year, I had a housing waiver so I could live at home with my mom, offset the cost a bit. But then, you know. I got more into it. More involved. Sophomore year, I was already in the lab working on the project that eventually turned into . . ."

He trailed off, flicked his wrist, sort of at the room he sat in, huge with a view, a drop in the bucket, really, nothing he couldn't afford. He cleared his throat, ashamed. One lucky break after another, that's what Rensselaer had been: the right school, the right mentor, the right game of pretend in his mind, the right time. A fucking fluke, really, and then another one, the worst fluke of all.

That he'd lived, and Sara Beth hadn't.

"My senior year, I rented in a house off campus. A real shithole. Cheap and falling apart, but we—my roommates and I—didn't fucking care, most of us were never home. And I had—I had a sense things were about to break open for me. My mentor and I had the idea out there, we had interest. I was going to stay on for my master's, that was settled, so I didn't really give a fuck about where I lived."

He could see the house in his mind: peeling countertops, no baseboards, vinyl siding falling off the side. *Shithole* was an understatement.

It was a hazard, and he should've known.

"I graduated at the beginning of May, but had the lease until August. Had a way nicer apartment lined up for the fall, since we had investors locked in by then, money coming in, but it seemed stupid to waste what I'd already paid for."

Harder now. Hurting more now, but he wanted to tell it to her, because he thought, somewhere in this city, Michael was telling Emily, and he did not want his friend to be doing it alone.

"Sara Beth did classes at Hudson Valley Community College. Real nearby, and by then, she was close to finishing an associate's. It took her longer, with the way she worked, and how she was still commuting from a fair ways away. But that summer, if she took three classes, she'd be finished. Ready to go when it was time for her and Michael to move on to their next stop. So it made sense. It made sense for her to live with me for a bit."

Michael thought it was such a good idea. He hated Sara Beth's commute, how she took night classes, how she was tired from work when she drove back and forth.

He'd been so grateful.

"She moved in right after my graduation. Took the—" He broke off again, a wet catch in his throat. He could picture this, too. It *haunted* him. The cheap paneled walls, a poorly done "finish" to part of the space, the rest of which was a utility room.

"Took the basement room," he rushed out. "It was the nicest one, if you can believe it. Had its own entrance. And a bathroom, so she wouldn't have to share."

Layla made a noise. A knowing sound. *The basement room*.

"Michael's graduation was later. End of May, but he was going to come home after. I figured, for however long he had at home, he could stay there, too, with Sara Beth. That would be good. Better than staying with Fitz and Paula."

One thing I love about you, Griffy, Sara Beth had said, *is that you stay committed to pissing Fitz and Paula off*.

He'd laughed, playfully pushing her away from the microwave, which she'd bent to peek into, trying to see what he was heating up, to decide whether she'd want to share—steal—it. The kitchen light above them was flickering temperamentally like it always did in that house, especially when any appliance was running. He'd said, *I don't stay committed. I don't even have to* try *pissing them off*, and she'd laughed, too, because both of them knew it was true.

He could hear Sara Beth's laugh, still. Could call it up easily. But he realized now that he couldn't remember Emily's, and he'd probably heard it more than once in the last few days. He thought that was not good of him, not to remember. He would probably never have occasion to hear it again, though at least she *would* laugh again. Someday.

He would do this next part quick. Brutally quick.

"The fire was the third week of May. The middle of the night.

Just me and Sara Beth in the house that weekend. Electrical. It started in the basement."

The basement room, he bet Layla was thinking, but he was thinking more about that word, *started*. It made the whole thing seem slow. A little spark, a smoldering maybe, until there was a point of *catching*, a point of spreading.

But it hadn't been like that. In that house—a shithole, a hazard, everything old, already rotted, not up to code—it had not been a *starting*. It started and ended at the same time, that's how it seemed. A conflagration, an explosion. To this day, Griffin could not say if he smelled smoke first, or if the fire was already *there*, coming up through the floor, too fast-moving to bother with a warning odor.

They said she probably didn't suffer, Michael told him, one of those days after, Griffin in the bed paralyzed with pain, every kind of pain, pain he knew would never leave him, worse for the way Michael came every day, sitting and sitting, talking to Griffin as though he had not once considered being angry. *They said it was very quick.*

"I couldn't have saved her that night," Griffin said now. "I know that. I—I did try to get to her. I got out of my window and went around to her entrance."

The T-shirt he'd been sleeping in balled haphazardly over his left hand, a desperate, meaningless effort to spare himself pain. He had not *known* pain. He had opened that door and *become* fire. He could not remember anything after that, for days and days.

But he'd known, even as it consumed one whole side of him, blasting him backward into the night, that Sara Beth was gone. He'd known that before everything inside him—his body, his brain—went black.

"But I could have saved her before. Never letting her move in.

Not giving her that room. I could have. That's why—Paula and Fitz."

He figured he didn't need to complete that thought. She'd seen Paula and Fitz with him. It didn't matter, really, that they'd both once cared about him, too, or at least they'd seemed to. When he was younger, sweet-faced and lonely, when he probably seemed like a pleasant, harmless charity case. It didn't matter that well before the fire—middle school, probably—they'd started to sour on him, to see him as a bad influence, to look scornfully down on his mother, as though they'd run out of patience for the fact that she hadn't yet managed to bootstrap herself out of being poor, or maybe for the fact that Griffin hadn't turned his back on her in favor of them.

"And Michael?" Layla said softly.

Even with two words, he knew what she was asking.

He shook his head. He'd heard people use this expression, that their eyes *burned* with tears. But he would not say that.

He would not say that's how it felt at all.

"Michael never blamed me. He has always stood . . . he has always sat beside me. For forever."

It felt over for him then. A breaking. He bent himself forward in the chair, set his elbows on his thighs and his head in his hands, knowing it felt all wrong, pain and parts of him all out of proportion, exactly like one of those sculptures in the museum garden.

He was thinking, *I can't believe I did it. I can't believe I did this to Michael. My best friend.*

Or maybe—he wouldn't ever be sure—maybe he said it through the wet catch in his throat, maybe he said it to the floor between his spread knees.

Because before he knew it, Layla was there. Not touching him, but kneeling before him. He could see her pale, beautiful hands resting on her thighs, waiting. He thought, *Get up from there*, the first command he'd ever given her, but he couldn't bring himself to say it. He stared at her hands, blurry through his wet vision, grateful when—after he didn't know how long—they started to come back into focus.

"Griffin," she finally said, and then one of her hands lifted. She set it so gently on his right leg, curving her fingers around his calf, her thumb resting on his shin. "You did the right thing."

"I told him," he said, embarrassed at the sound of his voice, but not so embarrassed that he didn't keep going. "Tonight, in his room. After we got back from getting your perfume. I told him if he didn't tell her, I would."

"That was good," she said, so soft—*god*, she must be such a good fucking doctor, and this was humiliating, for her to talk to him this way.

Five minutes, and it would get more humiliating. He would be insensate with the pain coming. She would see it all. He was going to let her. He *wanted* to let her. He deserved it.

"*Then tell her*," he said now. "That's what Michael said to me, before he left the room. *Then tell her*."

Layla rubbed her thumb back and forth across his shin. He could only assume it was from the years he'd spent being specially tuned to everything that touched him, but he somehow thought he could feel the bewilderment in that small movement, a confusion that mimicked his own. Why would Michael have said that? And not like a dare, but almost like an invitation? Why did he seem to *accept*, after all this time he'd kept it from Emily, that Griffin would be the one to tell her?

"I don't think he's himself," Layla said finally, which is probably the sort of thing he would've been insulted by only a few days ago.

You don't know him, he would've snarled, monstrous and overprotective, clawing at anything that got in his best friend's way.

Now, he wasn't insulted. He wouldn't quite call himself *comforted*, either, but he was not angry that she'd said it. He thought, *He isn't himself. He maybe hasn't been himself since he bought Emily that ring. Since he decided to give her that ring, without telling her the truth.*

"Griff," she said, her fingers pressing more firmly into his calf, hugging him in the only way she could right now. "Listen to me."

He must've shaken his head, given some indication that he couldn't. Inside him, it was all going wrong now, wires crossing along the left side, creeping strangely and inexplicably into the right.

"Listen," she said again, more firmly, keeping her hand on him, as though that one point of contact could neutralize every other sensation that was screaming along his nerve endings. "It wasn't just right for Emily. It was right for Michael, too. You did *right* by them."

Dimly, he thought of another strange irony: that without her, without Layla, he would not have done right. If Layla had not been here, he doubted he would've ever known that Michael had not told Emily about Sara Beth. And even if, somehow, he *had* known, he would not have ever breathed a word.

Not if he hadn't met Layla.

He would not have ever been able to see anything beyond seeing Michael through the wedding.

It was *something you said*, he thought, no anger, no ire in it now. *It was everything you said to me, ever.*

With effort, he moved, only enough to get his right hand down to where her left rested on him. He linked their fingers awkwardly, uncomfortably, but no kind of discomfort like this mattered to him now. The two of them, linked forever for having ruined this wedding, not that he'd ever tell her so. Not that it would ever really be anyone's fault but his.

"We just have to wait," she said, holding his hand tight, her thumb smoothing over the back of it rhythmically. *We just have to wait* was another real doctor-like thing to say. Will the skin graft take, will the antibiotics work, will the tissue soften? *We just have to wait.* But he didn't mind. By now, he was almost outside of his mind, parts of him beading with sweat, his body in charge.

"We'll keep our phones on, and we'll wait to hear. They need to talk, and we need to wait."

He wished he could reassure her of that. The *we* part. He wished he could say he'd wait with her, he'd wander with her all night like they'd done yesterday, he'd take out his phone and check it every time she checked hers. He'd kiss her and touch her when the hours got long so she would forget; he would turn her into that tower of light.

But he hadn't spent the whole night being brutally honest—wrecking ball to someone's life honest—to start lying again.

Not to her, not now.

So he squeezed her hand and told her the truth.

"I'm probably going to need some help."

Chapter Twenty-Nine

For the second morning in a row, she woke up in Griffin's bed.

This time, it was not a slow waking, not sleepy and stretching. It was more of a snapping to, her breath catching as soon as her consciousness came online. She sat up quickly with the sense she'd overslept, but when she turned to look out the windows—the curtains undrawn—it was still dark, though after many years of odd hours, Layla knew it was close to dawn. Soon enough, that sky would turn, casting pastels all over Paris, the only place in the world, she thought, where color looked quite like this.

Beside her, Griffin slept.

He *slept*.

She could admit, in a dark, selfish corner of her heart, newly discovered to her, that she felt a sense of pride over his slumber—his slack face, his deep breathing, his left hand resting lightly on his abdomen, rising and falling with the movement of his lungs.

I won't sleep, he'd insisted so many times, during the worst of last night, when it seemed like he would never stop gritting his teeth, when he kept lapsing into short, shallow breaths, when the parts of him that hurt the most seemed to twitch and curl without any intention or purpose.

She hadn't argued with him about that, of course. He knew himself; he knew his pain. And *she* knew it, too—that people with pain like Griffin understood the tides of it the way no one else ever would. This kind of pain had, she'd thought at one point last night—with no small sense of the irony—its own gravity. To the person experiencing it, it was its own universe.

But even as she expected to stay up with him all night—to walk, if that's what he wanted, to wrap the leg again, if that would help, whatever—she also started, around midnight, to see signs of him slowing down, mostly in what he was able to say to her. Once, he said, "How do you like it in here?" and she looked up at him, confused and concerned. It would not be good, if he started getting disoriented.

She said, "In your hotel room?"

"In my bell tower," he answered.

I might not be able to handle this here, she thought. *I might need to take him somewhere else.*

But he had not been disoriented. If anything, it was the beginning of him slowly coming around. He stopped pacing back and forth in front of the long bank of windows, and pointed. Then, he explained to her about the bell tower. About playing pretend, about the movie he remembered watching with Michael on an Easter weekend a long time ago, about calling his mother the morning they went to Versailles.

You'll sleep, she thought as she listened. She thought it again over the next hour, as they stayed near the windows, as they watched the city together in a new way, wandered through it from above. *You'll sleep*, she didn't say, when he grudgingly agreed to lying down with her—"Five minutes," she said. "Just until *I* fall asleep"—even though, by then, she could see his eyelids growing heavy, his movements growing more careless.

"Go on vacation," he murmured, maybe four minutes later, and by then she'd learned to wait before assuming disorientation. "You go on vacation, and take care of sick people."

"You're not sick," she said back, and she thought the snort he made in response had a sense of humor in it.

In the end, he was asleep before she was.

Now, assured that he still was, she sank back into the bed, reaching for her phone. Before she drifted off last night, she'd changed the notification alert for texts on her phone to the same sound her pager app made, determined not to accidentally sleep through anything that might come: from Emily, from any of the MacKenzies, from Rosie, even.

But there had been nothing, and now—only four thirty a.m., to be fair—there was still nothing.

We just have to wait, she told herself, the same thing she told Griff, but it wasn't so easy now. She was *awake*, awake at four thirty, which everyone knew was like a witching hour for worrying about things, your personal laundry list of very stupid things, every insecurity or unsolvable problem or devastating mistake of your life, unless you were up to actually *do* something. Without the immediacy of helping Griff, her brain whirred with everything she'd learned in the last few hours, and everything she still didn't know.

The things Griffin told her . . . *god*.

The way Emily must be feeling. The way *Michael* must be feeling. Whether he would be able to see what Griffin had done for him. Whether Emily would.

And even after everything—after that conversation with Griffin in the café yesterday, after realizing, well and truly, that she *wasn't* a MacKenzie anymore—the silence of her phone still felt painful, or at least . . . revealing. Surely, someone knew something; *someone* had heard from Em, or Michael, and maybe there had been some kind of *consensus* about her and Griffin, maybe Jamie told everyone and they all thought . . .

"Layla."

Ridiculously, she automatically slammed her eyes shut. Like he was going to scold her for being awake. Like she was actually going to try and fake it.

She opened them again. She said, "Yes?" in a way that sounded *extremely* prim. Way too prim for being in his bed in nothing but her underwear and one of his excellent, nearly seamless black shirts.

He made that snort again. "I can hear you over there."

"No, you can't."

He made a noise. A doubtful *Hm*. When he was waking up, the register of his voice was so much deeper, and a deranged vibration settled between her legs. *After everything!* she scolded herself. *It's not the time!*

"What can you hear?" she finally said.

"Your mind."

The flat tone of it was so unexpectedly funny that she had to press her lips together. *Mind over matter*, she thought, and almost laughed again.

"Come over here," he said. In this huge bed, after everything last night, she'd stayed pretty firmly on her own side, worried about disturbing him. No part of her touched him now, and she hated that. But also, she didn't want to hurt him.

She could hear him shifting in the covers.

"I'm okay," he said. "Come over."

What happened next was so . . . she did not have another word for it other than to say that it was *intimate*—shifting toward him, saying, *Where*, the shared knowledge that a moment like this could not be automatic for them, the shame he seemed to let go of, enough that he could say, *Not there* or *Here, put your leg here*. All this for something couples took for granted every night, every morning.

All this for a *cuddle*.

The best one she'd ever had.

"Does it hurt?" she whispered, when they settled into it.

"No." He pressed a kiss against the top of her head. She thought the kiss might be him silently adding, *It doesn't hurt enough to stop.*

"Nothing from Em," she said.

He didn't say anything for a long time. She knew it was for Michael, that silence. She knew it was so heavy on him.

"We just have to wait," he finally replied. "Like you said."

She nodded, but she thought now they were both in the four thirty a.m. thick of it, picking through their individual laundry lists.

"Layla," he said again.

"Sorry," she answered this time. "I'm—"

"Roll over," he said gruffly. "On your back."

"Oh! Sorry, am I—"

"No," he answered, then he shifted, moving more swiftly than she was anticipating, and in a second she was on her back, Griffin leaning on his right elbow over her. Beneath the sheet, his left hand moved; he found the hem of her—*his*—shirt, and she thought, *Oh, thank god. Thank god he can touch that fabric so easily, that he can push it up over my stomach, that he—*

"Help me out," he said, when he had the shirt pushed up enough to expose her breasts, and *yes*, she was so glad he asked; he would have to get used to asking her things like this; she would have to get used to anticipating it—

She cut off that train of thought, that *get used to*. She lifted herself enough to take off the shirt, felt his palm settle against her sternum, pressing her down again. She was already breathing hard, already desperately wet—the worry, the intensity of *everything*, the temptation to think about getting used to him—all of it short-circuited her, driving a need for a release.

"Is this okay?" she said, but when he answered, his mouth was already on her right breast, a muffled *Mm-hmm* that intensified the sensation of his wet sucking.

He stayed there for so long—alternating between her breasts, leaving a mark at one point, she was certain; he stayed through all the times she begged him to do something else—to let her come, to *please* let her come—as though he would not indulge her until he was sure, completely sure, that he had destroyed her laundry list, every single item on it. He stayed until she maybe did not know what a list was, until *she* was disoriented, unsure of any place in the world except the expanse of this bed.

And then he finally, finally lowered his head and licked right through the center of her, one time and she was coming—so quick it would have been humiliating except that he simply kept going, as though he had moved on from her list and was now hell-bent on destroying his own, eating her even as she knew he had also reached down to touch himself, groaning into her as his own pleasure crested, and as she came again—fast and forceful this time, obliterating. Distantly, she felt him move over her, felt the warm wetness of his release on her abdomen, felt him finally flatten himself beside her on his back, out of breath and she thought—she hoped—sated.

"I'll get up," he said. "One minute."

She reached back, grabbed for the shirt. Shoved it beneath the sheets and cleaned herself off.

He chuckled.

"You have so many, what does it matter?" she said, and he laughed again, then quieted. A serious quiet that settled over them, as sure as the sheets on their bodies. Outside, the sky was growing lighter and lighter. Pink-purple, Paris dawn.

"Thank you," he finally said. "For last night."

She turned her head, looked over at him. She wanted to say something like, *What if it wasn't just last night?* but that wasn't right; she knew it wasn't quite right. She wasn't trying to say that she wanted him to have more nights like that, or that it had been good or interesting or even rewarding to care for him that way.

She wanted to say, *Just so you know, last night sucked, but I do not care. I would never care. A million more nights like that, and I don't think I would ever care.*

But maybe that wasn't right, either. Maybe it was too big for only knowing him as long as she had. Too big for only minutes after having her mind blown by him again, and probably only a few hours from finding out whether this wedding had been blown apart.

So she would try saying it smaller. She whispered his name, barely more than an exhalation. A test, maybe. A question.

"Griff?"

The pause was so long she thought he might not have heard.

But he finally said, "Yeah?" in that rough voice, rougher now from his breathlessness.

"I would do it again," she said, and as it turned out, when she said it, she realized it wasn't small at all. It was not last night: It was this whole *week* that she would do again; it was maybe even every single thing, good and bad, that got her to this week in the first place. She would do it again. Get scolded by him on the plane, get shocked to her core to see him again. Get dragged off a boat, get danced with in a garden ballroom. Get kissed in a doorway, get left alone in a rideshare, get her cracked heart patched up while looking at a piece of art.

Get lost with him in Paris. Get found for who she really was.

Everything, she would do again.

She stayed still, flat on her back and naked beneath the sheet, now not touching him at all. It was scary, but she knew already that she didn't regret it.

He moved his hand, sliding it across the expanse of mattress between them. Taking hers, and twining their fingers together.

"I would, too."

It was no kind of vow, not that she wanted one. Not that she was sure whether she would ever want one of those again.

But it was something. Something beyond this week. Beyond whatever happened today.

And that's when her phone—newly set with its pager-sound notification—blared its intrusion into the room.

Chapter Thirty

Rehearsal breakfast is on! said the text, which Layla looked at for a long time, unsure about that exclamation.

On the one hand, Manon was an exclamation-type person: how she delivered compliments, welcomes; how she received gifts, new people, news. So getting a text from her with one—a group text, no less, sent to all the guests—was not surprising.

On the other hand, Layla simply could not grasp how it was an exclamation-type morning.

Not after the looks on everyone's faces at the open house last night, once it was clear that Michael and Emily were leaving, looking taut and pale and doomed.

Not after knowing what Michael had to tell Emily.

Even if they *had* patched it up—and Layla genuinely hoped they had—the breeziness from Manon struck her oddly.

Still, she was resolved as she walked back to the rental: freshly showered and back in her spreadsheet-planned outfit ("Rehearsal Morning: cream cardigan, olive green midi, beige heels"), prepared for what certainly sounded—judging by that exclamation—like a long day of pre-wedding and actual wedding events.

Were it not for the man walking beside her, she might have mistaken herself for the Layla of a few days ago, determined to plaster on an amicable smile, wearing her neutrals and wanting to *go along*, to *get through it*.

But she was not that Layla anymore.

And Griffin was beside her.

Quiet—increasingly, concerningly quiet—but still.

Beside her.

She stopped at the last turnoff, the one that would take them the remaining few steps to the apartment, and turned to him.

"I can go in first. If you want."

A double-checking, that's what she was doing. Earlier this morning, before she'd left his room to go back to her own, he'd been the one to suggest it—them going in together.

It's not a secret, he said. *I'm tired of secrets.*

She'd been happy to say yes. Relieved and also strangely hopeful—as though their shared decision to show up to the breakfast together would somehow be the right sort of omen for how it worked out between Michael and Emily, free of their own secrets now, too.

Newly committed, about to be newlyweds.

Now, though, only a few steps away—already running a few minutes behind—Layla could not be sure he hadn't changed his mind. It was his reticence, but it was also something else. Last-minute nerves, insecurity, cold feet. Like a groom on his wedding day.

"No," he answered, which—even after every other interaction she'd had with him—seemed unusually curt.

Something must've shown on her face, and he reached up a hand, scrubbed it over the right side of his own.

"Sorry. Just, you know. Not sure what we'll find in there.

Would've rather—" He broke off, dropped his hand and cleared his throat. "Would've rather heard from Michael."

She nodded, getting it. His own way of being bothered by that exclamation point. She waited for whatever his next move would be, but fortunately, she didn't have to wait for long. After only a few seconds, he stepped forward and took her hand in his before they continued on their way.

Almost as soon as they walked in, though, Layla was no longer hopeful.

Not at all.

The space had been reset since last night—the couches and chairs no longer in the large living room, all of it replaced with a long, rustic wood dining table. That might've been a good sign, a place for the breakfast they were meant to have after quickly running through the ceremony program in the courtyard, but the problem was, the table was totally blank. No centerpieces, no place settings.

And then there was the company. Griff and Layla didn't seem to be the last to arrive—she didn't spot the Nantes cousins, nor Miranda and Finance Guy. Michael's uncle and cousin—she'd met them briefly last night—were there, but Damaris and Abram weren't.

Most importantly: neither were Michael and Emily.

And those who were there did not look as though they expected the bride and groom to arrive anytime soon.

Or ever.

A quick scan of faces revealed varying degrees of bewilderment and concern, and that was before any of them even noticed Griffin and Layla.

Once that happened, at least a few expressions transformed: Rosie with an eyebrow raise, Fitz with a jaw-clench, Jamie—with his eyes drifting down to their joined hands before coming back to Layla's face—with a frown of . . . of *something*. Judgment or disappointment or worry or some other thing he had no right to.

Robert cleared his throat, breaking the silence.

"Layla," he said, the lack of nickname as sure a sign as anything else. "Michael and Emily are not here."

I see that, she didn't say.

"Their things are also no longer here."

Layla swallowed, feeling Griff's hand dampen in hers. Yesterday, after the spa, Emily and Michael both were relocating most of their things to their rooms here. Certainly all the things they would need for today's events.

"Oh," she said, and silence fell again, which she guessed meant that she was now as caught up as everyone else who'd arrived here this morning.

Layla darted her eyes to Rosie, who no longer had her eyebrows raised in surprise at seeing Layla and Griffin together. But still, her expression was speaking: not *quite* as concerned as everyone else's. Carefully neutral.

A very not-Rosie-like expression, and that's when Layla knew.

That's when Layla knew that Rosie—the maid of honor, of course the maid of honor, that's how it *always* should have been, from that very first morning after—already knew whatever was about to happen next. Rosie had probably been the one to tell Manon that the rehearsal was on, to get everyone here.

As if on cue, Layla's phone blared again in her purse—*god*, she'd forgotten the pager notification noise—and she rushed to the chair where she'd set it, rifling through the front pocket to get to her phone. As she did, she became aware of other notifications, too: a ding there, a vibration over there, a trilling bell close by.

Everyone was getting a message.

Even Griffin.

They were no longer holding hands—he'd dropped hers, or she'd dropped his during the frantic phone-silencing—and Layla's were shaking as she swiped across her screen.

As she scrolled in silence over the same message she assumed everyone else was seeing, too.

Dear family,

Michael and I are so sorry to tell you that we have mutually decided not to be married today.

We owe you all a much longer explanation and a much fuller apology for bringing you so far away for this magical week, only to have it end this way. We promise we will be in contact with each of you individually to do that, as soon as we are able.

I have asked Rosie to begin canceling various services that were set up for today, and I insisted that she not inform anyone until we sent this message. Breakfast will still be served at the apartment shortly, and we ask that you do your best to enjoy yourselves and one another's company in our absence.

By the time you receive this note, you should know that we are no longer in Paris. We are taking some time to make a decision about our respective futures.

We love you, and we thank you for supporting us throughout this past week, and in whatever comes next for us.

Emily & Michael

Layla was *aware*, as she read, that there were reactions—a gasp giving way to a little sob from Manon, a soothing cluck from Robert. A "Well!" from Céline, a whispered "Which one is Rosie, again?" from Michael's cousin, an unpleasant, gurgly squeak from someone whose sounds she did not know well enough to identify.

But mostly, she was focused on her own.

Her own, and Griffin's.

She'd brought her hand up to her mouth as she read, lingering over the words that seemed to matter most—some that she wanted to see as optimistic, some that insinuated a more permanent severing.

Today.

We.

A decision.

Respective.

But Griffin had not moved at all. Not beyond looking—quickly, there was no way he could have read the whole thing—and sliding his phone into his back pocket.

Now, he was a statue. Like he would stay here forever, waiting.

After a few more seconds—when everyone seemed to finish reading—the room exploded with conversation, with movement. Snippets of reaction while reading now became full-on sentences of disbelief, coming from all corners. *Which one is Rosie, again?* transformed into a lot of questions aimed directly at the woman in question, who had clearly prepared herself to repeatedly say, "My job is to do what Em wanted." Manon was crying in full punctuation now, Robert and Céline flanking her. Poor Samantha had slumped into one of the chairs, shaking her head, Jamie setting a hand on her shoulder.

What do you mean, *breakfast will be served?*

Did they leave the country?

Rosie, are they somewhere together, at least?

My goodness, all this money spent!

It was like being inside a dishwasher cycle. And all Layla wanted was to *go*.

Almost as soon as she thought it, she realized—she could, in fact, go.

She did not have to stay for this. She loved Manon and Robert. She could even admit that she still loved Jamie, if not in the same way she thought she had when she'd arrived here in Paris. But the person that meant the most to her in this whole mess was Emily, and Emily was not here anymore. Emily would *be in contact*. Emily was *taking some time*.

She would be there for Emily, when the time came.

But for now, she and Griffin could go.

She and Griffin could—

Suddenly, a voice burst forth above the others. Hard and unexpectedly close.

"What did you do?"

Fitz.

He was standing almost directly in front of her, but with his body turned toward someone else.

"What did you do, Griffin?" he repeated, brandishing his phone, screen lit, Em's message there like an accusation. "What did you do to her?"

"Fitz," said Paula softly, coming up from behind, taking her husband's elbow. "Let's not—"

Fitz stepped back, looked down at his wife. "Let's not what, Paula? Make *assumptions*? Everyone saw him come in here last night—"

"Let's—" she tried again, but Fitz was beyond hearing her, his face red now. Layla thought of Em in the spa yesterday, saying, *that got Fitz going.*

A mention of Griffin. That's what got Fitz going.

And she could see it now. It *going*. She could see that this is what Griffin was waiting for, what he had turned into a statue for. Preparing himself, hardening himself.

"What did you say to her?" Fitz shouted, his anger ratcheting up with the knowledge that Griffin was not going to answer.

"Mr. Pl—" Layla began, cutting herself off as she realized she was not quite sure how to address him—Sergeant? Fitz, even though she didn't know him?—but it didn't matter. She definitely had not spoken loudly enough to interrupt this.

"I could've called this on Wednesday, that you would wreck this. I could've seen it from a hundred miles away, that if something went wrong for my son again—that if he lost someone again—I'd find *you* at the end of it. *You!*"

"Hey," Layla said, still not loud enough.

"You have been a *curse* to Michael. A goddamned curse! Why he defends you at every turn, despite everything you took from him, I'll never goddamn know, but if there's one good thing that comes out of this, I hope it's that he finally sees—"

"Hey!" Layla shouted now, and actually—actually, she had not *only* shouted.

She had also set her hand on Fitz's shoulder.

And *shoved* him. Out of Griffin's statue-still face.

"Layla," someone said—she thought Robert, but honestly, it could have been Jamie, too. She was beyond caring. She was beyond anything remotely amicable in this situation.

She was mind under matter. A one-woman mob.

Fitz was staring down at her, shocked.

"That. Is. *Enough*. You obviously have no idea about who Griffin is, or possibly who your *son* is, so if you'll—"

"Layla!" This time, the voice was Manon's, unmistakable in its exclamation. A not-complimentary one. A not-welcoming one.

A *scolding* one.

She was so surprised she finally shifted her gaze away from red-faced Fitz. Manon was looking at her as though she was a stranger.

As though she'd never been family at all.

Robert cleared his throat. "Layla," he repeated, his tone more soothing, but somehow still with that scolding note folded in. "We realize you've . . . well, it's clear you're having some kind of dalliance here—"

Griffin made a noise.

Low and warning. A statue creaking to life.

"Robert, come *on*," she said quickly, her voice cutting through it. She looked between him and Fitz, trying somehow to remind Robert who he *really* was, at least in all the years she'd known him. He'd never been the sort of man to talk to someone like Fitz had just talked to Griffin. He'd always hated that sort of dominance, that particular brand of toxicity.

But she couldn't find that Robert now. Too upset by or worried for Emily, maybe, but it didn't matter. What mattered was that, in this moment, he seemed to think *she* was the toxic one.

Shockingly, it didn't even hurt.

"Oh my god," she muttered, and turned her attention back to Fitz. One more thing, and then they could go. "You need to talk to *Michael*," she said. "Not Griffin. You don't have anything to say to—"

She was interrupted by that gurgling squeak again, and then, a sound and movement she'd heard and seen once before on this trip. A chair being shoved back, a sudden standing.

And Sam, streaking past everyone, hand over her mouth.

"Oh, for goodness' sake!" Manon shouted, even more scolding-sounding than she had been to Layla, clearly at the end of some kind of wedding-cancellation rope. "How many times is she going to do this?"

Unkind, Layla was thinking as she heard a door slam, but also, was she going to have to go in there and check on Sam again? Because—

"Mom," Jamie snapped angrily, which was good, already a better showing than the boat deck, but actually he should probably save this for later and get over his weak-stomached fear long enough to follow Sam, who . . .

Oh, she thought, with dawning realization, at the same time Jamie yelled, exasperated-sounding, "She's *pregnant*."

Another round of noisy reaction. Rosie said, "I fucking *knew* it," and Céline said, "Oh, Jamie," like she was very disappointed in this whole thing. Robert coughed and Manon started crying again, and they did not seem like happy tears. Shockingly—or perhaps not—Paula was no longer holding on to Fitz's elbow; she was clasping her hands at her chest and saying, "Aww," as though she herself was about to be this child's grandmother.

Layla felt something bubble up inside her, and at first, she thought it must be a bad sensation. It could only be a bad sensation, surely, upon figuring out that her ex-husband was about to have the baby that he'd broken his vows to her for.

But no. It was not, in fact, a bad sensation. It was a sparkling-water sensation, a fizzy desire to explode in hysterical, exhausted laughter.

Pregnant, of course!

She was well over halfway to doing it, to letting out that laugh, a not-very-amicable reaction to the news, but then, a lot happened all at once.

Fitz shoved again, out of the way.

A fast crossing of the room.

One punch, a chorus of shrieks and gasps.

Jamie on the floor, clutching his nose, howling dramatically.

A statue standing over him.

"What did I *tell* you?" boomed Fitz, seemingly directing that comment to everyone before turning back to the statue—to Griffin. "You can't *help* but burn everything to the ground, can you? *Can* you?"

Layla wanted to intervene again. She wanted that impulse to shove, to shout back at Fitz, but it had momentarily abandoned her. She could only look at Griffin, standing over Jamie, shock on his face, as though he could not remember how he'd gotten there, as though he could not remember throwing the punch.

But she could tell he'd heard.

You can't help but burn everything to the ground.

"Griff," she said, but she knew he wasn't listening. He was probably hearing Fitz on a loop. Fresh salt in a wound that he had opened again—for her—only last night.

He kept his head down. He said, "I'm sorry," to Jamie, even though Jamie was still making a lot of noise down there and probably didn't hear. She couldn't even see any blood. She thought he was probably fine. Actually, she thought he might be milking it, staving off any obligation to check on Sam.

"I'm sorry," Griffin repeated, this time raising his head, both of his hands. "I'll go."

"No," Layla said, at the same time Robert said, "That seems like the best idea," and also at the same time Michael's cousin said, "Wait, didn't he pay for this wedding?"

Rosie heard that. She said, "Oh my god, he *did*?"

"*Some* of it," Manon clarified, and Robert said, "Well," in a corrective way.

A way that suggested it was more than *some*.

By now, it didn't surprise Layla. It made sense: not because she knew about his money, but because she knew about *him*, and how much he loved Michael. He would do anything for Michael.

Pay for the wedding.

But also, break up the wedding.

"It doesn't matter," she thought he said, but there was no knife-edge in his voice now. It was hard to hear him over another burst of chaos: the Nantes cousins arriving at some point in the last few seconds, adding to the flurry of shocked conversation with their fast, confused French, Robert kneeling to help Jamie up, Sam emerging from somewhere, gray-faced, Rosie rushing over to her with a glass of water. Layla felt distant from it all, watching Griffin take in the scene as though he was looking at something else entirely, as though he was seeing some long-ago night come roaring back, hot and destructive and never-ending.

No, she thought. *No, no, no.*

He took a step back, and she followed.

Then, Manon practically shrieked her name, shocking her enough to turn away—a second of distraction that some part of her knew Griffin would use to his advantage.

"Can you check him?" Manon said, still shrieky, having joined Robert in flanking Jamie, who was still holding a hand over his nose, staring miserably at Layla. "What if his nose is broken?"

"It's not," Layla said flatly, which she supposed she could not really know for sure. She'd make her apologies to Hippocrates later.

Or maybe she wouldn't. Maybe she was fine breaking her vow to that guy, just this once.

Jamie had dropped his hand from his nose, finally, but still, Layla did not really look at the damage. She said, "I'm going to go," and then she turned, knowing already Griffin had beat her to it—that he was already out the door, alone in the Paris morning, but also alone somewhere else entirely, in the middle of a fiery spring night.

She barely looked at anyone as she strode back through the room, grabbing her purse up again and passing Rosie and Sam in the hallway. "Carry alcohol wipes," she said to Sam, because she could not help it—could not help feeling for this woman and the Paris crucible she'd been put through this week. "Waft one under your nose when you feel sick."

Sam may have murmured her thanks, but Layla was out the door, stepping into the street with a sinking feeling in her stomach at not being able to see Griffin straightaway.

She would find him; she would try to the right at first, and—

"Lay, wait!"

She groaned. Actually *groaned*: a not-calm, extremely bothered *Arrrgh* at being held up, in this moment, by *him*.

The husband who had—she could see it so clearly now—held her up for so *long*.

For a second, she thought of simply speeding up—of ignoring him, of running away, of refusing to give him even a second more of her time this morning.

But just as quickly, she rethought it.

She thought, *This isn't just about a second more of this morning. This is about a second more of forever.*

So, she stopped where she stood. Turned to face him: Jamie and his soft, light eyes that had welled with tears on their wedding day; Jamie and his safe, sweet handsomeness, even with a swollen, already bruised bridge of his nose; Jamie's quick-to-smile mouth turned down in a pouting frown of sadness and disappointment and concern.

She had so truly loved him, once.

"I'm sorry," he said, his voice cracking. "I'm sorry you found out that way about the baby. I didn't mean for you—"

"Jamie," she interrupted, and *yes*—yes, there it was, the blade in her voice, the one she'd learned over the last few days how to sharpen—"I do not care about the baby."

He stared. Like Robert, like Manon. Stared like he didn't know her at all.

And maybe he didn't.

Not anymore.

"I hope the very best for you, and for Samantha, and for your baby. But it is none of my business anymore. It has not been my business for a long time, and I should've said that to you sooner."

"Lay," he said again, and she decided that she didn't like that nickname. Did not like the diminutive, the way it chopped her almost in half, the way it *flattened* her. "Of course it's your business. We said we would always be—"

"Family," she finished for him, but in this bladelike version of her voice it was a new word. A severing, rather than a joining.

"Yeah," he said. He sounded so small and lost and sad that a part of her—the part of her that had been in love with him once, that had planned a life with him once—ached for him, and despite everything, she was glad not to have lost that aching. She was glad that this severing was leaving something behind in her. Something that would hurt a little forever.

Sometimes, that was all you could keep from the things that happened to you.

"I lied," she said, still sharp, because it was a kindness to keep it that way for him, too. "Or I changed my mind, maybe. It doesn't really matter which. What matters is that I should've known that when we got divorced, we couldn't be a family anymore. Maybe someone else could do it, Jamie, but I can't, and you know why I can't. You know what it meant to me to call you—to call your mom, your dad, your sister—family. And that's why you should've known that it wouldn't work to change your mind about us. To change your mind, and still get to keep me."

He made a noise—a scoff, maybe, but there was a weak, nasally whistle that accompanied it, the swelling doing its work.

"If this is about *him*—" he began, and Layla held up a hand, stopping him.

"This is about you, Jamie," she said. "This is about your loss, and why it's not my job to make it easier for you. Nicer, more amicable, whatever. We are *divorced*."

He winced at the word, one she realized they had only ever said rarely to each other. Euphemisms, that's what they'd preferred: *I think it's time* or *going our separate ways* or even the somewhat-harsh *splitting up*.

But to her, it felt so good to say it: straight to his face, while they stood across from each other, a reverse ritual that maybe would have helped her on that day when she'd just scrawled her signature across a tab-tipped set of documents.

The restlessness was back in her now—the need to go, to find the man she'd actually come out here for. She looked at her ex-husband and heard his whistling nose and thought of all the ways the MacKenzies left in that apartment would talk about her today, once the dust settled.

Can you believe she—
I've never known her to—

That isn't the Layla—

But there was no part of her that cared.

"Jamie," she said, and waited until he met her eyes to speak again. "Get a stronger stomach, and go take care of your family."

Then, she finally turned and ran.

Chapter Thirty-One

She caught up to him on her first try, no backtracking necessary.

Around a curve, a half block until the hotel, and the streets of the Marais were still quiet, so it sounded extra loud when she called out to him, the black line of his body hunched in such a specific way, a *leave me alone* way.

But he did stop when he heard her.

He turned and looked at her across the expanse of street, and she thought, *Don't leave. If you leave now, like this, that'll be the end of it with us.*

She knew that deep down.

A knowing more certain, maybe, from having just ended it—really, truly, ended what was left of it—with Jamie.

Griffin started walking toward her.

They met in the middle, in the center of the narrow street, neither of them, apparently, worried about traffic passing through. On either side of them, the stone sidewalks were lined with those hip-height, painted-black guard stones, a relic from another time, like the buildings that rose up to enclose them—cream and tan and gray-white with age, the most gorgeous, showy neutrality. Above were balconies, trailing ivies, lanterns spaced evenly and hanging elegantly from black wrought iron brackets, and, at the very, very top of it all, a curving river of bright blue morning light.

She thought, *This would be the place. This would be the place to tell someone you love them.*

Paris. Je t'aime.

No translation needed.

But something else she knew deep down was that she would not be telling him that today.

Not in any language.

And she knew that he would not be telling her, either.

"He wasn't right," she said, which—what with *Je t'aime* on her mind—certainly felt too blunt for this perfect, poetic street. But it was still important, so she kept going. "What Fitz said. He was not right."

You do not burn everything to the ground, part of her wanted to say, but she could not bring herself to voice even a contradictory echo of Fitz's vitriol. Could not bring herself to say *burn* in Griffin's presence.

He was looking at her with such brutal, bleak sadness: his gaze moving over her face as if he was memorizing her, his mouth set as if it helped him concentrate. It was so overwhelming that she dropped her eyes, desperate to think of something, *anything* to say that would make him forget about all the ugliness Fitz had aimed his way.

Because that ugliness, she suspected, was about to suck every scrap of beauty out of what she and Griffin had found here together in Paris.

"I know that," he said finally, surprising her, and she snapped her eyes up to his.

She probably looked ten kinds of hopeful. *Too hopeful.* And she thought, maybe—*maybe*—she saw a ghost of that Versailles quirk.

"I think I'm more family to Michael than Fitz has maybe ever been," he added.

"I think so, too," she said, surprised to hear tears gathering in her voice. Relief and pride and happiness for him. Too much *t'aime* for her to acknowledge.

But if he knew this—if he knew that it had been good to tell Emily, that he had done right by Michael, that he was in fact more family than Fitz ever was, then maybe, for the two of them—for Griff and Layla, Layla who needed someone who understood family in exactly this way, there was a chance. A chance for them to—

"Your ex-husband," Griffin said, and the ghost of that quirk was gone. The bleakness back.

"He's fine," she blurted, thinking of that funny little wheeze, that still-shocked look on his face as she'd turned to leave.

"I figured," Griffin said. "I didn't hit him that hard, despite his carrying on."

"You didn't have to, you know. Hit him. It doesn't bother me, that she's pregnant."

He shrugged, looked toward the curve of the street, his gaze distant. She wondered if he even realized that he had the left side of his face facing her. He hardly ever did that, before.

"I figured that, too. I lost my head for a second."

It was so quiet, so preternaturally quiet. As though all of Paris had slept in. Or as though all of its residents were sitting inside and waiting for whatever was next, the same way Layla was, even as she stood outside, so exposed.

"Your ex-husband," he said again, and she almost rolled her eyes. She almost said, *How many ways do I have to tell you? I am not worried about him*, but then he looked back at her, and she realized that, when he'd said this before, he hadn't really been asking for a status report on the man's face.

It'd only been the beginning of a sentence. The beginning of something bleaker.

"He said something to me yesterday."

"Griffin, he doesn't—"

"He said you deserve someone good. Someone reliable."

She swallowed. Dread and frustration and anger gathering within her anew. If she'd stayed behind to shut the door on Jamie, only to have Griffin open it again, she thought she might scream.

"I *hope* you are not about to tell me what I *deserve*," she said. "I hope you do not think I'm incapable of determining that for *myself*. Not after everything I've told you about how I got here. How I knew what I *didn't* want for my life."

Something flickered in his expression, chasing away the bleakness for a split second, buoying her with a too-transitory hope.

He shoved his hands deeper in his pockets, shook his head. "I'm not about to tell you that," he said. "I think you do deserve those things. But your choices are yours."

They are, she thought mulishly. *And I'd choose you, if you'd let me.*

But he wouldn't. She knew he wouldn't.

"There's something that guy and I have in common," he said, and she had to admire how he still, even after punching him in the actual face, would not say Jamie's name out loud. "Beyond having ideas about what you deserve."

She didn't answer. She was too stymied, her brain searching fruitlessly for comparisons between Jamie and Griffin.

She could not think of a single one.

"I don't think either of us are good. I don't think either of us are reliable."

"That isn't tr—"

"But here's the difference between me and him, Layla. I *know* it. I know I've got a half dozen problems I've never bothered to deal with, because all I've been doing is worrying about how bad I hurt. And I know I can't be counted on to fix them. I know that next week I could have a bad day, ten times worse than what you saw last night, and all I'd do is start thinking again about whether I could somehow get the gates of hell to open up for good this time. To keep me in and never let me out again, until I got so used to it that it would feel like the only forever I'd ever get. I *know* it."

Something inside her shook to hear that: *get the gates of hell to open up for good this time.* She knew what he was saying without him having to say it so plainly. That the worst of his pain had included thoughts like this, however passing, and she knew that wasn't good, though she supposed she meant the word differently than he did, or differently than Jamie did, with his *someone good* bullshit.

She meant that it was not *okay* for Griff to feel that way.

But she didn't have time to explain that, because Griff was in it now, and if there was any hope to be found in this path they were on, it was that he didn't look quite so bleak anymore. He looked more like the man she'd first seen on the plane—taut and determined—mixed with the man who'd once dragged her down the Boulevard Saint-Germain to kiss her.

"That guy you were married to—it wasn't good, what he did to you. The position he put you in, the way he said *family* and meant something other than what he promised you the day you got married. That wasn't fucking reliable, making those vows to you and deciding that changing his mind was enough of a reason to stop honoring them. And I won't do that to you. I *won't.*"

That last part, he said as though he was convincing himself, and she thought, at first, that maybe what he was looking for was for her to help—for *her* to step in and do the convincing.

And she almost did. She almost opened her mouth and said, *Of course you won't*. She almost *soothed* him, made herself a sort of sacrifice to him. Not in the same way she had with Jamie—not saying, *Of course we can stay friends* or *Of course there's nothing to forgive*.

Still, she almost said to Griffin that she believed him, when she couldn't be sure that she did.

When she couldn't be sure he believed himself yet.

And she thought—she *decided*—that she would never make that mistake again.

So she didn't say anything. She stood there and felt her eyes well up with tears she knew would fall.

His throat worked as he stepped closer. He took her hand, but in a particular way—the same way he had by the Seine. A slow, careful braiding, step by careful step until they were folded into each other.

She did the same thing she had that night.

Waited until he got close enough, then rested her forehead against his chest.

This time, what she felt there was only his burning, breaking heart.

This time, she thought she could soak it in her tears.

He spoke to her in a low voice, low like it was when they were in bed, but stripped of eroticism. A private voice.

"I don't ever want to see you burned to the ground because of me. Out in the world on your own, trying to build yourself back up with your plans and your nice smiles and your never staying mad at anyone."

They were dangerously close to *him deciding for her* territory again, him deciding what she did and didn't deserve. But only close, not quite there, at least not for her, because she was thinking about that phrase: *Out in the world on your own.* She was turning it over in her mind, thinking of all the ways after her divorce that she'd made herself *more* alone. Those choices, she knew, were hers alone to own, not Jamie's: taking the new job, moving all the time, not staying close to Cara, not trying anything new, not doing anything but working, all because it felt to her like . . .

It felt to her like she'd failed.

Like her struggles with staying close to the MacKenzies—all the missed family dinners, the coffee check-ins, whatever—were proof that she didn't deserve a family.

That she didn't deserve to be close to anyone at all.

I guess I'm not actually good, either. I'm not even all that reliable.

Her tears were coming in earnest now, soaking into Griffin's shirt. She wished she'd stolen one of them, because she had the feeling she wouldn't see one again for a while.

She had the fear that she wouldn't see one again for forever.

"Layla," he said, that particular way he had of shaping the sound of her name. She squeezed her eyes shut, *tight tight tight* to get a couple more of the tears out, and then looked up, bracing herself.

Don't say I won't see one of these shirts again for forever, she thought.

"I want to know what promises I can make to you," he said, and ironically, it was as grave and serious as hearing a vow itself being made. "And what ones I can't. I have to know that, first."

She nodded. She had his shirt clutched in her fists, a tiny, sad celebration. *He didn't say for forever,* she said to the shirt. *Maybe I'll touch your nice seamless softness again.*

He must've misread her silence, because his face hardened

again, his brow furrowing. His right hand was still tangled with hers, so he lifted his left and put it against her cheek, tipping her face up, his eyes on hers intense.

"And in case it's not clear," he said, "if I didn't make it clear, that first night I kissed you—"

Her eyes slid closed, remembering it.

There shouldn't be anything amicable about losing you.

He stroked her cheekbone until she looked at him again.

"If I had you, the only force in this world that could get me to let you go is my own pain. *Nothing* else."

She knew what he meant, saying that. She knew he was reassuring her, even if it was premature. Even if it would turn out to be impossible.

He would never leave her the way Jamie had, he was saying.

He would never change his mind. Not for anything, real or imagined.

She kissed him, because she could not help it, because she wanted to seal this: this street that was not an aisle, these not-promises, this sadness way deep down, and the seed of hope she knew some part of her was planting in her soul, small and sacred.

When he broke away, it was with a groan, a pleading whisper of her name that she knew meant they were out of time.

She loosened her fingers, letting his slip free.

She thought, *I am not going to let this burn me to the ground.*

"What will you do now?"

He tucked his hands back into his pockets, straightened his shoulders. Looked down the street, toward the hotel.

"Go home," he said. "Hope Michael doesn't hate me." He brought his eyes back to hers. "Do a hundred other things that people have been telling me to do for a long time, but that I've never wanted to do."

A long pause.

"Not until you," he added.

Maybe a few more tears slipped down her cheeks. Maybe she brushed them away sloppily. Maybe she couldn't think of a single thing to say.

"Will you go back?" he asked her, after a few silent seconds. "To the apartment?"

She shook her head, a finality to the small movement that would be almost impossible to explain to anyone but him.

"I think I'll walk for a while," she said.

Until I know you're gone, she didn't add.

As though he'd heard her, he said, "Layla. Don't wait for me."

He wasn't talking about her walk. He wasn't saying, *Come back to the hotel whenever you want, whether I've gone or not.*

He was warning her of something else.

"I won't," she said, and she thought it sounded very convincing. She thought he would not dare guess that no matter what he said, no matter how long it took, she would keep watering that seed of hope for him—for *them*—inside her soul.

But just in case—in case something might give her away—she said, "You should probably go."

One last long look before he nodded. Before he did not say goodbye.

Before he turned away.

She did not want to watch him go, not this time—not like the times she'd watched him walk away before she ever truly knew him, not like the times when she hadn't known yet what kept him running scared. So after a beat, she turned, too, planning to follow the street's curve and turn the opposite direction from the apartment.

Before she got quite there, she heard Griffin call her name again.

She turned, saw him standing on this perfect Paris street she would remember forever.

"Yeah?" she called.

"Would you still do it again?"

The question she'd asked this morning, in the bed that would always be theirs. Before the mess in that apartment, before the wrenching pain of this inevitable conversation.

She couldn't quite say she smiled. She was still too sad and raw for that.

But her voice was clear when she called back to him with her answer.

"I would."

Less than ten hours later, Layla left Paris, seemingly the exact same way she'd come.

A late-booked middle seat in the back. A neutral outfit.

All alone.

But somehow, she knew, nothing about her would ever be the same.

Chapter Thirty-Two

Well.

He was fucking miserable.

Tuesdays were almost exclusively miserable now, not that he could really remember Tuesdays *before*. But Tuesdays now were absolute bullshit for him, sunup to sundown of coming face-to-face with his own limitations. He drove a far way on Tuesdays, which was part of the problem; driving was uncomfortable unless he stopped frequently, which he did now, goddammit, because *A person cannot expect to change without making changes.*

If there was a positive to the stopping frequently, he supposed it was that he'd gotten familiar with a few of the places along the way. A gas station that was clean if he needed to take a leak, a good Dunkin' drive-through where there was always decaf, never one of those *Oh, we'll have to make a pot* situations. There was even a little shop he'd found one day on the way home when he'd had a particularly bad moment, needing to get out and walk up and down a street in a way that absolutely looked suspicious unless he eventually found a convincing-looking reason to stop in somewhere.

It was a model train shop, which honestly was very fucking

annoying at first, really ratcheting things up on the don't-think-about-Paris pain scale, but in the end, it was still model trains, and he still had his pretend brain, which always enjoyed a 3D model. There was a kid who worked there, a teenager, and Griffin thought that was extremely strange, because in Paris the man in the model train shop had been—well, it didn't fucking matter, did it? The point was, a teenager named Kevin—sort of an old man name, to be honest—worked in this one, or at least he worked there on Tuesday afternoons. Whatever Griffin thought his own interest in 3D models was, this kid's was a different order of magnitude. The first time Griffin went in there it took him a full fucking hour to get back out. This despite the fact that Kevin literally called him Scarface, to his actual face. As in, "Hey, I'm going to call you Scarface!" No pause after to see if Griffin would laugh or maybe strangle him to death, just a turn of his avid attention to the next model he wanted to show off.

Anyway, he eventually bought a set to build.

He worked on it on Thursdays, which were objectively better than Tuesdays.

The reason he had to go so far on Tuesdays was for the pain management specialist he'd ghosted all those years ago, when his injuries were fresher and also easier to treat. That guy did not, thankfully, call him Scarface, but at times some garden-variety insults would not have gone amiss, since pretty much every other second of the time they spent in each other's company was challenging either physically or emotionally, and sometimes both at the same time.

Or, actually, as the specialist would probably say, it was always both at the same time.

One pain feeding the other, which didn't mean either one was less real.

For a long time on Tuesdays—the first six, at least—the most miserable part had been the reckoning with that in a way he'd avoided doing before. He'd always had good doctors, good therapists, so it wasn't as though no one had ever told him about the link between his mental health and his neuropathic pain.

But he hadn't wanted to hear it. He hadn't wanted to *practice* it. He had always held fast to his pain.

Now, it had been eleven Tuesdays, and he was learning to let it go. He stayed all day, did *the works*, which actually meant meditation *and* a group session with other chronic pain patients, both of which took more collective time than any of the other stuff—water tank, ultrasound therapy, whatever. It hurt, and some days it humiliated him, and on two specific Tuesdays he'd gotten back to his car and fucking *cried* in the front seat, and the worst part of that was how he felt better afterward, and also that his mother could tell when he arrived, two hours later, to her house for dinner.

He always went to dinner at her house on Tuesdays now. Peter usually came, one of his two Mom-allowed nights per week. Before—before the place he still could not think about much in the presence of other people—Griffin had sometimes come to dinner. But he'd never stayed beyond the meal, and now, on Tuesdays, he did, which made it so he and his mother could talk about other things besides what number he was on the pain scale.

These days, sometimes she didn't even ask at all.

Sometimes she asked about Paris. About the Placketts—about whom she no longer curbed her tongue—and about whether he'd heard anything from Michael.

Usually, he said little.

He saved that for his Fridays for now—individual therapy, here in town. Not too hard to get to, and not near as bad as Tuesdays.

Almost exclusively miserable Tuesdays.

Tonight, he was getting restless for the part of Tuesday that kept it in *almost* territory. He was sitting on the couch with Peter, Mom in her recliner working on a crochet blanket for Leonard, who "did like to be cozy!" Peter was asking Griffin about whether he'd thought any more about school, about Griffin going back to work on that master's degree he'd never gotten started on because of the fire, and despite himself—despite the way he was thinking about how, at group therapy, one of his cohort had talked about this sort of conversation, the well-meaning people in your life wanting timelines for what you were doing because of their own fears, their own confrontation with the reality that life sometimes didn't live itself according to anyone's timelines—he was still weighted with annoyance. Maybe at Peter, and maybe at himself, maybe at his mentor for even suggesting the thing about the master's program— six Wednesdays ago, that's when he'd made the suggestion, because Wednesdays were Griffin's day to work, to actually involve himself more meaningfully in the business that made him enough money for things like all-day pain management therapy.

"No decisions yet, Pete," Griff said, softening the curtness with the nickname, which Peter genuinely seemed to like, probably because it wasn't something like *Scarface*.

Almost exclusively miserable, he thought, taking the last swig of his bottled root beer and standing from the couch.

"Well," he said, which over the course of now eleven Tuesdays he had come to understand was a more polite way to warm up to his exit, as opposed to simply walking out the door.

"Wait a minute," his mother said, and he suppressed a groan. Thirteen Tuesdays ago—before, before—he might have released it. But he didn't now.

He didn't really have anything to groan at his mother about. He never had.

He was lucky she was his family.

She was balling up Leonard's blanket haphazardly, shoving it into the basket she kept by her chair. Outside, with everything for the animals, his mother was almost ruthlessly organized. But in the house, she had a much more . . . casual approach. So when she stood and drew him back toward her small den, he was not surprised by the mess on her desk. She had her fists set on her hips and she was saying, "Now where did I—oh, there it is," then she was bending over and shoving a stack of god knew what out of the way.

When she straightened, she was holding a few crinkled sheets of white paper, paper-clipped messily together.

"Printed this out at the library!" she said.

Again, he did not groan. In fairness to the impulse, though, his mother printing out things at the library for him did have a groan-worthy history, back in the early days after the fire. Anything she could find—treatments, testimonials from victims with similar injuries, sometimes even accounts of other fires, as though it would soothe him to know that the one he'd lived through wasn't unique—she would bring to him like this, on these white sheets, with these little paper clips.

"It's about something called the Paris Syndrome," she said, and then she was doing the thing that she did back in those early days. Licking her index finger and paging right into the thing, like she was getting ready to read it off. "You ever hear of that?"

"Don't think so," he said, but already he didn't like this—what it meant, that his mom printed out this article the same way she'd printed out articles about burn trauma. He knew he had not told her much about Paris; he knew what she knew was mostly confined to Michael.

And sure.

Not talking to Michael in twelve weeks was pretty traumatic.

But he didn't want her to think he had some kind of syndrome.

"Well, I thought you'd enjoy it," she said. "It's about how people get this big idea about Paris, about how perfect it'll be. And when they get there, it's a complete disappointment! It's more complex than that, actually, there's an actual psychiatric condition, but—"

He took the article from her. Folded it longways and tucked it into his back pocket.

That is definitely not what I have from Paris, he thought. *It isn't a disappointment at all. You'd hardly believe how not-disappointing it is.*

"I'll read it," he promised her gently, then he bent and kissed her wrinkled cheek, and she patted his scarred one. Ten Tuesdays, they'd done that, and every time she looked like he'd held out the whole world to her. Happier than she had looked even on the day he'd bought her this farm.

He waved at Peter as he left, made his way back home, his heart kicking up as he got closer. It was a ritual, waiting until he got home, until the hardest parts of the hardest day of his week were over, until he finally walked in his front door and realized that, this time, it had not been quite as hard as the week before, or the week before that.

Until he realized that he was not, in fact, really miserable at all.

But he was not . . . he was not *not miserable* enough. Not yet.

He wasn't quite sure what it would take.

But he knew it would take something.

So he kept this ritual.

He went to the small table in his kitchen. He slid the article from his mom out of one of his back pockets and set it down—he would read it, eventually, since she'd gone to the trouble, but not tonight—and from the other, he drew out his phone.

A swipe, a tap. A text box that only ever had one of two messages. The same two, over and over again. Ten times, so far.

Would you still do it again? he wrote, pressing send, and then he darkened the screen, leaving the phone on top of the still-folded article about a syndrome he wouldn't ever understand, no matter what he eventually read in there. He didn't get nervous or miserable not to get an immediate reply.

Ten Tuesdays taught him that she didn't always respond quickly.

So he took a long shower, washed off the day. Thought about all the places and people he tried not to let intrude too much on the difficult parts of his Tuesday. Thought about how much longer it might be until his Tuesdays could look different.

Not yet. Not quite yet.

Still, when he finally made his way back to the kitchen, he breathed a sigh of relief to see that she'd replied.

Eleventh time, two words.

I would.

Michael called him on the thirteenth Thursday, when Griffin had his hands in a particularly delicate piece of his model train set.

He dropped what he'd been holding.

He probably broke what he'd been holding, which Kevin was going to give him hell about on Tuesday, the little shit.

But he did not care.

"Mikey," he said, when he got the phone up to his ear, and another thing that he did not care about was that he sounded slightly out of breath. Inside his chest, his heart was pounding, and along his left side, he felt a strange, uncomfortable skittering that no longer filled him immediately with dread, with frantic anticipation.

"Hey," Michael said back, a single syllable that Griffin could not really read anything from.

There was dead air between them—a game of chicken, a game of *who will say how are you* first.

Griffin. Griffin would.

"You all right?" he said, which was basically the same. Gruff, maybe, but whatever. He wasn't meant to become a different *person* with all this therapy.

Michael laughed. A huffing, sarcastic laugh. "Been better. You?"

He could've said, *Same*. Let the dead air stretch again, and it would have been *fine*. It would've been familiar, even: almost every hospital room visit, Griffin getting ruder and ruder, daring Michael, *begging* Michael, in the only way he knew how through all that pain, to get fucking *angry*. To yell or scream or destroy something about Sara Beth being gone, the way Griffin sometimes wanted to.

Even though he really had no right to.

Even though he physically *couldn't*.

He couldn't ever do anything but *lie* there.

He took a deep breath and did not let the dead air stretch.

"I'm sorry for Paris," he said.

But immediately, he disliked the taste of it in his mouth. It had the flavor of a lie he didn't want to tell. The sort that didn't help anyone, especially not himself.

"No, I'm not," he corrected, and talk about gruff, Jesus. "I mean that I'm sorry you got hurt. That it happened the way it did. That's—that's really all I mean. About being sorry."

Good thing Fridays were for therapy. Tomorrow he would have to talk about being bad at apologies.

"You did what you had to do," said Michael, followed by a long pause. Like he, too, was rolling around the taste of something bad.

Eventually, Michael cleared his throat. He said, "You did the only thing you could do. It was the right thing to do."

Griffin was glad to be alone. Glad to let his eyes close in pure, simple relief.

He felt something move through him. The beginning of something he'd been waiting for. *Scanning* for, every single day. A new scale, and all the levels between *Not yet* and *Now*.

He thought of a dark hotel room. Felt a slim, longed-for hand squeeze around his calf and heard a soft, longed-for voice say, *You did right by them.*

"I dared you," intruded a different voice—another one he'd missed, sure, but right this second, it was no small effort to focus back on his best friend, who had maybe just said—

"I dared you to do it," Michael repeated, "because I knew it had to be done. I knew it did, and I was too much of a coward to do it myself."

After that, it was different.

The conversation, that was. No more dead air. It was Griffin saying, *Mikey, you're not a fucking coward*, and Michael pushing back, Michael saying that he maybe had always been a coward, that he'd always put Griffin between himself and the hardest things— the pressure he got from Fitz, the grief over Sara Beth, this wedding—and Griffin saying, *That's not how I see it*, but also, after listening, sort of seeing it, too. They talked about that night, first about the things they'd said to each other and then about the one thing Griffin had said to Emily—*You need to ask him about Sara Beth*—and how Michael was mad about that at first, how he'd wished Griffin had said the whole thing so he wouldn't have to, and Griffin said, *How do you think I fucking felt*, in a sort of deadpan quip, and Michael actually laughed for real.

Then, Michael told Griffin about Emily.

He stayed to the broad strokes of it. *Out of respect*, he said, and for the first time in Griffin's life, or maybe since the first time he'd gone to fucking therapy on Fridays and talked about how he loved Layla Bailey in the broadest strokes possible, he fucking *got it*, got something about how Michael felt toward Sara Beth all those years ago and how he felt toward Emily now.

How precious it was.

How much he wanted to protect it.

"We're taking it slow," Michael said eventually. "Starting over."

"Germany?" Griffin asked, and he could practically see his best friend shake his head.

"Not going," he answered. "It's caused some fucking problems, to be honest, but it's fine. It's worth it. She's worth it."

Griffin was about to default to an old pattern, to say, *What kind of fucking problems?* and then offer to throw money at them. But he stopped himself in time, which maybe he would brag about tomorrow. Just to take the sting out of having to ask how to do a proper apolo—

"My new therapist says we might have—had, I don't know—a codependent relationship," Michael blurted. "You and me, I mean. Not me and Emily."

Now that they'd talked for a while, Griffin could hear how Michael had been working up to it. How hard it was to say. How he thought it would be a surprise to Griffin.

Or that it would hurt.

But Michael didn't know about the last three and a half months. The work of the last three and a half months. He didn't know that Griffin had learned that a lot of things about Michael *did* hurt, that sometimes, just remembering certain things about Michael—about Michael and Sara Beth—could be like a huge, heaping meal for the pain he had to work so hard not to feed.

So he said, "My therapist said the same."

They both laughed, and Griffin told him a bit about it—fucking Tuesdays, and the work stuff, and even Kevin and his Scarface shit, about the decisions he still wasn't ready to make about school, about how he was, almost every single day, leaving the house.

Getting out of his bell tower, all by himself.

Not for Michael.

Not even for Layla.

By himself, *for* himself.

He remembered that first day, that hotel lobby, him and Michael and Layla and Emily. Layla calling him *heroic*, and how he bristled then—how that bristling turned into a blade, cutting him deep, making him lash out.

But now, he felt it. Felt the heroism in himself, for all he'd done, all he knew he was capable of doing.

Now, he thought. *Now.* Crystal clear. No *Not yet* in sight anymore.

"You sound good," Michael said, when it seemed to be winding down. "Different."

"Yeah," he managed through the *Now*.

Michael laughed again. "Not that different, though. Just one more thing."

Christ, Griffin thought. He should've tried the *Well*, like he did on Tuesdays with Mom and Peter, but it probably wouldn't work over the phone.

"Layla's here," Michael said. "Not, you know, in my house. But in Boston."

Now, now, now, he thought.

He was already moving toward his computer, opening the lid.

"Not sure if she's got a placement here," Michael was saying, "or if it's a longer-term thing or what. She and Em went to dinner last night."

Griffin set the phone down, put it on speaker. He was moving his fingers across the keys on his computer.

"Are you listening?" Michael said, obviously hearing the tapping sounds.

"I'm getting a fucking flight. A train, I don't know."

Michael laughed again. "You're in a hurry now, after three months?"

"Three and a half. And yeah. I'm in a fucking hurry now."

He scanned the screen, making sense of the times and numbers before him. On the other end of the phone, he heard the sound of what he thought was a door opening. Michael's voice again, muffled, like he'd pressed his hand over the speaker.

Then—unmuffled—a delighted laugh Griffin once thought he might not ever get the chance to commit to memory.

Emily's.

"I told you!" he heard her say. "I told you he was only waiting for *you* to call."

"You catch that?" Michael asked.

This time, Griffin was the one to laugh.

"Yeah," he said, clicking on one of the options in front of him. "I heard her. And Michael?"

"Yeah?"

"You had better fucking marry that woman someday."

Chapter Thirty-Three

There was a lot to like about a walk along the Esplanade.

The Charles River Esplanade, that was.

Esplanade was a French word, or at least it came from French. Middle French, if she was remembering right from looking it up this morning, when she'd agreed to meet Cara here.

She did that a lot these days: look up words. English ones she wanted to know the French for, or French-sounding words she wanted to know the origin of.

She had a new app, a better one that her conversation partner told her about during their first FaceTime meeting, back when Layla was still at her placement in Chico. That had been challenging, what with a nine-hour time difference between there and Paris, but for five weeks they made it work. When Layla got back on Eastern time, the lessons became much easier to schedule.

They also became easier to *do*.

After five weeks, she'd broken herself of the habit to apologize for every clumsy pronunciation, every botched verb tense, every dropped word or failure to remember the French one. Her conversation partner—a forty-two-year-old woman named Sabine who had the best shag haircut Layla had ever seen in her life—had helped with that, since she did something like seven French lesson FaceTimes a day and did not have a lot of patience for Layla's repetitive *I'm sorry!*

By the time Layla left Chico, she'd dropped the apologies. She'd even incorporated some French curses for when it all got too frustrating.

She worried, at first, about taking the French lessons. Worried it was way too MacKenzie-adjacent.

But no, she decided.

No, it did not have to be MacKenzie-adjacent. It did not even have to be Griffin-adjacent.

It only had to be *Layla-liked-learning-it*-adjacent.

And so far, she found that she did.

"These runners," Cara said, clucking her tongue. Layla thought of the word *courir*, but she did not know the word for *runner*. *Courier*? Probably not, too easy. Next week she would ask Sabine, who would probably make that funny *p*-heavy noise of exasperation and say, *We say* jogger, as though it was the most obvious thing in the world.

"Like what are they fucking doing?" said Cara. "It's four o'clock in the afternoon on a Friday! Not working, I guess!"

Layla smiled and took a sip of her coffee. Complaining about people running for exercise was a *very* Cara thing to do, one of the many things she'd missed about her friend. Layla happened to know that Cara had a Peloton (also a French word: *small ball*) in her apartment, which she rode at weird hours to accommodate her working, which was not always in the middle of the afternoon.

"It's a nice day for it," said Layla.

Cara snorted. "You would say that."

Layla smiled into her to-go cup. Cara was grouchy today, sleep-deprived after too many long shifts in a row. But she'd been the one to suggest the Esplanade, texting Layla that the hospital had turned her into a fluorescent-light, stale-air gremlin, and she needed to get outside.

And Layla, who had two whole weeks here with no work schedule, was happy to oblige.

"I mean," Layla said, gesturing toward the water. "Look at this. The trees, the boats, the city. It feels almost . . ."

She trailed off. It did not really feel Parisian, which was fine. It was nice enough on its own. Though sometimes, if she squinted at that bridge up ahead, say, the curving arch over the water, the—

"Let's talk about your shitty apartment," Cara said. A mercy.

Layla left a beat of silence, building the suspense before saying, "In ten days, it is officially no longer my shitty apartment."

"Layla!" Cara exclaimed, grabbing her arm and shaking her, nearly upsetting Layla's coffee. "That's so good! So, you decided?"

Layla nodded, looking up ahead at the bridge, not squinting.

She did love Boston. Or liked it, at least. But over the last couple of months—since Paris—she'd been thinking about whether Boston was really her home base. Whether keeping a *shitty apartment* here for in between her placements made any sense, or whether she had done it as some kind of deferent, amicable monument to the fact that her home with Jamie had been here, to the fact that the MacKenzies were here.

"And you re-signed your contract?"

Layla swallowed, nodding again. This, she was less sure about: one more year, at least, as a locum tenens, though she had negotiated fewer total placements, with more time in between. Her salary was still more than she needed, certainly as a single person, and enough to make the most of the time in between with travel.

But not enough to keep renting a shitty apartment she didn't even want anymore, in an expensive city she didn't think she wanted to call home.

"C'est bon!" Cara said teasingly, knowing about the conversation-partner stuff. "How do I say *I'm proud of you* in French?"

Layla rolled her eyes and didn't answer. But she thought, *Je suis fière de toi.*

Je suis fière de moi.

She linked her arm with Cara's, and said, "Thank you. For everything."

She said it seriously, quietly, squeezing Cara's arm as she did, so her friend would know the depth of it. It wasn't the first time she'd said it to Cara since she'd been back from Paris, and it was the short version—the one that held all the other thank-yous Layla had offered to her friend in recent weeks.

Thank you for still being my friend for all that time, even when I couldn't be a good one back.

Thank you for waiting for me to stop being so amicable.

Thank you for being there when I could finally admit that Jamie was not actually as good as I always said he was.

Thank you for not saying I told you so.

Merci, merci, merci, merci.

Cara was the first person Layla texted when she got back from Paris. Cara had been there through it all. Not often in person—that was not how their friendship worked, not with their jobs and their schedules—but so often, in long text threads, voice notes, occasional calls. It was clear that Cara had, until then, actually been practicing great restraint when it came to Jamie—to the MacKenzies in general—and sometimes, she set forth with a torrent of complaint that truly made Layla laugh.

And that reminded her of someone, too.

Someone else who could be grouchy. Tilting toward cruel, at times, but only ever out of fierce, focused protectiveness. Kinder than most people could see.

She took a breath of fresh air—not even a trace of cigarette out here, not that she should be disappointed—and focused on Cara. She did not want to be thinking about a man when she was out with Cara, not after all the times she'd done that in the past, and all the harm it had caused their friendship.

Layla was learning how to be a better friend now. A friend who knew better what family *really* was.

So she said, "Do we have a destination today?"

Cara gave a dramatic scoff. *Dramatic*.

"What?" Layla said.

"A *destination*, Layla? Really?"

"I'm—yes? Like do you want to go eat, or shop, or—"

Cara groaned. "Here I am, *trying* to show *interest* in your *interests*, and you ask me if we have a fucking *destination*, I can't believe it!"

"My interests?"

Cara stopped and took out her phone, swiped and tapped at the screen for a few seconds, then turned it and held it up in front of Layla's face.

It was a translation app.

The one Layla used to use.

The word on the screen was *flâner*.

Layla flushed.

"To stroll, right?" Cara said, still exasperated. "Like, without a destination? That's what it means?"

Only sort of, she thought, but she nodded. Sabine had been the one to teach her the word, only a few weeks ago now. The funny thing about having Sabine—well, maybe not Sabine specifically, but having a French conversation partner in *general*—was that sometimes, Layla ended up telling her more *details* about her days in Paris than she actually told Cara. They were good conversation prompts: She could describe, for example, a boat cruise, the sights seen, the food served, the disastrous moment when someone threw up over the side, and work out how to say it all in the tongue of the place where it had all happened.

And one day, only a couple of weeks ago now, when Layla's conversation appointment had coincided with a particularly aching, lonely feeling, a restless impatience, a *worry*—she'd told Sabine about that day alone with Griffin. The walking, the shops, the random restaurants, the people-watching, the complete abandonment of the itinerary for the day. And Sabine had said, "Ah! You are *une flâneuse*!"

It didn't really mean *someone who strolls*. It meant more than that, a French something, something Layla suspected would be difficult to *be* anywhere else. It meant . . .

Well.

To her, it meant *someone who wanders*.

Flâner, the verb form. *Wandering*.

To her, it would always mean *wandering*.

With a specific person.

With whom she still, absolutely, would.

She swallowed, unexpectedly emotional. Grateful and also heartachy. Cara was not making it easy to focus right now.

"You remembered," she said to Cara, then added, "Je suis fière de toi."

Cara linked her arm through Layla's again, moving them back into their walk. Their *stroll*. The truth was, it was a little too fast-paced to be called that. Cara—and also Boston, and all these runners—had limitations, when it came to being without a destination.

After a few minutes of walking quietly, Cara said, "I know I've talked a lot of shit lately. About your ex-in-laws."

Layla laughed, remembering some of the greatest hits: Cara's angry-face emoji response to the long email Manon had sent to Layla after Paris, part apology and part guilt trip over Layla's "unceremonious departure," her doubt about Layla's decision to talk to Robert and Manon on the phone one day a few weeks ago, a painful but necessary conversation in which Layla had set some new boundaries, and, finally, her gasping proclamation of the MacKenzies as *cheap-ass motherfuckers* when Layla revealed that Griffin had been the one to pay for most of the wedding. Layla thought that last one was pretty unfair, but now, she didn't always so readily push back on anything negative about the MacKenzies.

Sometimes, she'd learned, you had to let your friends—your family—howl at the moon for you.

Especially when you weren't capable, at first, of doing it for yourself.

"You have," Layla said.

"But I have to admit, I've been wrong about your sister-in-law. *Ex*-sister-in-law, whatever."

Layla smiled, thinking of Em at dinner last night. A tearful reunion. A happy one. She *did* still think of Emily as a sister; that was the nice thing to come out of all of this.

Separate from anyone else in the MacKenzie family, she still felt that way about Em.

"Oh?" Layla said. "What brought this on?"

Cara's steps slowed, more like a stroll now. She shrugged casually, was quiet for a few seconds, clearly distracted by something on her phone. She slowed to a stop, and Layla figured it was work.

Then she tucked her phone away, looked up at Layla, and said, "I think she really cares about you. Just for you. Whether you're sisters or not, you know?" She was smiling widely, excitedly. "I really think that."

"Okay?" Layla said, but also—she felt it. A warmth moving inside her.

Not from Cara's smile. Not from the nice things she said about Em. Not from the sunny day or the not-cigarette smell of the Esplanade or the breeze off the water.

A crackle in the air, like lightning.

A fae prince, a column of smoke, a shade from heaven.

Come to get his mortal girl.

She turned, and there was Griffin.

Cara left with only a brief explanation: a text she'd gotten late last night from Emily, the two still in each other's contacts from way back when there were still pre-wedding events for Layla being scheduled; some hasty planning to make sure Layla would be here when someone else—someone *special*—would be waiting. After that, a quick blown kiss, an assessing gaze at Griffin in his all-black, his baseball cap. A declaration that she had not, in fact, enjoyed a *stroll*, and actually she did have a destination to get to, *thankyouverymuch*, and Layla would *need to call extremely soon, okay?*

Then, Cara left them alone together.

Or as alone together as you could be in a city of people, which—as Layla and Griffin both knew—was actually quite a lot.

"Hi," she said, half disbelieving. Him, *here*. She had never seen him here.

She had never seen him anywhere but in the air, and then in Paris.

She found herself profoundly, overwhelmingly relieved to know that he had the exact same effect on her in this place. She knew for certain now—in a way she couldn't possibly have known three and a half months ago—that he would have this effect on her anywhere.

After any amount of time.

"Sorry it took me so long," he said, which, as an opener, was not particularly profound.

But he had his ball cap low, his hands in his pockets. Nervous. And maybe also feeling some pain. Travel, a new place, a walk from wherever. It could be pain.

"It wasn't that long," she said.

He blew out a breath. "It felt long to me."

She smiled. Part of her wanted to say, *Oh my god, for me, too; it's felt like forever*; part of her wanted to close the distance between them *now*, to throw her arms around him and squeeze and squeeze until she could assure herself that he wasn't a hallucination, that the magic heaven of him wouldn't simply disappear into the air.

But another part of her felt a *Not yet* from him. That's what she was reading in his ball cap, his hands tucked away.

So she stayed quiet. When her smile started to feel unwieldy, she lifted her coffee to her mouth, and watched as he tracked the movement: her lips around the lid, her careful sip on an indrawn breath, her throat moving in a swallow.

He said, "Back to American habits already."

A teasing note. She heard it.

She shrugged. Still smiling, probably. "Maybe it *did* take you too long."

At that, he looked suddenly . . . stricken.

Absolutely *stricken*.

"No!" she said, overloud, way too loud for being alone together. She took a step closer to him, and repeated it. "I was kidding. I only meant—"

He took off his hat. Turned and tossed it onto the dark green bench behind him, which she hadn't even noticed until now.

He took her hand. No step-by-step, no careful braiding. His warm, damp palm pressed to hers, a clasp. He tugged her closer, still keeping some space between them.

"I can make you these promises," he said firmly.

And then, he listed them. Like he'd been practicing and practicing. Like he'd had a hundred conversation partners since he left her.

I can promise that I'm learning to take better care of myself.

I can promise that I've accepted it'll always hurt.

I can promise to admit when it does.

I can promise that I want to be here. That I want to have a life. That I deserve a life.

I can promise that I'll want that even if you don't want to share some of yours with me.

"But god," he said, after that last one. "God, Layla, I hope you do."

She would not risk that stricken face again.

She would not, even for a smile.

So she leaned in, and pressed her mouth to his. She said, "I really, really do."

At that, he let go of her hand. He wrapped his arms around her, hugged her close, so close that she could feel his heart beating and burning in a new way, not at all broken.

They stood that way for a long time, holding each other along the banks of the Charles, both of them probably pretending that they could somehow be somewhere else together, too—a different river in a very different city.

She smiled against his chest, the smooth, soft, seamless shirt she would not miss her next opportunity to steal. She said, "I have a list, too."

She looked up at him—his handsome, sculptural, *perfect* face, *god*. Her whole list flew out of her mind for a second, and she thought maybe she would have to do it later. When she did not want to kiss and kiss him, to remind herself what her mouth could do when it was pressed against his.

But Griffin had not forgotten. "What kind of list?"

"Not promises," she said, scrutinizing him as she did, waiting to see if he was disappointed.

But he wasn't. She could tell that even before he said, "I didn't expect any. I think the thing about us is, it's me who'll need to make the promises at first. I think maybe you've had enough of making your own for a while."

She lowered her head again, let him kiss the top of it. He rubbed his palm down her back as she let out a relieved breath.

"List," he finally said. "Go."

She couldn't help her laugh. He still talked like Griffin—Paris Griffin, the man she'd met all those months ago, curt and commanding and impatient.

She was so glad for that.

So she did her list, too.

Every French word and phrase she'd learned over the last three and a half months that she'd longed to say to him. The places they'd gone together, the things they'd seen and done, the way she'd *felt*. She said things like *flâner* but she also said *manquer*; she said *la souffrance, la joie, la tristesse, l'espoir*. She said all the words she liked the sound of and the meaning of; she thought Sabine would probably hate it all, as a list, but also she thought her pronunciation was getting better and better.

There was one more thing, too—something she hadn't dared to ask Sabine if she was grammatically correct about, something she'd checked and double-checked so many times online.

"*J'ai envie de toi,*" she said against his skin, along the right side of his neck. She hoped she'd said it with all the longing and desire she felt. Hoped that somehow, underneath it, he could feel the other thing—the bigger thing—she wanted to say waiting just beneath the surface. Waiting for sometime later, sometime in the future, when she would be ready to make promises again.

He held her tighter, dipped his head close to her ear. Let her feel what all that French did to him.

"Jesus," he breathed. "I haven't been learning any more French."

"No?"

"No. I've built a few model trains."

She laughed and pulled back to look at him. "Really? You'll have to show me." She frowned dramatically and added, "*Le train*. Not much of an effort there."

He kissed the word from her mouth.

"I will show you," he promised. And then he added, seriously, "I've done some other things."

"I can tell."

She could see it in him, those things. She could not quite articulate *how* she could see them, because he looked the same: the clothes, the coiled tension, the care he still took with his movements.

But she could see them. In his eyes, or in the set of his mouth. Something.

It was ineffable. Untranslatable.

She said, "You look so good. Tu es si beau."

He gave her a specific smile. The Versailles one. Grudging but earnest.

"You have no idea how you look to me," he replied.

"How?" she said, and he took her face in both his hands, a more complete holding than he'd done that last day in the Marais. He looked at her for so long.

Not memorizing, though.

Not looking as though he was getting ready to say goodbye.

He was looking at her as though he was making a promise.

"A city of light," he said. "A tower of gold."

He bent his head and kissed her. Long and full of promises she knew he would never break.

"Like Paris," he said, when he took a breath, and then he kissed her again, before adding something else. A final, perfect set of things, maybe the only things she ever wanted a man to promise her, ever again.

"Like yourself. Like the woman I love. Like Layla Bailey."

Epilogue

Fine, she was right.

They were at the airport too early.

Griffin stood, alone, before the sparsely populated gate, frowning at the screen that said it was still ninety minutes to boarding, and suppressed a sigh.

If he was honest, he didn't really need the confirmation of the time. After all, barely ten minutes ago, when he'd made it out the other end of security, Layla had been waiting to wave her lit-up watch in his face, her smile smug.

"Told you we were leaving too early," she'd said, and he'd grunted back in acknowledgment, too nervous to say much of anything else. But he liked the way she shuffled her feet in something like victory. "I'm a travel expert!"

Fucking cute, her braggy little dance.

And anyway, between the two of them, she *was* the travel expert, no argument there. Over the last year and a half—ever since that day he'd shown up in Boston—Layla had kept on with her work as a locum tenens, an arrangement that had been both difficult and right for the two of them. In their weeks apart, he missed her—sometimes, enough to get his wires crossed, his pain kicking up strangely—but it was good for him to deal with it, to keep talking about it at his appointments, to distract himself with his work, to tell her about it without shame. It was good for them to talk on the phone, for him to see his own face on a screen for video calls and how she smiled with delight at it; it was good to think of ways to stay close to someone, to get to know someone who was—especially in those early months—still so new to him.

Even if that someone was often far away.

But when Layla wasn't far away—when she flew to him in between, when she started staying longer, when she agreed to move the things she had in storage to his place—that was better than good; that was how he learned her best. That's how he knew all the sounds she could truly sleep through, the candy wrappers she always had in her scrubs pockets, the way she made a grilled cheese all wrong, the quickness with which she could pick up something like crocheting, at least as long as his mom was showing her. That's how he knew that she had it in her to do a goofy dance when she was right about something, that her real, honest laugh was louder than he would have ever guessed, that sometimes, she liked to be held so close and tight that he thought it might hurt her.

"I'm not so bad anymore," he'd said back to her, after the little *travel expert* dance, and she'd made a *Hmm*ing noise, conceding the point.

They were, after all, about to board an international flight.

He *wasn't* so bad anymore about traveling, not after he'd also gone to see her in various cities, each time a little easier. He couldn't say he liked it—the bland apartments she stayed in, the beds he hated except that she was in them, all the new things there were to get used to in every place—but Layla was worth it. Seeing her off to work, taking care of her after a shift, that was worth it.

Making plans to take her places—restaurants, parks, whatever he could find in whatever town she was in—that was worth it. Every time, she was happy. Every time, it reminded him of how she'd built a bell tower for herself once, too.

It reminded him of how they'd climbed down together.

And anyway, it'd been good practice for this. The trip they'd planned together, for one of her longer breaks between placements.

The trip for which he'd tacked something extra on.

"*Mom*," a small voice whispered nearby, a note to it that was well familiar to him by now—more so, surely, for all the time he spent outside, no hat, these days. Subtly, he turned his face and saw the source: a kid whose age he couldn't guess, but stood only knee-high to his mother, who was holding his hand tightly, obviously trying to rush him past where Griffin stood.

"Look at his—" the kid was saying, as his mother *shushed* him harshly, giving Griffin a weak, apologetic smile, her eyes cast mostly down as she passed.

Griffin waited, knowing the lagging kid would eventually look back.

When he did, Griffin lifted his left hand and waved, stifling a laugh when the kid squeaked—in delight or fear, or some combination—and stumbled against his mother's leg.

"I better savor this," Layla announced, coming back to his side after her trip to the nearest coffee kiosk. She had a to-go cup large enough to give a lesser person—him, certainly—a caffeine-induced heart event. "My last *real* coffee for *two weeks*!"

He smiled down at her, leaned in to press a kiss to the corner of her mouth. "Don't let anyone there hear you say that."

She mimed zipping her lips shut, gave a passing glance at the kid and his mom before turning back to Griffin, unbothered. Another good thing between them, how they'd gotten through this: Layla's anxiety, in the first year or so they were together, about the kids question. For a while, it felt like anytime they were in the presence of any random kid, Layla would watch him too close—waiting for some tell, some look of longing in him.

He had not been lying to her in Paris: There was no future, real or imagined, he wanted more than he wanted to be with Layla. But it'd taken a lot of convincing to get her to understand that it went beyond that: that he had not, even before her, even before the fire, ever seen himself with kids, that it was not something he wanted for his life.

I'll tell you however many times you need to hear it, he'd told her one night, a few months ago. *I'll keep pulling you back from whatever gate you're thinking of going through.*

That, finally—after all the nights she'd hung in there with him, waiting while he fought off the shades—seemed to get through to her.

It was part of why this particular trip felt special. Important.

Only part, though.

The other part, he had been keeping a secret.

He took what he hoped was a subtle breath through his nose, made note of the needle-feeling under his left armpit, didn't dwell.

He said, "Eighty-eight minutes," in a way that he hoped betrayed nothing of his nervous anticipation.

"Okay," Layla said, taking a sip of her coffee. "Let's walk for a while."

Even for first class, boarding had been touch and go.

Meaning, Griffin had been touched a lot, by accident—by a fellow passenger, by a flight attendant who moved carelessly, by more than one suitcase—and he wanted to *go*.

In his seat, he was sweating a little—trying to control it so his skin wouldn't react, his left leg feeling preternaturally long, a psychosomatic consequence of adjusting to an unfamiliar chair, however comfortable. He thought of the extra clothes he kept in his carry-on now, in case these got damp, the prescription he had if his stress got out of control, the fact that the woman sitting beside him had seen him way worse, and never cared.

He breathed easier, but still.

He was fucking nervous.

This whole thing—he might've overshot it. It might be too soon. Too complicated.

Against his right leg, his phone vibrated with a notification, and he was pretty sure he knew who it was. He slid his eyes to Layla, who was smiling down at her own phone, probably texting with Cara, so he reached into his pocket and took his out, too, tilting the screen slightly away from her.

> Did you do it yet?

Michael, as expected.

Not until we're in the air, Griff replied.

He watched as the bubbles popped up, then disappeared. Popped up again. Disappeared.

Christ, Griffin thought. *He's going to tell me not to do it. Waits until I'm on the plane to tell me not to do it.*

I told Em, came Michael's eventual reply. SORRY

Griffin smiled as he typed back: I knew you would.

Michael and Emily were pretty anti-secrets these days, at least when it came to each other. About six months ago, they'd pulled off a pretty big one, sneaking away—alone—to City Hall on a

Thursday afternoon to get married, hopping a flight for a weekend trip right after. They hadn't told anyone until they were safely ensconced in their beachside hotel room, sending around a set of photos: hands joined as they stood before the judge, their first kiss as husband and wife, a selfie from their honeymoon balcony, backlit by an orange sunset over the glowing ocean.

In the weeks after, Griffin and Layla had heard about the fallout—Griff from Michael, Layla from Emily—that had come from both the MacKenzies and the Placketts, no matter that Michael and Emily had promised a small family celebration later. Whether that would eventually happen—and whether Griff and Layla would make an appearance at it—was still up in the air.

She's gonna like it, Michael texted.

She likes her plans, Griffin replied.

She'll like it, Michael texted. Em says so. Good luck.

Then, the flight attendant—speaking first in rich, musical-sounding Italian before switching to accented English—announced that the cabin door was closing.

Thanks, Mikey, Griffin typed, and shut off his phone.

Thirty minutes later, he was ready to do it.

He had a window for making it work, he knew. In first class, no matter the amount of coffee, Layla would fall asleep, out like a light, no eye mask necessary. She had her book out already, a Rick Steves guide to Florence and Tuscany, which she'd already tabbed with brightly colored sticky notes. By this point, she had to have been over this book so many times that it would bore her into sleep.

Because she likes plans, he thought, and almost lost his nerve.

But then he remembered.

He remembered that she liked him—no, she *loved* him—she had told him hundreds of times now, the first time carved like a sculpture set on his heart. He remembered her skin under a specific sky, remembered a tower of gold. He remembered how they'd started, how they'd both become something new.

He remembered that she liked when he made plans of his own. For himself or for her or for them both.

So he leaned forward in his seat, reached around to his back pocket.

Stopped when the plane's speaker crackled to life. When he heard the word *medico*, and felt Layla straighten in her seat beside him.

No, Griffin thought. *Fucking* no.

"Seriously?" Layla whispered in stunned disbelief, which at least made him feel less alone in his knee-jerk annoyed response to a medical emergency.

The announcement was in English now, a call for a doctor on the plane, and Griffin sat back, deflated but resigned. Obviously, if someone was in need of—

"Anyone?" the flight attendant said now, and Griffin raised his eyes as Layla was unhooking her seat belt. The flight attendant, he thought, looked a little cheeky for making this sort of announcement—he didn't see what there was to fucking smile about, if someone needed a doctor.

But then, two rows up from where Layla and Griffin sat, a woman rose from her seat: blond, pink-cheeked as she turned to the side to make her way to the flight attendant.

"Maybe you'll get the day off after all," Griffin said, though he knew that wasn't accurate—he knew Layla would go, too, even if there was another doctor on board. Anyway, now that he had a better look at the woman ahead, he figured she was fresh out of med school, and might need some help with whatever was happening.

He'd taken Layla's book from her, figured he'd look at it again for however long she was gone. It'd be fine to do it different than he'd planned; it would—

"Oh," said Layla, stilling where she was, and then slowly sitting down again. He looked over at her—her wide eyes, her soft smile—and she nodded toward the flight attendant, who was now speaking softly to the blond woman.

And directing her to turn around.

Where a man knelt on one knee, his hands raised, a ring box held between them.

It only took a few seconds for the whole first-class cabin to catch on, for the blond woman to gasp and nod and then start crying, for a smatter of applause to build as the flight attendant announced that this request was for one very *specific* doctor, who had said yes to the proposal from her boyfriend—an airline employee who'd surprised her on today's flight.

Layla said, "That's sweet," and Griffin cursed the very stupid thing he'd been reaching in his back pocket for.

"That floor," Griffin said, nodding toward the still-kneeling man, "is probably—"

Layla laughed, leaning in to kiss him—a hard press of her lips first, and then a secret swipe of her tongue across his bottom lip—and it was enough, it was always enough, to jolt him back to reality.

To sensibility.

Layla did not want him to *propose*.

Not now, not for a long while. They'd *talked* about it; they'd gone over it. Their next big decision was about whether she'd do another year traveling, or whether it was time to settle somewhere—a hospital near him, or maybe somewhere new for them both. Not *marriage*.

He knew that, and that's why he'd—

Well. That's why he'd done what was in his back pocket.

That's why he'd made this plan.

And that's why he knew she'd love it.

So he leaned forward again, took the folded sheet out of his back pocket. Before, he was going to say something first, something clever and romantic that he'd practiced just for her, but speaking in anything other than his native language right now—after the nerves, after that interruption—was impossible.

"Layla," he said, which was a word he could say no matter what.

He slid the paper into her palm.

And when she smiled down at it—the secret folded square of it—he thought maybe she already knew.

Still, she unfolded it slowly, calmly, stealing glances at him, her cheeks a prettier pink than the blond who was still giggling and crying up ahead.

"An itinerary," she said, when she had it open.

She was not giggling or crying, but he thought the curve of her lips, the dampness at the edges of her eyes, was his favorite sort of enthusiasm from Layla.

When they were in public, at least. When they were outside of whatever bed they found themselves in.

"A few extra days after Italy," he said. "A little apartment for the two of us."

"Paris," she said. "Griff!"

She kissed him again—harder this time, longer. Very close to a not-in-public kiss.

He had to adjust himself when she finally pulled away.

"We can wander," he said. "No pressure. You can think about what's next."

She smiled. A city of light all on her own, his Layla.

She said, "I know what's next."

And then she whispered it to him, the same way she had the very first time, in the language she'd learned only for herself.

"Griffin," she said. "Je t'aime."

Acknowledgments

As always, I have many people to thank for making each one of my books possible, and for this one, which came at a point of personal and professional transition, the list is so long that I want to acknowledge up top that it will almost certainly be incomplete.

First, I extend endless gratitude to the two people who are most responsible for making my books a reality: Taylor Haggerty, my agent, and Esi Sogah, who was my first editor and is now my editor again. Thank you both for believing in my work, and for always saying to me the things I always need to hear (such things include: *yes you can have more time, no you are not bad at this, yes it's still a good idea, no I will not burn the draft/contract and pretend it never existed, yes it is too much information on that one niche topic, no you should not disappear into the woods*, etc.). I love you both, ew.

Taylor and Esi are at the front line of a team that does an incredible amount of skilled work on my behalf. Root Literary is agency excellence personified; I am especially grateful to Holly Root, who stepped in during a crucial period of seeing *The Paris Match* to its final form. Speaking of final forms, I want to thank Kristin Dwyer and Molly Mitchell at LEO PR, who make sure I am out there for publicity in a more final form than I would be if left to my own devices (my own devices: not showing any version of my form anywhere); to Kristin especially, thank you for giving me the confidence and the regular reality checks I need to be the face and voice of these books I love so much. I am also grateful to Heather Baror-Shapiro and Alice Lawson, who work to bring my books to new audiences and into new formats.

To the entire team at Berkley, thank you so much for welcoming me to your list, and for bringing this book so beautifully into the world. For their early and ongoing support, I thank Ivan Held, Christine Ball, Jeanne-Marie Hudson, Cindy Hwang, and Claire Zion; I also thank Genni Eccles and Naira Mirza for their amazing work in assisting throughout the editorial process. I am so grateful to all those at Berkley and beyond who helped create such a gorgeous package for *The Paris Match*: That includes managing editor Christine Legon; production manager Katheryn Gao and production editor Lindsey Tulloch; copy editor Marianne Aguiar; jacket designer and interior designer Sarah Oberrender and Kristin del Rosario, respectively; and the incredibly talented Enya Todd, who captured the magic of Paris in her art, illustrating the cover of my dreams. Thank you to everyone who had a role in shepherding this book into the hands of readers, especially Craig Burke, a very early reader and supporter of this manuscript; my indispensable in-house publicist, Kristin Cipolla; and marketers Jessica Mangicaro and Kalie Barnes-Young.

My too-smart-to-truly-contemplate husband has helped me with many research tasks over the course of my fiction-writing career, but for this one especially, I offer him endless thanks for the expertise he provided on medical matters—when medical matters were probably the last thing he wanted to talk about after work!—and for the connections he helped me make for additional research on burn trauma and associated chronic pain. Any mistakes I've made in this area are, of course, my own.

I am so grateful to the very brilliant and very thorough Charlotte—brought into my life via the wonderful online romance community—for helping with a final read-through to check on my French, and my version of Paris.

Over the years I've come to think of two "beta" readers as, ironically, my A-Team: To the two A's in my life who read as I write, thank you for your cheerleading, your insights, your willingness to gut check as I go. I could not do this without you. I also thank Jennifer Prokop, Sarah MacLean, and Lauren Billings, all of whom read portions of *The Paris Match* as I drafted it, and all of whom know me well enough to know what I needed to keep going. Alyssa Cole, Tarah DeWitt, Kennedy Ryan, and Alicia Thompson have my gratitude for walking through the drafting trenches with me at critical moments, when things felt unsalvageable (Alyssa, I hope you recognize some portions of this book, and think of our day walking around Paris!).

I am fortunate to have a network of family, friends, and colleagues near and far who support and uplift me. This includes my mom and dad and brother, my extended family of in-laws, and my dear friends Elizabeth and Joan and Amy and Sarah and so many more. For all those who know about and welcome this part of my life—especially when it can make me more scarce in yours—I am eternally grateful.

For my best friend Jackie, to whom this book is dedicated, thank you for visiting Paris with me as I prepared to write this book, for inspiring me with your adventurous spirit and your bravery and your love for the world outside of your home. I can only hope you're half as proud of me and this book as I always have been—and forever am—of you. I add my sincere thanks to your wonderful husband, John, who helped with some crucial research questions for this book.

Always, I thank the readers, reviewers, bloggers, librarians, and booksellers who help bring books to life—not just mine, but *all* books. Your work in bookish spaces—online or in stores and in libraries—nurtures readers, writers, and humanity in general. Without your respect for and attentiveness to books, and without your enthusiasm for the ones you love, my life—and this world!—would be so much emptier.

Finally, an acknowledgment I've saved for last, if only for how much it aches to write. When I began drafting this book—my ninth novel—I had by my side the companion who had been with me for the writing of all my novels so far. But when I completed *The Paris Match*, that same companion was no longer with me, and the time in between was marked by deep grief for his gentle spirit, and the unconditional love, patience, and comforting steadiness he always offered to me. So, a loving thank-you to my late dog Owen, who on my most difficult, isolated days always reminded me that it was worthy work to make even one other person in the world feel less alone. Thanks for helping me write these books, pal. I'll be missing you forever, and writing with the hope that I'm helping someone the way you always helped me.

Praise for Kate Clayborn

'A classic author writing in the modern age, Clayborn is in a league entirely her own.'
Christina Lauren, *New York Times* bestselling author of *The Paradise Problem*

'Kate Clayborn's writing is magnetic and witty and expansive, and her characters feel as real and solid to me as my own limbs.'
Ali Hazelwood, #1 *New York Times* bestselling author of *Problematic Summer Romance*

'Totally original and so romantic.'
Beth O'Leary, international bestselling author of *Swept Away*

'I never disappear into a book the way I do into Clayborn's.'
Alicia Thompson, bestselling author of *Never Been Shipped*

'Kate Clayborn's writing is uniquely, intensely beautiful.'
Sonali Dev, bestselling author of *There's Something About Mira*

'Gorgeously written romance.' NPR

'A warm, witty, complex voice, and I cannot get enough.'
The New York Times

'Clayborn's characters are bright and nuanced, her dialogue quick and clever, and the world she builds warm and welcoming.'
The Washington Post